Julia Golding is a multi-award win... young adults. She also writes under... and Eve Edwards. Well over half a m... sold worldwide in more than twenty different languages.

The Persephone Code is her first adult historical fiction novel.

www.goldinggateway.com

facebook.com/jgoldingauthor

THE PERSEPHONE CODE

JULIA GOLDING

One More Chapter
a division of HarperCollins*Publishers* Ltd
1 London Bridge Street
London SE1 9GF
www.harpercollins.co.uk
HarperCollins*Publishers*
Macken House, 39/40 Mayor Street Upper,
Dublin 1, D01 C9W8, Ireland

This paperback edition 2024

1

First published in Great Britain in ebook format
by HarperCollins*Publishers* 2024
Copyright © Julia Golding 2024
Julia Golding asserts the moral right to
be identified as the author of this work

A catalogue record of this book is available from the British Library

ISBN: 978-0-00-863687-6

This novel is entirely a work of fiction. The names, characters and incidents portrayed in it are the work of the author's imagination. Any resemblance to actual persons, living or dead, events or localities is entirely coincidental.

Printed and bound in the UK using 100% Renewable Electricity
by CPI Group (UK) Ltd

All rights reserved. No part of this publication may be reproduced, stored in a retrieval system, or transmitted, in any form or by any means, electronic, mechanical, photocopying, recording or otherwise, without the prior permission of the publishers.

For Richard Blackford

Chapter One

APRIL 1812

Hellfire Caves, Buckinghamshire

A fire flickered on the altar at the base of the inverted cross. Two men stood facing each other, their shadows dancing on the cavern roof though their bodies were eerily still.

The younger man was the first to break the silence. 'I've kept my side of the bargain and brought the book. Do your part!'

'Oh, I will!'

The strike came from within the folds of a cloak. With brute force, blade grated against rib. It shoved the Warden of the Hellfire Caves backwards. The stroke had missed the heart, piercing to the right of the sternum.

Anthony Pennington stared in disbelief at the dagger protruding from his chest. So wrong. Was it only three nights ago his lover had kissed that same spot?

His shirtfront swiftly turned scarlet. He clamped a hand to the wound, clutching his cravat to staunch the flow. There was too much blood.

The man stepped back from the puddle. 'Save your wants and wishes, Pennington, for the afterlife.'

Anthony's knees gave way.

Strength left but pain was late arriving, like a duke knowing the ball would wait for him. Feeling nothing was a bad sign. Was he going to die here? How could he? He was only twenty-eight. He'd done nothing of note – barely lived. He'd been in the army and seen his share of battlefield injuries, though he was no one's hero. Under his command, men had been slaughtered by Napoleon's soldiers or died of gangrene after the butchery of field doctors. Experience asserted that it was already over for him. To escape Old Boney only to find his end in Buckinghamshire? What a grim joke.

All he could do was protect the others.

The man Anthony had come here to meet picked up the book his victim had let fall. He smeared the cover with blood as he attempted to wipe it clean. It wasn't the first blood the book had seen. Tradition demanded the ink be mixed with the faithful's own when they made their pledge. Anthony's signature had been in there. He had thought to use the book to buy his freedom. How blind he had been! Good breeding did not mean honourable behaviour. Had his common sense not told him that blackmailers don't release their victims so easily?

The man flicked through the pages. Anthony wanted to rip it from him, but his arms wouldn't obey. They hung like hams on hooks at his side.

A cruel smile lit the man's face. He glanced up. 'Rejoice! You have played with hellfire and now you go to meet it. By your lights, I've done you a service.'

Finally, Lord Pain entered and made his bow. Anthony gasped, then gave an agonised cry. Every breath he took was like being stabbed anew. The pressure in his chest indicated a lung had collapsed.

'Getting a taste of the devil's whip, are you?' The man seemed intrigued. 'Tell me: what is it like?' He pushed his face nearer, the reek of civet too strong in his pomade.

How humiliating to be killed by someone who didn't know how a true gentleman dressed; by someone who had no style.

Such a disappointment not to score a better calibre of assassin, Anthony thought grimly.

'Go to hell!' he spat.

The man tsked. 'I thought we'd covered that. That's *your* destination. Frankly, I don't believe in such superstitious nonsense. All the names and their pledges are here, I trust?'

Anthony wasn't going to give his murderer the satisfaction of an explanation. He had fulfilled his part by bringing Sir Francis Dashwood's diary to the meeting. He hadn't promised to reveal how to read it. A rag of honour remained, and he would cling to it until his last breath. Let his killer find that out himself.

The man negligently flipped the leaves. He glanced at Anthony and smiled.

'Still alive? Well then, tell your master, Beelzebub, that you have served into my hands the means to destroy the Hellfire Club – with the chaser of bringing down the government as their wicked practices are revealed. He might let you have time off for infernal behaviour.' He chuckled at his own joke.

Anthony's head swam. His knees were wet as a pool of blood formed on the floor of the cave. Skulls grinned from the altar. The lewd carvings quivered and cavorted – demons tupping maidens, boys servicing old men, drunkards pissing on sacred symbols…

The man found the list of those who had belonged to the Hellfire Club since it began. He gloated with sick joy.

'Really? The Duke of Wharton was the founder?' He tapped his lips with a bloody forefinger. 'Shame that line is extinct. It would have been my greatest pleasure to bring it down.' He turned a page.

Anthony grimaced at his red-kneed breeches. He knew that book as well as his own chin in the shaving mirror so he could predict what the man would see next.

Gloating turned to alarm. 'Where are the pages for the current members?'

Oh, the uses of a razor blade. Anthony thought he should write an ode on the subject in the style of Pope. Or Cowper. He was good at imitation. A family trait. Anthony shook his head. Thoughts tangled. Knowing he was taking his leave of life's assembly, he couldn't bring himself to care. He'd be out of this man's reach so very soon.

A hand gripped the hilt of the knife.

'No, you don't escape that easily, Pennington! It's not too late for you to suffer beyond your imaginings. I'll make you cry for your mother!' The murderer shoved the knife deeper and sent pain ricocheting. Anthony could hear the sawing against the bone, but the dagger was still not near enough to the heart to kill him quickly.

Dear God, it hurts so much!

'Tell me!'

The diary had been Anthony's sacred charge. He hadn't had time to pass on the knowledge that was his responsibility. It spelt the ruin of so many; it threatened the kingdom. What was written there would make the world burn until there was nothing but ashes.

He hated to fail.

'So sorry.' He addressed his brethren, wildly thinking that he saw them crowding him. No, those were only the club's paintings, decorating the walls of this chamber of revelry. No one else was here but him and his killer – he'd made sure of that.

'Tell me – or I will make everyone you love suffer!'

'I have ... no one.' Some comfort in that thought.

'Everyone has someone! You have a lover, don't you?'

He did, but no one would know the name – they'd been careful. His lover had the wits to disappear back into the crowd once they heard what had happened to him.

'A father?'

Anthony gave a gurgle of laughter. 'Good luck ... taking *him* on. I almost ... want to ... live to ... see that.'

'Your sister?' The man's voice was a snake's hiss.

A chill spread through Anthony's limbs. Horror came with death biting its heels. He sought the man's face but there was no mercy to be found there. 'How...?'

'How do I know about your father's bastard? Society talks, you fool! And she hardly hid the connection, flaunting her bastard name.' The man kicked him in the stomach. 'I'll make you tell, or she'll suffer next!'

Dora, Dora, why did you not hide as I begged you? You chose defiance over safety. Anthony shuddered. Would this man torture the answer from him, piling pain upon pain in Anthony's last moments? Did he have the strength to hold out?

He should protect Dora. He had failed to do so in life, and now he was failing her in death. But his secret—!

Confusion muddled the path ahead.

There was one step left that he could take. He'd already left the letter. It would put her in danger, but he'd had no choice. He had sworn an oath. She had to understand, but he would leave as many clues as he could. Anthony put his hands on the hilt over the killer's and twisted, angling it up. He chose a soldier's death.

'No time... Tell her... Not Dora...' His last words came in an agonised whisper as he ruptured his heart. Consciousness trickled away with the massive outflow of blood.

'Dammit!' The murderer freed his hand and wiped it on the young man's jacket. 'You can't do a thing right, can you, Pennington? You even died too soon.'

Chapter Two

Lake Windermere

'Sir!' The messenger loped up the steep path, waving his hat. Late afternoon sun behind him cast a spider-limbed shadow on the rocky ground.

'Damn you,' muttered Dr Jacob Sandys, putting down his brush. There went his pleasant day of trying to capture the Lakes in their majesty. Someone was sick and the locals had not taken him at his word that he had quit the medical profession. It had proved too dangerous a life for him. Why could he not be left alone?

Because the world carried on turning. Babies insisted on being born. People had the unfortunate habit of dying.

Resigned to his duty, Jacob stood up and waved back. A phalanx of rainclouds marched in over Ambleside, the surface of Windermere dulling from navy to grey. The wind whipped his collar-length dark hair into his eyes. He needed to visit a barber but had let himself grow a little wild out here. Ah well. Nature was conspiring to cut short his session. Maybe that was for the best. He had become an indifferent landscape artist, worsening with every attempt. Was that because he had wrenched shut the gates of Paradise and lost the brilliant vision once given him? Or had he overestimated his skill back then, one of the many delusions of the opium-eater?

'A letter, sir! Express – from London.' The messenger, Ned Black from the inn, waved the envelope like a flag of truce. The locals knew Jacob had a temper when interrupted.

Not sickness then, or at least not a patient he could reach in time. He wiped off his brush and stowed it in the travel-sized art box. His father? Lord Sandys had been declining for some years, lingering in Bath or Harrogate. Had his mother finally sent for him? He snatched the letter from Ned and cracked the seal. Not his mother's handwriting – or anyone in his family. He'd not seen this signature for a decade. George, now Reverend Leighton of West Wycombe, his old friend from Oxford.

Whatever had prompted George to write to him express?

My dear Sandys,

I apologise for the alarm I have no doubt caused you with the receipt of a sudden letter from one from whom you have not heard for an age. The truth is that I am in urgent need of your assistance and beg your forgiveness for my presumption. My problem is twofold – two devil's horns, I could call it. I will start with the unfortunate events that occurred in my parish last night. A young gentleman who was leasing a house in the village was found dead in the West Wycombe Caves (though you may have heard of them under their infamous title of the Hellfire Caves). I had only recently made the acquaintance of Anthony Pennington, the victim – an officer on half-pay, a young captain battered by the wars. I had been visiting him in the hopes of curing him of his infatuation with this impious group, but I was too late to save him.

It now seems to me that his murder is connected to similar questionable deaths in my parish over the last eighteen months – all young men or women associated with the caves. These poor lost children of God have been worrying my conscience as no effective action has been taken to discover the cause and punish the guilty. Having such a place of riotous behaviour within the parish bounds attracts the licentious, and though I had expected drunkards and impropriety on the nights that the Hellfire fraternity gathered, I did not expect death. The local magistrate refuses to act – and indeed I suspect him of being amongst the revellers. He dismissed it as a robbery gone awry. I stand as the lone gentleman wishing to get to the bottom of this crime.

At a loss to know to whom I should turn, I recalled how you helped the Dean at Trinity solve the mystery of the disappearance of Havers while we were undergraduates. That emboldened me to appeal to you now to come and help me in my time of need. Somerton told me that you are living quietly in the Lake District, rubbing shoulders with that poetical lot, Wordsworth, Southey and their ilk. He said you are not currently employed on any more worthy endeavour. For friendship's sake, I beg you to emerge from seclusion just this once.

Jacob grimaced. He remembered well how impressed Leighton had been that he had discovered that Donald Havers had staged a drowning accident and fled to Ireland to escape his creditors. Leighton's praise had not been merited; the deduction had been nothing but pure logic. Havers had been the last man to go for a swim on a cold day and the first man to run at the sign of trouble.

He turned to the second side.

My other request I beg you to carry out even if friendship cannot persuade you to travel south. The young gentleman, Anthony Pennington, left a message for a lady who I believe is his sister from the wrong side of the blanket – a Miss Dora Fitz-Pennington. The surname says it all, does it not? He once told me that he was related to an actress in one of the touring companies and, putting two and two together, I saw he had a playbill advertising a circuit this summer amongst his possessions. That bill states that the company will be in Kendal next week so, by the time my message reaches you, she will be a short ride from your cottage if you act quickly. I see God's hand in that. Would you bear the burden of Christian service and break the melancholy news to the poor man's sister? She is estranged from her family so there is a danger she will first hear the news in the papers – a shock I'm sure you would wish to spare her.

He left her a message amongst his effects that I will preserve until she can come to fetch it herself. The instruction is to hand it to her in person and trust it to no other, not even her father, though I prefer not to have to refuse a pointed request from that gentleman in his time of trouble. He too must wish to see his son's last words.

I remain, my dear sir,
Your very much obliged and sincere friend,
George Leighton

Bloody Leighton. The appeal to friendship would make Jacob an impious cad if he ignored it. He uttered a stronger swear word that made the messenger flinch.

'Sorry, Ned.' He folded up the letter.

'Bad news, sir?'

'Does good news ever travel express?'

'True enough.' Ned picked up the painting stool and easel as Jacob shouldered his satchel and portfolio.

'It appears I'm going on a journey.' They started down the path back to the village, Jacob a step in the lead.

'I'll fetch your horse from the stable.'

'Good man.' They reached the path where it divided, one way to the village, the other to his home. Jacob tossed Ned a shilling for his pains. 'Bring him to Cragside. It'll save me half an hour.'

Passing Jacob the artist's gear, Ned ran off in the direction of the White Hart. Jacob hastened to his house, duty rather than desire driving him. So, he was to tell some actress that her brother was dead? He could think of happier ways of spending his evening. He didn't care for the theatre. Jacob preferred antiquarian collecting – there was not much a relic could do to you other than intrigue the intellect. It certainly didn't demand you stand up and perform in front of strangers. Still, he acknowledged that he did have the skill Leighton ascribed to him. He could ferret out a fraud – person or parchment – better than most men.

The church clock tolled five as he reached his cottage. He'd better hurry if he was to make Kendal before nightfall. Dora Fitz-Pennington didn't yet know it, but her life was about to take a turn for the worse.

Chapter Three

Kendal

Dora dipped the nib in the inkwell and gave the last D a final flourish. At least the Kendal management had furnished her little cupboard of a dressing room with wax candles rather than tallow – an improvement on the theatre at Carlisle. The light was good enough to work right to curtain-up. Would the piece pass judgement?

She nibbled the top of her pen, assessing as a buyer would. The paper had been cut from the back of an old hymnal in Keswick parish church so it had the right vintage. Once the surface had been distressed, the odd word smudged, perhaps an artistic burn as if it had only just been snatched from the fire, then it would be ready. A little singeing would go with the story of its origins, which she had decided was that the writer had condemned the draft to the flames, but an enterprising servant had rescued it. Ben Jonson had been known for his temper. He'd killed a man – hardly one of literature's most admirable souls. He was a rogue of the theatre, like her. Jonson was not as collectable as Shakespeare, but there was still a market amongst antiquarians for his work and they were less suspicious when a new document emerged. They should lap up this early draft of 'To Celia'. *Drink to me only with thine eyes...*

She would laugh if someone tried that line on her to get her into bed, but it was the kind of sentimental claptrap that her agent in London liked best. He would be pleased that she was varying her 'finds'. He had complained in his last letter that she had done too much Dryden (she had to agree), so she had reached further back for her newest piece. She loved this game of fooling the experts and imagining what her favourite authors would write if only they'd had an extra day and a bit of paper in front of them... The right paper was always a challenge but touring with the Northern Players did mean she had the chance to call in on many an unlocked church and liberate a few blank pages from old bibles without anyone being the wiser. Or if they did realise, by then she would be long gone, playing Richmond or York by the time they thought to ask what had brought the actress to spend so long on her knees in front of their lectern.

Better than being on her knees backstage earning a coin that way. Men were pigs.

The youngest stagehand, son of the company's manager, knocked and put his head around the door.

'Miss Fitzy, you're on in five.'

At least, the older ones were swine. Young, they could be tolerable.

'Thank you, Jem.' She slid the Jonson poem into her writing case inside the battered leather album she and her brother had created. Travelling with their father around English estates, they had sought out samples of the handwriting of the great and the good in libraries for their little hobby. No one noticed two children rummaging along the shelves and in desks, or if they did, just sent them away with a box on the ear. Anthony had given the keepsake book to her as a parting gift when she had made the final break with her family. Five years had passed since that tumultuous Christmas Day. She missed her big brother, even if she understood his reasons for keeping his distance. Threat of disinheritance held even the boldest in line. He was a rebel, but only up to a point.

No good dwelling on past disappointments. People did tend to let you down, even those you loved most. A brother in thrall to the poppy was never going to be a hero. She turned the key and dropped that into her cleavage, checking it was secure. Her fellow actors, fine friends though they were, could be notorious spies and gossips. More than one had tried to open her case, knowing that she kept her valuables within. So far, they had not guessed that her extra income came from literary forgery rather than gentlemen callers. Let them carry on speculating.

Jem dipped back in without knocking.

'Miss Fitzy? There's a gentleman to see you.'

Speak of the devil. Dora checked her costume, buckskins ready under the skirt she wore in the first act for a quick change. They were a little tight around her thighs, being cut for a man. The breeches parts always drew the crowds, which was why Mr Thomas insisted on repeating *As You Like It* and *Twelfth Night* every week in abbreviated form. It was a rare man who passed up the opportunity to admire her ... ehem ... Rosalind.

'He'll have to wait.' She stuffed her spiralling brown hair under her hat. One man whose advances she had rejected last week had called her Medusa, saying that her hair was like the gorgon's snakes, escaping every which way when not tamed. Sour grapes, no doubt, disparaging what she had kept out of reach.

She smiled at herself in the mirror, checking she had not smudged her stage makeup. Brown eyes outlined in kohl smiled back. She'd enjoyed her set-down of that last suitor and thanked him for his insult. She had told him a gorgon was no bad role model for a female. It meant she was empowered to bite a few annoying people or put them out of countenance with a stony glare.

'He says it's urgent.' Jem twisted his cap. The poor boy had a soft spot for her. He would be better sighing for someone nearer his age. Dora patted his shoulder as she passed. Her mind was already summoning up her first line. Having to remember so many scripts did wonders for the memory. She could scan a page and recall it with few errors.

'The play's the thing, my lad. I'll speak to the gentleman afterwards.'

Chapter Four

Jacob arrived too late to catch the actress before she went on stage. Resigned to spending the evening in this damp northern town of grey buildings and greyer streets, he wondered what to do with himself. He paused outside the druggist's shop, knowing that one form of escape was always available there. Sapphire- and emerald-coloured glass jars in the window put him more in mind of a confectioner's, but it was greedy adults rather than children who crowded around the counter for their lozenges to be weighed out for them. He saw in the opium-eaters' desperate faces an echo of his own. Before he could move on, a familiar devil crept out from its hiding place inside his brain, pitchfork pricking him in the stomach as the pains began – an excuse to dull them with the poppy. He *needed* the pain relief. Who would know he had broken his own promise to himself? Who would care? Was he not a happier sailor on life's voyage when he took a mere drop or two – cleverer – more perceptive? The tug to go in was visceral, his feet already turning in that direction.

Tincture or tablet – happiness could be bought for a penny and carried off in a coat pocket.

A man came out and jostled Jacob in his rush to get home to take his medicine and enjoy his dreams in private. That was enough to bring Jacob to his senses. He had been down that path. It might lead to a few hours of euphoria, his mind spinning like a Catherine Wheel with ideas and insights, but the payment would go on long after. He forced himself to send the devil back to the corner of his brain that he had never entirely managed to cleanse. His time would be better spent watching the actress perform and gauging her character by mundane means, not drugged perceptions. He felt pity for her, naturally, but the last thing he wanted was some sentimental Miss weeping on his shoulder all night. There had been too much loss and grief in his life to rush to embrace a stranger's pain.

He looked back at the druggist. No, stop: he would *not* go there! Setting his shoulders in a firm line, he marched on, a prisoner under his own guard.

Jacob took a seat in the pit at the Woolpack Yard theatre, exchanging a nod with the clerk perched on the bench next to him. The play was already underway, the auditorium hot and smelling of too many bodies crushed in close proximity. Compared to Drury Lane, this was a very poor relation, the auditorium no bigger than his father's ballroom – not that Lord Sandys would thank him for that comparison. On the other hand, you could see and hear the actors with greater ease. Thank God someone had burned down Sheridan's monstrosity of a Theatre Royal and caused it to require rebuilding. Jacob hoped the new theatre would be an improvement and that having a box would finally be a worthwhile investment for his family after they had spent a decade struggling to hear the dialogue.

No danger of that in Kendal. The actors declaimed as if they were performing in a gale, captains on the poop deck of a warship. All subtlety was lost, and Shakespeare reduced to a parade of fools in one of his wittiest plays. Jacob was relieved to see that the women were of a higher quality. The two playing Rosalind and Celia were the stars of the show. It was only a shame that Rosalind had to pretend to be the boy Ganymede, and then pretended to be a girl for Orlando to woo...

Really, Shakespeare?

Despite that nonsense, she was witty and warm with a magnificent head of dark curls and a shapely feminine form very well displayed in her men's clothes. Her dark eyes were framed by long lashes, reminiscent of a doe, but there was nothing shy or meek about her to continue that comparison. On the contrary, her skin glowed with a summery tan that made Jacob think of meadow romps long ago with a willing lass, and her eyes sparkled with humour. She was more alive than anyone else in the entire theatre. You knew that she would be a handful in all the best ways and her lucky partner would love every moment of the challenge. Looking around at the appreciation on the faces of the men around him, he could tell he was not the only one to notice and he feared he would have to beat back the stage-door admirers if she was the one for whom he had bad news.

Or was Pennington's sister Celia? A black-haired girl with porcelain skin and big blue eyes, the kind of frail female so many of his acquaintance would pay royally to take under their protection. He knew her type. Her expression did not mask the experience and calculation. Of course, the lady was concentrating on remembering her part, but Jacob guessed that her intelligence went beyond stagecraft. She would know very well how to wrap fools around her little finger. Once bitten...

'Do you know the name of the actress playing Celia?' he asked the clerk as the play wound up to its happy resolution. The manager had taken liberties with the cuts as it had lasted barely two hours.

'Miss Plum?' The clerk waggled his eyebrows and Jacob had to smile at the absurd sobriquet. 'Apparently that is her true name and no stage affectation.'

'Then nature has been very apt in the way she has grown into it.'

'Are you here for the picking?'

Jacob was beginning to wish he hadn't started this conversation. He had grown to dislike the trade that went on in the Green Room at theatres with actresses treated as little more than courtesans. Only such luminaries as Mrs Siddons had avoided that path and maintained a respectable standing.

'No. I'm merely a messenger – and the lady is not my target.'

'Then the delightful Dora?' The clerk nodded without waiting for confirmation. 'I hear she is discriminating as to whom she lets into her dressing room, unlike her cousin.'

'I'd better make an early start then.'

The clerk put a hand on his arm.

'The evening's not over, my friend. They're doing *Castle Spectre* as an afterpiece.'

Jacob stifled a groan. The playwright, 'Monk' Lewis, was his least favourite author. His school friends had been obsessed by his gothic novel of rape and murder, with its cast of virginal victims, devilish monks, and corrupted nuns. They'd acted out satanic rites and drinking games in his honour, forming a club which they had called the Eton Monks, a cub version of the Hellfire wolves. Jacob had been withering in his scorn and had earned a broken nose as a result.

Then again, you should have seen the other boy. Ben Knighton still carried the scar on his lip.

This play was not much better, with a Welsh castle, ghosts and a wicked earl to titillate the audience. If he had to go to the theatre, Jacob preferred sparkling comedies or Shakespeare well done, not this highly spiced fare delivered by an incompetent cast.

More to the point, how long was this all to last? He had hoped for an early night so he could rise at dawn to catch the stage to London because, damn his eyes, he had not yet repented of his decision to answer the call of friendship. Leighton had left him little choice when he had played that card.

During the shifting of the set, a tumbler came on to entertain the audience with feats of agility, somersaulting like a jester of old in front of the painted vista of a haunted castle. Jacob relinquished his seat to try his luck with Miss Fitz-Pennington in the interval but had no joy. The stage door was guarded by a cyclops of a man – his arms folded and a black eyepatch giving him a piratical look. He told Jacob, and the other hopefuls, to bugger off until the end. The management clearly didn't want their actresses engaged on their backs when they should be on their feet on stage.

Rather than return to his seat on the bench, Jacob stood at the rear to watch the play without paying much attention to the execrable dialogue. It dawned on him that Dora Fitz-Pennington was actually a very fine actress, surely far above this cackle. She was mesmerising to watch, her movements graceful and somehow knowing, as if she were sharing a joke with the audience as to how silly the piece was. He didn't blame her for the arch performance. If he had to deliver lines like 'from good spirits I have nothing to fear, and heaven and my innocence will protect me against bad', which anyone who had lived more than five minutes in the world would know was a bouncer, he too would be laughing inside.

Or crying.

And he very much feared she would be crying when he spoke to her.

Chapter Five

Ruby Plum jostled Dora in the corridor backstage – no mean feat as her friend was barely five feet and Dora was tall for a woman.

'Did you see him?'

'See whom?' Dora was going to be late for her final scene but her Lilliputian friend was determined to share the news.

'That gorgeous man standing at the back!'

'Gorgeous? In Kendal?'

Ruby wrinkled her brow. 'Perhaps I meant rich?'

'You definitely meant rich.' Ruby chose her conquests by the depth of their purses, and Dora could not fault her for it. They each did what they had to survive.

'Dora!' hissed Jack Lammas, her stage lover, beckoning her on. 'Move your arse!'

'Remember I saw him first,' called Ruby.

Dora gave her a mock salute and entered for her final scene. At least in this play she got to stab a villain – and then plead that he be spared death so he could repent. The latter part was a disappointment. Angela would be a better character if she enjoyed her moment of heroism and sent the evil to perdition.

She plunged her dagger into the bosom of Earl Osmond, piercing the blood bag for the gory effect. From her fellow actor's glare, maybe she had been a little too enthusiastic with the thrust. The play wrapped up quickly afterwards as she had saved her lost father and earned the hand of her lover in a nice swap of the usual roles. The applause was generous for their bloody resolution to the problems facing the inhabitants of Castle Spectre. The men in the pit even stood and cheered. Some threw flowers at her feet, which was far better than the rotten fruit that had assailed them in Richmond. Jack had been having one of his self-destructive spells and had slept with the mayor's wife.

A cast note had gone round after that: *do not dally with the wives and daughters of the men who decide our welcome in a town.*

She gathered up the flowers, gave a final curtsy and left the stage well pleased. It was the kind of play that regional theatregoers enjoyed – the portrayals of isolated great houses ruled over by despotic men being not that far from their reality. Dora knew that the London sophisticates rubbished such things as far-fetched, but in her experience, gothic dilemmas were all too common. Men did want to take you against your will. Noble houses were not havens of manners and culture but more often than not hid ugly secrets. As for ghosts, there were uncanny stories told in all corners of the country so it would be unwise to dismiss those cavalierly. What did the city critics know in any case? Give her the theatrical splendour of this ragamuffin troupe – who watched your back and were open about their dishonesty – over the polished lies of the rational gentlemen of parliament who ruled the nation.

Not that she harboured a grudge, of course.

Wiping her hands and leaving the prop knife on the table for cleaning, Dora set about removing her costume. She was just struggling with the laces of her costume when Jem knocked on the door again.

'Another gentleman to see you, Miss Fitzy. Shall I tell him to take his horn colic elsewhere?'

She had been entertaining Jem with a variety of colourful rebuffs all of which added up to refusals of amorous advances. She laughed to hear one of her phrases repeated back to her.

'You liked that one, did you?'

Jem rubbed his sleeve over his nose and gave her a Shakespearian bow. 'Excellent, i'faith. Almost as good as "Take your peppered pego to the pushing school!"'

She had indeed been rather proud of that one.

She put her finger to her lips in mock thought. 'Then how about this? Tell the dangler to take his cock-a-doodle elsewhere.' She waggled a finger to underline the meaning.

He snorted, bowed and ran off on his mission.

The laces finally unknotted, she threw on a dressing gown, giving herself a moment of unconfined joy before facing the annoyance of having to don her street clothes. She sometimes wished nature had not endowed her so copiously in the bust.

Jem knocked quickly and put his head round the door.

'Really sorry, Miss Fitzy, but he says—'

The door banged open.

'—He says that he's no dangler and won't even touch the cock-a-doodle comment.' A stranger stood in the entrance. This had to be Ruby's gorgeously rich gentleman. Wavy dark hair kissed his collar, but his pale blue eyes were cold, like one of the Westmoreland lakes on a spring day before summer had warmed it. He was tall and wore his clothes well. He was, she surmised, someone who understood the importance of tailoring. The cut of his cloth screamed Bond Street and his boots were Hoby's. Round these parts, this suggested he either belonged to the rising class of factory owners or was a scion of an old family.

That didn't mean he could get away with having no manners. A lady's no meant no.

Dora pulled the front of her dressing gown closed. 'I fear touching your own cock-a-doodle is exactly what lies in your future because I'll have none of it. Get out of my dressing room.'

'Very witty, Miss Fitz-Pennington, but you have misunderstood this situation.'

When would men learn?

'Of course, it has to be my problem, doesn't it? Well, I have the solution. She's next door and very desirous to make your acquaintance. I, however, have better things to do. Jem, please ask Harding to remove the gentleman if he refuses to go willingly.'

'Come along, sir.' Jem pulled at his elbow. 'She's not like that. Come see Ruby. She'll appreciate you.'

The man pulled his arm free.

'I don't want *appreciating* by Miss Fitz-Pennington, Ruby or anyone else for that matter. I'm here to deliver a message.'

That was a likely story.

'Oh? And who, pray, is using you as a messenger to me?'

Jem gave her a look, asking if he should go for Harding. She held up a hand, interested as to what latest twist the man would give to his tale.

'My message is from Reverend Leighton of West Wycombe.'

Dora groaned and spun away to the mirror to remove her stage makeup. The gentleman caller was one of the worst: a moralist.

'At least you don't claim an acquaintance with the Archbishop of Canterbury. What's the message? Don't tell me, I can guess.' She ran a damp cloth over one eyelid, the first swipe turning her into Cleopatra with kohl winged around her eye.

'I very much doubt that.' He met her gaze in the mirror, an ironic arch to his brow.

She rubbed away the makeup, her own brown eyes now clear

of enhancement. 'You want me to repent of my wicked ways and stop distressing my father with my choice of profession.'

He seemed amused rather than offended by her words.

'I would rather hope we all repent of our wicked ways.'

She threw the used cloth in the wash basket. 'Tell Reverend Leighton to inform my father I am completely content with my life and would not crawl back to live under his roof if you paid me.' She gestured for Jem to fetch Harding. The boy hurried away.

'As I said, Miss Fitz-Pennington, you mistake me. I'm here about your brother.' He was using his height to loom over her like some lord dominating an uppity peasant.

She could do uppity. It was one of her favourite roles.

'Get your story straight, sir.' She moved to command the stage – the mirror in this case – putting a chair between them. 'First you are here for the church, now my brother. I advise you never to stand for parliament. You are a terrible liar and would not flourish there.'

Harding entered, pushing up his sleeves.

'Shall I get rid of the nuisance, Miss Fitzy?'

'Hold, man.' The visitor's eyes narrowed. He didn't look like he would be that easy to remove. His stance had shifted to that of a military man, or pugilist, hands held loosely by his sides, ready to react to her giant. 'She may not want to hear my message, but I am honour bound to deliver it.'

Dora was not the kind of woman to enjoy provoking fisticuffs. Letting him speak seemed the quickest way to get rid of him.

She gave a weary sigh. 'Very well. Deliver your sermon and be gone.'

Harding scowled but stood back.

The gentleman glanced at the big man.

'You may wish to hear this in private.'

Her laugh was sardonic.

'No, I really would not.'

He hesitated, then continued.

'Very well then. Miss Fitz-Pennington, I very much regret to inform you that your brother is dead.'

'What?' Dora swayed, the room spinning like a child's top. No, it couldn't be.

'Get a seat for the lady,' snapped the man.

Jem wormed past Harding and pushed her dressing table chair behind her suddenly weak knees.

'Sit down, miss,' he whispered, pulling her into the chair.

'Is this a horrible joke?' Anthony had developed a very bleak sense of humour since leaving the army and she wouldn't put it past him to test her. 'Did Anthony put you up to this?'

The man bristled.

'I do not amuse myself by going around telling young ladies that their relatives have died unless it is the case. I have no acquaintance with your brother. The news came from the rector of his parish—'

'Reverend Leighton.' Now it all made horrible sense. 'I owe you an apology—'

'It was a misunderstanding. My condolences for your loss.' He gave her a clipped bow.

'I... Thank you.' She rubbed her hands together, belatedly aware she had not yet cleaned off all the blood. An emptiness filled her chest. Anthony ... gone. 'How did he die? Do you know?'

The man looked away over her head.

'I understand that he was killed. Possibly by footpads.'

'In London? I thought he was living in the countryside and had given up on city life?' She had indeed fretted about his companions when he had been roistering around Covent Garden and St Giles, but had worried far less of late.

'Not there. In some caves near his home.'

'Caves? In Buckinghamshire?'

'The Hellfire Caves.'

The news stunned her. Everyone who followed the scandal sheets had heard of those infamous caves, haunt of the idle rich who liked to shock society. She had warned Anthony that they were dangerous circles in which to move. The rich men who dabbled in the orgies fuelled by drink laced with drugs and the performance of satanic rituals to spice up the occasion were the worst that 'the quality' had to offer. Anthony had countered that the members were the only honest men in the Ton and that they were only what he, a sinner, deserved. Already a laudanum addict, he'd found them accepting of his habit. Yet, after her entreaties, he had promised to stop.

But that was five years ago, on the occasion of their last face-to-face meeting. The gulf between them had widened since then, he entangled in his world of high society, she in her workaday role slogging between towns and bringing Shakespeare to the labouring classes. They still loved each other, but from a distance.

The pain grew – she hadn't known grief would feel like this. Oh God: it wasn't fair! She hadn't been there to save him. She had been familiar with his periods of blank desolation but had been too far away to shake him out of them. Her influence had waned, and he had been left to punish himself as he saw fit.

Oh Anthony. The emptiness expanded into an ugly hole, her happiness buried six feet under.

'My friend, Reverend Leighton, says he will tend to the body for interment and expects your family to arrive shortly.' The messenger's voice was almost gentle. 'He also wrote that he has a letter for you from your brother.'

Dora steeled herself. Pride dictated that she mourn in private. She held out a hand, clinging desperately to her dignity.

'The letter is held for collection in West Wycombe.'

'Of course it is,' she said wearily, letting her hand fall. 'Will the reverend keep it until I can fetch it?'

The Persephone Code

'Yes, if he can. I'll tell him your wishes when I see him.'

'You're going south?' Dora sat up. Here was the answer. 'Would you fetch it for me?'

Her lordly messenger went poker stiff. 'Miss Fitz-Pennington, I doubt very much that Leighton will hand it over. He stressed that it was to be delivered to you in person and that he will hold it for you alone, unless your father demands it.'

'And you wouldn't want to play carrier pigeon either.' Next week the troupe would probably be in Lancaster. No, this was something she would have to do herself when she could.

The man tugged at his cravat, disordering the perfect knot. 'You ... could come with me. I mean, I could escort you, if you so wish.'

She gave a hollow laugh, her suspicions returning.

'I have employment, sir. I cannot abandon my people so lightly.'

'Indeed. Well then, I will leave you to your friends.'

Jem crept to her side and put his hand on her shoulder. She patted it in thanks but all she wanted to do was curl around her pain.

'Thank you. Most kind. I'd prefer to be alone.'

'In that case, I will leave you in peace. I go to London on the coach tomorrow morning, should you change your mind. You can find me at The Golden Fleece.' He gave her a shallow bow.

Left to herself as she had asked, Jem and Harding escorting the visitor out, Dora bent her head to her hands. Her eyes were dry but only because she was still too stunned to comprehend the message. It seemed absurd. Anthony, dead? It had been a common fear when he was in the army, but she had got used of late to the idea that he was a survivor. She expected him to outlive his wild days and become a fat alderman in Liverpool with a flock of children and a tolerant wife. When her father predeceased him, she had hoped to be allowed back as wicked Aunt Dora, entertaining his children with tales of the stage and spoiling them terribly.

It hurt so badly that this future was ripped apart.

With Anthony gone, she was alone in the world.

She got up abruptly. *Her father*. In her shock, she had forgotten to wonder what her sire would do at the news. It was simple to guess – the messenger had already hinted. He would sweep in and clear Anthony's house of anything that might drag the family name into disrepute.

More disrepute.

Would Anthony's letter to her survive? Oh, she could see him opening it, or destroying it, but not keeping it aside for her. Only a man of the cloth stood between the letter and destruction and how reliable would the clergyman be when faced with the tempest that was Ezra Pennington?

That messenger was right. She would have to go and retrieve it herself if she wished to know her brother's last words to her. She hadn't been thinking straight. Time was against her. Her father had advance notice and would already be on his way – or would have sent someone in his place. They might have already arrived.

But she couldn't give up without trying. Thanks to her last imaginative reconstruction of a Dryden letter, she had enough funds to travel to London. She could even take her latest Jonson piece and so pay for her return. She just had to tell her friends that her absence was unavoidable. Mr Thomas would fuss but he wouldn't want to lose one of his best actresses, not if she promised to return as soon as possible.

'Mr Thomas!' She ran from the dressing room. 'Mr Thomas!'

Only when she had received permission to take a leave of absence did she realise that the gentleman who had brought the message had not thought to give his name.

Typical. Bloody gents and their presumption.

Collecting her writing case and personal items into a bag, she set about packing up the costumes that would stay with the company until her return. If she left Ruby to do it, some of the nicer items would doubtless relocate to her trunk. Ruby had the soul of a magpie.

Chest packed and strapped shut, Dora did a last sweep of her dressing room. The rest of the company had already left for their lodgings, so the theatre was quiet and dark.

As she turned to leave, a crash reverberated through the building. Someone had just kicked in the stage door.

Chapter Six

Stirring the lamb and thyme stew the innkeeper had served him for a late supper, Jacob wrestled with his conscience. He was aware that he had treated the actress with only cursory kindness. Her luminous dark eyes had held worlds of pain – he knew the look, having had to deliver bad news many times to patients and their loved ones. It was little wonder she had refused his offer to escort her south. He hadn't made it clear that he would fund her trip – he was not short of money thanks to his inheritance and could spare the price of a coach ticket for the sister of a murder victim.

Had his wartime experience hardened him so much that he had lost the last shreds of his humanity? He should have offered more than scant words and shallow concern. He hadn't even mentioned that his friend found the circumstances of the man's death suspicious.

Badly done, Jacob, he chided himself.

Pushing the empty bowl aside, he resolved to return to the theatre. She would probably already have left for her lodgings, but the nightwatchman might be able to tell him where that was. He could send up a note and a more generous offer.

The front doors of the theatre were padlocked and the lights extinguished, just as he had expected. It was gone eleven, which was late for a rural town, and the only people out and about at this time were gathered at the inns. Jacob walked around to the rear, planning to knock on the stage door as he had earlier, but found it gaping open.

Strange.

He stepped inside. Caution bred of years spent with the army made him stop, old instincts firing. If he were interrupting a burglary, he needed more than his fists. He would be better off going for aid – or his pistols. Yet if someone had merely failed to secure the door after returning to pick up a forgotten item, he would not be thanked for over-reacting.

A woman's scream settled the question for him. Breaking into a sprint, he headed towards the cry. He passed the open door to Dora's dressing room and saw that a candle still burned inside. A chair had been overturned and a shoe lay on the floor. Evidence of a scuffle?

The scream came again. It sounded like it was in an echoing space.

The stage.

Jacob slowed as he reached the wings. Inexperienced soldiers died by running into battle without assessing the threat; veterans knew better. Taking cover in the shadows, he peeked out at the bare boards of the performance space. What the devil? Dora was on her knees, her arms tied behind her with a scarf, a pose that thrust her chest forward and made her neck vulnerable. A man straddled her from behind. He had a knife to her bare throat and her magnificent hair bunched in his fist to pull her head back and expose her neck further. He was not alone. Two companions flanked him, but that was all Jacob could tell about them because they wore long black cloaks and expressionless Venetian masks that covered their faces.

He checked his instinct to rush to intervene. The scene was too bizarre for workaday Kendal. Was this the next play? Was he interrupting a late-night rehearsal? The lady was a good actress and her fear looked genuine, and he did not want to make an ass of himself.

But the single shoe...

'Tell us what you know!' hissed the one who held her.

'I don't know anything!' Dora pleaded. 'Let me go!'

'What did he give you?' He twisted his fist in her hair and she screamed again.

'Nothing! I don't even know the man!'

This was no rehearsal.

Three against one. He needed a weapon. Jacob looked around him and saw a dagger on the props table. Better than nothing. He grabbed it and dashed onto the stage, taking the closest of the man's associates by surprise. Holding the blade to the assailant's jugular, Jacob trapped his arms in the folds of his cloak. There was a reason soldiers didn't go into battle wearing voluminous garments.

'Release her!' He called on the commanding tone he'd used to daunt rioting soldiers in Portugal.

Unfortunately, these were no raw conscripts. The man holding Dora looked up, the barest hint of dark eyes shining behind the white mask.

'Get him!' The leader clearly had no concern for his friend, or he had guessed that Jacob would not in truth cut his throat. He was correct, but Jacob *could* put the man out of action, and even the odds a little. He shifted his grip on the dagger and plunged it into the man's shoulder where it would immobilise him and cause maximum pain.

At least, that was the plan. What happened was that the blade disappeared up into the hilt and all he did was deliver a hearty thump.

'Hell!' A blasted prop!

It took Jacob's prisoner only a second to realise he wasn't injured. He spun round with a grunt of laughter and tackled Jacob to the floor. The other man joined in the fun, kicking him in the ribs. They were enthusiastic, he would grant them that. Jacob tried to squirm free but the best he could do from his position was protect his head against the men's boots.

'Soften him up, but I don't want him unconscious. I need to talk to him,' said the leader, thrusting Dora onto her face. With her hands tied, she took the impact on her cheek, unable to control her fall. 'We'll come back to her later.' He sheathed his knife. 'Maybe she'll like to spend the night telling us what we want to know, eh?'

Jacob swore at them.

The leader crossed the stage to kick Jacob in the kidneys. Pain exploded in a rocket burst.

Jacob couldn't keep count of the blows – chest, ribs, back, right arm, groin. His vision had blurred and he was light-headed with agony. Only the strictest discipline kept him from crying out. He would not give these bastards the satisfaction. What could he do? He would almost have welcomed blacking out if he didn't have both Dora and himself to save. He tried rolling into their legs to bring at least one down but that ended with a kick to the back of his head that made him see stars. He hadn't been on the end of a beating like this since he had been unhorsed in a cavalry charge.

Then came a thud and he was pinned under something flexible but heavy. Confusingly, a black bat fluttered by his nose. A painted backdrop covered him. Next, someone gripped his arm and pulled him out.

'Run!' cried Dora.

Following her cue, he glanced back to see their attackers floundering under the canvas for Castle Spectre. She'd dropped the scenery on them. Brilliant – and resourceful. She led him back via her dressing room where she grabbed a bag and her shoe, not stopping long to put it on. He snatched up her coat for her, guessing neither of them would want to return this evening. His body ached and his eye was swelling, but he couldn't afford the time to stop and treat his injuries. Nothing serious, he didn't think, though a cracked rib was possible.

'The inn?' he asked, once they were on the street. 'Safety in numbers?'

They could hear shouts behind them. The backdrop had only delayed their assailants, not put them out of action.

'Yes. I can't think of a better place. Do you know who they are?' Dora walked swiftly but didn't run once they were out of the alley and in the high street. He appreciated that she understood running where others sauntered would merely alert their followers to their position. Mingling with the people going in and out of the tavern was their best choice. There was a ballad singer with a violin entertaining the crowd with an Irish jig so that made their job a little easier.

'No idea. How could I?'

'They were asking about you.'

'Me?'

A man staggered up to Dora, reaching for her arm.

'Wonderful performance, mish. Buy you a drink?'

The actress deftly side-stepped him.

'No thank you. I'm already engaged for the evening.' She carried on walking as if such annoyances were standard fare and not worth mentioning or calling upon Jacob to repel. Actresses were exotic visitors to quiet towns like this one.

They entered the public bar. Pipe smoke made a welcome cloud. Jacob looked for the tallest customers he could find.

Dora continued her account without a hitch. 'I stayed late and they found me. They wanted to know what you'd given me.'

Jacob frowned, guiding her to the far side of the bar.

'I didn't give you anything.'

'Apart from news.' She glanced over her shoulder. 'Is that them?'

Three men entered the taproom, scanning the crowd. If it was the attackers from the theatre, they had dumped their cloaks and masks and Jacob got a better look at them. None of them were known to him but they were too richly turned-out to be mere hired hands. Watchchains, snowy cravats, tie pins – they had money. One had his black hair tied back, one was balding with a crooked nose and the last, the youngest, was auburn-headed and looked slightly familiar but not in a way Jacob could pin down. The redhead had marks on his pale cheeks.

As though he had recently been wearing a mask tied behind his head.

'It's them.' With a nod to the innkeeper, Jacob kept walking. 'My horse and my account immediately. I'm leaving.'

The innkeeper, a rotund host with a grimy apron, threw down the rag he was holding and followed them out into the yard.

'I hope we've given satisfaction, sir?'

Jacob dug into his pocket, knowing his sudden departure would be greatly smoothed by the application of gold.

'Completely. Family emergency.'

The innkeeper took the coin and smiled. A guinea always had that effect. He whistled to the stableboy.

'The master's horse, Robbie.'

The assailants would be through the bar shortly. He had to risk it.

'There are some men I really don't want to meet. They are no friends of the lady here either. Would you delay them for me?' This time he offered five shillings.

The host nodded at Jacob's black eye.

'Looks like you've met them already. Well then.' The innkeeper gave him and Dora a swift look, probably spinning some explanation for himself about jealous suitors or disgruntled husbands. 'I can do that, sir. You duck in the stable and I'll send the lad for your bags. Love conquers all, eh?'

Jacob really did like an innkeeper who could think on his feet.

'Thank you.' Taking the lady's arm, he led her into the stable where his horse was being saddled. His ribs were protesting but he still couldn't stop to assess his wounds.

'Are you well enough to travel?' she asked, noticing his wince as he reached up to check the halter. Nero had a tender mouth.

'I will be.'

'Can you not take some laudanum for the pain?'

That way lay demons. 'Right now, I only want to get enough distance between us and Kendal so we can work out precisely what is going on. Can you ride?'

Dora shrugged. 'A little.'

'A horse for the lady,' said Jacob to the groom. 'We'll send it back from the next inn.'

When the groom looked uncertain, more money exchanged hands. This evening was going to leave him seriously short in funds until he could apply to his bank.

The groom touched his forehead and hurriedly finished saddling Nero.

'I've got just the horse for her,' he said.

'Thank you. Haste is appreciated.'

'Sir!' The actress was hunkered down by the door, watching the yard through the crack. Jacob joined her, leaning over her to look out from above her head. He shouldn't stand so close that her curls tickled his chin and clung to his bristles, but this was an exceptional situation – proprieties be damned.

The innkeeper was talking to the three assailants in the yard. Jacob could hear his answers but not the questions as the men were facing away.

'He was a guest, aye, but he's gone. Left a full five minutes ago to head back home. Where's that? He's from near Keswick, he said. Or was it Carlisle? You have to forgive my memory – so many people coming through here. He'll be taking the Northern Lakes road. A woman? I can't go giving out particulars about my customers.' Jacob blanched as coins exchanged hands. Would the host give them away, taking bribes from both sides and ending up twice as rich? 'Well, there might've been some bouncing lass with him but who am I to judge? Probably why he wanted to rush home, if you get my meaning?'

Jacob's companion sucked in a breath. He couldn't blame her for objecting to the description but if it served to send them off on a wild goose chase, all the better.

The innkeeper rocked on his heels, seeming impatient to get back to his customers. 'Thank you, sir. I'm only too pleased to be of service to your good selves. If you hurry, you should be able to catch them at the turnpike.'

The men conferred briefly, and two of them headed out, presumably to collect their horses from whichever stable they had left them in for their evening of assaulting innocent bystanders. The last, the bald man with the broken nose, turned towards the stable. They weren't trusting the helpful innkeeper. Very sensible but very inconvenient.

'He's coming to check on the horses,' hissed Jacob.

'In here, sir,' said the groom. He opened the stall where Nero had been stabled. 'Quick, miss.'

There was no time to second-guess the groom's suggestion. Jacob dived inside, keeping to the wall to make use of the shadows. Dora crouched down beside him. This close, even over the reek of the stable, he could make out her light scent of rosewater and powder. Damn enticing woman, this one.

The groom started taking the saddle off Nero.

'Here, boy, whose horse is that?' asked the bald man in a growl of a voice.

'This one? He's the squire's hunter.' The groom dropped the saddle on the wall of the stall where it would hide their heads if anyone looked over. 'Squire's up for the assizes so this one isn't for hire. Do you need a horse, sir?'

'No. Did a man and a woman leave here a few minutes ago?'

Jacob couldn't see the questioner, but he could tell from his voice that the man was moving, scouting out the stable. His diction was that of the Ton, and the product of an expensive education; very similar to Jacob's own, if truth be told. Jacob's northern vowels, learned from his nanny, had been beaten out of him by a succession of schoolmasters.

'Right before you arrived, sir,' confirmed the groom. 'They were in a right lather. Rode out on the same horse, him carrying her like a parcel, would you believe it? Whoa, you're not allowed back there!'

Jacob held his breath. From the absolute stillness of his companion, she had too. One more curl had fallen and now tickled his nose. He prayed he wouldn't sneeze. There was a sound from much further in of a bucket being kicked over.

'I'm getting Mr Bennet. You can't go tossing things around in our tack room!'

'Keep your wig on, boy. I'm done looking. But if I find out you've been lying...!'

'About what, sir?'

'Humph!' The man clattered out, kicking the wooden pail in front of him.

'Bloody southerners,' said the groom, letting Jacob and Dora out once the man had gone. 'Think they own the fecking place.'

Jacob met Dora's eyes for one charged moment, the two of them suddenly aware of their proximity. He tucked the curl back over her ear, though it clung to his lips as if it didn't want to let go. It was a strangely intimate gesture amidst the peril. She touched the ear he had brushed, an adorably confused look crossing her face. He would have said something, a half-hearted apology maybe, but then the groom heaved the saddle off the partition in front of the stall under which they had been sheltering. He put it back on a patient Nero.

'I'll fetch Astarte for you, miss,' he said.

In five minutes flat, they were ready to leave, Dora seated on a sturdy-looking grey mare. She appeared to know one end of a bridle from another, which was good news. Jacob had been prepared to take her on a leading rein if necessary but now he had hopes she would keep her seat.

'The roads south are clear, sir. One of my lads followed them and they're scouting up to the turnpike north,' said the innkeeper.

'Thank you, Bennet. I'll make sure I tip you all well on my return. Are you ready, Miss Fitz-Pennington?'

His companion gave him an inscrutable look.

'Probably not but I can't see how they've left us any choice.' She kicked her horse into motion, further proof she had at least the rudiments of riding under her belt. She had a mannish silhouette in what he now saw was a military greatcoat with brass buttons, and she rode astride as no sidesaddle was available. Tall for a woman, a cursory glance might suggest a boy or young man. That might be helpful in evading pursuers. 'We head south?'

'Yes,' Jacob said loudly as they waved farewell to the innkeeper and his servants. As soon as they were out of sight, he turned the horses east at the next crossroads, taking the fingerpost to Middleshaw.

'Really?' she asked, suspicion plain. 'I've walked most of these roads and I know that's not south.'

'The landlord has taken two bribes already in one night. I don't want to test his moral fibre when he is offered a third.'

'Good point.' She kicked her horse into a trot and followed without further argument. They had only gone another hundred yards when she said, 'Who exactly are you?'

Chapter Seven

Road to Middleshaw

Dora couldn't believe that she was following a gentleman she had only just met – and didn't even know by name – down a dark country lane with unknown enemies on their trail.

Clearly, she had missed out on a guardian angel when they had been allocated. If the angels had done their job properly, Dora would be tucked up in bed right now, her thoughts on the next performance – and her brother would still be alive.

'I'm Dr Jacob Sandys, of course. Who did you think I was?' He growled like a bee-stung bear.

'There is no "of course" about it. You never introduced yourself.' She corrected her mare's amble towards the hedge. Now that they had slowed, the mare was showing a tendency to think grazing was part of the ride. She loved horses and had ridden many a thoroughbred when she was younger, but this one reminded her of the recalcitrant pony on which she had learned to ride, Sugar Lump. The name revealed everything one needed to know about the beast. Such stubbornness was admirable if inconvenient.

Her companion was silent for a few yards. Was he reviewing their exchanges to date?

'I apologise. You are correct. Our introductions were somewhat diverted by our misunderstanding.'

By Dora's calculations, they both had something to apologise for in the short period of their acquaintance, which made them even.

'Dr Sandys, I know speed is imperative, but are you in need of medical attention?' She gestured to his battered body. His horse had a smooth gait, but she could see he was in pain from the hiss of his breathing and he no longer held himself with that aristocratic poker-stiffness of their first meeting. 'From a fellow professional, perhaps? I wouldn't want you to fall off your horse in a swoon.'

Dr Sandys felt his ribs experimentally.

'I think the risks of stopping to find one outweigh that of riding on. When we reach a safe place to rest, I will look to my bruises then.'

'I can tell you now that you have the beginnings of a nice shiner.' Indeed, the moonlight did paint his face with a garish collection of bruises. 'Brings out the colour of your eyes.' In truth she couldn't see either eye, thanks to the swelling.

'Your flattery is too much, my dear,' Sandys said in a rakish drawl.

She laughed, pleased to find her prickly companion had a sense of humour.

'But I'm relieved you aren't seriously hurt. They went at you with gusto.'

'*Con furioso*. It's not my first beating – though I hope it's my last. At my age, I thought such things behind me.'

Dora glanced at him speculatively. He didn't look that old to her. In his thirties perhaps, but not much advanced. Ruby had been right that he was attractive, but it was the allure of an interesting face rather than a classically handsome one. The bend in his nose attested to previous fights. He had a dimple in his chin that made her want to press a finger into it. Stupid thought. He was dangerous to her as a woman, though – the shared moment in the stable had proved that.

'No one would fault you for taking the Kendal Black Drop to get yourself through the next hours.'

He muttered something that sounded distinctly like 'Get behind me, Satan' but he made no direct comment.

If he preferred pain to the strange dreams brought by opium, then so be it.

'Do you have any idea why those men were after you?' she asked.

He shrugged, then winced, the least movement paining him. Riding must be purgatory.

'I thought they were after you – it was you they came for.'

'Only after you'd visited me, and it was you they asked about.'

'And yet not by name?' He frowned, and she caught what he meant. 'Tell me exactly what happened after I left to return to the inn.'

Dora sighed as she looked back over the Rubicon she had accidentally crossed from a quiet life to this.

'I changed my mind about travelling. My father is likely to destroy the letter if he gets his hands on it first.' Any mention of her parent was like opening a door onto a blast furnace of disappointment and anger. She shoved it closed. Not now.

'Why—?' He cut himself off. 'We'll return to that later. Carry on.'

'They burst in and dragged me from my dressing room. They judged it too small a space for three men to sufficiently terrorise a lone woman.'

He huffed at her sardonic tone.

'They tied my hands behind me with one of my own neckerchiefs, the bastards, and then started barking questions.' She shook her head. It all felt so strange, like a nightmare. 'I was in shock, I think. They were so intimidating in their cloaks – I couldn't see their faces and that made it a hundred times worse.'

'Tell me what you remember about the cloaks.'

'Do you know something?' She swung round to study him.

'I only caught a glimpse. Please describe what you saw.'

She closed her eyes, trusting her mare to keep to the track, and summoned up what she could recall. This was how she learned her lines, visualising them on the page. A useful trick for one in her position.

'They were black but lined with white satin. Expensive, I would say. The one that held me had an odd fastening on his cloak. It was an eye set in a triangle, the apex pointing upwards. The eye was the pin, the triangle the buckle.'

'Impressive.'

'I have a good memory.'

'Satin?'

'Yes, the genuine article.' She smiled wryly. 'You have to know these things when making costumes.' Everyone helped out in the Northern Players, with the girls often called on to use their sewing skills in the wardrobe. 'The eye looked familiar. I haven't seen it in church but I'm sure I've come across it before.'

Dr Sandys gingerly probed his swollen eye socket before dropping his hand.

'That's because it is the Eye of Providence. It has a long lineage. Some antiquarians believe it came into common usage in the Mediterranean, thanks to the example of Egyptian hieroglyphs. You can see the Eye of Horus on the temples of Egypt and the shape and intention is similar.'

'You've been to Egypt?'

'I have – with the army.'

'My goodness – a traveller! Dr Sandys, you are more interesting than you seem.'

He quirked a brow.

'Thank you for that backhanded compliment. But the Eye didn't stop there. It found its way into Christian iconography. One of the most famous examples is the painting of the Supper at Emmaus by the Italian Renaissance artist Pontormo. In the place more usually given over to the hovering dove, or Holy Spirit, he painted an eye in a triangle, symbol of an all-seeing God within a shape representing the Trinity.'

'You've seen that too?'

He shook his head. 'A reproduction only.'

'It's a Christian symbol then?'

'Not exclusively. Its use is more widespread than that, popular with Deists and rationalists too. The Americans use it on their great seal, chosen to represent all-seeing God watching over us.' He spoke clearly and concisely, a talent she admired. He had the cadence of one of Shakespeare's better orators, an Anthony or a Jacques. Why couldn't he look like a Falstaff or a Sir Andrew Aguecheek? Then she could push aside her inconvenient attraction to him.

What had he been saying? Oh yes.

'I expect they picked it as the opposite to the lion and the unicorn shield of King George; you've got a king, we've got God.'

'Or because the colonists were riddled with Freemasons and Illuminati when their nation was founded.'

That was a disappointing thought. She had rather hoped America would be different.

'Boys do love their clubs.' She paused. 'You're not one of them, are you?'

'One of what?'

'One of those men who join some foolish club for the thrill of associating secretly with each other.'

'You sound as if you've had experience of such a one?'

Her heart twisted at the memories called up by that question.

'My brother, of course. He threw in his lot with that fast set – rakes and drunkards with more money than sense. They were nicknamed the Hellfire Club in the newspapers.' God help her if Dr Sandys proved to be one of them. She didn't fancy her chances of outpacing him on her mare.

'Ah yes. They are but one of many such clubs that break out like a rash from time to time.'

He sounded indifferent to them, but was he really? 'Anthony told me that they had their own secret name.'

He looked interested by this revelation, but not involved. 'Indeed? Another subject to which we must return. Please go on with your account of what happened tonight.'

She pulled Astarte to a stop.

'You haven't answered me. I need to know more about the man with whom I'm travelling or I am a fool. Do you belong to one of these clubs?'

'No, I do not belong to a secret club.' He sounded annoyed to be quizzed, which made him more believable.

'But you wouldn't tell me if you did, would you?'

He chuckled at that.

'You have a cutting wit. Someone will get hurt.'

'So my father always told me.' She urged the mare onwards.

'Heaven forbid I should sound like your father. What else do you remember?'

'Only one spoke. He held a knife to my throat – not a prop one like you tried to use—'

'Thank you for reminding me. Not my finest hour.'

'He asked me for what "he" had given me.'

'Exact words?'

'"You had a caller tonight who brought news of your brother. What did he give you?" Oh.' She could see the ambiguity now. 'Do you think they know about Anthony's letter? And why would they want it?'

'I'm sorry, Miss Fitz-Pennington, I didn't explain myself properly when I delivered the news.' Dr Sandys looked out over the dark fields with their ghostly sheep, a grim line notching his brow. Fortunately, there was enough moonlight to see their way but not enough to read the expression in his eyes. 'The circumstances surrounding your brother's death have raised questions.'

Her fears returned. 'What kind of questions?'

'He was murdered in the caves, all that is true, but my friend believes it wasn't the action of footpads. He thinks it connects to other deaths in the area – ones linked to the activities of the Hellfire Club. That's why he asked me to go to him, so we could look at the evidence together. I believe he wants to present a cogent case to the authorities.'

'I see.' Dr Sandys was here out of duty, not because he was involved. She hated to admit it but, if there was trouble locally, Anthony would be exactly the kind of man to find it. It would be no shock to find that her brother's death had not been a random piece of bad luck. However, perhaps that meant that the perpetrator could be traced? She owed Anthony that much at least. She would find his killer and see he had an appointment with the hangman.

'Let us finish with what you remember.'

'Very well.' She battened down her rage and grief. That would have to wait. 'Your intervention gave me the opportunity I needed to escape the scarf. I think they were used to finer stuff than I can afford – my neckerchief is flimsy muslin and frayed. I was able to tear it to free my hands.' She held up her right hand. 'Broke a couple of fingernails but I thought that worth it, seeing what they had planned for us.'

'Indeed.' His lips curled in disdain.

'Then I came up with the quickest way of immobilising them so we could escape.'

'The backdrop? Very well done indeed, Miss Fitz-Pennington.'

The compliment was welcome as it was the last she was likely to receive for the ruin of a stage prop.

She sighed. 'Mr Thomas is going to kill me. He had that painted in York. Cost a fortune.'

'I will send him payment with you when you return. I wouldn't want you to be unfairly blamed for the damage.'

'You are very kind.' It stuck in her craw but she would accept, even though it had been her choice to sacrifice the scenery. Her reasoning was simple: Dr Sandys had deeper pockets than Mr Thomas. 'Gathering all that together, you say we are being chased by men who masquerade as cloaked villains, and they think either you or my brother have given me something. They want that something, but we do not have a clue what that something is – unless it is the letter?'

He shot her an astute look. 'You don't think it's the letter?'

'My brother cut off all official communication with me five years ago on the orders of our father.' Covert messages had been passed, naturally, when a reliable messenger could be found, but Anthony had explained that he had to make out in public that he held to the family line and had separated himself from her. 'No one should expect him to write to me.' That they would know of the letter didn't feel right to her, but how could she be certain? 'Unless they raided your friend's house earlier and he told them about it?'

'Raiding a theatre after hours is very different from attacking a clergyman in his parish. And a gentleman wouldn't place his friend in trouble like that,' Dr Sandys said loftily.

'Hah!' The man didn't know gentlemen very well if he thought that.

'Not George Leighton. He has very strict morals. I've seen them tested. The unknown assailants might have picked up on local gossip about it and leapt to conclusions when he sent me a letter by express. That would set tongues wagging.'

'I pray he still has my brother's letter in his possession. We must make haste to reach him before my father or these play-actors get to him.'

Dr Sandys rubbed his brow in what she realised was a habitual gesture of frustration at the world.

'Not play-actors, Miss Fitz-Pennington. I very much fear we have attracted the attention of the Illuminati.'

Chapter Eight

'Illuminati?' Dora snorted. Ridiculous. 'Is this another club with orgies, opium and drinking games because that's what attracted my brother to the Hellfire Club.' It all sounded foolish to her, cementing her already low opinion of the upper classes.

He gave her a stern look. Dr Sandys did not like her mockery. Bad luck. Sarcasm was her speciality, served up to all.

'I'm afraid nothing as simple. They exist because people love to congregate with like-minded souls. Hellfire Clubs set out to shock. They thumb their nose at society. I doubt very much any of them believe in the satanic rituals they conduct, or the oaths they take to each other.'

Dora didn't agree. She'd met enough devils in her lifetime to convince her of the existence of evil and those who believed in demons. But Sandys was a rationalist; she would leave him his illusions.

'What is the point of their rebellion? They are hardly bettering society.'

'Quite the opposite. It is about the individual. Their motto is "Do what you will" – the ultimate cry of the rebellious child or

The Persephone Code

morally bankrupt adult. If they ever had a wider aspiration, it is that of a bull in a china shop.'

That did sound like a group who would attract Anthony, gnawed at by his black dog of low spirits. 'And the Illuminati?'

'They are the opposite of the Hellfire Club in many respects – their natural enemy. They claim to be servants of reason. If a few believe in anything, it is in the form of Deism, a generalised sense of the divine, rather than the God of the Christian Bible.'

In Dora's experience, true atheists were rare. Most people she met travelling the country kept religion at a distance until needed and didn't hold a strong view, leaving belief to those paid to have the cure of their souls.

Still, this didn't make sense.

'Atheists meeting under a symbol of the Eye of Providence? How does that work?'

'It stands for opening the eye of the mind. If they have a motto, it is "Do what reason tells you".'

'Whose reason?' She was enjoying this to and fro with him. Nothing more seductive than a well-informed man.

'Ah, I see you've hit on the problem. *Their* reason – and theirs tends to want to fashion society to their own benefit so in the end both groups do what they wish.'

And wasn't that a grim verdict on the state of the nation? Dora had long felt Britain was on a wild ride, far out of her control, what with war against Napoleon and a repressive government prosecuting anyone who dared stand up for radical causes, such as the rights of the common people.

'Who are *they*?'

'No one knows. A small, rich elite.'

'No change there then.'

He shook his head at her mocking tone. He would have looked more censorious if not for his rakish black eye blooming quite spectacularly.

'It's the secret nature of the groups that differs from other clubs. Most times we see what men are after as they act in the open. They debate in parliament, in court, or in the newspapers. If the real decision-makers hide in the shadows, how are we to protest against moves they make, or even understand how we are being manipulated? I believe they dress it up in high-sounding language and symbols to excuse what is really a shameless plot to enrich themselves at our expense. There are few true believers.'

Dora breathed on her fingers. The night was turning chilly and her wrists were sore. She had lost some skin as she pulled her way out of the scarf that had bound her in the theatre. What he was saying was interesting, but such matters felt beyond her, a lowly actress on an obscure theatrical circuit. Her priority was a place to sleep and recoup her strength.

'You might feel that way, but I've never had any power even if I see it being abused openly.'

'I see I am riding with a *sans-culotte*.'

'Hardly.' She grinned as she showed a flash of the breeches under her skirt – ones she had not had time to remove after the performance. The warmth and protection for her thighs were welcome. They were far out of Kendal now and into a landscape of isolated farms in hidden valleys.

'Hah!' He chuckled then held his ribs with a grimace. 'However, Miss Égalité, you might feel differently if you had lived through the French Revolution. Would you have cared then? Many say the Illuminati were the ones who steered that business, before it went off course so spectacularly.'

'Who knows? Most of us feel powerless, and the actions of the men in power happen without explanation. They certainly don't feel accountable to someone like me, so what difference if they are open or secret about it?' She glanced at him, this well-turned-out gentleman with no lack of funds. She couldn't resist a little dig. 'I would imagine that you feel very differently. What is your family background, Dr Sandys?'

He shrugged, not willing to share. She found that annoying, as he seemed very well-informed about her.

'All right then. I will guess and you can tell me if I'm hot or cold.' She flexed her hands to stop them freezing. 'You're a doctor, so that means you are educated, but not the eldest son of some noble line because they wouldn't allow such a one to follow a profession if he is in line to inherit an estate. Am I correct?'

'Not the oldest. My brother, Arthur, has that dubious privilege.'

'Ah, so you are from the gentry?'

He shook his head.

She couldn't imagine him being any lower, so that left...

'Nobility?'

He nodded. 'My father is Viscount Sandys.'

She had been right. An impressive title but she quickly reminded herself that she made it a point of pride not to show deference unless someone earned her respect.

'And they allowed you to be a doctor? I thought such things beneath them.'

'There was no "allowed" about it. I forged my own path.' He sounded nettled and defensive. She sensed that this had been a topic of much debate in his own family. 'I was bound for the military, so I thought to be of use saving lives rather than taking them.'

A sentiment she agreed with, though not going to war at all might be better. She nudged Astarte away from the hawthorn hedge.

'And did you?'

'Did I what?'

'Save lives.'

'You don't have a very high opinion of doctors.'

'From what I see, the outcome of an illness is rarely changed by the visit of a doctor, except that the family is much poorer for it.'

'And yet on a battlefield, bullets must be dug out and shattered limbs splinted or removed. Better to go to the man with the tools than try to do it yourself. Speed is essential – and only experience teaches that.'

Dora wondered at herself. She was attacking a man for his profession when in truth she had little to hold against doctors, not having had much contact with them. Her brother had been scathing about army sawbones but, as he had been wrong in many of his opinions, his views should not guide her own.

'I'm sure you were greatly valued.'

'Oh, I wouldn't go that far. I tried not to kill my patients – that is the best that could be said of me. What about here?' It was an abrupt change of subject, but he pointed now to a barn that sat close to the side of the road with no farmhouse in sight, unless it was hidden by the little wood further on. There was light from a nearly full moon but not enough to make out the details of the landscape. A few bleats told her that sheep were close by, probably sheltering behind the stone walls of this landscape of hills and crags.

She knew barns well, and could foresee the lack of any food or drink, not to mention bedding. 'Not an inn?'

'I think it would be wise to avoid a public place tonight. Best to avoid news of our direction, should we be chased this far.'

Her agreement was signalled by turning the mare towards the barn.

'You really think they will keep after us?'

'If they thought their errand worth coming all the way to Kendal, I doubt they will give up so easily.'

'But surely we will be safe now? They have no way of knowing our route and there are only three of them.'

'Yet they can reason a shrewd guess at our destination, and we don't know if we met the entire company. Our best plan would be to wait them out before heading south.'

'We cannot tarry. My father will get to the message first – if he hasn't already.' She could imagine the letter even now curling in the flames. The thought burned her, though she knew they had to rest. Dora dismounted and opened the gate for the two horses.

Sandys laid a fleeting hand on her shoulder – a touch that shivered through her, raising the hairs on the back of her neck.

'We must rest the horses, and we also need our wits about us. Let's sleep here for the remainder of the night and set off early before a farmer comes calling.' She admired the way he steered his horse with just the pressure of his knees – no hauling on the reins for him. 'With any luck, we will be fifty miles from Kendal before our foes think to look for us in this direction.'

She pushed open the barn door so he could ride in without dismounting. Sandys looked around him.

'Good enough but I apologise for the standard of accommodation.'

'It is by no means the first night I've spent in a barn. Nor the last, I daresay.' She rummaged in her bag for a candle and tinderbox.

The barn, with its thick walls built of local stone and roofed with slate, was ideal for an overnight stay, being dry and with a pile of hay in the loft. No other animals were in residence so the horses had the ground floor to themselves.

'These are presumably winter quarters for the cows out on the pasture,' said Sandys, answering the thought that had been in her mind too. A few weeks earlier and they would not have found the barn so sweet-smelling, though it might have been a great deal warmer with a herd sheltering beneath.

Dora insisted on unsaddling both horses while her companion looked to his wounds. She watched out of the corner of an eye while, with his back to her, he stripped off his coat, waistcoat and shirt, then used his long cravat to strap up his ribs. Even by the light of the single candle she had lit, she could see that his skin was mottled with bruises.

'Anything broken?' she asked, filling a nosebag for Astarte.

'No – at least not as far as I can tell. Possibly a cracked rib or two.' He turned to pick up his shirt, revealing a long scar that ran from his collarbone to his navel. She couldn't hide a sympathetic wince. 'The retreat at Corunna, January 1809,' he said in response. 'We rescued twenty-five thousand men from the beach under fire of the enemy. A miracle, considering it was winter and a quarter of the soldiers were sick or injured.' He said it as if he'd recounted the same thing many times before.

'I thought you were a non-combatant.'

'In which case the Frenchman who tried to cut me down had not received the dispatch.'

'How foolish of him.'

'But understandable. We saved the army so they could go back and fight up through the Peninsula. It was a victory for us in the long view, even though at the time it felt like the bitterest of losses.' He covered a very praiseworthy chest with his shirt. Dora tried not to notice her disappointment. 'I sewed myself up.' He said it as if almost to himself as his memories took him back to that battle and its aftermath.

'You did *what*?'

He flashed her a smile, coming out of his reverie.

'I wouldn't recommend it, but I trusted my hand more than that of the soldiers I was with on the hospital ship. I did a fine job and earned the nickname of Stitch amongst the men.' He laughed – he *actually* laughed – as if that was a good memory. 'Ouch.' His hand went to his ribs.

'You are...' She swallowed back the rude words she was about to say.

'Fit for Bedlam? I daresay. After you.' He gestured her to go ahead up the ladder. Dora picked up the candle but realised her skirts were going to be difficult if she didn't have a hand free.

'Let me.' Sandys took the candle and she hitched up her petticoats to make the ascent. 'Going to war is a mad proposition but far too often necessary.' He followed with his saddlebag slung across his back. She took the candle once he came within reach. 'Thank you.' He unrolled a blanket from his saddlebag with the ease of practice and spread it on the straw. 'Your bed awaits, madame.'

'What about you?'

'I'll use my coat.'

She was truly bone-tired so had no wish to argue.

'Thank you.' She lay down and used her own greatcoat as a cover. Sandys groaned as he lowered himself onto the hay at a respectful distance from her. A true gentleman – what a rarity. She blew out the candle, letting the moonlight creep back in through a high window.

'Now, Miss Fitz-Pennington, tell me about your father.'

Chapter Nine

Middleshaw

Jacob had been wondering about his companion, hoping that divulging some of his own past would encourage her to confide in him. So far, she had been sparing with her conversation – and he'd much prefer to talk than let his mind circle back to the nagging thought that the answer to his pain lay in finding the nearest druggist. He had to stick to less difficult topics – like murder.

If Leighton was correct that Pennington's death was suspicious – and the attack in Kendal did prove him to be right – then anything she knew about Anthony and the Pennington family might provide clues. Did their father have important connections that Jacob needed to know about? Why had her brother mixed in such dangerous company? What could Pennington possibly have in his possession the retrieval of which was worth sending Illuminati across England to terrorise his sister on the chance that she held it? Jacob was somewhat slower to admit that he had grown curious about the lady in her own right. Her wit and quick thinking recommended her to his favour – a pleasant change from the hothouse flowers that so many women pretended to be in the Ton.

He preferred tougher plants that stood on their own, whatever the climate – particularly golden-skinned, generously curved blooms like the lady resting in the straw but a few feet away.

'My father is a monster.' Dora pulled the collar of the coat higher and turned over, signalling that, in her opinion, this was all he needed to know.

'I was hoping for a little more than that,' he said with a smile, gazing up at the rafters. A barn owl blinked back at him, eyes reflecting the moonlight streaming in from a high window. He hadn't even noticed the bird until that moment. 'Look.' He pointed upwards.

She turned onto her back, and they watched as the creature gave them a last scornful survey and took off on velvet wings to hunt.

'Beautiful,' whispered Dora. 'And on that note ... goodnight.'

Unfortunately, she wasn't going to enjoy sleep yet. There were things he had to know if he was to keep her safe.

'Please, Miss Fitz-Pennington, I have questions.'

She gave a feminine grumble, before saying, 'Go on then – if you must.'

She would lead her lover in a merry dance, this one, never giving an inch without making him work for it. 'You ascribe to your father great persuasive powers, enough to wrest the letter from my friend. What are these? Position? Money? Force of character?'

'A pox on him. Do we have to discuss this? I'm tired and would very much prefer to spend the hours between now and dawn asleep.'

'Miss Fitz-Pennington, it appears that the Illuminati, or possibly his Hellfire associates, killed your brother. Whoever wielded the blade, we know that the Illuminati are hunting something of his; maybe the letter, maybe something else. It is fair to assume that they will have gone after all his close connections. I understand that you may not like your father' – she snorted at this – 'but it may be that he needs to be warned because, if I were them, I'd seek you both out in case your brother sent this thing they want to his father instead.'

Silence fell between them, broken only by her rapid breathing.

'Miss Fitz-Pennington?' Was she panicking? He wouldn't blame her after the night they had just endured. 'Are you well?' He wondered if he should offer her a shot from his brandy flask.

Her gasps became sobs… No, not sobs but laughs – the dark kind that he had heard from soldiers when they were told they were to set off again in a rainstorm after barely an hour's rest.

'The Illuminati after our father! Well, for once they might have bitten off more *illumination* than they can chew.'

Who the devil was Pennington senior? Jacob thought he knew most of the key people in London and government, even if not personally, and the name rang no bells.

'You don't believe the Illuminati pose any danger to him?'

She sat up, the coat pooling about her waist, and drew her knees to her chest. Her hair tumbled around her shoulders having given up any pretence of staying pinned back.

'All right, Dr Sandys, let me tell you a little about my father, then maybe you will let me sleep. Ezra Pennington is a merchant in Liverpool. An alderman, mayor for a few years, hoping to be so again, and owner of ships, but most of his holdings are in the West Indies. That is where I was born and where my mother came from.'

Jacob had a sinking feeling he knew where her story was going. He had spent his early twenties working with Wilberforce and the abolitionists to end the slave trade, which had been achieved in 1807; but slavery persisted in the Indies with untold numbers suffering on the plantations. The nightmares from what he had learned of the plight of the slaves had become mingled with the horrors of war – another monstrosity. Thankfully, the dreams were no longer as vivid as during those years when he had fallen into the habit of dulling his despair in opium.

'He keeps slaves?'

'Who doesn't?' She shrugged as if to say he shouldn't need to ask the question.

'Those who think it is evil.'

'Then I wish more people took their money out of plantations. But as his bastard, he did not feel my view worth taking into account when ordering his affairs.'

Jacob wondered if she had closer ties to slavery than she perhaps knew. Her hair was curled and her skin tone a little darker than the average young lady in England. Many merchant families in the West Indies had African ancestors in their lineage. That might have made further difficulties with her father.

'Who was your mother, if you don't mind me asking?'

'A foolish sixteen-year-old girl from Kingston just out of the schoolroom when she was seduced by the rich merchant from Liverpool.' Her tone was sardonic – a habitual note for her, he realised. 'I think she believed they were to be married, unaware of the little obstacle of a wife back in the old country.'

'There's a name for such men.'

'Indeed. I've called him that many times and been whipped for it.' She grimaced. 'She died in childbirth, leaving me alive, much to everyone's surprise and regret. Her father – my grandfather – took me from my poor mother, roaring with grief, and dumped me in my father's arms. My father said that my grandfather gave a great speech about how Pennington had made this bed and would have to lie in it – I think my father almost admired him as he also has a temper.' She hugged her knees closer. 'I sometimes wonder if my grandfather regretted that rashness. I would have infinitely preferred to be raised by my mother's parents rather than... Well, I suppose I will never know for certain.'

'And your father raised you with his legitimate family?'

Her lips twisted into a bitter smile.

'You could say that. He had to pretend to look after me or lose his reputation in Jamaica. My mother was dismissed as a lightskirt who deserved her fate, while he was toasted in the clubs as a dashing rake, but even rakes have to pay their dues. I left Port Royal as his daughter and arrived in England as his ward. Daughter of a dear colleague who died of Yellow Fever. There was just enough plausibility in the lie for people to pretend they believed it, even his wife.'

Many of the noble families had a miscellany of legitimate and illegitimate children in the nursery but it was more unusual for one of the merchant class to do so. Morals in the provinces were usually stricter than in the capital.

'You were accepted by your siblings?'

'There was only Anthony.' Her voice caught on his name. 'He ... he was two years older than me so it was natural that we should band together, with the adults as our adversaries. As we grew older and the family resemblance became obvious,' she touched her cheek, then ran a finger down the profile of her nose, as if remembering her brother's features, 'we both realised that my wardship was a lie, but we rarely spoke of it. What was the use?'

'Indeed. And yet you were never acknowledged publicly?'

'Do you think the Mayor of Liverpool, magistrate for our district and staunch member of the parish council, would parade his by-blow before his neighbours? You don't need to answer that.'

'Yet you kept his name?'

She chuckled at that.

'Oh no. That was my choice once I broke with him. I was Dora Smith for the first twenty years of my life.'

'Very original.'

'Indeed. I decided to go on stage as Fitz-Pennington, child of Pennington, because I knew it would infuriate him. But he has no power over me, and what could he do? Take me to court? That would only make the connection even more infamous. No, he chose silence and ignorance of my fate. Dora Smith died the day I left his house. He even forced the family to wear a black armband and go into mourning as if for a distant relation.'

Jacob could well imagine the young Dora defying her father as she strode out of Liverpool in search of her fortune. Yet the risk she had taken! Something told him she would not appreciate his commentary on her choice that could have seen her on the streets or dead in a ditch. Better to concentrate on the present danger than pick a quarrel about the past.

'He sounds like a big fish in his world, but the Illuminati are a school of sharks. I fear even your father is in danger.'

'Then I will leave you to tell him.' She bunched back her hair then rolled over. 'He wouldn't listen to anything I have to say. I would be wasting ink and paper. Now, goodnight. Save your other questions until the morning. I've had enough of today.'

Jacob reminded himself that in addition to the assault, she was also dealing with the news that her only brother was dead. Again, he was falling severely short of compassion.

'Sleep well, Miss Fitz-Pennington.'

She huffed a laugh at his careful use of her surname.

He closed his eyes. What an interminable day. He had no energy to continue. The beating he had received had reawakened the pull towards opium that he had successfully buried in the Lakes. One lure of the drug had been that it at first had made him a better doctor, able to push through a long shift at the hospital with waves of battlefield casualties being brought in. Opium had separated him from the suffering and pain by what felt like a pane of glass, allowing him to operate. The irony was that he had had to give up his business of doctoring to avoid being around the temptation of self-medication every day. He did not feel like the victor, despite having won his personal battle against the drug.

Added to that, he had got caught in a web that clung all the harder when he tried to pull free. Chivalry meant he could not retreat to Hawkshead and leave Dora to puzzle this out alone, nor, now he had met her, did he want to abandon her. Besides, he had no confidence that the Illuminati, now they had scented his part in this business, would not seek him out there. The answer lay in solving the mystery. Only then could he return home and put this episode behind him. And for the next few hours, there was nothing else to do but rest and ready himself for the trials of the coming days.

Barely had he let the tension seep out of his bruised body when the ladder to the hayloft rattled and a rifle appeared at the top, followed by a head. The gun was pointing straight at him.

Chapter Ten

'What the devil are thee doin' in here? Get on wi' thee!'

Jacob's pulse returned to something like normal when he realised it was a farmer rather than the men from earlier. Quite rightly, the landowner was objecting to them taking a night's lodging for free. He could sympathise. He no more wanted vagrants in his barn than the next man.

He held up his hands, palms open.

'Apologies. We lost our way.'

Hearing the refined tones, the farmer dipped the muzzle of the gun – not that the current trajectory between Jacob's legs was much comfort. 'What's wrong with yer face?'

Jacob could hear the rustle and quickened breathing of Dora beside him but he daren't draw attention to her.

'I...'

'My husband took a tumble from his horse,' said Dora quickly, getting to her knees to show that she was decently dressed. She quickly patted her hair over one shoulder to tame the masses. 'I've been very worried about him – he seemed quite addled. The best I could do was get him under shelter. Do you know where there's a doctor?'

Now his gallantry was appealed to, the farmer's attitude underwent a sea-change.

'He's taken a clowt, has he? Aye, that'll do it. Come down, lass. Ar'll make sure yer man divn't fall.'

Dora shot Jacob a look to tell him to act his part. He was a little surprised to see the initiative taken from him, but he had to admit her story was plausible and helpful. He had to remember that about her.

Dora climbed down the ladder, continuing to tell her story.

'We were making for the road to York, sir, but I'm quite turned around and don't know where we are. Do you live nearby? I looked about for a house but could only find this barn. I do hope we haven't disturbed you?'

The farmer passed Dora the gun and helped Jacob to his feet. A trusting man, this one.

'Our house is o'er yon beck, reet hard to see in the dark after we shut up for the night. But I saw a light and thought the tramp had come back. He's taken a liking to this barn, he has.'

'A very fine barn,' Dora agreed.

Jacob positioned himself at the top of the ladder and found the farmer underneath him, ready to catch him if he fell.

'Mind yer step, sir.' His strong hands guided Jacob's feet to the next rung. 'I have to chase him off – or set the dogs on him.'

'I, for one, am very grateful that you came yourself to see us off.' Dora gave him a smile that revealed dimples in her cheek.

'They divn't chase the ladies, Mrs…?'

'Mrs Sandys. This is my husband, Dr Sandys, a physician.'

Jacob marvelled at the ease with which she announced these lies.

She's an actress, you fool. It would be more surprising if she fluffed her lines.

The farmer patted Jacob's shoulder to signal that he'd arrived on the ground.

'It's a case of physician, heal thyself, eh?'

'My wife worries,' Jacob said gruffly. 'Mr...?'

'Clegg.'

'I will be fine, after a night's rest. We must be on our way at first light.'

The farmer sniffed, not agreeing with this prognosis.

'We'll see what thee says after we've looked at thy injuries. My wife knows a thing or two about doctoring, having me and our lads to look after. Leave the horses here. They'll come to nae harm.'

Jacob accepted the neighbourly arm to help him navigate his way along the track to the farmhouse, Dora carrying the farmer's lantern and gun. Clegg shouldered their bags, refusing to let either of them take the extra weight.

'I lug yon sheep that get stuck in snowdrifts. This is nowt,' he declared.

They arrived in the snug farmhouse built of stone and slate, very like the barn. Mr Clegg woke the household. The farmer's wife bustled down on her husband's shout that she was needed. That call also brought her two sons and a shy daughter. The girl took charge of Dora, leading her away to change her clothes and take a bed for the night with her.

Mrs Clegg clucked over his bruises and slathered them with an ointment she had on hand. When he asked what was in it, she smiled, eyes twinkling.

'Blackwort, witch hazel and a bit of this an' that. It's a family secret.'

Relieved, he returned her smile.

'By all means, keep your secrets.' And he hoped she would let him keep his. At least it wasn't one of the opium-based preparations that you could buy from every druggist, barber or tobacconist. Most thought them harmless, even giving them to babies as a cure-all, but Jacob knew from bitter experience the cure could be worse than the original injury. Despite temptation, he'd made a vow of total abstinence and intended to keep it.

Mr Clegg placed a mug of beer before him.

'I reckon that'll speed thy recovery, e'en more than my wife's doctoring.'

'Thank you.'

'Our Joe will make a place for thee in his bed,' said Mrs Clegg.

'I'd be happy to sleep in a chair.'

'Whisht, lad,' said the farmer. 'Thee's in a bad way and my wife has spoken. Divn't cross my wife.' He patted his lady on the arm as she chuckled.

'Aye, thee needs a bed.'

That sounded heavenly. Jacob was just beginning to count his blessings when the door banged open and one of the farmer's sons rushed in from outside.

'Da! The barn's ablaze!'

'Eh?'

Jacob and the farmer hurried into the yard. Beyond the trees an orange glow illuminated the night. The barn where they had taken shelter was ablaze.

'The horses!' Jacob broke into a run. He kicked himself for leaving them behind when he'd known there was a chance they were being hunted. His injuries must have addled his brains. Nero deserved far better from him.

The men raced along the track, Jacob limping and stumbling in potholes where the others ran surefooted around them. His mind continued to work through the fact that this might not be a coincidence, meaning—

'Wait! There may be...' But they were out of sight.

'Dammit all to hell!' He turned to go back to fetch his pistols only to find Dora had once again anticipated him. She met him with the farmer's rifle, white nightdress flapping about her in the stiff breeze. She'd only stopped to don her boots, neglecting a coat. The direction of the wind changed. The smell of smoke was strong, embers flitting in the sky. As they fluttered by her, her hair streamed in the wind, so she looked like an avenging goddess descended to wreak havoc – Athena in the battle for Troy.

'Do you know how to use this?' she asked.

'I do.'

She shoved it into his arms.

'Quick! I couldn't live with myself if the Cleggs are hurt.'

Gritting his teeth against the pain of his ribs, he began running again and realised she was still with him.

'Go back!'

'No.' She was outpacing him.

Damned obstinate female! Having no breath for an argument, he hobbled as fast as he was able into the barnyard. The fire had taken hold and they could hear the panicked neighs of their horses.

'Gad, Absalom, break down that door!' roared the farmer.

His two sons, big lads, threw aside the hurdles and barrels that had been laid across the entrance. Someone had been trying to shut the horses inside. Had they hoped to kill their riders too? Maybe not: a window on the roadside had been left clear. It looked like an attempt to funnel them in that direction. Mr Clegg dragged open the doors and Nero thundered out, the whites of the stallion's eyes showing. He reared and bucked, making it hard for anyone to get past him.

'Astarte!' Dora dodged Jacob's grasp, attempting to find a way behind the horse.

'Miss...' She was supposed to be his wife! 'Dora! Come away!' called Jacob.

A sharp crack split the night and the stone by his foot

splintered, shards stinging his calf. Jacob dived behind a sheep pen. This was all going to hell in a handbasket.

'Take cover!' he shouted. The shot had come from the direction of the road. The shooter was hiding in darkness, while he, Dora and the men were all lit for targeting by the fire. His voice had carried to the nearest of the boys, but not to Mr Clegg, Dora and the remaining son, who were trying to calm Nero.

'Da! Gad!' The boy bellowed. 'Gunshots!'

'Leave the damn horse!' Jacob added. 'Save yourselves!'

Another shot drove home his message. The bullet clipped the top of the wall behind him. At least he knew who they had on their kill list. Dora, spot-lit in her nightgown, appeared safe. Unfortunately, he only had one shot loaded in the old rifle Dora had thrust at him, so he could not afford to waste it by firing blind.

Then Dora proved that, though she might be an actress, she did not take direction, as she slipped behind Nero and headed into the barn.

Chapter Eleven

The smoke hung in the air, thickest near the doors where the fire had been set. It was a huge risk to enter but there was no way that Dora would let a horse burn to death if she could do anything about it. It was their fault the mare was in this predicament. Gathering her skirt and taking a run at the entrance, Dora leapt over the burning timbers. Heat singed her ankles, but she landed inside without setting herself aflame. Good enough. There she found Astarte backed into a corner, eyes rolling in fright. Nero's theatrics at the door had driven her back inside, poor girl. Soot smudged the mare's pearly flanks and she twitched and bucked in her panic.

Dora reached out.

'There now, pretty girl, there now.' She pitched her voice low, like she'd used to do with her father's highly strung thoroughbreds. 'You're safe now.'

They were far from safe, but she had to make the mare believe it. If an animal trusted you, it would follow you into cannon fire, as the cavalry proved over and over. She could hear shouts and what sounded like gunshots from outside, but that wasn't her problem. Hers was a horse who had done nothing to deserve this.

Glancing up to assess how long they had, Dora saw the flames had made it to the hayloft. There seemed little chance that the building could be saved. The barn owl flew once over her head and out the open doors, unimpressed by the disaster they had brought upon it. Poor Astarte was too scared to follow. The fire hadn't reached her corner and no amount of tugging would persuade her that she had to go through the flames to get out.

I'll have to ride her, Dora realised. Riding bareback wasn't something she had done since she was a child, risking the groom's wrath as she stole rides from her father's favourite mounts. She wondered if she still had the knack.

'Only one way to find out.' Eyes stinging, lungs labouring, she hauled herself onto the mare's back with the help of a trough. Taking a grip on the mane, she dug her heels into the horse's side. 'Yah!'

Instinct to cower battled with the instinct to obey. Dora could feel the horse wavering as she spun in a circle.

'Yah!' she urged again, and this time Astarte bolted for the door, jumping the bonfire in the entrance with more grace than Dora had done.

'You stupid woman! Get down!' a man shouted.

Dr Sandys didn't take disobedience well. He hadn't worked out that she had no reason to obey him. Feeling a bit of the devil in her tonight, Dora urged the mare on, turning her towards the farmhouse.

A crack split the night.

A spurt of earth three yards away told her that had been close. She thought she'd not been the target. Muttering curses on the Illuminati, she lay low against Astarte's neck. The house was a very good idea, if their enemies had not got there before her. She rode the mare into the yard and steered her to the back of the house. With their enemies lying in wait, her party would need more than a single shotgun to drive them off. Did Sandys travel with a brace of pistols? Many gentlemen took them on journeys as there were footpads and highwaymen aplenty on the bleaker stretches of road.

Having secured Astarte in the pig pen so she wouldn't bolt again, Dora dashed into the house. There was no sign that enemies had come here yet. She saw through the kitchen window that Mrs Clegg and her daughter were outside filling up buckets at the well. Running upstairs to where Sandys' kitbag had been taken, she tipped it out onto the bed. Possessions went flying. Her gaze ran over the fine cambric shirts and soft buckskin breeches, a notebook, a case... Grabbing that, she opened it, intrigued but disappointed to find it full of artist's materials – pigments, paint brushes, little bottles. No guns.

She then spied the saddle bags. Of course! He'd want weapons to hand. She treated those with the same disrespect as she had his kitbag and was finally rewarded. A case of pistols. She flipped it open and quickly primed the guns, thankful that her miscellaneous education had included such necessities. Travelling theatrical companies were seen as soft targets for thieves and it was assumed, correctly, that they carried their takings from the box office until they could be banked. They all kept their pistols loaded on the journey over the Pennines.

Catching a flash of white at her ankles as she turned for the door, Dora was reminded how cold and visible she was in her nightgown. She grabbed her coat from a peg and hurried back out.

There was no need for the moon as the burning stable lit her way. Stopping at the edge of the copse of oak and holly that hid the house from the road, she could see that her allies were pinned down. They were angled so that they looked away from her to the hillside opposite. That gave her the clue as to where their enemies had set up. Was there more than one? Now she had had a moment to consider, it seemed unlikely that the Illuminati would have so many men searching for them. Maybe there was only a single shooter out there? Otherwise, they would have already circled round, wouldn't they, and taken a shot from the rear? This plan – to set fire to the stables to flush them out – seemed more like the action of a single person knowing he was outnumbered. More men and they would have liked their odds of bursting in and taking them captive.

Time then to make the hunter the hunted.

Dora cut through the trees. The holly conspired to hold her up, and it was hard going off the path. She stuck one of the pistols in the deep pocket of the coat to free up a hand to push branches out of her way. After scrambling through the prickly lower branches and sacrificing several strands of hair, she came out onto the road further down from the barn, out of the reach of the firelight. Her legs were scratched but she ignored the pain. She crossed swiftly and climbed the bank opposite. Her aim was to get above the shooter and take him captive from behind. That achieved the goal of rescuing Sandys and the Cleggs, as well as giving them a chance to find out what exactly was going on.

A dry-stone wall barred her progress. A few of the rocks tumbled as she bellied over it, making a clatter that she feared their assailant would hear. Pausing, she strained her ears and eyes to search for movement over the ridge. When no one approached, she judged it safe to go on.

Another shot split the night, followed by a shout from the barn. Dora instinctively ducked but it wasn't aimed in her direction. She prayed no one had been hit. The shooter would have to reload – now was the best chance she would get. Staying low, Dora ran to the edge of the ridge where she hoped she would be able to look down on the enemy. Her guess was right. He had set up in a sheep fold, using the walls to protect him from return fire from the men in the barnyard. He hadn't thought, or didn't have the capacity, to defend himself from the rear. A horse was tied to the open gate, still steaming from a brisk ride. Dora slid past it while the attacker was engaged with reloading. She pressed the muzzle of the pistol against the back of his neck and he spilled the cartridge he was pouring into the priming pan.

'Drop your weapon or I'll drop you.' She kept her tone low and calm. She had to convince him she meant every word.

'Go to the devil!' he spat.

'Less talk, more action.' She pressed the barrel into his skin so he could not mistake the cold touch of steel. The satisfying clunk of a rifle against the stone followed.

'I have him!' she shouted.

'A woman?' This gave the man foolish confidence. He lunged, as if her gender meant he no longer had to fear her.

Dora lowered her aim and shot his foot.

Chapter Twelve

He screamed as she took out the second pistol.
'You were warned. Don't move.'

Heart drumming, she couldn't do anything about the fact he was now writhing in pain, yelling and cursing. Apparently, she was a whore and a punk, which was rich coming from the man who had but a moment ago been trying to shoot her and her friends. Stepping back, she kicked his rifle out of reach because, once his fog of pain lifted, he likely would make a grab for it and swing it at her. Even unloaded, it could serve as a club. Without taking him out of her sights, she crouched to sweep it up.

'I'd be obliged if you bloody well hurried!' she shouted to the men in the barnyard.

A figure vaulted over the wall, landing almost on top of the injured shooter.

'What the—?' Dr Sandys looked between the downed man and Dora with his pistols as if they were specimens in a zoological garden.

'What the Devil, yes, I know. All very surprising etcetera

etcetera. But perhaps you could secure our prisoner, then offer him some assistance? He appears to have injured his foot.'

'Injured his foot?'

'Dr Sandys, I'm pleased to report that you have no need to get yourself a parrot as you fulfil that function very well for yourself. Yes, he has been shot in the boot. I suspect his big toe was the casualty. That was where the gun was aimed. More importantly, I thought he could tell us exactly what is going on.'

Sandys swung into action, taking off the man's cravat and using it to bind his hands.

'Stop that noise, man. It's just a scratch.'

Dora approved of his bedside manner.

'A scratch? She blew my bloody foot off!' The crack in the man's voice revealed him to be little more than a youth, perhaps only in his early twenties. Red hair was plastered to his brow and his face was pale. Dora found herself devoid of pity for his tender years, given what he'd just put them through.

Surprised, Sandys glanced up at her. Had he thought the injury was self-inflicted in the hurry to reload?

Dora shrugged.

'I doubt he'll lose the foot unless he is stupid enough not to accept the aid of a doctor.' She prodded the young man with her toecap. 'That's this person – the one you were trying to kill – if you haven't worked it out yet.'

The two Clegg boys appeared at the other side of the wall.

'Everything all right, missus?' one asked.

'I've caught you your arsonist. You are welcome to him after we've got the answers to our questions.' She uncocked the pistol and put it in her pocket so she could rub some warmth back into her fingers. 'He owes you a barn at least and, from the cut of his clothing, I'd hazard that he can afford it.'

The boys exchanged grim looks and between them heaved the captive up to carry him back to the yard. Dora and Jacob followed, a strange procession in the gaudy light of the burning barn. Mr and Mrs Clegg and daughter had given up trying to extinguish it. Their pails of water were no match for the flames.

'Here's the one responsible, courtesy of the lady here,' said Dr Sandys when they reached the farmer.

Clegg scratched the back of his head, gazing mournfully at the barn.

'Bad business, this. I never seen owt like it. He could've killed someone.'

'I rather thought the gunshots gave that intention away,' murmured Dora.

'What do we do, Da?' asked one of Clegg's sons. 'That bloody villain – pardon my French, Ma – must pay for this!'

'Not much to be done. Absalom, bide thee here and see it doesna spread. We'll take this one back to the house and find out what mad devil sent him to make trouble on our land.'

Dora touched Sandys's elbow and whispered in her ear.

'What do we say? They think we're a married couple. That won't last long if he starts bleating about Kendal and what happened with his friends.'

Sandys glanced down at her, a crease deepening the frown on his brow.

'Something's been bothering me about him.'

'Something more than his penchant for trying to kill us?'

His sour smile acknowledged the comment. Good; he appreciated her sarcasm. It was her favourite mode of speech.

'I recognise him – at least, I'm sure I've met his father or close kin in society. He won't like that as his kind thrive on anonymity. I just need to drag the connection out of my memory. And to put your mind at rest, I imagine he will not wish to say any more than he has to in front of these worthy people.'

'But still—'

He rested his hand on her wrist in a comforting gesture, letting it linger.

'If the truth of our relationship comes out, then we admit it. We have nothing to be ashamed about.'

That was correct. And, if she were the young man, she would attempt to pass this off as a bit of high spirits that got out of hand and say no more about it. The best tactic would be to apply money to the situation and pay off the farmer and his family. It would remain to be seen if the young man had the sense to do that.

Chapter Thirteen

Cradling the cup of tea Mrs Clegg had brewed for her, Dora watched Sandys bind the assailant's foot with brisk care. The injured man's face was waxen. Sweat beaded on his brow and he made no secret of his pain as he yelled at every tug of the bandage.

'Enough caterwauling. You brought this upon yourself. You'll get no sympathy here.' Sandys rinsed his hands in the basin and dried them on a linen towel. He rolled his shirtsleeves back down and fastened the cuffs.

'Mug of beer, doctor?' said Clegg.

'Thank you.' Sandys took a seat in the chair on the opposite side of the hearth from their captive, the Cleggs standing as witnesses behind him. He let the full weight of the silence rest on the captive's shoulders, ratcheting up the tension until Dora was tempted to break it herself. The prisoner looked from face to face, to the drinks that had been offered to everyone but him, and finally down at his foot.

'I'm maimed for life.' He sounded petulant.

'And whose fault is that? If you want to blame someone, blame those that sent you after us.' Sandys looked up at the farmer. 'I apologise for not warning you earlier. We were aware that we had attracted hostile attention when we were in Kendal last night but thought we'd left it behind. We had no idea they had followed us so far out of town and had no desire to bring the trouble to your door. Believe me when I say that you will not suffer any ill consequences from this night's work.'

'Ill consequences?' spluttered Mrs Clegg. 'Where's the herd going to shelter come winter?'

'In the new barn that this young man is going to pay for.'

'I say we pack him off to the magistrate,' said Mr Clegg. He folded his arms, standing like the stump of a tree that refused to be grubbed up.

'In normal circumstances, I would agree, but there is more to this business than I can explain to you.' Sandys turned his attention back to the prisoner. 'So, is Major Fosse your uncle or your father? You are his image.'

The prisoner flinched.

A hit, a very palpable hit, as they say in Hamlet, thought Dora.

'I'm doing my best to summon up everything I know about the Fosse family.' Sandys was putting on more of a Ton accent than he used with her and the Cleggs, sounding like the typical bored gentleman from high society. 'I knew Major Fosse in Portugal. A fine officer. But I cannot recall that he had any family back in England. That rather increases the odds that you are the son of his older brother, does it not?'

Their captive looked past Sandys, refusing to meet his eye. His whining and whimpering had given way to a sulk. From the set of his shoulders, he was not going to crack; he was locked up tighter than a Newgate cell.

Dora wondered if she could open the door. Could she provoke him into confirming his identity or divulging more useful information?

'Oh, so we have a minor Fosse rather than a major one?' drawled Dora, acting like a duchess who had been accosted by a puppy that had dared address her. 'How disappointing. If one is to be burnt out of house and home and then shot at, one would rather prefer to be the victim of a more notable character. It adds more cachet to the suffering. Don't you think so, Minor Fosse?'

The man glared at her.

'It's the Honourable Mr Fosse to you.' His voice had the snap of a whip about it; he was clearly a man used to underlings running around after him. He probably couldn't even dress himself without a valet handing him his undergarments.

'An honourable dishonourable, or is it a dishonourable honourable? I can never get these titles straight in my head. Does that not mean that he is the son of a lord?' She turned her question to Sandys.

'Indeed. And as I recall there are two sons of Lord Fosse, Peter and Jason. Which is it?' The minor Fosse glared mulishly. 'Never mind. I think I remember. Peter Fosse, I wager. There was some scandal last year, I do recall, that saw him sent down from Cambridge. It makes it unsurprising to find him caught up in bad company.'

'The older son?' Dora marvelled. 'Then I fear for the future of the Fosse estate. It will be a smoking pile of embers by the time he is through with it.'

Fosse scowled. He really did not like them talking over his head. Good.

'You cannot hold me here. My father will hear of this and then you will all be sorry!'

'Minor Fosse, you are labouring under a misapprehension.' Sandys repeated the nickname Dora had given Fosse with relish. 'Your father may be an important personage in the southwest, but here his name carries little weight. By contrast, my own family are the largest landowners in the area. I feel sure that the local magistrate, who also happens to be my godfather, will be very happy to oblige me in incarcerating the man who tried to murder me. He will be veritably disturbed that one of his neighbour's tenants has lost such a valuable farm building and will also wish to take that out of your hide. I'd say you are looking at committal to a Crown Court and transportation to Australia at the very least.'

Godfather? Dora wondered if Jacob had conjured that up or if it was the truth. She hoped not to meet this godfather, as she had the greatest aversion towards anyone enforcing the law in such a fashion.

'It won't get that far,' Fosse said sulkily. 'We know people. I'll be out before you know it.'

He might very well be right. In her experience, rich men rarely suffered for their crimes, but let a starving man steal a loaf of bread and he would be sent off to Botany Bay.

Sandys had tired of playing 'Who's the biggest landowner?' with the man. His voice turned steely.

'How did you follow us here?'

'Wouldn't you like to know!' sneered Fosse.

'Yes, I would, and you are going to tell me.'

'Oh, will I?'

Enough. Dora got up and swept the family Bible from a shelf. Stepping forward, she dropped it on the man's injured foot. He screamed like a stuck pig.

'The doctor here may be reluctant to force you to answer but I have no such qualms. How did you follow us?' She knelt, picked up the Bible and handed it to an astonished Mrs Clegg. 'Sorry about that, but needs must.'

'I suppose so, Mrs Sandys,' Mrs Clegg said warily.

'Mrs Sandys! Is that what she told you?' said Fosse. 'That's not a respectable wife but an actress, a whore—'

Dora grabbed the Bible back and dropped it on his foot a

second time. He yelled and made to strike her, but Sandys shoved him back in the chair.

'You really are a slow learner, aren't you?' Collecting the book again, she passed it to Mrs Clegg. 'We apologise that we weren't entirely straight with you earlier. I have only just met Dr Sandys. There is no connection, proper or improper, between us. We were thrown together by chance when this man and his friends decided they wanted something and we refused to give it to them.'

The Cleggs exchanged a glance, but it seemed they were more worried about the arsonist than the play-actors in their midst because they didn't demand Dora and the doctor instantly leave their house.

'I add my apologies to Miss Fitz-Pennington's.' Dr Sandys bowed to Mrs Clegg. 'But let us turn to the matter at hand. Fosse, how did you follow us? Did the landlord tell you where we were going? How did you catch up when we made the turn east?' Fosse sank into his seat, lips pressed together. 'If you don't answer, I will let Miss Fitz-Pennington loose with the Bible again.' He gave Dora a crooked smile.

Mrs Clegg clutched the book to her chest and pushed a fire iron closer.

'She can use that, she can.'

Fosse was still snivelling and clutching his foot. He really was a sorry specimen of a gentleman.

'We don't have all night,' said Dora, reaching for the iron.

'It was the horse from the inn,' he gabbled. 'All the mounts they hire out have a nick on their shoe so that they can be tracked – and it wasn't the innkeeper but the groom who told me.'

Sandys frowned.

'How much did you pay him?'

'I didn't pay him anything!'

'I expect he just threatened to burn down the stables,' said Dora, and from the flicker of cunning in the man's eyes, she knew

The Persephone Code

she was right. 'I really think that godfather of yours might be a good idea, Dr Sandys. Minor Fosse shouldn't be allowed to run loose if he's got it into his head that fire is a legitimate form of persuasion.'

'We should listen to the lady,' said Mrs Clegg. 'He's a menace.'

'A menace?' Fosse closed his eyes and smiled sourly. 'Someone like you dares label a man of my station a menace?' A change came over him. His demeanour was no longer so pathetic. His spine straightened and he set his foot on the floor. It appeared that he'd decided to give up on the role he'd been playing, finding it brought him no success with this audience. His expression was oddly empty, cold as a December night. A shiver passed down her spine. Dora's friends amongst the demimonde had warned her of such men. *If you come across someone who seems to have no human warmth, don't take him to bed, if you can help it.*

'I want to make a deal.' His tone was clipped, assuming an authority it had previously lacked. Finally, they were meeting a brother of the Illuminati. It was about time he showed up.

'We have no interest in you, Sandys. You've only been caught up in this affair by chance. You can turn around now, go back home and forget all about it. All we want is the girl.'

Sandys flicked a glance in her direction. Dora couldn't read his expression.

'Is that all? Well, why didn't you say so? How much is she worth to you?'

There was a gasp from Mrs Clegg. Dora did not blame her because it did sound as if the good doctor was cheerfully contemplating selling her off. As he was an acquaintance of hers of only a few hours, Dora lacked the confidence that he would not take the easy way out. Reaching down into her coat pocket, Dora curled her hand around the stock of the loaded pistol that she still carried. Whom would she shoot first? Fosse? No, if Sandys betrayed her, she'd go for him.

Fosse smiled coldly, doubtless thinking that all men were as venal as he.

'What sum would buy your silence?'

Sandys looked like he was considering it. The rotten pig.

'How much are you good for? I would not trust you to send money on afterwards, so how much do you have on you now?'

Fosse shrugged.

'I can give you a banker's draft for a hundred guineas. That's all I have with me. Will that be enough?

Sandys held out a hand.

'Make it over to me and that will do very well indeed.'

Chapter Fourteen

Road to the Devil's Bridge

Knowing he would catch it from Dora for this, Jacob waited for the man to make his bargain. Slowly, Fosse reached into his breast pocket and drew out a banker's draft.

'Pen?' Fosse asked.

When no one in the Clegg family looked like they were willing to aid this transaction, Jacob himself took down the quill and ink that stood on a shelf with the farm's accounts book. He could feel all eyes on him – loathing in Dora's and bewilderment in the Cleggs'. It couldn't be helped. Dipping the end in the ink, he passed the quill to Fosse. The man scratched out his name and made it over to Sandys.

'First name?'

'Dr Jacob Sandys.'

'No honourable?' he sneered.

'Never felt the need to use it.' Jacob kept his eye on their audience. The last thing he needed at this delicate moment was for one of them to snap.

JULIA GOLDING

'There!' Fosse held out the banknote.

'Excellent.' He refused to thank the bastard. Twitching it from the young man's fingers, he smoothed it out on the kitchen table.

'If you think I'm going to go quietly with that man, you have another thing coming!' spluttered Dora. He was surprised she had held her peace so long. 'I'll ruin you for this, you cowardly cully!'

He coolly took the quill and scratched out his name and made it over to the farmer.

'There. That is for your barn, Mr Clegg.'

The farmer took it and gazed at the largest sum he had ever seen in his life, then up at Jacob.

'I canna be accepting this, not if the lady—'

'Rest assured, Mr Clegg, the lady is not in danger.' At least not from this transaction. 'I made no promise. I merely asked him how much he was good for. This way you won't have to beat the money out of him.'

'I would've enjoyed that,' muttered the more hot-tempered of Clegg's sons. Jacob sympathised.

'It was a ruse?' Dora still did not trust him. He would have to do better at impressing on her his credentials as a gentleman.

'Indeed. I needed your fuming outrage for him to believe me.'

A slight smile curved her lips.

'You gulled him?'

'I gulled him.' It was the first of his schemes that had gone well this evening.

'You bastard!' Fosse leapt up, hands outstretched to throttle. A fire iron connected with his temple and he fell down unconscious, slumping onto Jacob. From target to physician in a split second, Jacob caught Fosse, checked his pulse and laid him out on the floor to recover.

Dora looked over at Mrs Clegg and swung the implement thoughtfully.

'You're right; this worked very well.'

Day was dawning and they could not stay at the Cleggs' cottage, not now they knew Fosse's companions might soon be looking for him. They decided to leave the mare with the notched shoe in the care of the farmer to be sent back to the inn, and to take Fosse's horse in her place.

'Will you be all right on a gelding?' asked Jacob, helping her mount.

Dora patted the chestnut's neck. 'We'll be fine, won't we, boy?'

Jacob took her at her word, having no time to worry that she might be overestimating her skills as a horsewoman. They'd go slowly at first so she could get used to a livelier mount, but they would have to increase the speed as soon as she got to grips with it. He hoped she was a fast learner. He slung his saddlebags over Nero – his newly repacked saddlebags. He hadn't yet mentioned the ransacking of his room to his companion, but she had gone through his belongings like a whirlwind. She was clearly not a woman who passed through the world without leaving her mark.

The farmer's wife handed Dora a basket of provisions.

'For the road, miss.'

'Thank you, Mrs Clegg. And I'm so sorry we dragged you into this.' His Athena was looking magnificent this morning, defiant despite her traumatic night. He wondered when the crash would come.

'Seems like we're going to get a new barn, and maybe a washhouse out of it,' said the farmer's wife, 'so don't fret about us. Worry about thyself and that doctor of thine.'

'Not mine.' Dora turned and winked at him. 'Just borrowed for a short while.'

He wanted to laugh but contained himself so they could complete their farewells. Mr Clegg held Nero's head while Jacob mounted.

'What does thee want us to do with that man?' Clegg jerked his head to the kitchen where Fosse was still lying by the fire. He'd woken up a few minutes after the blow but said he felt sick and dizzy. A concussion, Jacob had diagnosed, and told him to keep still.

'You could take him to Kendal. My godfather really would see him locked up if you mention my name, but...'

'But...?'

'Clegg, these are powerful people. Your interests might be best served by being shot of him as soon as possible. You have your damages so you've got what you might expect out of him and much sooner than the law would allow.'

'I doubt the law would've got round to it.'

Jacob tended to agree. 'My advice? Keep him resting for as long as you can, then kick him out on foot. That should delay him and give us a chance to get a head start. Don't make yourself matter to him. He's the sort who will forget as soon as he sets out on our trail. He's not from these parts so I doubt he'll come back to make life any more difficult for you – and if he does, I'll speak up for you.'

The farmer nodded.

'Aye, I can do that. Godspeed.'

'Thank you.' Jacob urged his horse into a walk. 'Come along, Miss Fitz-Pennington.'

Dora kicked her mount to follow. 'Which way?'

'We'll head east.'

She turned her horse onto the farm track leading to the road. 'Very well.' Finding the surface well-maintained, she upped the pace, going from a walk to a trot to a canter. 'Keep up, doctor. We haven't got all day!'

Soon he was looking at her disappearing back. Jacob shook his head. Her claim to have ridden 'a little' appeared to be nothing but another of her artful lies.

'Thee'll have thy hands full wi' that 'un!' called the farmer.

Jacob waved an acknowledgement with his hat and set off in pursuit. That was a challenge he was looking forward to meeting.

The horses could not gallop all the way to West Wycombe, of course, so they slowed after a couple of miles.

'How are you managing?' he asked when he drew level. Annoyingly, Nero had not been able to catch the requisitioned horse.

'Caligula and I are doing well.' Dora offered Jacob a hunk of bread, torn from the provisions in the basket. She had the rakish air of an experienced camp follower, seated comfortably astride her mount, greatcoat buttoned tight, squashy hat pulled over her wild locks.

'Caligula?' He chewed, remembering now that he was hungry. Events had driven that from his mind. Dora was more attuned to the practicalities of travelling than he. Eat when you could.

'If you are to have a mad emperor for a mount, I should too.' Shading her eyes, she looked at the sun rising before them. A molten circle, it rose over the Pennines like a door opening to a blast furnace. 'Where to?'

Jacob had been turning over an idea in his mind. They needed help. Fosse had caught up with them much sooner than he had thought possible. The Illuminati were a well-financed group with the ability to buy information at every inn and tollbooth on the roads south. If he and Dora had any hope of reaching their destination without another altercation – one which they might well lose this time – they needed to take an unexpected path.

'I have a friend in Kirkby Lonsdale who might help. It's on this road and we will pass the door.' Was this a good idea? He had not parted from his acquaintance on the best terms. The chances of this turning out well were, at best, in the balance.

'I second appealing to a friend in Kirkby Lonsdale,' said Dora, sagging forward a little. 'I'm exhausted but we daren't risk an inn.'

Her vote in favour bolstered Jacob's resolve.

'Very well. We head for the Devil's Bridge.'

'Really? Your friend lives by the Devil's Bridge? And that doesn't sound ominous to you?' She shook her head and sank her teeth into a wrinkled apple with a crunch.

'You'll like them. They'll like you. I think.'

She swallowed. 'You don't sound very sure.' She tossed him an apple, which he just managed to catch.

'Only because they hate my guts – or so they told me on our last meeting.'

Another woman might have pressed for details, but she contented herself with: 'No doubt you deserved it.'

His pretence to sell her for barn money was clearly not yet forgiven. He was too much of a gentleman to chuckle.

―――――

It took a couple of hours to find the way to Kirkby Lonsdale. It was market day, so they were far from the only people on the road this early. Dora was yawning as they rode through the sellers setting out their wares in the square, low sun casting long shadows behind so they looked like they were being stalked by giants. Jacob rubbed his eyes, determined not to give in to his tiredness. He would need his wits about him.

They attracted interested looks as they trotted through. A lady riding astride would do that, but they were also strangers in a place where people knew every face that turned up to market day. Jacob scanned the crowd. No one showed unusual levels of hostility. He would have to hope that the Illuminati had not got here before them. Paranoia that his adversaries could somehow read his mind had edged in after their near disastrous stop at the barn.

He turned to find his companion had lagged behind.

'How are you faring, Miss Fitz-Pennington?'

She kicked her horse to draw level. 'I'm dreaming about a bed and lying horizontal for an hour or two.'

And what wouldn't he give to be lying in it beside her?

'I hope I can achieve that much for you.' He might well end up back on the road with a flea in his ear, but Dora would probably receive a warmer welcome. His acquaintance would enjoy her plucky character.

They crossed the Lune on the high bridge with its three arches that gave the spot its name. Dora looked about her, taking in the churning waters of the river and the banks where sheep grazed.

'Doesn't seem very devilish to me.'

'The name refers to the local story about how a woman outwitted the devil.'

'Oh, I like it already.'

To help her along, he'd finish the tale. 'One of her cows strayed to the other side and she didn't want to get wet following it.'

'I can imagine.' They both looked over; the water was an uninviting peaty brown.

'She struck a deal with the devil. He would build a bridge in exchange for the first soul that crossed it. He completed it overnight and the next day the woman came to admire her new bridge.'

'And fetch her cow.'

'Indeed. The devil was flapping his wings and brandishing his pitchfork, ready to scoop up the woman's soul.' He paused teasingly.

'And?' Her brown eyes narrowed at him. She was seconds from swatting him for delaying her gratification.

Stop thinking about how much fun she would be to bed. 'The woman threw a bread roll ahead, her little dog gave chase, so the devil got its soul instead and disappeared in a blast of temper.'

Dora huffed. 'I'm rapidly going off her.'

'Really? I would have thought being the devil's dog would be more fun than belonging to that fearsome woman.'

'You make a good point. And tell me, Dr Sandys, how do you know this story?'

He turned Nero down the drive of the house he'd once known very well.

'I collect stories and books. It's a hobby of mine.'

'You're a collector?' Her voice sounded a little strained. Was she laughing at him for his less-than-rakish behaviour?

'I do. If we don't know our history, we are blind to our past and future mistakes.'

She said nothing more, merely turned her head away.

Jacob refused to apologise for his interests. He had an extensive collection that was the envy of those who knew the value of genuine manuscripts of rare tales, songs or poems. Like the poets – the late Rabbie Burns and Jacob's neighbours the gruff Wordsworth and urbane Southey – he believed there was more raw power in these stories than polite tales from the Ton. 'I always admired how folk heroes can triumph against the odds.'

The house came into view – three storeys with eight windows on each level and a porched doorway in the middle. It was the dower house to a much larger estate some miles away.

'And are we meeting a folk hero?'

Jacob laughed dryly. 'No, Miss Fitz-Pennington. We are meeting a grand lady of the Ton. She is the widow of the last lord of Tolworth.' He dismounted and helped her down.

Dora pursed her lips. 'I'll mind my Ps and Qs then, with the old lady.'

He was about to correct her misapprehension, when the lady herself came striding out of the house, brandishing a horsewhip, dogs boiling at her heels. Her blond curls were as dishevelled as ever, though, unlike their last encounter, she was fully clothed.

'Is that you, you bastard! Get off my land!'

Jacob turned to an astonished Dora.

'Meet Virginia, the dowager Lady Tolworth.'

Chapter Fifteen

Devil's Bridge House

Jacob was making a fair attempt at hiding his consternation, but he knew that the next few minutes would be humiliating and possibly dangerous, if the lady lived up to her reputation. She would happily put a round of buckshot in his arse if he got this wrong.

Dora dipped a curtsy.

'Lady Tolworth.'

Ginnie looked down her nose at Jacob's companion.

'Don't tell me you brought your latest conquest to my door, Sandys?'

'You make it sound like I have so many,' said Jacob wryly. He noted the crow's feet at her eyes and the hint of a few white hairs, none of which detracted from her beauty. She had matured well, as he had suspected she would.

'Have you no shame?'

'Not in this case. This is Miss Fitz-Pennington, a lady I have known for all of' – he checked his pocket watch – 'twelve hours. None of which has been spent in bed.' Tragically.

Ginnie curled her lip.

'Who said a bed was necessary?'

Dora was looking between them like a spectator at a shuttlecock game, bemused by the innuendo.

He held up his hands, placating. 'Ginnie, please, the lady and I are chance companions, driven to your door by necessity.'

She tapped the whip against her boot.

'I warned you that if I saw you again, I would beat you senseless.'

'As much as I adore your displays of emotion, this is serious.'

'So am I.'

A chill breeze wrapped Dora's skirt around her legs, and she shivered. Jacob was failing her again, he knew. He'd promised shelter, but Ginnie held a grudge like no other. She did not take rejection well.

'Excuse me, my lady, Dr Sandys, but may we continue this reunion somewhere warmer?' Dora turned to him – when had she become *Dora* in his thoughts? Jacob wondered. Probably when she dropped the Bible on that idiot's foot. 'Or perhaps we should travel on if the lady does not wish to welcome us?'

Her calm and reasonable tone was met with a huff from Ginnie.

'Oh, very well. Come in.'

With poor grace, the Dowager Lady Tolworth turned on her heel and headed inside. Dora caught up with Jacob as they followed.

'Oh my, Dr Sandys, whatever did you fall out about?'

'Politics,' he said, while at that same moment, Ginnie said: 'Everything.'

With Lady Tolworth's staff hurrying to open doors for them, they entered her parlour as smoothly as two frigates arriving in port. This had a fine view across her grounds to the Devil's Bridge, a picturesque landscape that was quintessentially northern English with its pasture, oak grove and plump sheep. The parlour, however, spoke to more cosmopolitan tastes. It had been recently refurbished with pale blue drapes and Empire furniture, sphinxes holding up tables and winged lions for armrests. Ginnie might be a staunch Tory, but she was not immune to fashion that had its origins in Napoleon's campaign in Egypt.

'Yarton, bring tea for our guests,' she ordered. The butler hurried away to carry out her wishes. Ginnie had always run a tight ship when she had been the reigning Lady Tolworth. Her late husband had been elderly when she married him, and he'd spent the last decade of his life in a state of confusion. While he was cared for on his estates by a loyal band of servants, his wife had been left free in London. That was when Jacob had met her, he a newly commissioned medical officer in the army, and she a dashing lady of the Ton who knew what she wanted from a personable young man. It had been an education.

'You must be desperate if you have come here in search of sanctuary.' Ginnie sat down and cast the whip on a side table. It knocked over a vase of bluebells that Dora quickly righted. 'Oh, do sit, the pair of you. I can't stand having people looming over me.'

Dora perched at the end of a sofa that had a scrolled arm. Jacob took a seat at the other end, forming a triangle with the two women.

Ginnie pointed a finger at Dora. 'What are you?'

She didn't miss a beat. 'An actress in the Northern Circuit.'

'Your egalitarian principles have gone even further than I thought, Sandys.' Ginnie might ignore marital laws, but she did not bend class ones.

Enough of her nonsense. The whip had been put down, so Jacob no longer feared for his person. 'An old friend who is a vicar in Buckinghamshire asked me to break the news of the death of the lady's brother,' he said soberly. 'I'm escorting the lady to the place where he died.'

Ginnie's demeanour changed immediately. She might be a termagant, but she had a heart. Her eyes lost their snapping fire and softened with sympathy.

'I'm sincerely sorry to hear of your loss, Miss Pennington.'

'*Fitz*-Pennington,' Dora corrected. 'Anthony was my half-brother.' Her pinched expression showed how deeply she grieved. Swallowing hard, she struggled to contain her emotion.

'You're Anthony Pennington's sister? Oh lord, don't tell me Bullroarer is dead?' Ginnie looked shocked as she put two and two together. 'How?'

'He was stabbed to death in the Hellfire Caves,' said Jacob, relieving Dora of the burden of the conversation.

'The ... what? Oh, that place. Damn uncomfortable spot for an orgy. Never went, but I heard stories, of course.'

'You knew my brother?' Dora asked.

'Not in the Biblical sense, my dear, but he was an amusing partner in a hand of cards and a decent dancer.' She tilted her head. 'I can see the resemblance now. Your profile – the Penningtons always have a fine nose, not like my little bit of nothing.' She brushed her own snub nose in disgust. 'Your father is that objectionable alderman from Liverpool, is he not? Ezra Pennington?'

Dora nodded, but she was stiff with tension at the reminder of her sire.

'You have my pity. Anthony used to tell me of his tyranny. He couldn't escape into the army quickly enough. Poor boy. Who killed him?'

'We don't know,' said Jacob. 'Footpads possibly, but we've had people on our tail ever since I delivered the news to Miss Fitz-Pennington. Cloaked figures set upon her at the theatre in Kendal.

We fled and then they set fire to the barn in which we took shelter.'

'Good lord! The country really is going to the dogs. Radicals, I suppose? Frame-breakers or Jacobins?' The butler came in with the tea and set it by the lady. She briskly served, passing a cup to Dora. 'I told you that reform would open the floodgates, Jacob. Edmund Burke had it right.'

'These weren't revolutionaries, my lady,' said Dora meekly, a new act for her but one, Jacob thought, she had calculated would appeal to the forthright dame. 'They were well-educated men from Society. The one we caught was the son of a lord.'

'Peter Fosse,' added Jacob.

Ginnie snorted. 'That horrible weasel.'

'I believe he's got himself mixed up in the Illuminati,' explained Jacob. 'I've seen it happen to those men who don't feel happy with their privileged lot, and who don't have the qualities to rise on their own merit. They band with fellow conspirators who like to feel they have their secret circles running the rest of us.'

'I'll have no dealing with that kind.' She waved a slim hand in a vaguely southerly direction. '"King and country" is my motto, not "all bow" to Robespierre, or Napoleon, or some foolish cabal of those in love with themselves.' Ginnie offered Dora sugar, which the actress refused. 'Sweet enough?'

Dora looked at the bowl. 'I prefer not to take it.'

'Ah, one of them, are you? An abolitionist?' Ginnie stirred her tea. 'Our people are very well treated. I make sure of that – at least, I did when I had the running of the estate.' A frown wrinkled her brow as she considered the current state of affairs in the Caribbean. Dora's own expression was grim but, thankfully, she did not contradict their headstrong hostess. 'Can't answer for the new Lord Tolworth, spineless fool that he is.' Ginnie waved her teaspoon at Jacob. 'At least Prinny hasn't turned out so bad now he has the Regency. I thought he'd bring in all your fellow radicals and turn the country into a hotbed of revolution. But no, he even left his Falstaff out in the cold.'

'It was a matter of conscience for Mr Sheridan to remain outside the administration,' said Jacob, 'because he disagrees with the Regent on the principle of Catholic Emancipation.' Many had been surprised when the Prince Regent had let down his Whig allies, friends for decades, and kept the arch-conservative Spencer Perceval in government. Richard Brinsley Sheridan, the surviving leading figure in opposition since the 1780s, had been expected to reap the reward for his faithfulness. Instead, he was out in the cold like Falstaff in *Henry IV Part II*. The reformers were angry and disappointed, but Jacob had been too cynical to share their sense of betrayal.

Ginnie glowered. 'You and Sherry would have the Pope telling us what to do, would you?'

'No. I merely think it is wrong to bar decent men from public office because they are not Church of England.'

'See!' Ginnie turned to Dora. 'This is why he and I would never last. He's a radical. He'd see my kind sent to the guillotine.'

At least Ginnie now recognised what he had realised when he'd broken it off: fireworks in bed did not make for a compatible life outside of the bedroom. 'Hardly, as I would be in the tumbrel with you, thanks to my own bloodlines.'

Ginnie gave him one of her sly smiles. 'Ah, but I do miss making up with you after a quarrel.'

Jacob could feel the heat rising in his cheeks as his thoughts darted back to some of their more sensual encounters. He didn't want to think about them, especially not with Dora here.

'My lady, we came here hoping for a safe place to rest. Neither of us has slept,' said Dora, rescuing him from his embarrassment. 'Separate rooms, of course, so I'm not in the way if you wish to revisit fond memories...?'

Or maybe not.

Ginnie assessed her. 'Not so meek then. Good. It sounds like you will need to be strong if you've got people hunting you. Yes, you may both rest here. None of my household will tattle. Have you thought how you will reach your destination?'

'We are bound for West Wycombe,' said Jacob. 'I was hoping we could catch a stage, perhaps in Lancaster?'

'Nonsense.' Ginnie downed her cup of tea like it was a belt of whisky. 'It's time I visited my stepson, Lord Tolworth, in London and shook him up a bit. You will travel in my carriage – with me.'

Chapter Sixteen

Road to West Wycombe

'We can rest when we are dead,' said Dora when she was offered the choice of delaying their departure for a few hours or setting off as soon as the carriage could be brought round. The saying, a favourite of her brother's, rang hollow after his murder. Neither his soul nor hers would be at peace until she found out who had killed him and why.

She had been planning to sleep on the way, leaving the former lovers to settle their differences in whatever way they felt appropriate, but discovered that Dr Sandys had opted to ride Nero for the first part of the journey. Coward. This left her at the mercy of Lady Tolworth's inquisition. She had no choice in this because Caligula had been consigned to the stables. Dr Sandys had argued that it was better not to be charged with horse thieving, not when the details of how she came into possession of a nobleman's mount involved shooting Fosse in the foot.

Her rear-facing seat was well padded and for the first time she did not have to worry about where she was going. Responsibility had been handed over to a competent coachman. Her eyes drifted closed as they took the turnpike to Lancaster.

'Is what he said true?' Lady Tolworth asked.

Dora jolted awake. 'Which part, my lady?'

'That you aren't his mistress?'

'Oh, that.' She yawned, belatedly covering it with her hand. 'No. I'm nobody's mistress, nor angling to be one. My lady.' She had to remember who she was talking to but her manners with the nobility were never very reliable. She had too much resentment to make obeisance a natural stance for her.

The lady nodded and turned her gaze out of the window.

'Good for you. I'm sorry about your brother. I liked him, though he had a cruel side. And a wicked wit.'

Dora had been trying not to think about that. Anthony had blurted out to her on his first home leave some of the things he'd seen in the war, and she guessed he'd been part of them. No one was innocent on a battlefield, he had said.

'He could be. Mostly it was directed at himself. He was kind to me.' Though he hadn't chosen her over their family and its fortune. That had been the deepest cut. He had never been a hero, just her brother.

'No doubt he loved you in his own way. We don't mean as much to them as they do to us.' Her ladyship's eyes were on Sandys riding on the grassy stretch beside the carriage. There was more emotion there than the good doctor had suggested.

Dora needed to distract herself from her hopeless thoughts about Anthony.

'What happened between you and Dr Sandys, if you don't mind me asking?' It was a long coach journey, at least a day and a half with a necessary stop to rest at a coaching inn, and Dora could think of worse ways of passing the time.

Tapping her gloved fingers on the sill, Lady Tolworth considered how to respond. Dora thought for a moment that her

The Persephone Code

question would be knocked back with a regal arch of an eyebrow, but the privacy of the carriage, with a listener who did not matter in the least in Society, encouraged confidence.

'I fell in love but pretended it was just another intrigue.' She toyed with the fringe of the window blind. 'Tolworth was still with us then, so I had no real liberty to act. And Jacob was so free, defying his noble family to be an army doctor, of all things.' She chuckled. 'I thought it a rebellion, but I think he liked the intellectual challenge and the sense of purpose.'

Dr Sandys sent them both a look as if he could feel them talking about him. He spurred his horse to ride ahead. The mud he kicked up splattered against the doors of the carriage.

Lady Tolworth grimaced at the dirt. Not that his was the only mud on the window by now. Travelling was a messy business, even on the toll roads. 'I hope he tips my coachman well.' She rubbed the glass, but the smear was on the other side, of course. 'His family votes with the Whigs, but I believe Sandys is a radical, a medical Cobbett, who thinks most hospitals are pits of disease in dire need of sanitary reform.'

'They are.' Few chose to go unless at the last extreme.

'But why bleat about it in London?' Her tone had resumed its waspish sting. 'Sort out the ones in your own county first. Lead by example. I don't believe the government should meddle in such things. A good landlord should see to his own estates. I hope no one ever offers Jacob a seat in the Commons.'

Dora didn't agree but she wished to keep the lady on the topic of Jacob so resisted the temptation to argue. 'And yet you and he...?'

'And yet I fell for the tall, blue-eyed officer with integrity and passion.'

'Described like that, who wouldn't?' Dora wondered what the age gap had been – ten, fifteen years?

'I haven't forgiven him for ending it. I should have been the one to give him his congé.'

'Why did he?'

Her expression turned wistful. 'You'll have to ask him.'

'We aren't on those terms, my lady.'

Pale blue eyes turned to her, the colour of a break in the clouds on a rainy day. 'Not yet, maybe, but I can see that you intrigue him, and that you are interested too, despite your protestations. Just don't fall in love with him. He holds us all to strict standards and is disappointed when we inevitably fall short. Spare yourself the heartache.'

Dora thought of her career as a forger of the very items that Sandys had said he liked collecting. She enjoyed watching the so-called experts crow over the latest 'finds' she invented for them. It was like taking a secret bow after a masterful performance. He would not forgive her for that.

'I have no intention of doing so.'

Lady Tolworth shook her head. 'That's how it always starts, but our hearts undermine us.'

Lady Tolworth's coachman had long journeys down to a fine art. He was wasted on serving her ladyship, thought Dora, and would be better used helping Wellington move troops up through Portugal. He sent stableboys ahead with teams of horses, so they had fresh ones to change at the inns along the way. Windows were wiped and mud removed so the carriage sparkled again. Well-compensated innkeepers delivered refreshments and hot bricks to put by cold feet as soon as the conveyance clattered into the innyard. Dora was astonished how quickly the miles passed. At this rate they would reach their destination well within the two days.

'How the other half live,' she murmured, as their carriage horses were exchanged in record time in Manchester. Her hopes rose that she could get to her brother's letter in time.

Dr Sandys had to rest Nero so joined them in the coach for the next stage. He entered as one would a bear's den, praying that the creature would remain in hibernation. Fortunately for him, Lady Tolworth chose not to awaken the resentment of their parting.

'Tell me more about poor Anthony,' said Lady Tolworth once he had settled next to Dora, facing their hostess.

Jacob unwound his muffler. Spring was a chancy companion on English roads, blowing hot and cold, wet and dry. 'I only know what Reverend Leighton told me. Pennington had become mixed up with the circle that frequented the caves. Leighton was trying to persuade him to cut his ties but failed.'

Just like she had failed, thought Dora. Sometimes the pull to danger could not be eradicated from the one addicted to the thrill. Anthony had not wanted the escape rope she and others had thrown to him.

'An overdose? Victim of a party that got out of hand, perhaps?' Lady Tolworth mused. 'Hellfire events are known for their drinking, liaisons, high-stakes gambling, dares and anything that raises the blood.'

'Sounds riotous,' said Dora, deadpan.

'The people that go are so deadened to the world by ennui that they will do anything for excitement.'

'Even kill a man?' She hated to think of Anthony in such company, but she had to admit that he would have felt at home and probably led the charge to dissipation.

'I'm afraid so, Miss Fitz-Pennington. It would not be the first such death in Society. Fools, drink and weapons – an unholy trinity.'

'A duel, or a misfire, I could understand, but Pennington was stabbed,' said Jacob. 'That does not sound like any party dare I've heard of.'

Lady Tolworth waved off the doctor's remark, indicating that, if this was opinion, then he hadn't been to the same kind of parties as her. 'Did your brother have any enemies, Miss Fitz-Pennington?'

Dora wished she had more she could say. It felt so wrong not to know what her brother was thinking in his last days, not after two decades of being each other's best friend. That didn't mean he'd been the perfect brother, of course. He'd played his share of cruel pranks on her. She had no illusions.

'We have not been close for years, my lady, not since I broke with my family. However, as a child, he did make enemies almost as easily as he made friends.' To his schoolmates, he had been either a brave fellow or a bully – she had heard tales of both. 'I imagine he would have continued on the same path in the army and elsewhere.'

In the lull in the conversation that followed, she remembered how Anthony had filled her ears with his exploits at Westminster School, not realising that some of the stories in which weaker boys were picked on did not do him credit. She had often wished he would protect rather than punish such lads, but he had sworn that it was the only way to toughen them up.

Those were the years when the distance had begun to grow between them. He would come home from the holidays, swaggering with the confidence of the fifteen-year-old just coming into his powers, carrying tales of the younger boys who fagged for him at school. He was doing them a favour, he claimed, just as his jokes at her expense were to prepare her for a world that looked down on bastard daughters. So when he'd stolen her clothes at their favourite bathing spot and left her to walk home in a carter's smock, that had been to train her for the kind of humiliation she could expect in life, had it?

She'd cut a hole in his favourite breeches in retaliation, saying that if she had to walk through the village showing her legs, he would parade with his bum hanging out.

'You know everyone in Society, Lady Tolworth,' said Dr Sandys. The lady raised a brow at that formality from him – ridiculous when they had both been naked together. 'Ginnie,' he conceded. 'Who else do you know in the Hellfire Club?'

'Word is that the new poet has fired up the younger set. You know him? Lord Byron – a minor title but the boy is making a major splash.'

'The man who kept a bear at Trinity because the rules forbade dogs?'

'Yes, him. An amusing fellow. In bed with all and sundry. Age no barrier.' Ginnie looked briefly interested as she considered Byron's potential as a future bedmate. 'His father died in a gambling den in Ireland, blind drunk and fighting his best friend, so Byron junior has the perfect qualifications to be a Hellfire member. It used to be much more serious though, back in my late husband's youth.'

'Serious?' asked Dora.

'Wilkes and Liberty? Does that ring any bells?'

'I'm sorry, no.'

'You make me feel old.' Lady Tolworth sighed. '1768, that year we almost had another revolution. John Wilkes, the radical Member of Parliament and ugliest man in England, fell out with the government over free speech.' She curled her lip. 'Free speech? Who ever heard such nonsense? No speech is free. Someone always has to foot the bill.'

'His case did change the law for the better,' said Dr Sandys. 'He challenged the use of general warrants, which gave the law officers *carte blanche* to enter premises and make mass arrests. We are all much safer from incarceration now.'

Lady Tolworth's rings glittered as she wafted her hand in disdain. 'Safer? Pah! Only the treasonous benefited.'

Dora could see they were going to descend into another argument on the rights of men.

'What was Wilkes' connection to the Hellfire Club, my lady?' she asked quickly.

'He belonged for a time. How else would he get women into bed? In addition to being a troublemaker, he was also a writer of obscene material. His fellow members of the Hellfire club had a grudge against him for some tasteless tricks he played, so pursued their revenge in the House of Lords.'

'As one would, being a lord,' murmured Dora.

'It was an odd revenge: Lord Sandwich read out Wilkes' obscene parody of Pope's "An Essay on Man", the subject being Woman, about which he knew nothing at all. They all agreed Wilkes was a bad lot, and he was outlawed. He had to flee the country.'

'Wilkes didn't circulate it – the lords made it famous?'

'*Exactement*. Ironic, isn't it?'

And unfair, thought Dora.

'Tolworth said it was a foolish move. Hellfire Club business should have remained private. That was the code of a *secret* club, after all. Instead, Sandwich raised the dirty linen on a flagpole and made Wilkes into a radical hero. Wilkes' response was to publish the details of the Hellfire Club antics and shame many famous men – a betrayal from the inside, and therefore all the more powerful. The rest you can imagine.' Lady Tolworth smiled bitterly. 'The press got hold of it and the public went on one of its periodic fits of moral outrage. Not that any of the great men involved – Sandwich, Dashwood and others – suffered noticeably. It was more the idea that the nobility were satanic worshippers who gathered for orgies, sacrificing virgins and whatnot, that remained to undermine respect for the natural order. It all weakens the sinews of what binds us together as a society – blood and breeding, and knowing one's place.'

'I rather thought the Hellfire Club fame had all died down with the passing of the generation, becoming an idea to excite boys, not a pursuit of men. It appears I was wrong,' said Dr Sandys.

Lady Tolworth leaned towards him and touched his knee. 'Sex and defiance of the rules never go out of fashion, Jacob.' Dora was sure she was not the only one to hear the invitation. 'It might go underground for a while, but the Hellfire Club always exists in some form. The question is only how powerful the members are and what they stand to lose if they are publicly exposed.'

'Sexual peccadilloes aren't enough?' asked Dora.

Lady Tolworth shook her head. 'Who cares about that? Lord, the antics in most noble bedrooms break the laws of decency in every way imaginable.' She shot a mischievous look at Dora. 'And I've imagined a lot, believe me.'

Dora couldn't resist a snigger. 'You should write a tell-all for the press and make a fortune.'

'Tempting, but no. Yet if something truly criminal goes on – a rape, a murder or treason – then there will be lots of influential people trying to hide their involvement.'

'Hellfire burns all members even if only a few are implicated?'

'Exactly, Miss Fitz-Pennington. If your brother was killed for what he knew, then look to those who had the most to lose.'

Chapter Seventeen

St James's Street, London

After the disappointment of Pennington dying without revealing his secrets in the caves, his murderer had sent his best men after the sister. An actress should be easy pickings. He'd chosen to go himself to track down the tougher nut to crack – Ezra Pennington. Anthony Pennington would likely have confided his most important secret in his father, surely, rather than his disgrace of a half-sister?

He smiled as he walked through St James's with its gentlemen's clubs, tobacconists' and vintners', thinking what a sorry lot the leisured classes really were with their braying laughs and pampered lives. The Hellfire Club was the worse secretion of that culture, like the whiff of gangrene in a wound. Still, there was a cure for every ill. An informant from within the ranks of the club had told him – under extreme duress, it must be acknowledged – that as a pledge to keep the secrets of the club, each member handed over something incriminating or embarrassing about himself. To betray the club was to ensure your own destruction.

Among those things gathered were the latest plans for Wellington's campaign on the Peninsula, handed over as a pledge by one foolish aide-de-camp. Useful treason – and pure temptation. If he obtained those, he could strike a deal with Napoleon, ensuring the swift defeat of the allies and his own ascendency in Britain as Napoleon backed his claim to rule.

Next step would be to eliminate Napoleon, but that was a matter for another year, another scheme. Old Boney had enough foibles to make that easy enough to achieve.

He looked about him and over the treetops of St James's Park to where he imagined the complacent cabinet gathered in Downing Street. Soon all this would be swept away, falling into the Thames just as the young man had, shock on his white face as he was let go, his usefulness exhausted.

The merchant was not hard to run to ground. The murderer's informers had told him that the Liverpool tradesman had bribed his way into Boodle's – not quite as prestigious as White's Club, but normally a member still needed a title to enter. Word was that Prinny would grant Pennington senior one soon, thanks to some timely loans when the Prince Regent had outspent his allowance. It was another sign that things needed shaking up. Money was now the key that opened society doors. The government borrowed heavily from men like that upstart Rothschild to fund a hopeless war. None of them gave serious thought to the crippling debts they incurred. Private citizens were just as bad. Impoverished gentry required rich tradesmen's daughters for their wastrel sons to marry. Did one need more signs than this that the country was going downhill and urgently needed a better calibre of leader?

He entered the club, where he, of course, was well known.

'Evening, sir. Will you be wanting dinner?'

'No thank you, Robertson.' He unclasped his cloak, revealing a flash of white satin. 'I'm looking for Mr Ezra Pennington, the Liverpool shipping man.'

The doorman sniffed as he stowed the cane, hat and cloak. He was no more enamoured of the idea of bringing a commoner into the hallowed grounds of his club than the original members.

'I believe Mr Pennington is in the Coffee Room, sir. There was a meeting with his investors and he is yet to depart.'

'Thank you, Robertson.' He pressed a sovereign into the man's gloved hand. It always paid to grease the palms of London's doorkeepers. Knowing their names was another investment that cost little and bore much fruit. He took the stairs two at a time and entered the leather-upholstered and oak-panelled haven of the Coffee Room. A footman pointed out his target. Pennington was sitting amidst a cluster of armchairs, a snifter of brandy swirling in his hand as he held forth to his acquaintances. As the visitor recognised none of them from Society, he decided these must be men of Pennington's kind – tradesmen, merchants and bankers. Not a hereditary landowner among them. His Illuminati philosophy taught that by logic he should respect the rising classes but he couldn't get over his prejudice that they just did not know how to behave in public. Take Pennington now – he was speaking at the top of his voice even though others were reading the papers and conducting quiet conversations not six feet away. The merchant looked like a badger with his black hair striped white at the temples. He spoke with that creature's vicious persistence, snapping out each word.

'Perceval is mad, *mad*, to bait the Americans! He wants war? Haven't we got enough of that on the Continent without dragging the damned Colonies into it too? War is bad for business.'

'Not for everyone. Galton's doing quite well for himself,' said another.

'Galton? I tell you, Bellingham, that Quaker from Birmingham is a sanctimonious devil. He took me to task for my dealings in the West Indies – and him an arms manufacturer! He literally profits from bloodshed!'

There was a round of mutterings against the Quakers, Evangelicals and Abolitionists, which made the onlooker smile.

Bellingham, a febrile man with curling sideburns, shook his head. 'They've ruined the Baltic trade.'

'Damn shame,' muttered another.

'And where's our money going?' Bellingham continued. 'To Johnny foreigner. Britain can't afford to subsidise all the armies fighting Bonaparte – Russians, Austrians, you name it, we are paying for them! Spencer Perceval should be shot with the guns he's ordered for the allies.'

'And we should be shot of this damned war in Spain!' said Ezra, topping the comment of his colleague. 'I say we make peace with Napoleon, leave the seas free for trade and liberate ourselves of the fear of having our cargo stolen by privateers.'

'Hear, hear,' murmured Pennington's allies.

Amused by the little cabal of merchants and their gripes, the onlooker cleared his throat.

'Mr Pennington?'

The merchant looked up, no trace of recognition on his face. They hadn't to his knowledge met before, but you could never be sure in Society whom you had met once and swiftly forgotten.

'Yes, sir?'

'I wonder if you could spare me a moment? It is about your late son.'

Pennington's expression dimmed as recollection of his recent loss clouded his evening. His colleagues looked grimly into their glasses, death subduing their vigour. Pennington's gaze swept him, took in the cut of his visitor's jacket, the style of his boots and breeches, the gleam of his watch chain, and evidently concluded that this was an acquaintance worth cultivating. He got up and bowed to his friends.

'Keep my seat for me, would you?'

'This way, sir.' He led Pennington to a couple of armchairs at the far end of the room. With the potential for eavesdroppers, distance was preferable. He wanted to assess the man without interruption. He hadn't yet decided if Pennington needed killing or if he would be more of an asset alive.

He introduced himself and noted the impressed and calculating gleam in his quarry's eyes. A bid to persuade him to invest in Pennington's ventures would probably follow sharpish if their paths crossed again.

'Mr Pennington, my condolences on your loss. Your son was a fine man.' He signalled to the waiter to bring them a round of drinks.

'You knew him, sir? He didn't mention you, not that I can recall.' Pennington picked up his brandy and warmed it in his palm.

'How odd. Though he did have many friends. Had you talked to him of late? Our acquaintance was fairly recent.'

Pennington huffed. 'Unfortunately, Anthony and I were too alike. Both stubborn.'

'You were at odds when he died?'

'It's no secret that we fell out over the conduct of the war and had not yet reconciled. I was hoping to see him this month and mend our fences. Then he went and got himself killed – damned foolish business.'

The man was obviously already well-oiled by his drinking with his friends and ready to talk.

'Your son supported the Earl of Wellington's attempt to drive the French out of Spain?'

'Forget Wellington. The blame lies with Prime Minister Perceval. The politicians are pulling the strings, not the military.' Pennington sipped his drink. 'They're idiots. Napoleon would make peace if it were offered. Let him keep the Continent; we have markets overseas to develop. The sea campaign is ruining free trade and adding to costs. Something drastic must be done – a change at the top.' He caught himself before he went too far. 'What's your view?'

'Oh yes, I quite agree.' He didn't agree about Napoleon, but he wanted the man to consider him an ally. 'It's a sorry business.' He took out a card and handed it to Pennington. 'Men of clear thinking should stick together.'

Pennington tucked the card away, very satisfied to have won another ally, or so he thought.

'Actually, Mr Pennington, I approached you because I was wondering when your son's funeral will take place.' He hoped he looked suitably sorrowful.

'I'm having him brought to our London home. He'll be interred in our family vault next Tuesday.'

'Which church would that be?'

'St Bartholomew the Great.'

'Smithfield?' It would follow that the tradesman had an address in the mercantile district of London rather than the fashionable West End.

'Indeed. The ceremony is at noon.' Pennington glared at his brandy. 'I never thought I'd bury my son.' It was the first hint of genuine grief.

'You have no other children to console you?' Didn't he sound the concerned citizen?

'No.'

'I thought I heard of a daughter...'

'She's dead.'

'I'm certain I heard it said that she had left home to go on stage...'

'My daughter can go to perdition for all I care.' He threw back the last of his drink in one swallow. 'If that is all, sir, I'll return to my meeting.'

'Indeed. Thank you. My deepest condolences once again.'

Pennington replied with a sharp nod then strutted over to his little gaggle of malcontents. His visitor savoured his own brandy, rolling the taste on his tongue. That had been useful. Pennington and his son had been at odds for a while. That reduced the likelihood that Anthony would have entrusted him with the missing papers. The tradesman also seemed like a poor candidate for being a member of the Hellfire Club, too focused on his business and not in the right circles to be invited. Anthony had possessed a certain military glamour that had gained him entrée. He would hardly want his provincial father along for nights of debauchery, no matter how deep his pockets were. Pennington might have spawned a bastard once, but he didn't look like the kind of man to find sex a temptation now. Money was his mistress. That was fine, as that was something one could work with, should it become necessary.

He downed his drink and waved away the offer of another. Pennington could live for now. His plots with his fellow merchants could create problems for the government. If they built enough opposition in the quarters that counted, such as amongst bankers, then Perceval's policies would founder and his credit would dry up. The resulting chaos would be fertile ground for the Illuminati to flourish. If he and his associates kept their heads, they could position themselves as the ones to step in and steady the ship of state in the face of economic storms. And if Napoleon reversed Wellington's gains and Britain was once again under threat of invasion…

The prospects were very rosy for advancement.

All he had to do was crack the sister and get at those secrets.

Chapter Eighteen

Road to West Wycombe

Something was very wrong. Matt Jenkins slogged his way along the path leading to West Wycombe, mud clinging to his boots, making them twice as heavy. He had begged Mary not to go but she had insisted, promising she would be back in a week or two. Many months had passed and there had been no word. Why hadn't she come back? Surely she would realise that she'd lose her job at the inn? Jerry, the landlord, was furious that he was missing his best maid, but no one had been worried for Mary. Not like Matt. Mary sought finer things. She enjoyed a glimpse of the high life. Maybe she had hooked onto a rich lord and was enjoying the life of a pampered mistress? She would be back when her payday came, or so they said even as they sniggered at him behind their hands. Jerry had also mentioned to Matt's face that he might be able to take her back if she asked nicely. Matt had almost knocked off his blockhead because he knew exactly how Mary had got the job in the first place – behind the pub, on her knees, with Jerry's cock in her mouth. She'd laughed when she told him, saying she'd known worse.

They thought him simple, harbouring romantic feelings for one of Henley's harlots, but Matt knew Mary was far more than that. He wasn't the quickest man – things came to him slowly – but he was true to his girl and Mary knew that. Reliable like an oak tree, she had said, hugging him, her blonde head tucked against his chest.

Sex had been a small matter for Mary, and Matt had tried to understand it as she did. She thought it a game, or a way of enriching herself, as she had the kind of looks and body that appealed to men – a milkmaid freshness with plump curves. God had given her these advantages and she wanted to use them, like this chance to join a party of gentlemen. She had said it would be a giggle and an opportunity for them to put some money aside for the day when they could afford to be married. She had said that, once they wed, she would stop all of it, but he had wondered if she really would. He hated that she took men into the back room at the inn in Henley, but that was how he had met the girl who had stolen his heart after she had lightened his purse considerably of his harvest earnings.

He wiped his brow, getting hot even though the day was miserably chilly. What did it matter that she had known other men? They did not know her – not really. Mary was the kind of girl who would give her last shilling to a widow with five children to raise. He knew this because he'd seen her do it only last spring. The kind of girl who understood that a slow-witted man could still love and cherish her for the rest of her life. He would make sure she wanted for nothing once they got that cottage on the estate he'd been promised by Viscount Hambleden. She wouldn't need to go into the back room then. She would be Mrs Jenkins and he would belt anyone who disrespected his wife.

The golden ball on top of the church appeared over the trees.

Good; he was in the right place. He hadn't been sure he would be able to find it on his own. His dad had rolled his eyes when he'd said he was going after Mary and predicted that nothing good would come of it. It was cheering to prove his father wrong.

'If by some miracle you do get there, Matt,' his dad had said, 'go to the main house and ask one of the servants if they know Mary. But prepare yourself for bad news. That Mary is a greedy lass. She won't come back if she's fallen into clover.'

Matt settled his knapsack more comfortably on his back and headed into the village.

Chapter Nineteen

Lady Tolworth left them at the coaching inn at High Wycombe, extracting promises that they would both call on her if they came to town.

'My stepson is a tedious fellow. I will need the distraction,' she called as the carriage pulled back out onto the London Road.

Dora looked at Dr Sandys. 'Well? Does she stand a chance?'

'We'd better hurry. I hope the inn has a chaise for hire.' He appeared distinctly hot under the collar at the lady's clear interest in rekindling their romance.

'She's a lovely woman.' Dora hurried after him as he waved to catch a groom's attention. 'Rich. Independent.'

'I'm glad you liked her. I thought you'd get on well.' He tossed this over his shoulder, not wanting to engage in the nub of the matter.

'She still likes you.'

He swung around, an amused light in his eyes. 'Miss Fitz-Pennington, if you are going to turn adviser on my amours, I really think I should call you something else. What was it the theatre people called you?'

He'd noticed that, had he? 'Fitzy. Or Dora.'

'Miss Dora. It suits you. And you can drop the "doctor". I'm Jacob.'

'Perhaps.' That was an intimacy reserved for close friends and lovers, and she was neither.

Lady Tolworth's prophecy echoed in her mind: *yet*.

He looked a little chagrined by her cool answer. 'Naturally, you don't have to.'

'I know. I'll see if the mood takes me.' With a smile, she walked on. Jacob was the kind of domineering man you needed to keep guessing.

The inn did indeed have a chaise for hire. With Nero stabled to recover from the long journey south, they were soon rattling out of High Wycombe for the short one to the village. The inn provided two chestnut horses in the traces, feathery hair around their hooves denoting their Clydesdale breed. Dora was still struggling with how quickly they had swapped the harsher landscape of the north, with its stony fields and sheep, for this landscape where the crops were already planted and the hedges budding. The land folded and swelled like high seas of grass. You couldn't see what was over the next rise, making each valley strangely private while still being near the main road to London. That was why the Hellfire Club had chosen it for their parties, she realised; a quick escape from censorious town society to let their more scandalous urges out to play.

A spring downpour prompted them to pause under an overhanging tree to wait for it to pass. Fat raindrops hammered puddles and the ditches filled up to spill over the road. Then the skies turned back to ragged blue.

'You drive well,' she commented as he avoided the worst of the ruts and puddles with skill. She still held on to her seat as even the best driver couldn't make this road a smooth experience.

He shook rain off the brim of his black top hat and replaced it with a firm tap. 'I've steered a wagon through a battlefield many a time. This is nothing.'

'Collecting the injured?'

He nodded. 'You can make a great difference to the chances someone has of surviving if you see to them before they are moved.'

No wonder he got the scar from the French soldier. He hadn't stayed tucked away in his hospital, far from the front line, as most surgeons would have done.

'That was very courageous. I'd take *my* hat off to you if it hadn't been so fiercely pinned to my head by Lady Tolworth's maid.' She was pleased that her jaunty smile elicited a warm one in response. This felt very like flirting.

Were they flirting?

They definitely were, she decided.

'Not courageous,' Jacob said. 'I was just scared of the nightmares I would be sure to have if I knew I hadn't done everything I could.'

She doubted that was his only reason. She squeezed his forearm in sympathy and he put his gloved palm over hers and kept her hand there.

As they neared West Wycombe and the caves, her thoughts turned back to her brother and what he might have left for her. It couldn't be something as simple as money as that wouldn't have brought the Illuminati to Kendal. Unease crept over her. As much as she wanted his letter, she didn't want to be in possession of someone else's secrets, especially not dangerous ones. It was like having a bomb tossed to you with the fuse lit and no one to pass it to.

'There it is, Miss Dora: St Lawrence Church, where George Leighton is the rector.'

Following his whip, Dora spotted a square tower with a golden ball at its summit rising over the treetops. A six-sided mausoleum, built of flint and Portland stone, stood beside the church. To her it looked like an old-fashioned lady in a panniered gown next to a tall one in the new Empire line fashion.

'The church looks more like something you'd see in Italy.'

'You've been?'

'Of course not, but I've painted my fair share of Italianate backdrops.'

He chuckled. 'I recall that the church was embellished by the infamous Sir Francis Dashwood, and he was inspired by Venice. Aren't we all?'

Dora shrugged. 'If you say so, Jacob.'

He grinned at her familiar form of address. 'Good, we're battle comrades now. I think we've earned the familiarity, Dora.'

She liked the sound of her name on his lips but put her nose in the air to pretend otherwise. 'I'd hardly call that tussle in the barn a battle.'

'Oh, but it was. Battles are made up of skirmishes like that. Believe me. I've lived through enough of them to know. You would have earned a mention in dispatches with your defeat of Fosse and the inspired use of a family Bible.'

She had to return him to the subject at hand or she was in danger of developing cracks in her defences against him. He was being too charming for her own good. 'And what purpose does that ball on top of that church serve? Is it a weathervane?'

'Not at all. That ball is hollow and can seat a small party. The view is supposed to be magnificent. I had heard that the Hellfire Club used to meet there.'

'In a church?'

'On top of a church. I think it appealed to their sense of sacrilege.'

'Good Lord.'

'I think the Good Lord had nothing to do with it. Dashwood

had his infernal one in mind as he cavorted in public, but remained hidden.'

'How very ... Hellfire.' Dora considered the logistics of fitting enough men and women in the golden ball to qualify for an orgy. She would prefer a bed and only one partner. Perhaps they kept their activities to infernal toasts in wine mixed with brimstone? 'How on earth did he get permission?'

'Permission? My dear Dora, you don't ask permission if you are Sir Francis Dashwood, largest landowner, Chancellor of the Exchequer, the one who has the rectory in his gift. You do what you will.' He tapped the horses into motion again. 'I believe the caves are actually under the hill on which the church is built – more symbolism for you.'

'And the Church didn't stop him?'

'How could it? The caves were the result of Dashwood digging out the chalk to improve the road to Oxford.'

'And I'm sure he did none of the digging himself.'

'I did not realise you were a pedant, Miss Dora. He had his men dig out, if you wish to be precise. He provided work in a time of hunger during the 1750s.'

She snorted. 'See! The devil's in the details, though that was a rather angelic motive.'

'How apt. Howsoever the excavation occurred, he was left with a complex of tunnels and his thoughts turned to bacchanalian revels. What power did the clergyman at the time have to stop him? His club included many of the notable men of his day – members of parliament, lords, a son of the Archbishop of Canterbury, and even such luminaries as Benjamin Franklin attended the revels.'

'Ben Franklin? You mean the hero of the American Wars of Independence and Founding Father?' Dora shook her head in disbelief. 'He was here with his breeches around his ankles tupping the ladies of the night?'

His blue eyes sparkled with amusement. 'History does not record. Perhaps he played backgammon?'

'I've heard it called that too.'

Jacob chuckled. 'Franklin was flesh and blood like all men, so I will not pry into his private activities with willing partners. You might be interested to know that he and Sir Francis did emerge from the parties long enough to make a serious attempt at reforming the prayer book.'

'In what way reforming? Making orgies permissible?'

'Nothing so shocking. They shortened the services to make them more appealing to the younger generation, taking out some of the crustier language. It was printed in 1773 but wasn't adopted. It is a curiosity of the times – I have a copy in my library and think it an admirable undertaking.'

'You're not one for long services?'

'Not much of a one for attending church.' He brushed a catkin from his shoulder where it had sprinkled its pollen. 'I think that was rather the point of the Hellfire Club – cocking a snook at episcopal flummery. The one time a devil did show up they all went on their knees and begged forgiveness. They weren't as wild as history maintains.'

'Really? What devil?'

'Legend says John Wilkes hid a baboon in a box dressed as the devil when the Hellfire Club members were at their principal site of revelry, a few miles away at the ruin of Medmenham Abbey. He released it as a practical joke but it caused Lord Sandwich to fall on his knees and beg forgiveness.'

'Ouch. That must've been embarrassing.'

'It is said to have been the start of the great enmity between the men, which led to the public exposure of the private club.'

That was exactly the kind of prank Anthony might have dreamt up. 'My brother would've loved that, but I rather pity the poor baboon. You aren't a religious man, Jacob?'

His expression turned defensive. 'I didn't say that. I prefer to take my worship out of doors and away from clerical hypocrisy.'

She arched a brow. 'Excuse me, but aren't we just about to meet your clergyman friend?'

'There are some exceptions to my rule. Leighton is admirably upright. He was trying to persuade this generation not to frequent the Hellfire meetings, but with little success. Ah, here's the rectory now.'

The rectory was just over the brow of the hill from the church, hidden behind an ivy-covered wall. She couldn't even spot a chimney pot.

'Not one to want his parishioners peering in at what he's doing?' said Dora as Jacob jumped down to open the gates. He was moving more easily now, recovering quickly from his beating.

'He is a private man, though I would hazard this privacy was the choice of his predecessor. The ivy looks as old as the wall and probably dates from Dashwood's time.'

'Then that must've been what the good rector did about the scandalous behaviour. He couldn't beat them, didn't want to join them, so he hid from them.'

'There are plenty in society of that view. If you can't see it, you can ignore it.'

Jacob touched her glove. 'Will you take the reins and drive through so I can close the gate behind us?'

Dora had included cart driving in her life on the road so was able to do this without lessons in holding the ribbons. She squeezed their chaise through the entrance with an inch to spare, and not a scratch added to the paintwork.

'I take it the narrow gate is another ecclesiastical reference?' she said as Jacob climbed back into the driving seat. She shifted over to make room, aware that their thighs were touching.

'Undoubtedly. I'll suggest it to Leighton for his next sermon.' He flicked the ribbons and the horses clattered obediently into the forecourt. The timber and redbrick house with a terracotta tiled roof was nothing like the Italianate church and mausoleum at the top of the hill. It belonged to an older era, probably with medieval foundations, and appeared to have grown organically from the landscape rather than been dropped on top of it. The glass in the windows was held in a leaded lattice, several having the bullseye pattern of crown glass that distorted the view out. Spring flowers – daffodils and primroses – sprouted under the windows on the south side, though the snowdrops and celandines lingered in the shadows cast by the walls around the courtyard. It was pretty but Dora judged it a damp and cold place with so many rooms to heat on a clergyman's wage. Perhaps Jacob's friend had a private fortune? Many did, and were gentlemen who treated their parish duties as a sideshow to their biblical studies or antiquarian pursuits. They were some of her best customers.

Anthony had encouraged her to fleece the shepherds. It had appealed to his naughty sense of humour. And yet he had made friends with one.

Jacob jumped down and helped her descend without damage to her skirt.

'Ready?' he asked in a low voice.

She nodded, grateful he had noticed her emotions were close to the surface now that she had reached her destination. Was Anthony still here or had her father already fetched the body? And the letter?

Chapter Twenty

Hellfire Caves

'She's just down here.' The man laid a comforting hand on Matt's forearm as he hesitated at the mouth of the caves. It was a queer place and he wanted nothing to do with it.

'Why would my Mary be down there?' The passageway was scary and narrow for a man of his height and breadth. His ploughman's muscles often made him feel unwelcome in places where other people fitted without a murmur, like the pews at church that creaked if he sat down. He'd taken to standing at the back near the bellringers.

'Oh, it is much pleasanter further on. She has a fine little nest, snug and welcoming. She said to expect you.'

'She did?' Matt was pleased that Mary had come to trust him so far that she knew he would wade through water and walk on hot coals to reach her if she needed him. 'But she's all right?'

'Indeed. I imagine she's resting at this hour. Come, let's go and find out.'

Some part of Matt's trusting brain was waving a warning. This felt like one of the tricks the boys might have played on him before he grew big enough to thump them, like the dare to swim in the Thames when they ran off with his clothes or shutting him in with Farmer Barnsley's bull. He glanced at the gentleman beside him. A grand man like this wouldn't stoop to play a joke on a foolish fellow like him, surely?

'You say you are to be wed?' said the man cheerfully, holding up the lantern to light the way.

'I hope so. Very soon.'

'How fortunate for her, to have a solid man like you at her side.'

Matt liked the sound of that; him a 'solid man'. His fears left him and he strode on to prove that he was just such a one.

'Do you read and write?' the man asked, though what prompted the question Matt was not sure.

'Not me, sir.'

'Shame. Ah well.'

'But Mary can. She's clever that way. She'll teach our children to be more learned than their father.' He could imagine it now, them all teasing him as a big lummox while he gave them piggybacks around their orchard. They'd have an orchard by then, and bees. He liked bees and had a hive of his own already. He didn't mind the stings. He didn't mind if his family laughed at him as long as they loved him.

The passageway took a turn to the right.

'Creepy place this,' he said aloud. His doubts that Mary would be down here returned now that they were far from the entrance. It didn't feel like her kind of place at all. She would have been more at home at the inn he'd visited earlier to ask after her.

'Not much further.'

They passed through a larger space, though he couldn't see much of it in the lantern light, then they made a couple of sharp turns. The final step was to get on board a small boat and cross a waterway. A boat underground! Who would've thought of such a thing?

'She's in here,' the man said, going into another bigger space, though this one Matt could make out in the light. It was about the size of the squire's dovecot.

'Mary? Honeybee, it's Matt.' His voice echoed around the space but, unless she was pressed against the wall in the shadows, there was nowhere for her to hide. Maybe this was a cruel trick after all? 'Where's Mary?'

'Look up,' said the man calmly.

Matt did as he was told, but all he could see was a rope hanging from a hook in the ceiling.

'She's above us on the hill, but six feet from the surface.'

'I ... I don't understand.'

A sharp blow to the back of his head left Matt Jenkins in the dark.

Chapter Twenty-One

West Wycombe

Jacob pulled the doorbell and it jangled inside brightly. Footsteps approached and a person, blurred by the thick glass in the door, rattled the locks.

'Yes, sir?' A sour-faced housekeeper stood in the entrance.

Unmarried rectors had to have ones with faces that would curdle milk, or else risk tongues wagging, reasoned Dora. From the look sent her way, she knew the woman for the kind who chased theatre troupes out of a village if they dared pitch up uninvited.

'Please tell the rector that Jacob Sandys is here, with Miss Fitz-Pennington,' said Jacob in his best stiff-necked aristocratic tone.

'I doubt the rector is at home, sir, to visitors. Wait here.'

She snapped the door closed and left them on the step.

'Friendly soul,' murmured Jacob.

When the door opened again some long minutes later, their reception was much warmer.

'Sandys!' A hulking man in black emerged from a room at the end of the corridor, a quill in his hand, his wig slightly askew. 'What favourable wind blew you into my harbour? I wasn't expecting you for days – if you came at all.' He glanced down at the quill in his hand. 'Oh, forgive me. I was working on my book and told Mrs Stock to deter all boarders.' He passed the quill to his housekeeper, leaving her with the problem of what to do with it, and held out his hand to Jacob. 'So pleased you came.' His gaze had already gone to Dora. 'And this is Miss Fitz-Pennington, you say? You went far beyond what I anticipated, accompanying her here. Charmed, my dear, charmed.' He gave her a neat bow, hand to his breast. She bobbed a curtsy. He had the air of Mr Hardcastle of *She Stoops to Conquer*, an old-fashioned country gent, middle-aged before his time, but there was something impressive about him. Perhaps it was his height? He matched Sandys with his six feet and outdid him in breadth. The sedentary life of a clergyman had added some pounds around his middle.

'Mrs Stock, please send Truman to see to Dr Sandys's carriage,' he continued, waving them on. 'Then tea and some of your scones in the parlour. Did you light a fire in there yet? No? Then I'll do that for you while you carry out my orders.' And in this bustling manner that left little room for replies, he shepherded them into the room that looked out over the garden. 'Sit down, sit down. Rest yourself after your journey. You will of course be staying here? I ordered a room to be prepared for you, Sandys, just in case you came, but will make sure Miss Fitz-Pennington's chamber is made up so she can rest before dinner.'

'I'm to stay here?' asked Dora. She had not been expecting that. Rectors didn't normally welcome actresses into their households. It sounded like the beginning of a risqué joke.

'Oh, it is all very decent, I assure you. My aunt lives with me, Miss Helen Leighton, my father's sister. She's a little vague these days but she has the presence of mind to serve as chaperone.'

That hadn't been what she was thinking at all. The days when anyone worried about decency as regards her had long since passed. Perhaps it was the gentleman's own reputation they were guarding?

Leighton sat down in a winged armchair by the hearth, before leaping up again. 'The fire!' He rummaged around on the mantlepiece, found flint and tinder, and soon had a blaze going. 'I know it is spring, but this side of the house stays cool and a little damp until May arrives.'

Dora wanted desperately to ask immediately about Anthony, but good manners meant she had to sit through Leighton and Jacob exchanging pleasantries and catching up briefly on what had happened to them both in the years since they had last met.

'Served in the navy for a while as chaplain, Algeciras, Trafalgar,' said Leighton after Jacob gave the facts of his military service. 'Like you, I saw enough conflict to last me a lifetime. Did we think that would be our future back at college when what was to come seemed like sunny uplands?'

'Bliss was it in that dawn to be alive, But to be young was very heaven!' murmured Jacob.

Leighton straightened his wig, which had travelled back on his head in his enthusiastic fire-starting. 'What's that? Not heard that before.'

'My neighbour, the poet Wordsworth, has a long poem with which he is tinkering incessantly. He read me some of it – very fine indeed – and those lines stuck with me.'

'Ah yes. That chap. Clever man; fond of wilder landscapes than you'll meet round here.' Leighton gestured out of the window. 'Coming to West Wycombe felt like an early entrance to Paradise, or at least some kind of Elysian Fields where blood is rarely spilt.' His grey-green eyes turned to Dora, a clergyman's well-worn expression of sorrow. 'I am very sorry about your brother. He was a fine man at heart.'

'Yes, he was.' Dora swallowed against the obstruction in her throat. She envied the man having had such recent memories of Anthony. She would give a year of her life to have had that privilege. 'Not perfect, but he had his redeeming side. Loyal to a fault to his comrades.'

'Indeed.' Leighton studied her kindly, fingers steepled. 'You are probably wondering what has happened to him?'

'I am, sir.' She looked up sharply. 'Did my father come?'

'He sent word he was too caught up with business in London and dispatched his private secretary in his place to make the arrangements to retrieve Anthony's personal effects and move the body to the family home in London. There is to be a funeral at St Bartholomew the Great, I believe.'

That settled that question. Anthony was to be laid to rest in the family vault. The Penningtons had two places where members were customarily buried: Smithfield in London, where their fortune had been founded some fifty years ago by Ezra's father, or Liverpool, where they had bought their estate to be near their dockyard. Ezra Pennington was practical rather than sentimental. Though, if asked, Anthony would have said he had more connection to the chapel in the grounds at Butterworth Manor, their father would not want the cost and delay of taking him so far.

She would say her brother's goodbyes to their childhood haunts for him, she vowed, next time she was in Liverpool.

'The coffin is in the church rooms, in the lockup, if you wish to pay your respects?' Leighton suggested delicately.

She couldn't speak, just nodded. That was more than she had hoped – a chance to say goodbye. There was no way she would be welcome at the funeral service. Her father would see to that.

'Very well. I'll escort you there myself so you can visit him. You are just in time. The body is being moved tomorrow.'

Dora cleared her throat. 'And the letter you mentioned – do you still have it?'

Leighton looked away, his friendly expression clouding. 'Ah. About that.'

Chapter Twenty-Two

Was that guilt in his friend's voice, wondered Jacob. He wouldn't be surprised if Leighton had given in to demands from Ezra Pennington to return all effects, including correspondence. If Anthony had been mixed up in the scandalous goings-on of the Hellfire Club, his father would want all incriminating papers destroyed to preserve his son's posthumous reputation.

Dora pressed her hand to her breast as if it pained her. Jacob wished he could comfort her but there was nothing to ease murder. 'Please tell me you have it still.'

Leighton got up and disappeared into the corridor outside. She turned to Jacob.

'What does that mean?'

'I don't know.' He reached over and squeezed her hand briefly. 'I don't really know him all that well.' That was what Jacob had realised, listening to Leighton recount his naval career. Jacob hadn't even been aware that he'd joined the service and certainly wouldn't have expected the bookish man he'd known at Oxford to take such a course. They'd both been under orders at the same time, but in very different military theatres, and not known about each other.

Leighton came back with a letter. He didn't hand it over immediately but looked down at it in doubt.

'Miss Fitz-Pennington, this note has been weighing on my mind. I wonder if it is quite safe to give it to you. Your brother was killed, perhaps because of what he knew. If I hand you this, am I putting you in further danger?'

In the few words he had said about their journey to their host, Jacob had not mentioned their problems in the north, hoping they'd left them behind. He was glad now that he had omitted that part, or Leighton might have been tempted to throw the letter on the fire in this blooming of gallantry.

As Jacob had come to expect, Dora took such sentiments as a challenge rather than a warning. She immediately held out her hand. 'I will take that risk. Anthony was my only family. I'd read a letter from him even if it leads me into a den of lions.'

Leighton reluctantly passed it over. She looked critically at the seal.

'This has been broken.'

The rector held up his hands. 'I hope you do not suspect me. It is exactly how I found it at your brother's house.'

That opened the possibility that someone already knew the contents. The Illuminati? That might explain why they had tracked Dora all the way to Kendal.

'Where was his house?' asked Jacob.

'On the Dashwood estate that borders the village, about half a mile from here. I'm afraid I can't say who else had access to his rooms, but you can imagine a fair number of people – servants, friends and the like – came and went unquestioned.'

Dora slid her finger under the damaged seal and flicked the pages open. Reading it swiftly, she paused, went to the window and held it to the light, then turned it over.

'Looking for something?' asked Jacob.

'My brother was fond of puzzles and ciphers. What he writes makes little sense, so I wondered if perhaps he'd hidden a further message.' Hesitating, she then passed the note to Jacob. He was gratified by the show of trust.

It was dated some ten days ago, the night Anthony was killed.

Dearest Sister Dora,

Forgive my long silence. I have been cloistered with the monks and had scant time to send up my orisons to your northern hermitage. I am a bad Saint Anthony, deserving of whipping. I fear I might not get the chance to hear the penance you set me for my neglect.

My dear brave sister, I have followed your appearances on stage from afar and hope that pious life has given you pleasure and pleasant company.

'Pleasure, or wrong or rightly understood,

Our greatest evil, or our greatest good.'

I hope you have chosen well.

How things have changed for me. Inscribing this Bull, I see only troubled times ahead for my service as Shepherd of Sinners. Our father is wading in dangerous waters and there is no haven there if things turn sour. I urge you to keep close to such friends you have who are not beholden to anyone in society. You cannot tell where the enemies lie when everyone around you wears a mask.

You may know by now that I did not part ways from my Monks of Medmenham Abbey as you urged. Do not frown at me for I have risen to the top of my order and been given the honour of Custodian of Sir Francis Dashwood's diary and Warden of the Caves – the Hades in charge of their Underworld. You would scoff at such a promotion, I know; but for me, this is a worthy role, and one I will not dishonour as many have held it faithfully before me. I do not wish to be the one who fails my brethren.

Then why this letter? A very good question – and even now I think it might be better to cast it into the fire. But would that save you? Maybe it is preferable that you should be warned? I will leave it for you and trust that your God has not wholly abandoned you even though He might have given up on me.

My reckoning is due. You need to know that I have attracted the attention of an enemy who believes I hold a secret that would destroy the great men in power. Many innocents could die as a result. He is not wrong. Men will do in the dark what they will not own in the light. Some acts that even I do not condone have occurred, but who am I to cast the first stone? I trust I can hold off my enemy and reach a deal, giving him what he asks for but not what he desires. I pray that will be enough.

I cannot write more in case this falls into the wrong hands, but I have shown you the Great key to a place nearby. I could not destroy my charge as I had sworn to defend it. You will remember the key if you think hard enough about what we shared together. Find it and take it to my successor as Hades. Sheridan will know who that is.

A papal blessing from your loving brother
Anthony

Jacob turned the pages as she had done. The dead man's handwriting was strong and even. This was written with a clear head. There was no code that he could immediately decipher, and he could not smell lemon juice, suggesting no invisible message was included.

Leighton held out a hand. 'May I?'

Jacob waited for a signal from Dora, which she gave, then passed it to his friend. Dora stood with her arms wrapped around herself, teeth biting into her lower lip as she held her grief tight.

'See, Sandys, I was right!' Leighton brandished the letter. 'This wasn't the random act of footpads. Anthony Pennington was murdered at that meeting. Who on earth could he have arranged to see?'

No one knew the answer to that so Jacob turned to what they might be able to puzzle out.

'Do you understand it?' asked Jacob. 'This talk of a key – a great key?'

'I don't,' she said. 'He writes that I'll remember but he never gave me a key to anything. Unless he left one for me somewhere?'

'Then the references to penance and papal blessing – are you Roman Catholic? Is it the crossed keys of St Peter, perhaps? Some religious keepsake?'

Dora shook her head. 'My brother believed in nothing. You can take those as part of his mockery of religion. He would playact pope, priest and king when we were young, staging mock ceremonies to shock me. He discovered it took a lot to do so. He always called me Sister Dora as if I were a nun, so I started calling him Saint Anthony.' She pulled a wry face. 'Children are naturally ironic.'

'We should go to his house and see if there is anything there that jogs your memory.'

'But I thought his effects had already been collected?'

The rector handed her back the letter. 'They have, but they are to be sent with his – with him. I cannot see any objection to you looking for something he wished to give you.'

'And we should search his house as well,' said Jacob, 'in case he has hidden this key in a place only you will be able to guess.'

She rubbed her brow. 'I doubt very much it is as simple as a real key, but we have to look.'

'You are tired, Miss Fitz-Pennington,' said Leighton. 'Do you wish to rest before we go out?'

'No, no, not tired in that way,' Dora said. 'I'm just … sad.' Jacob watched with respect as she breathed through a swell of emotion, driving off the tears by sheer force of will. 'This is Anthony's world, Anthony's … Anthony's bequest. I don't even want it.'

There wasn't anything either of the men could say to that. Jacob could understand how she might resent being pulled away from the little pond in which she swam happily to be dumped in the cold ocean thrashing with sharks. Anthony Pennington had a lot to answer for.

'Then let us go while we have daylight,' said the rector. 'Where first? My advice is that the caves can wait as they can be seen as well by night as by day.'

'My brother's body,' said Dora. 'I want to see Anthony.'

The lock-up lay at the end of the lane and was easily reached on foot. Carriages could pass under this timber and brick building and join the main road. To Jacob, it resembled many an inn in which he had passed uncomfortable nights while on campaign in the Peninsular War. The rooms were largely empty, with no fires in the grates, adding to the gloomy feel.

'He is in the coldest room,' said Leighton, choosing an iron key from a ring and unlocking the door. 'We use it as a storeroom and occasional gaol.' The door creaked open. 'As you can see, I provided a simple coffin at my own expense for the removal to London. Doubtless your father will prepare something better for his final resting place.'

A plain deal coffin lay on the table, the lid already fitted but not nailed shut.

'Shall we uncover him?' Leighton asked.

Dora nodded.

He took one end while Jacob seized the other. They lifted off the lid and set it aside. Dora approached and gazed at her brother's face in the grey light coming through the barred windows. She gave a choked sob and rested her hand against his lips as if hoping against hope that there might be breath stirring there. Jacob could have told her from the lividity and greenish tinge to Anthony's skin – and the rank odour that crept from the corpse – that he was already decomposing. The man's face had the bloated look that settles in after death, turning what once must have been handsome features into a mockery of themselves. He looked like a dissipated man of middle age, not a young man in his prime.

'Oh Jacob,' Dora whispered. Tears brimmed and slid down her cheeks. 'It's really him.'

Of course, Jacob realised. She had held out that frail hope that so many did, that this wasn't real. The lumpen fact of a body took that away from the mourner.

'I'm sorry.' In the long run, it would be better that she saw Anthony like this, Jacob reminded himself, so that no doubt remained.

Leighton put a fatherly hand on her shoulder and whispered some words of comfort and prayers taken from the burial rite. It was not fair to expect Dora to search her own brother's body for a key, so Jacob took over the duty of patting down the man's clothes. Moving aside the waistcoat and shirt, he spied the entry wound, the blood having been cleaned off by whoever had laid him out. He noticed that it was off-centre and longer than he had expected.

'Odd,' he said, before he thought to censor his words.

'Odd?' echoed Leighton. 'In what way?'

Jacob hovered his finger over the wound, estimating the length of the cut. 'This missed the heart at first. See the widening to the entrance. It was then thrust up and into the heart.' He reached out and turned over Anthony's palms. 'Defensive wounds. He held the blade where it entered, perhaps trying to stop the thrust.' He didn't add that death would not have been instantaneous as it had not hit its target immediately. There were some things that a sister need not know. 'He might not have had time to feel any pain.' He said the latter for Dora's benefit. Better for her to imagine the best case. He could imagine a worst where the pain had been prolonged in order to make Pennington talk. Had he? It was impossible to say, when they did not know what explosive secret he had been hiding. He couldn't have said very much because the Illuminati were still hunting for the pieces of the puzzle.

'He is at peace now,' said Leighton. 'Our Master is a merciful judge. If he turned to Him at the end, he will be at His side in Paradise, even as the thief that hung on the cross beside Jesus.'

Dora touched her brother's hair in farewell, then stepped back. She ran her wrist under her eyes, swiping away tears. 'A key?' She sounded almost angry, but that was just her defences going up.

'No, not on him,' said Jacob. 'But I don't see any belongings here.'

'Maybe Mr Pennington's man of business has them in his room at the George and Dragon?' suggested Leighton.

'Then how can we check them?' Dora glanced at Jacob, tears sparkling on her long lashes. He dipped his head at the rector and hoped she would get his hint. They might be able to investigate later, but only when the law-abiding reverend was abed. 'Oh, but of course, we can't,' she corrected herself. 'Let's go to Anthony's house.'

As Jacob reached for the coffin lid, a man entered the room with a determined step.

'What the blazes are you doing here?' he demanded.

Chapter Twenty-Three

Startled, Dora swung round to greet the newcomer.

'Mr Gatskill, this is Anthony's sister, and her escort, Dr Sandys,' said the rector, interposing his considerable bulk between the open coffin and the man.

Her father's man from the inn, come to check on his charge. Dora rubbed her chest, hoping her pulse would settle to a pace that would allow her to respond calmly. She didn't know this man, but anyone who worked for her devil of a father needed firm handling.

'The deceased had no sister,' sneered Gatskill.

He had no right to her brother, nor her grief. Snatching a last glimpse of Anthony's changed features, Dora went forward as Jacob placed the lid over him. 'He most assuredly did, sir.'

The coffin closed with a final thump – a blow to her heart. If she gave in to her grief, she'd be caught in memories of Anthony's laugh, his teasing, sitting cross-legged on the floor of a library with him, but there was no time. She had to concentrate on the enemy before her. Gatskill was a dyspeptic individual, slight and pale with fair hair standing up from his scalp as though he'd been playing with one of Galvani's electrical devices. She was one more thing to shock him if he did not know his employer had strayed from the marital bed.

'Miss Fitz-Pennington. A half-sister,' amended Leighton.

'Oh, the actress.' Gatskill sniffed like he'd said 'the prostitute' or 'the beggar woman'. 'She shouldn't be here. Mr Pennington has cut all ties with her.'

'*I* have cut all ties with *him*,' she corrected, 'but never with my brother. I have a greater right than any of you to be standing here. The right of blood.'

Gatskill refused to look at her. 'Get her out of here. She's a disgrace and shouldn't be allowed in decent company. I'm surprised at you, Reverend.'

'If you are surprised, then you cannot have read the Gospels,' said Leighton. 'Miss Fitz-Pennington, are you ready to leave?'

Gratitude warmed her chilled heart. 'Yes, thank you. I have said my goodbyes.' Neither her father nor his man could take that away from her.

Gatskill barely made room for her to pass so she bumped him with her shoulder. Sandys did likewise, though his was more of a shove. Only the rector paused to wait for room to be made for him.

'Outrageous!' spluttered Gatskill, stepping aside.

'Good afternoon,' returned the rector, tipping his hat.

'I won't have any qualms about raiding that man's room,' Dora muttered to Jacob.

'If the man is any guide to his employer, your father is an unfeeling brute.'

'I did warn you.'

Their route to Anthony's house took them along the village high street and to the park entrance. Inevitably, the rector couldn't walk five paces without being greeted by a parishioner. By mutual agreement, Dora and Jacob walked on.

'Is the big house still lived in by the Dashwoods?' she asked. They could see part of the long wall that circled the estate.

'They do still own it but the current holder of the title, Sir John Dashwood, is not fond of the place. I've heard that he often rents it out.'

'I take it he isn't like his grandfather?'

'Indeed not. The maternal side is descended from Milton so Puritanical blood has entered the Dashwood line.'

Dora's steps faltered. 'You aren't joking. The most colourful peer of the last century is linked to the puritanical poet of the one before. My word, life is full of irony.'

'Hang around the British aristocracy for long enough, my dear Dora, and you will find such coincidences are to be expected. It is a very small world.'

The rector caught up with them.

'I apologise. Problems with the May Day celebrations.'

'Leighton, is West Wycombe Park let at present?' asked Jacob.

'Oh yes, to a fine gentleman of seven thousand a year. Sir Fletcher Vane. He has a position in the Alien Office. Do you know him?'

Jacob shook his head. 'I keep away from the government men, though I understand enough to know that Vane must be handling the refugees from France and thus be involved in the domestic and foreign surveillance of people of interest.'

'The less said on that, the better,' said Leighton. 'There are French spies amongst us, they say.'

'And ours over in France,' said Jacob, not taking the warning seriously. There was no one within earshot. 'You may not know, Dora, but great sums of money are spent each year to gain the best intelligence of enemy movements and intentions. Back in 1794 the office gained fame for ejecting the French diplomat Talleyrand from England on account of his plotting. Talleyrand went on to assist Napoleon in his rise to power, so suspicion was probably justified.'

'Or did they merely create their enemy?' Dora suggested. 'It might've been better to keep him here.'

'True, though word is the Alien Office networks spread throughout the émigré community to the heart of Napoleon's regime.'

'Sir Fletcher is a most pleasant companion and a fair hand at whist,' said Leighton in an obvious attempt to change the subject from espionage. 'He's a vast improvement on the previous tenant, a Mr William Bates, who did us all a disservice reopening the caves for Hellfire revels. Bates brought your brother here, Miss Fitz-Pennington, and suggested Anthony rent Kitty's Lodge, one of the two gatehouses.'

'Kitty?' asked Dora, wondering if Anthony had been living with a lady.

'The lodge was named after Kitty Fisher, a famous courtesan of the last century, and a friend of Sir Francis. The other is called Daphne's Temple.'

'Now I begin to understand where the women who attended the parties came from. Miss Kitty was friends with Lucy Locket, I suppose?'

'Indeed. I understand that nursery rhyme had quite another meaning when it was first composed as a scurrilous poem.' Leighton frowned. 'I would tell the local children not to sing it, but maybe it is better for them to remain in ignorance.'

'The explanation would be worse than the song,' agreed Jacob.

Dora bit her lip, trying not to laugh at the image of the serious rector explaining female anatomy to young boys and girls. She felt as close to laughter as to tears.

The lodge was a small square building of two storeys, ochre walls, and a pyramid roof topped by a sphere. Anthony hadn't needed much space even as a boy, preferring to spend his hours outside, so she could see that it would appeal.

'This won't take long to search,' she said.

There was no entrance hall; one entered directly into the lower room. A daybed sat under one window, a fire with a toasting fork and kettle opposite it. The shelves were empty but there were rings showing where once bottles had stood. Without saying anything to Jacob, she took the stairs up to the bedroom, wanting to be alone with her brother for a moment – his memory, not that lifeless thing that was his body. The upper room was empty of everything but an iron bed. Ribbons hung from the struts. She took a moment to realise that these must have been for bed sport. Dora had not wanted to contemplate her brother's proclivities, but it wasn't hard to guess from the company he kept that he was the adventurous sort. Even he had not felt it decent to share the details with a sister.

Jacob followed and went to the bed. He tugged on a ribbon.

'Securely fastened.'

Dora turned away. 'That's a bowline. We are the children of a man who owns a shipping line. We had many hours to kill at the docks and Anthony loved nothing better than talking to the sailors.' She went to the window to look out at the view across the lake to the big house with its Palladian frontage, also painted ochre. She played with the tie on the curtains until she realised it was a sheet bend. The other one was missing. Anthony had been busy here too and she didn't want to think what other uses he might have made of the silk rope. 'I don't see any keys here, do you?' she said, cheeks flaming.

'No. Leighton is looking downstairs but that seemed picked clean to me.' Jacob was feeling around the mantlepiece, probing for cracks.

'He said he'd already given it to me,' she mused, perching on the window seat.

Jacob paused. 'Do you have anything of your brothers?'

'No, no, I've nothing... Wait!' She did have something, didn't she? The book of writing samples that they'd put together for their literary games. But how to explain to Jacob the collector that she had something that enabled her to make fraudulent documents?

'You've remembered?'

'I ... I don't know. Perhaps. I need to return to our lodgings and check.'

He held out a hand to help her up and kissed her knuckles. 'Very mysterious. You won't tell me?'

She shook her head. 'It might be nothing.' And she needed time to think up her explanation.

He kept hold of her hand for a moment.

'Dora, I haven't had the chance to say so, but I am sincerely sorry about your brother.'

She lowered her eyes. She wouldn't give in to those damn tears!

'I come from a large and annoying family so I cannot pretend to know what you feel now that you've lost the one member of yours that you could bear.'

She swallowed. 'He could be pretty objectionable too, but he was mine.'

'That I do understand. I'm sorry.' He pulled her gently towards him so she could, with the least pressure, escape and restore the distance between them should she wish it. She let herself accept the comfort that was offered, resting her head against his shoulder. It felt such a relief to have someone hold her. To have Jacob hold her. It had been far too long. Though there was a simmering attraction between them, this was not about that, not here in her dead brother's bedroom; this was about simple human sympathy.

His hand rubbed the small of her back. 'We'll solve this and see those responsible brought to justice.'

It was a wish rather than a vow. If he was right, the Illuminati were hidden and very powerful, creeping through society like dry rot. Justice was something that rarely touched the rich as they could throw all sorts of delays at the courts and call on their peers to let them go. Yet she appreciated the sentiment.

'Thank you,' she whispered.

He brushed her cheek with his fingertips, eyes locked on hers. 'If only there was more I could do.'

'Sandys, Miss Fitz-Pennington, have you finished up there?' called Leighton.

'Yes, we're coming down,' replied Jacob, setting her back on her feet. 'Miss Fitz-Pennington is somewhat overset and would like to rest now.' That would be the quickest way to reunite her with her belongings in the privacy of her bedroom.

'Overset?' she muttered.

Jacob flashed her an unrepentant grin and headed down the stairs.

'Ah, well, that's to be expected,' replied Leighton. 'The weaker sex should be protected and all that. However, Sir Fletcher Vane has sent a footman inviting us to call in on our way back. He wishes to convey his condolences. We might return to the rectory via the park, if the lady can manage it. It is but a slight detour.'

Dora had crossed the Pennines in winter, twice, so she thought a short trip across a landscaped park no hardship.

She joined the rector and Jacob in the lower room. 'I think I might be able to cope.'

Jacob's eyes danced with merriment as he heard her ironic tone.

'Excellent,' said Leighton, oblivious. 'Then let us go at once. We can do our duty by Sir Fletcher and still be in time for dinner at the rectory.'

They walked out of the chill of Kitty's Lodge back into the spring sunshine.

'What about the caves?' asked Jacob. 'I would like to see the location of the murder.'

'That will have to be after dinner, I'm afraid,' the rector said. 'We mustn't keep the great man waiting.'

Chapter Twenty-Four

West Wycombe Park

The footman who had come with the message led them to Sir Fletcher Vane. At this time of day, he was to be found in his gunroom – one of the offices in the wing at the side of the main house. It was a place that smelt of iron, dogs and leather, a masculine zone, far from the floral scents of a silk-lined parlour presided over by the lady of the manor. A tally of the winter's bag was chalked up on the wall behind him. Dora noted that he had the highest number of kills to his name – seventeen hares, five foxes and fifty-six partridges. With a jolt, she saw her brother's name up there. He was second on the hunters' list with a great many kills, mainly birds.

Vane looked up from his task, examining the condition of his rifle.

'A Manton. Quite a beauty,' he said, putting the gun to one side and coming to his feet. Dora was struck by his harsh features that would in his youth have added up to Grecian handsomeness but now veered towards severity. He wore a wig in the old style to

The Persephone Code

cover what might be a balding head. Dark brows framed intense jade-green eyes and he already had a shadow after his morning's shave as darker men often did. There was something of the classical hero or stoic about his square jaw and hollow cheeks. In her troupe, he would be cast as Coriolanus or Macbeth and be very popular with the ladies.

He came around the table to greet them. Dora was watchful for any sign of contempt as she was introduced but there was not a flicker in his eyes. He either did not know, or did not care, about her profession.

'Sir Fletcher, I see you have been busy,' said the rector, pointing to the chalkboard. 'Thank you for the game you have sent my way. Miss Fitz-Pennington, you will notice that I am at the bottom of the list, having bagged but a solitary partridge on my one and only hunt.'

'You are an appalling shot, Leighton,' Vane said cheerfully, 'but that is no hindrance to a man in your profession. Save your best shots for our consciences from the pulpit.'

Leighton bowed at this civil rejoinder.

'I have my own pack of hounds and am about to visit them. Would you care to accompany me, or would you prefer tea in the parlour? I'm afraid my wife is in town.' Vane addressed this query to Dora.

She was anxious to return to her room to examine the book she and her brother had made. A visit to the kennels should take less time than the ceremonies that accompanied tea.

'I would enjoy seeing your dogs, Sir Fletcher.'

'A woman after my own heart.' His smile was a little formal but perhaps his strong features could not relax into anything as common as a grin. He offered her his arm. 'You are the sister of the unfortunate man found in the caves, I understand?'

'Yes, sir.'

'May I express my condolences? I cannot claim to know

Pennington well, though we did hunt together this winter. On the few times we met, he always struck me as a stout fellow, the kind of person you would want at your back in a pinch.'

'He was indeed very dependable in that way,' agreed Dora. Her brother had a talent for male friendship. He would have appealed to a hunting enthusiast like Vane, able to keep up with any rider on horseback, or stalk for hours in all weathers with no complaint.

'Footpads, they say. It is shocking how lawless even a village like West Wycombe has become with desperate men roaming the countryside. I blame the blockade of the Continent. I tell you, Leighton, more trouble is coming. Frame breakers taking on the manufacturers, Luddites in Nottingham; the government should act to restore order.'

'There is indeed great suffering amongst the poor,' agreed the rector.

'I've seen it in my travels in the north,' said Dora. 'Many of the miners have nothing but rags to wear and their children no shoes.'

'You have toured the north?' Vane sounded intrigued.

She nodded.

'Did you see the Lakes? And the Border country? I hear it is very beautiful.'

Dora realised he was thinking of a tour as a lady would visit on her holiday, not as a working woman slogging through mud, pushing a cart loaded with props.

'It is majestic, though I believe Dr Sandys is better able to describe the beauties. He lives in the heart of the Lakes.'

'Sandys, Sandys…' Comprehension dawned. 'Son of Lord Sandys? I know your brother, Dr Sandys.'

'Which one – Arthur or William?' asked Jacob, drawing level at her side. She felt better for having him there.

'William. He's a noted expert on architecture and classical art, is he not? The Prince Regent has consulted him on numerous occasions. He said he wished to come here and study the gardens.'

'Yes, that would be William. Landscaping of this kind would appeal to his taste.'

Dora had already noted the scattering of follies and carefully planned surprises around the estate as they walked across it.

'The designer was Repton?' asked Jacob.

'Sir Francis Dashwood. The present Lord Dashwood said his grandfather employed fashionable gardeners mainly to disregard their advice and do what he wanted.'

Do what you will, thought Dora, *even in gardening*.

They reached the kennels, a long, low building with a fenced yard for exercise. The dogs sent up barks of excited welcome. The huntsman in charge strode forward, tugging on his cap.

'Master, Gentlemen, Lady.'

Behind the fence, whiplike tails flashed. Beagle snouts pressed forward but Dora knew better than to reach out to stroke one, no matter how appealing their big eyes. These were hunting dogs, loyal to their masters, but the pack was a killing machine and their training did not let them forget that.

Vane was watching her with a supercilious smile.

'Well done, Miss Fitz-Pennington. You are the first lady visitor I've had who didn't rush forward to pet the creatures, much to the detriment of their muslin gowns.'

Dora wondered why he hadn't bothered to warn her, unless he enjoyed seeing ladies having their dresses muddied and pawed. Perhaps he enjoyed the squeals and their appeals for his protection?

'I respect working animals, Sir Fletcher, and know what they are capable of doing.'

'And I admire sensible females, such as yourself.' He gave her a little bow. 'That puts me in mind – I'm holding a May Ball tomorrow night. Leighton, my invitation to you extends to *all* members of your household, guests included.'

'Most kind, sir,' said the rector.

'Oh, but I couldn't...' Dora could not dance when her brother was lying in his coffin but half a mile away.

'You would be very welcome, Miss Fitz-Pennington. My friends are not ones to turn up their noses to members of the demimonde; indeed, many of them will be bringing their ladies with them.'

The scales fell from her eyes. He thought her a mistress, did he? Most would assume that as she was an unmarried lady travelling in the company of a gentleman, what other explanation could there be?

'I am in mourning, sir.'

'Which we all respect, but many of the gentlemen knew your brother far better than I. My predecessor, Mr Bates, will be attending. If you wish to talk with those that loved him, this would be a perfect opportunity for you. Your brother is best remembered in a convivial setting rather than in the solemn trappings of a church service, is he not?' He turned to Jacob. 'Dr Sandys, are you a card player?'

'On occasion.' Jacob so far had kept aloof from the conversation. Did he not like their host? She agreed with him there.

'Excellent. We always welcome new blood at the tables. Stakes are capped to a hundred guineas, so no one loses their estates at my parties.'

'I'm not much of a gambler, Sir Fletcher. I did too much hazarding of my life on the Continent to think staking my wellbeing on the turn of a card amusing.'

'Then you may gamble your heart in the ballroom, dancing with the ladies who will be present.'

'You are very kind, but our plans—'

'No, no, I insist. One night of revelry! It will do you both good. An escape from melancholy for your lady and a chance for you to remind society of your existence, Sandys.'

'Moving to the north was very much intended to make them forget,' muttered Jacob, but Dora thought she was the only one to hear. Vane opened the gate to enter the kennel. He was greeted with rapture by his hounds, tails thrashing, barks booming.

'Besides, Leighton here said you were investigating the deaths in the caves,' called Vane. 'Where better to talk to the people who know the most than tomorrow night at my party?'

'Then I am pleased to accept,' said Jacob, sounding resigned.

'May we take our leave?' Dora asked in an undertone.

Leighton nodded. 'We've done our duty.'

'I will see you all tomorrow,' said their host, scratching the heads of his adoring pack. 'All of you.'

Chapter Twenty-Five

West Wycombe Rectory

Alone in her room to change for dinner, Dora dismissed the idea of attending the ball. If they were still here tomorrow, the menfolk could go. She had the excuse of having nothing to wear, and the rector would hardly have something in his closet to help her.

In her absence, the housekeeper had pressed the other gown that Dora had brought with her – a simple cotton dress, which she had made herself last winter from a bolt of sprigged muslin bought for a song in Edinburgh. It was secured with a ribbon beneath her bust. That left a wide expanse of neck which she covered with her last remaining fichu; the other had been shredded in the attack in Kendal. She still had her hair to deal with, but she had insufficient pins to tame it. Dividing it into three, she plaited the strands and wound them into a bun at the nape of her neck, using another ribbon to secure it. The bun wouldn't hold all evening like that but hopefully long enough not to shock the rector.

The Persephone Code

The rector dined fashionably late at five, so she had half an hour before the dinner gong would go. Taking the book of samples to the seat by the window, she turned the leaves. She and Anthony had added to it as chance brought different examples of the handwriting of famous individuals into their orbit so there was little organisation to the selection. Marvell sat beside Molière, Johnson with Jonson. Her pen could now act so many different hands, just as she could assume so many different roles. What had Anthony meant by a key? She knew this book so well that she did not have to hunt for any hidden messages; there were none. And how could a key mentioned in a letter last week be in a book he had last touched five years ago?

Unless he was pointing to the contents that he knew almost as well as she did?

With this new perspective in mind, she started again at the beginning. A sonnet, a fragment of a lost play, a ballad...

She was about to dismiss Pope – an author neither of them admired – when she remembered the oddly initialled 'the Great key' from his letter. Why lowercase the *k* if not to emphasise *Great*?

Who in history was known as The Great?

Alexander. First name of Alexander Pope.

She had been so blind. It was a long time since they'd traded puzzles and riddles; he had probably feared she had lost the knack of deciphering his way of thinking so he had risked underlining the linkage with his strange farewell of a papal blessing. She had thought it his usual blasphemy, but maybe he had meant it as a clue in case she missed the first. Pope.

'You made it so damned obvious, didn't you, Anthony?' she whispered. Any further clues he had left her would not be so easy to read, she was sure of that. Her brother did like to tease. Even in death.

Her grief welled up in her again.

No, she had something to do to honour his last request. Grief could go hang. Resolutely, she turned to the first piece by Pope that they'd copied, an extract from one of the poet's most famous poems, 'The Rape of the Lock'. It referred in mock-heroic style to the cutting of a lady's hair, but *lock*...?

How like her brother to have a double-layered pun in mind!

Thrilled that she had remembered, she turned to the passage:

'Close by those meads, for ever crowned with flow'rs,
  Where Thames with pride surveys his rising tow'rs,
  There stands a structure of majestic frame...'

The original poem referred to Hampton Court. Was there a further clue for her there? The palace was an enormous place and many miles from here. No sensible search could be made of so vast a structure. She didn't even know if Anthony had ever visited it. Her initial excitement turned to disappointment. It felt like a dead end.

Dora hung her head, the weight of her charge bowing her down.

Anthony, why did you have to be so clever? I don't know what you want me to do.

Perhaps Jacob would see something she did not?

Not wanting to ask him in front of Leighton, she checked the passage was clear before heading to Jacob's room. She tapped softly on the door.

'Come!'

She darted inside and held her finger to her lips. Jacob was at the washstand, cutthroat razor in hand, hair hanging free from restraint. She was glad he wore it long; it gave him a piratical look. His shirt was unbuttoned and the collar was turned back. Paler skin peeked out of the neck of the snowy linen and she could see a little dusting of chest hair.

She liked a little hair on a man's chest.

Oh, she was in so much trouble. She wetted her lips.

'Dora, you found it?' He put down the razor.

'Hadn't you better finish? You will look most odd if you go to dinner with only half your chin shaved.' And she was enjoying the show.

'True. Don't tell me anything exciting. I've reached the tricky part.'

She held her tongue while he finished around his neck. Did men enjoy dicing with death every day just to be clean-shaven? She remembered his dislike of gambling and decided he would probably not be one of the ones who enjoyed the thrill.

She perched on the edge of the chest of drawers by the door. 'You should grow a beard.'

'I did on campaign.' He angled his head in the mirror. 'Doesn't suit me. I look too much like my thespian uncle.'

'You have an uncle on the stage?'

'He wishes he could be.' He tapped the razor on the basin edge. 'At every family gathering he insists on making us all take part in one of his dramas. He won't stop pestering Sheridan with his execrable plays, none of which have a chance of surviving an unbiased critique. He is quite the family embarrassment.'

'I thought that was your role?'

He smirked. 'Minx. No, I'm the black sheep who goes his own way. He is the silly one who insists on running off cliffs.' He rubbed his face with a towel and threw it aside. 'What did you find?'

'My brother and I had a keepsake book of sorts.' She was bending the truth, but how else could she explain it without betraying her forgeries? 'He gave it to me when I left. I hadn't remembered exactly what was in it until this afternoon. Anthony went out of his way to remind me. The *Great* and *papal blessing* – Alexander Pope. The key? Well, we copied out an extract of "The Rape of the Lock".'

She watched as Jacob made the same punning link that she had done. His eyes gleamed with pleasure as the connections fell into place.

'Now we are in the chase! Which part did you copy?'

'The lines about the Thames and the rising towers. But that's Hampton Court, isn't it? My brother has no connections there.'

'It's years since I read it. Can I see the passage?'

She'd really rather he didn't as he would wonder why they'd written it in Alexander Pope's very fine looping style. He had one of the best hands of all the authors they had collected. Thankfully, her perfect recall came to her aid and she recited the three lines.

'Isn't the completion of the couplet something like *"Which from neighb'ring Hampton takes its name"* or is it *"fame"*?' asked Jacob.

'It's "name".'

'But you didn't have that down?'

'I think we tired of the piece. Not suited to the amusement of children on a wet afternoon. We went on to write out some of the finer passages in "An Essay on Man".'

'*"Know then thyself, presume not God to scan;*
The proper study of Mankind is Man."

'There are some fine things in that, but you must have been extraordinary children to take an interest in Pope's verse – full of philosophy and not much fun. Do you think Anthony would remember this scrap of poetry you wrote down together so long ago?'

'I'm sure of it.' If only because it was the first time that she had held the pen and did the copying while her brother kept watch for the owner of the fine collection of literary manuscripts. It had been a test of sorts, an initiation into his tricksy ways. He had acknowledged afterwards that she was the better forger with a fastidious eye for detail. 'Is the Thames or the towers the important phrase, do you think? He said it was nearby in his letter.'

'Could he mean Medmenham Abbey?' wondered Jacob. 'That stands on the banks of the Thames, belongs to the Dashwoods and is close by. The lines fit it very well.'

'Medmenham Abbey? My brother mentioned that in his letter, as did you. What is there to know about it?'

Jacob selected a new cravat and shirt from his wardrobe. 'It is a ruin and was the principal place for Hellfire Club rites even before the caves were excavated. The original members styled themselves on the Monks of Medmenham Abbey, which explains your brother's references to his brethren. Someone must've revived it for this generation. If your brother was warden, the Abbey would fall into his responsibilities.'

'It sounds very possible.' Dora's excitement returned. 'Can we go?' She wanted to get to the end of this; to find what her brother had hidden and expose his killer. Then her life could return to its old path.

'Yes, but tomorrow, in daylight, before the ball.' He pulled the fresh shirt over his head.

'I'm not going to the ball.'

'But I can't leave you here. What if the Illuminati catch up with us? With both Leighton and me at the Park, there would be no one to stop them.' He closed the distance between them. 'Dora, I'd prefer if you stayed by my side until the person who killed your brother is caught.'

'How do we know he won't be at the ball? Wouldn't I be safer behind a locked door in my bedroom?' She was suddenly very conscious that they were in a bedroom now. This was inappropriate but she had never been one to set store by propriety. She resolved not to care.

'They can't attack you in front of the local gentry even if they are there. Please come. It would make me feel much better about my participation.'

'But I have nothing to wear!'

He raised his eyes to the heavens, not understanding how vital that was for a female. 'If I solve that, will you come?'

She sighed. 'Very well. Protesting and reluctant, but I'll come.'

'Good.' Their eyes met. A question passed between them and she smiled her answer. He leant forward and kissed her, his lips lingering, savouring. As he moved away, he paused to brush his newly shaved cheek against hers, whispering in her ear. 'I can look forward to at least one dance with you.'

She returned the kiss and trailed a finger down his smooth neck. 'Only if I save it for you.'

With that last sally, she quit the room to his low laughter.

Dora had forgotten Miss Helen Leighton, the aunt who was supposed to be her chaperone, and only remembered her when she saw a wizened old lady at one end of the dinner table. Thank goodness she had not been there to stop that kiss – that had been the nicest thing to happen to Dora in a long time. Her body was still humming with the memory, like a harp after fingers have plucked the strings. Miss Leighton had a book open beside her as she made inroads into her soup before the rest of the diners had assembled. A quick glance in passing showed it to be a work on astronomy. Interesting.

'My aunt is hard of hearing,' explained Leighton, not bothering to lower his voice as he entered, 'and very particular about the times at which she eats. If dinner is late, as it is today, she forges on without me.' He touched his aunt's shoulder and gave her a buss on the cheek. 'How are you, Auntie?'

She must have read his lips, or expected the question, because she replied, 'Very well, George. Who are your friends?'

He introduced them briefly by name only, with no further explanation. Jacob held out Dora's seat on their host's right, then took his place opposite her. The prunish housekeeper and comely maidservant entered to serve the first course. Once the soup had been dispensed, Leighton turned to Jacob.

'What do you think now, Sandys? Was I right in thinking Anthony Pennington's death no chance encounter?' He caught himself. 'I hope you don't mind us discussing this distressing subject, Miss Fitz-Pennington?'

'No, indeed. I would be more distressed to be excluded from the discussion as it concerns me most nearly.'

Jacob gave her a nod of approval. 'I was convinced even before I arrived, Leighton. You see, we had some adventures on our way south.' He briefly summed up the attacks and the evidence that the Illuminati were on their trail.

Leighton abruptly set down his spoon, splattering his leek and potato soup onto the tablecloth. 'Illuminati? Those godless revolutionaries? What can they want with Pennington?' His expression changed. 'Oh, I see. The letter! They wanted whatever it was that Pennington held as Warden of the Hellfire Club. The two societies would seek each other's destruction as philosophical opposites.'

'We believe he was holding some information that could do serious damage – what, we don't know. Details of criminal activities committed by the current members, perhaps?' Jacob sipped his wine thoughtfully. 'Did you notice the hint that matters had gone on that Pennington did not condone? Have you heard of anything that rises to the level of a capital crime? You mentioned other deaths in the area. Could any of these have been at the hands of the Hellfire Club?'

Leighton dabbed at the soup on the table with his napkin and picked up his spoon again. 'That is possible. There are four more deaths that I know about since I came to the area, maybe more before that.'

'What kind of deaths?'

'Individually, they all seem unlucky or unsolved ones. A young man fell from the church tower last November. The locals thought he was trying to get into the golden ball while a meeting was being held.'

'What kind of meeting?'

'Not a parish council meeting.'

'The Hellfire Club still uses it?'

'I wouldn't like to say. When local men of standing ask for the key to show the view to their visitors, what am I to do? Their forefathers provided the funds to restore and embellish the church, and we will soon need a new roof.'

'Perhaps a Peeping Tom then. What about the other deaths?'

'The rest were young women not known in these parts. Their dress suggested they were ladies of...' – he glanced at Dora – 'courtesans.' He chose a kinder word than *whores*, but Dora guessed he meant the latter. Courtesans were not the sort who went missing with no one noticing. They had madams or protectors who controlled their careers, or they had money themselves and forged an independent path. Some were famous enough to be celebrated, like the previous generation's Kitty Fisher.

'How did they die?' Jacob asked.

'They were strangled.' Leighton sounded most uncomfortable making the admission.

'And no one has done anything about it?' asked Dora incredulously.

Leighton turned to her. 'Miss Fitz-Pennington, I'm afraid there is little in the way of law enforcement in these parts. It is down to the local magistrate to investigate, and Sir John Dashwood is rarely in residence. His tenants, like Sir Fletcher Vane, do not assume his duties when they occupy the house, so the nearest magistrate is in High Wycombe in the next valley over. The coroner does have some powers but I'm afraid he did not think it a priority to be looking into the deaths many months apart of women whom nobody knew.'

'They remain unidentified?'

Leighton nodded. 'They've been buried, naturally, but I had no name for them at the funerals and they have no headstones. I made sure they were in a peaceful part of the graveyard where the spring flowers bloom.'

Dora did not think that much of a comfort, prettifying an ugly end.

'And where were they found?' asked Jacob.

'One by the Park gates, one under the archway by the lock-up, and one in the caves where your brother was discovered.' He glanced at Dora, clearly regretful to mention the unpleasant subject. 'It has grieved me that no one cared for these women as they should. Our Lord knows the fall of the least sparrow, so He knows their names and judges us for our neglect.'

'Do you think they were killed during intercourse?' asked Dora bluntly.

Leighton's hand trembled and she feared for the tablecloth. 'Miss Fitz-Pennington!'

'Respectfully, Reverend, you and I both know that prostitutes cater for all kinds of appetites. I have not lived a sheltered life and am aware of what goes on in the brothels, bagnios and molly houses of Covent Garden. If all of them were strangled and they were all whores, then it must be possible that they were victims of a man, or men, who liked to choke their partners during the act?'

Miss Leighton turned the page of her astronomy book.

'It will be a waning gibbous moon tomorrow,' the old lady told the room. 'That is helpful to Sir Fletcher's ball guests, but not as good as a full moon. He ought to have held the ball a week earlier.'

'Thank you, Aunt,' said Leighton loudly. 'But you can hardly hold a May Ball in April.'

The lady had gone back to her star charts and did not reply. She probably hadn't heard.

'Miss Fitz-Pennington has a point, Leighton. Strangulation is associated with a perverted kind of intercourse, as much as we would like not to talk about it in polite society.' Jacob's face was set in deep lines. Had he seen such things in his military career? She suspected he had. 'Were the young women interfered with before death?'

Leighton looked highly unsettled by this turn of the conversation. 'I ... I wouldn't know. I did not lay out the bodies.'

'Who did?'

'Mrs Stock. She did them that service.'

The housekeeper. Dora did not fancy undertaking that conversation.

'I'll ask her in the morning,' said Jacob, showing that he was more forthright than she. He was doubtless used to nurses and other medical assistants discussing grisly details. 'It might be that the acts to which Pennington refers include these murders. Names of those who have attended Hellfire parties will do little damage – indeed, some men might even find their reputations burnished by the association – but rape and murder are another matter altogether.'

Chapter Twenty-Six

Hellfire Caves

As soon as dinner was cleared from the table, Leighton picked up his walking stick and gestured to the door.

'I find that a stroll after eating aids digestion,' he said for the benefit of the servants carrying off the plates. 'I'll fetch a lantern. Miss Fitz-Pennington, you really need not come.'

When, thought Jacob, would Leighton learn to understand the opposite sex?

'I'll fetch my coat.' Dora dashed upstairs.

Jacob smiled at the thought. Hers was a wonderfully disreputable greatcoat, not much improved by their time on horseback in the Lakes. It already looked like it had travelled the battlefields of Europe, and mud and smoke had further aged its patina. Had she been given it by a soldier sweetheart, or picked it up by chance on her travels? Since that electrifying kiss, the mysteries of Dora's past were suddenly of great interest to Jacob.

Leighton took one bewildered look at Dora's choice of garment but wisely said nothing. A raised brow was all he would allow himself.

'The caves are very close. Not even two minutes' walk up the hill.'

Handing Jacob a second lantern, he led the way to the entrance of the infamous Hellfire Caves. As they approached, Jacob noted carefully all that he could hear and see, gaining an understanding of the place and how easy it would be for a killer to come and go unseen. The caves were not isolated, located as they were at the edge of the village where the hill began its steep climb to the church and mausoleum on the top. People were a shout away if help were needed. Someone was chopping wood while a mother called her children in from the fields. An owl hooted, greeting the dusk. The sky was stained orange as the sun began to set behind the hill. The golden ball on top of the church burned like a beacon, but here, at its foot, shadows had lengthened.

'The entrance,' said the rector, holding up his lantern to illuminate the lower portion of the cave entrance.

'It looks like a chapel built into the hillside,' said Dora, hands tucked into her pockets. She looked like Wellington considering a difficult rampart to storm.

Leighton nodded grimly. 'That was Dashwood's impious jest. He had the local flint laid like the frontage of the chapels he saw in Italy on his Grand Tour – arched doorway, echoed by the shape of the embrasure for his coat of arms over that, and then three empty windows, elongated echoes of the arch.'

While Dora and the rector were thinking of ecclesiastical architecture, Sandys was thinking of something far earthier. Having attended the business end of many a childbirth, for him the entrance was far more feminine, especially with the flanking flint walls of the courtyard that could be imagined as parted legs. He dared not make that observation aloud lest Leighton completely dash his wig.

The rector reached for his keyring and drew out another to open the iron bars that stopped chance-comers wandering into the caves.

'Is it very easy to get lost?' asked Dora, looking apprehensively down the arched passageway. Pitch-black, it took little imagination to link this to the entrance of Hell. The complete absence of light crushed all hope and laughter. At least it wasn't the kind of tunnel to trigger a fear of enclosed spaces. Jacob could stand tall here. He estimated it to be at least ten feet high. The air felt damp, still and cool – not warm, windy and dusty like the coalmine he'd once had the misfortune to enter in order to help an injured miner. This felt almost wholesome.

'This is a single passageway rather than a network.' Leighton pulled out a notebook and opened it to a well-thumbed sketched plan of the caves. They weren't the first visitors he had shown around, deduced Jacob. 'Think of it like a bent leg of someone lying on their back. We enter at the foot. It goes steadily down to a round cavern at the equivalent of the calf, then on to a bigger junction at the knee. Then it changes direction, travelling down and along the thigh – that is the banqueting area. Then there is the triangle, the River Styx to cross with a boat, to the deepest part which is the Inner Temple.'

Surely, thought Jacob, this was all a continuation of the anatomical jest of the entrance. The triangle was a well-known representation of the womb. However, these men of leisure got their anatomy somewhat muddled, because in this metaphor the Styx and the Inner Temple would have been better coming before. Many men, for all their boasting, didn't really understand a woman's body, nor how to navigate it, so he wasn't surprised.

'Chalk,' said Leighton, patting the walls. 'The least bit of light reflects off the white so it is not as gloomy as you might fear. Follow me.'

Was it a schoolboy taste that was being exhibited here or were

Dashwood and his cronies tapping into something more atavistic, or indeed primal wondered Jacob. Other cultures used the same symbols in their sacred places – stone barrows that looked like the cervix or standing stones that were phallic. It would be too easy to dismiss it as a lord's whimsy until it was remembered that people had died here. Even if it had started as a smutty joke or lascivious taste, it had become deadly.

'How many hold a key to the entrance?' asked Dora.

'There's one at the rectory on my keyring, two at the great house and another in the George and Dragon in case visitors wish to make a tour. The landlord lets them in for a small fee.'

In other words, almost anyone could gain access to the caves.

'Oh, and Mr Pennington had one, naturally. He had the original,' continued the rector.

'Was it found on him?' asked Jacob.

Leighton paused, illuminating an empty side chamber. 'Actually, no, it wasn't. It was in the lock.'

'I find that strange.' Dora brushed the graffiti on the walls with her fingertips; names and signs that made little sense. 'My brother would surely have carried it with him for fear someone would steal it. He took his duties seriously.'

'Who has that key now?' asked Jacob.

'Why?' asked Leighton, sounding confused. 'Is this the key in the letter?'

'I don't know, but were all keys identical? Is it possible that it isn't his, after all? Has anyone checked how many are in the village?'

'You think the killer might have taken it and left another in its place? Why would anyone want to do that?'

Jacob shrugged. 'A trophy? To avoid having to go back and return the key he had used? Who knows. It's a loose end that I would rather tie off.'

Leighton jingled his own keyring thoughtfully as if the

The Persephone Code

sound would jog his memory. 'I think the key most likely went back to the big house because the caves belong to the Dashwoods.'

They reached the point that Leighton had designated as the knee and changed direction.

'How can anyone think this was an attack by footpads?' said Dora. 'You'd have to be a very bold thief to follow someone all the way down here. There's no easy escape except back the same way, or am I missing something?'

'There are rumours of another exit, but I've never found it,' said Leighton. 'To be frank, Miss Fitz-Pennington, such logic was not used in the inquest. I think the coroner who ruled on the death merely wanted to dismiss it as soon as possible.'

'He was sloppy,' said Jacob. 'Did he even come here?'

'No. The body was moved to the lock-up to wait for his examination.'

'It would've been cool enough down here to preserve a body. That was unnecessary.'

'Mistakes were undoubtedly made. I'm afraid I was from home when he was found.'

At the 'thigh', they reached the largest room in the cave complex – a banqueting hall with a domed roof. The walls held four large recesses furnished with mattresses. There was no need to imagine to what use they were put, and they did look particularly uninviting without the linen and cushions that presumably accompanied a party. One hellfire feature was the passageway that encircled the hall, allowing voyeurs to look in on the niches from the back, and onto whatever was happening in the bigger chamber. There was only an illusion of privacy. Every act could be seen from many directions.

'How quaint,' said Dora with a wry tone.

'I did say that you might be distressed by the caves.' The rector hurried them on.

'Not distressed – amused at the foolishness. Or I would be if I didn't also think of the women who are brought here.'

'I've not heard that the Hellfire Club struggles to find willing partners,' said Jacob.

'Oh yes, throw enough money at a desperate woman and she will be so pleased to come and shag a passel of rich men in a cave. How exciting. I bet that was her dream as a little girl before poverty drove her to sell herself.'

'I didn't mean—'

'No, you just meant that you rich men tell yourself these fairy tales that the women are willing. Agreeing to do something isn't the same as wanting it. And the dead whores buried nameless? That speaks loud and clear that no one cares what becomes of them.'

'Miss Fitz-Pennington...' said the rector, clearly intending to make peace, but Dora was having none of it. She took Jacob's lantern and stalked towards the far side of the room.

'Enough of these foolish party games. I want to see where my brother died.'

Silenced, Jacob followed her. She was magnificent in her anger – and she was also right. He had accepted the presence of women at these parties like a garland at a festival – part of the expected furnishing. Some women might enjoy sex with a thrill of voyeurism – he'd met a few in society – but Dora was only speaking the truth when she said that most female participants would be here because they had no better choices. Yet her reaction also felt personal. Had she ever found herself in such a position? Hardly something one could ask a lady, but he suspected that if her life were described as a bed of roses, she had experienced more thorns than petals.

The passageway broke into the two sides of the triangle then joined on the bottom length to conduct them to the River Styx.

Jacob held the lantern over the water. He couldn't tell how deep it was but the river wasn't very broad. One could jump it.

'This isn't natural?'

'No, I believe not. Usually there's a boat.' Leighton shone his lantern along the edge until he found the painter tied to an iron ring. He pulled a small craft to the bank. 'After you.' He handed Dora into the boat.

'This might be the shortest passage ever taken on Charon's ferry,' said Jacob.

'Just a convenience to prevent fine footwear getting damp.'

'How deep is it?'

'I've never tested it. Deep enough to drown a drunken man.'

'That's a cheery thought,' muttered Dora.

With a firm shove, the boat floated to the other side. No oars were needed. Dora hopped out and held the side steady as the rector and Jacob disembarked.

'This is the Inner Temple?' Dora said, unimpressed by the pitch-black surroundings.

'Just through here.' The rector held up his lantern and entered the chamber. 'Oh, my word! Sandys, quick! Help me cut him down.'

Chapter Twenty-Seven

Dora had seen enough death to know that this man had died hard. He was suspended from a noose, attached by a rope to the ceiling. His face was mottled, eyes bulging, tongue swollen. A big man, his own body weight would have asphyxiated him. An overturned barrel lay under his corpse. He could have kicked it over in his struggles. Jacob set it upright and reached for his pocketknife. The rector got under the man and lifted him to relieve the strain on the rope. Reaching up, Jacob sawed through the tough fibres of the noose until the man swung free. Leighton staggered but Dora was there to catch an arm and help him lower the man to the ground.

'He's dead. Has been for hours,' said Jacob, jumping down. 'Leighton, your lantern. Hold it up.' He lifted one of the man's arms. 'Rigor mortis. That means he hasn't been dead for more than twenty-four hours.'

Leighton crossed himself. 'The poor soul. To take his own life like this, in such a miserable place. What madness drove him to it?'

'You don't recognise him?' asked Dora, wiping her hands on her skirts.

'No, he's a stranger to me.'

'A big man like this would be a noted character in a small place like West Wycombe,' said Jacob. 'He's a working man from the clothes and state of his hands. Boots are caked in mud. Maybe he walked here?'

'That is very possible. The roads have been bad locally, thanks to all the rain we've been having,' said Leighton.

'Does he have anything in his pockets?' asked Dora. She moved away to shine the light around the chamber.

'An apple and a handkerchief. A pocketknife, kept sharp.' Jacob looked up at the hook. 'Why hang yourself when you could slit your own wrists and be done with it? Unless a hanged man falls far enough to break his neck, death is wretchedly slow that way.'

The walls were empty, but she could see pegs where wall hangings could be displayed. A low table had three large oil lamps evenly spaced, as on an altar. A wooden cross lay at the far side, leaning against the wall like a prop for a Mystery Play stowed until called on at Easter. The ring to suspend it was at the long end though, meaning it would hang upside down. The air smelt a little ... sulphurous.

She glanced at Leighton. Did he know? She should mention it, but not when they had a body to care for. Blasphemous ceremonies could wait. Dora shone her lantern over the last place to be examined: the statue of Venus that stood on a pedestal in the centre of the room.

'There's a note on her ... er ... on *her*.' She plucked the paper from the goddess' groin.

'He left a note?' asked Leighton. 'What does it say?'

'It's printed with no punctuation. I don't think he was much of a writer. *I am sorry I killed them I did it Forgive me.*' Though he had used capital letters, it was evidence of some education, thought Dora.

'Ah.' Leighton stood up and held his hands to his chest in a prayerful gesture. '*A fool returneth to his folly.* He punished himself in the place where he killed at least one of his victims.'

Jacob measured his hands against that of the dead man. 'Killed who? He would have little trouble strangling the girls, but I can't see him stabbing Pennington. That wound was from a dagger, or I'm no doctor.'

'How can you tell?' asked Dora.

'Entry wounds tell their own story. That was some long blade such as the Italians make for their assassins, not a labourer's knife, no matter how sharp this one was kept.' He tossed Dora the man's penknife.

The blade was only three inches long. She pocketed it and carried on with her search. The chamber yielded no more secrets. 'And if you don't recognise him, Rector, how could he have killed the women over a course of months – and Anthony? Could he come and go unnoticed?'

Leighton nodded. 'You both make very good points. Forgive my hasty conclusions. I will pray for the poor man.' He went down on his knees, administering a blessing.

A little too late for that, thought Dora grimly.

Jacob felt along the back of the man's skull. 'There's a knot from a blow – and dried blood. He was knocked unconscious by someone and then strung up here; that's how I read it.'

Dora considered the note again. 'Then maybe someone saw him writing his confession and took matters into their own hands – someone who cared for one of the girls?'

'Possibly. But my guess is that this is not the murderer, but another victim.'

Dora returned to the surface with the rector while Jacob waited with the body.

'There is something severely amiss in your parish, Reverend Leighton.'

'I am aware, as I also am now aware that you have a talent for understatement. I suspect the cause of all our woes comes from outside, carried in on hellfires.' He supported her with a hand on her elbow, though she felt in little danger of swooning. Working women didn't have time for that.

The servants were already in bed when they reached the rectory. She paused at the bottom of the stairs. 'I hope the magistrate and coroner will believe you now about Anthony and investigate properly?'

'Indeed. That will be one good thing to come out of this terrible business.' He handed her a candle and wished her a good night.

The lock-up would have a second body this evening. Dora retired to her room, leaving the rector to arrange for a stretcher to be taken down into the caves. There was a lot to do. Messengers had to be sent to alert the authorities, the coroner and the nearest magistrate.

She had taken the hint that he preferred her to leave him to do his work, but she would have liked to stay up and keep busy with him until Jacob returned. As soon as she stopped, grief for her brother edged back in. And so many questions.

Why was Leighton not a magistrate? Dora wondered as she shrugged off her coat. Clergymen often were, as they were likely to be the most educated man on hand when crimes took place in one of the country's parishes. Though if Leighton were known to disapprove of the Hellfire Club then the local gentlemen may have banded together to keep him out of their business. She would have to ask Jacob to make some discreet enquiries. That might give them the names of the men involved. William Bates, her brother's friend, who had been the Dashwoods' tenant, was he still in the area? He would be at the ball tomorrow. And what about Sir Fletcher Vane? Had he come to the area for the hunting as he claimed to the world, or did he have a darker secret?

Exhausted by all the questions, she flopped back on the bed. It had been distressing to find the body of that poor man, but it had driven away any melancholy that she might have experienced contemplating her brother's last moments alive in that wretched hole. Now she was angry. The killer – or was it killers – were so arrogant, carelessly dumping the bodies of those who got in their way. How had that farm boy upset them? Or had he just been a useful decoy, someone on whom to pin the other murders now that Leighton and Jacob had begun investigating? She couldn't imagine her brother writing such a letter as he had left for her if it had been that young man he was meeting.

A brief, terrible thought crossed her mind. Unless it was blackmail? Had Anthony been involved in the deaths of the women at some party that got out of hand? Had that labourer seen something and demanded to be paid for his silence?

But ignoring killings four times over the spread of years – the three prostitutes and the boy who fell from the tower? No, those deaths were no accident; that was someone who made a habit of killing. And sinful though her brother undoubtedly had been, his flaws were more commonplace – wenching and drinking, with some bullying behaviour in the mix when alcohol or the poppy lowered his inhibitions. Though no angel, he wasn't the wickedest devil either.

Or was she fooling herself? He had lived in the village and must have known about the women found strangled. Had he become so cynical that even that hadn't shocked him into disassociating from the Hellfire Club?

One thing she did know: he couldn't be the killer. The murderer had struck again days after her brother's death.

If only she could ask Anthony...

But it was too late.

She rubbed a hand up her arm, still feeling in her bones the sensation of riding in a lurching carriage. The body remembered where you had been, even if the events of the last few hours made Lady Tolworth's coach seem like days ago. Jacob had been quick to read the signs on the body of the hanged man. She had thought she knew death, as it was no stranger to the poor, carrying off children and women in childbirth with frightening regularity. She had known already that people stiffened a few hours after they passed, but not that the rigor mortis left after twenty-four hours. He'd spotted the blow to the head and the nature of the knife wound on her brother, breaking the awful silence of death. He was impressively competent.

Not that she didn't have her own more mundane powers of observation. One thing he had not mentioned but which she had noticed: the victim had no ink on his fingers, no pen and no paper in his pockets. So where had that come from?

A door banged below and she heard Jacob's voice in the passageway. He was talking to Leighton but, after a few exchanges, they bade each other goodnight. Good. Hopefully, their host would be too preoccupied with arrangements for the body to notice if his guests went wandering.

She slipped into Jacob's room once she heard him moving around in there.

'We need to go to the inn.'

He was just washing his hands but had not taken off his boots, a sign, she hoped, that he was prepared for another expedition.

'I think after everything that has happened this evening, you'd best stay here.'

Not this again. 'I thought you were too worried to leave me on my own?'

'Leighton is here, and half the village too from the sounds of people coming and going at the kitchen door.'

'None of whom you know. Any of them could be a danger to me. The only person you know to trust is yourself.'

'And you.'

'Oh no, definitely, don't trust me. Anyway, I'm going to the inn. Do you want to come with me or follow ten yards behind?'

He took her hands in his and squeezed. 'You are the stubbornest woman alive.'

'And you are the man with the shortest memory.' She freed a hand and tapped his nose. 'Giving me orders to stay out of my own business will never work.'

His laugh signalled his surrender.

'I'll meet you outside the gate. Best we leave the house separately.' Dora checked the corridor was free, then snuck back to her room to get her coat.

Chapter Twenty-Eight

The George and Dragon Inn

Jacob couldn't see Dora when he arrived at their rendezvous, just a man – possibly one of the messengers? – waiting at the gate.

'Psst!' The messenger beckoned him.

'Dora?' He glanced down at the breeches and greatcoat. Her hair was hidden by a cap.

'Don't look so surprised. I can hardly walk into the inn at this time of night in skirts without attracting undue attention. Nor can I scale a wall.'

'Who said anything about scaling walls?'

'You never know.'

She matched her stride to his, trying for a man's gait. Her long legs helped in that, as did the muffler hiding her chin and throat.

'We should ask if the man called in at the inn,' she said. 'As a stranger, he had to get his paper and pen from somewhere – and maybe he left behind a bag?'

'Agreed – but *I* will ask. Boyish though you may appear from a distance, you won't pass in the light.' Her form was far too female for that, praise be.

'All right. I will lurk outside and act like the boy you named me, spitting in the dirt, whistling at ladies and throwing stones at stray dogs.'

'You don't have a very high opinion of boys, I see.'

'Do you?'

Dora peeled away from his side as they reached the George and Dragon, drifting into the shadows of the yard, making herself inconspicuous in less objectionable ways than she had described. Jacob headed for the public bar, which was open late due to the shocking news of yet another death. The landlord had kept the fire going and men huddled at tables, sharing their theories. Faces were red with beer and anger, their fists curled. From snatches of conversation, Jacob gathered that most appeared to have adopted the idea that the man had killed the women, left a confession, and hanged himself in repentance. Death was too good for him. He shouldn't be in the lock-up but thrown in the rubbish ditch and burned with the rabid dogs.

Who was spreading that story? Jacob wondered. Both he and Leighton had told the men who carried the body out that it was unlikely to be suicide. They'd kept the details confidential in case the real killer might give himself away by divulging the information, but it seemed the perpetrator was a step ahead. In this cloud of accusation and rage, the origin of the story would be hard to pin down.

Jacob rapped a sovereign on the counter. 'Landlord!'

The spindly man with a head as bald as a billiard ball approached. He was the antithesis of the genial host who carried his beer around his gut. 'What can I get you, doctor?'

So his fame had preceded him? Just as well Dora had not shocked them by accompanying him inside. Her identity would have been sniffed out in seconds.

'A pint of your best, and information.'

'I can certainly provide the first, but I don't know what I can possibly have to tell you.'

'The man who died – did he come in here?'

'How would I know that? Lots of men come in here and I haven't seen that bastard who killed those poor girls.'

'We don't know that he did.' Jacob sensed that he would have little luck scotching that story.

'Who else would it be? No one round here goes about killing girls.' The landlord sighed. 'Well, at least he can explain himself to Satan when he gets to where he's bound. Shame we couldn't have our go first.'

'I'm asking after a big man about so high.' Jacob gestured to a few inches above his own height. 'Young – maybe twenty-five? Crop of fair hair and beginnings of a beard. Strong, probably a farm labourer from the looks of him.'

'What, him?' The landlord evidently knew immediately who Jacob was describing as he jolted the beer in his surprise. 'My apologies, doctor.' He wiped up the spillage. 'You mean that giant of a man and none too clever with it? He came in here yesterday, a bit confused like. I felt sorry for him. Let him sleep in the stables. He's the one that did it?'

'As I said, I don't think he did anything. Did he give a name?'

'Oh aye. Matthew Jenkins from Henley. Kept saying that, like it should mean something to us, but Henley's a good step from here.'

Near Medmenham Abbey, thought Jacob.

'Did he say what brought him to West Wycombe?'

'He was going on about some lass of his ... Mary.' Understanding dawned. 'Oh, you think he was looking for one of those poor girls? It didn't cross my mind that he might mean one of them harlots. His Mary was pure-hearted and kind, he said. I thought he was making it all up or was addled.'

'Did he ask for paper to write a note?'

The landlord snorted. 'Him? Nay, I'll drink a pint of my own slops if that one knew how to read and write. He couldn't even read the fingerposts. That's why he came in here, to check he was in the right place.'

Chapter Twenty-Nine

Dora was getting bored and cold. She stamped her feet and blew on her fingers. She'd had fingerless gloves in her pockets when she left Kendal but now wished she'd had her winter ones.

Waiting did not suit her. Time for curtain-up on the next act.

Where would Gatskill be lodging? She eyed the upper floor of the inn. The front room appeared to be a dining parlour. There were several patrons sitting at a table. They had reached the final stages of their meal as she could see a decanter of port being passed and pipes lit. Was Gatskill among them? The odds must be high as he would elect to be among the better sort, rather than in the public bar.

Which meant this was the best opportunity they would get to search his rooms.

Gnawing a fingernail for a second, she contemplated waiting for Jacob, knowing full well what he would say if she went without him. They'd left it vague as to how they would go about this, so it wasn't as if she was going against any carefully crafted plan, was it? Her defence? She couldn't go in to get him, not into a well-lit bar. No, she would seize the day.

A well-run inn, as this seemed to be, wouldn't let vagabonds just wander in and search guest rooms without a challenge. She needed a discreet way of entering. The cast-iron drainpipe looked possible, but what if someone saw? Then the jig would be up before it had started.

As she watched, a coach drew into the yard. Thank goodness she hadn't attempted the climb. The passengers tumbled out and the driver jumped down. The yard became a flurry of activity, with bags thrown to the servants and trunks unstrapped. Some of the passengers were staying.

Dumping her coat in the shadows, Dora walked purposely forwards and took a valise from a female guest.

'Let me take that for you, ma'am,' she said gruffly. Not giving the woman time to protest, she seized another bag and walked right into the inn and straight up the stairs. Those that did work there would assume she was a servant of one of the guests, whilst the owners of the bags would think she belonged to the inn. Sometimes the simplest plans, if done with no hesitation, were the easiest.

How long did she have before the landlord began showing people to their rooms? Not long. She dumped the bags at the top of the stairs and moved swiftly along the corridor. She would have to identify Gatskill's room quickly. He had worn a black overcoat with brass buttons, double-breasted, when he had interrupted them in the lock-up. If she found that, she found his room. He also came across as the kind of man to demand the best accommodation; so unless there was a nobleman passing by – and surely the village would be abuzz if that were the case – he was likely to be in the biggest room with the double windows overlooking the garden rather than the busy yard.

Ah no. That belonged to a lady and gentleman and they were

The Persephone Code

occupied. With each other. Vocally. She closed the door swiftly and lifted the latch on the one next to it. Bolted. That meant the occupant was inside. Shame the couple had been so eager to reach the bed that they hadn't locked theirs. She moved swiftly on, waiting to see if she had roused anyone. The door remained closed.

'Come on, come on,' Dora muttered as she tested the last of the doors at the back of the inn. This one opened into a darkened room with only firelight to illuminate the portion around the hearth. Gatskill's coat hung on the back of a chair, turned so that it would warm in the fire's heat. Did that mean he was intending on going out again? Or had he been out and got it damp? With a last look behind her, she slipped inside and felt the fabric. Dry.

She had to hurry. She patted the pockets of the coat but found nothing of interest. She then moved on to the trunk and bags that had to hold her brother's belongings. There was too much to search thoroughly in the short time she had. She decided to concentrate on documents and books. If he had left a diary, or copies of his correspondence, she would gain an insight into his last few weeks.

A locked writing case stood on the table by the window. Her brother's? Or Gatskill's? Did it matter? It would take too long to find the key to open it, so she took out two hairpins and bent them to pick the locks. Surprisingly this wasn't a skill learnt on the road; her brother had taught her the trick as it was the only way he could get money for his pleasures from their tight-fisted father.

The lock was simple – a deterrent to servants, but not proof against thieves. She finessed the lock, sweet talking it to give up its secrets, trying not to let it see that she was in a hurry. Inanimate objects could be buggers if they knew you wanted something quickly. This one proved a sweetheart. With a little click, it succumbed. She levered the lid open.

A burst of noise from downstairs and voices approaching told her the landlord was showing his guests upstairs.

'What is my bag doing in the corridor?' asked a woman in a quarrelsome tone.

Oops, the inn was going to be slandered for something of which it was innocent.

'I do apologise, my lady. I'll have words with my servants. Let me take you to your room. Hot water and a bit of supper will be carried up at once.'

The voices passed her door and Dora relaxed a fraction.

The first letter that met her gaze was in her father's spiky script and addressed to Gatskill. The handwriting was as unforgiving as the man himself. She scanned it: instructions to remove all traces of Anthony from West Wycombe. His effects were to be brought back intact, though any correspondence that wasn't financial was to be burnt.

Burnt! Damn her father. She dug through the box, finding Gatskill's tedious letters to investors, and financial forecasts for bankers, until she landed on a bundle at the bottom tied with a red satin bow. That did not seem very like Gatskill.

She pulled it out. Her brother's handwriting.

'You sly dog,' muttered Dora. Gatskill was planning on keeping the correspondence he had been instructed to destroy, was he? Perhaps he had a mind to see what leverage it would give him over his famously difficult employer?

'I'll take those.' She put them inside her shirt and buttoned her waistcoat to the top to keep them pressed against her skin.

More voices echoed outside with the clatter of footsteps. The sands in her hourglass were fast running out. But there was so much else to search! Dora couldn't resist looking in Anthony's trunk. It was unlocked. Lifting the lid, she was overcome with his scent, the most powerful reminder yet of her loss. She'd forgotten this, his smell of fine pomade – he'd had a fixation about the lack

The Persephone Code

of subtlety in other men's hair oil. This mixed with the odour of his favourite tobacco. Pulling out the shirt on the top, she held it to her face and breathed it in.

The latch on the door rattled.

Swearing, Dora dropped the lid of the trunk and scuttled under the bed, taking the shirt with her. Gatskill came in, his boots striding first to the writing desk, then to the fireplace where he poked the logs. Had she remembered to lock the desk? As he had not made a protest, she guessed she had. Satisfied with the renewed blaze, he patted his pockets and drew out a key on a chain. He went back to the desk.

Dora held her breath. If he saw the letters were missing...

He lifted the lid, dropped in a small purse, then locked it again.

Relief swamped Dora. He'd been putting his valuables in, not checking if anything had been removed.

But how was she going to get out? Would she have to wait until he went to sleep? Her theory that he might be warming his coat to head out for a midnight assignation was proved false when he removed the coat and spread it on the bed, under the covers. She'd done that herself when travelling; it removed the chill of the sheets. He then sat down by the fire, pulled off his boots and picked up a book.

Damn.

Dora held very still. The bed was high. He only had to look across and under to see her there.

A knock came on the door.

'That had better be the blasted warming pan,' muttered Gatskill, going to answer. 'Yes?'

'Mr Gatskill, we met earlier. Jacob Sandys.'

Chapter Thirty

The arrival of a coach had cut short Jacob's conversation with the landlord. Jacob had waited for the initial flurry to settle before he went in search of Dora.

She wasn't where he had left her. Of course she wasn't. Why had he expected her to stay put when they had a second task to complete? He hadn't mentioned he had a plan to draw Gatskill out of his room for a conversation while she searched, and now it was too late. She had seized the initiative.

They really needed to talk more about tactics *before* engaging with the enemy.

Meeting the landlord on the stairs, he got the man's room number from him. He knocked on the door.

'Yes?' Gatskill was readying for bed, boots already off. It was going to be difficult to persuade the man to return to the public rooms.

'Mr Gatskill, we met earlier. Jacob Sandys.' He held out a hand.

Gatskill shook it limply. A book dangled from his other hand. Gothic novel or economic treatise? Jacob rather hoped the former.

'It's rather late, Mr Sandys.'

This was the time to use the big guns. 'It's the Honourable Mr Jacob Sandys, MD. My father is Lord Sandys of Loughrigg.' He gave him the insouciant smile that worked for his older brothers.

'Oh, of course.' Gatskill was overcome with obsequiousness. 'What can I do for you, sir? Please take a seat.'

'I was hoping you would let me buy you a drink so we can have a talk about...' What business could he possibly have with Gatskill? '...About Miss Fitz-Pennington, my companion.' Jacob winced, knowing that didn't sound good.

Gatskill's smile was more a sneer. 'Oh, I'm a man of the world, sir. I quite understand. I'll ring for some hot punch to be brought up here. The fires are out in the dining parlour. Don't you find the country colder than Town?'

'Indeed, many think it so.' Jacob resigned himself to staying and so he settled himself into the armchair. An opportunity to search might present itself. He had already noted the trunk in the corner – too much luggage for a man on a short mission. That had to be Anthony's. Glancing across the room, looking for any indication that Dora had come and gone, he met her bright gaze from under the bed. She looked like a fox in its hole. It would have been funny if he hadn't desperately wanted to make sure she wouldn't get caught. But how to get this man out of his warm room? He was like a winkle in its shell: damn difficult to prise out.

He would have to try to rescue Dora from a very tricky explanation. Come to think of it, he would be implicated too if she were spotted. 'Are you sure I can't tempt you back to the public bar? There's a big fire there.'

'What? And rub shoulders with the yokels? No thank you. I've had my fill today of their onion breath and sweat. The punch won't be long. They add orange peel. It is the best thing about this place.'

'Been here long?'

'A couple of days. And you?'

'Rode in this morning.'

'How exactly did the girl find out about her brother?'

Jacob held up his hands. 'Not my fault. Leighton wrote asking me to pass on the message.' How to explain his presence? Play to the man's prejudices. 'Meeting the lady, I decided not to pass up the opportunity to accompany her south.'

Gatskill gave a dirty chuckle. 'Few men would.' He then recollected who she was and resumed his priggish disapproval. 'My employer has disowned her – you do know that? There's no money coming from that direction.'

'I'm not after her money.' God forgive him, that sounded awful.

'Quite. I've heard some connoisseurs prefer the dusky charms.'

Fortunately, at that moment the door opened and a maid came in with a bowl of steaming punch before Jacob punched the supercilious face of his host. She set it next to them.

'Will there be anything else, sir? Shall I turn down the bed for you?' She looked ready to toss the covers back and expose Dora. Jacob wondered how he could object to that, but Gatskill was there before him.

'No! All the heat will be lost. Bring up a warming pan, will you? Do you want your guests to catch chills and die of damp sheets? I've asked twice already.'

'Yes, sir. Right away, sir. What with all the guests arriving together, we've been run off our feet.'

'Well, don't dawdle now.' Gatskill waved her away.

Jacob contemplated the bowl. With that attitude, he had to hope the maid hadn't spat in it before she delivered it.

Gatskill played host, ladling a serving into a cup. 'Here; that will take off the edge. How can I help you, sir?'

Jacob accepted the punch and held it in his palms, warming his fingers. 'I was wondering, if I took a certain lady under my protection, would her family make any difficulties?' That was the best excuse he could come up with for this conversation.

'I think I can take it upon myself to say that Mr Pennington's main concern is that no scandal taints his name. He would be happier for her to be tucked away as some worthy man's ladybird than have her flaunting her charms on stage. You would be regarded as the lesser of two evils.'

A father who cared for his daughter, thought Jacob bitterly, would take such a presumptuous gentleman by the scruff of the neck and march him to the altar.

'I will see she doesn't bring his name into disrepute. A new name, perhaps, and a house in a quiet area of Town where my visits will not be noticed.' That was what his father had always done with his mistresses, and what his brothers did now.

'Quite so. That sounds very decent of you. He will be much relieved to know she is out of the public eye. And when you eventually come to marry?'

'A settlement, naturally. I'll see she is safe.'

'And after the honeymoon, the arrangement can quietly resume, am I correct?' Gatskill was enjoying this, believing he had Jacob's character.

'If the lady is willing. If we're still together.' How he hated this version of himself. This was what he could have been if he hadn't struck out on his own. The decent sort of rake who took responsibility for his sins. Dora would be fuming at hearing herself so described, but she should consider this her punishment for putting herself into such a stupid situation.

Gatskill checked his pocket watch. 'That sounds fair. If that is all you wanted to talk about, Dr Sandys, then perhaps we should call it a night? I'm leaving early in the morning.'

Seeing his chance to extricate Dora vanishing, Jacob swore silently. She would have to wait until the man was sound asleep to make her escape and hope he didn't grope under the bed for the chamber pot before retiring. Then an idea came to him.

'Actually, Mr Gatskill, I was also drawn here because I did notice some worrying signs this morning. On you.'

'On me?'

'Yes, we medical men are trained to spot these things.' He adopted the lofty tone of his profession – the air of mystery that usually resulted in a good payment. 'I detected a slight blueness to your lips and to the tips of your fingers.' Gatskill stared at his fingers in consternation. 'I wondered if you had any trouble with your heart?' Other than being heartless.

'You think I might be ill?'

He furrowed his brow. 'Have you caught a chill recently?'

'Oh yes – at Brighton in February.'

Jacob nodded sagely. 'Such things can travel to your heart. I could find out, if you would let me listen to your heartbeat.'

'You really think I might be in danger?' His voice rose in a panic.

Jacob winced at the medical ethics he was infringing. Still, it wasn't impossible... 'Indeed. Better safe than sorry.'

'What must I do?'

'Why don't you lie down on the bed and let your heartbeat steady. Yes, that's it. Close your eyes. Picture the most calming scene you can imagine – spring meadows, a warm fire on a winter's day, a lazy day in summer...' Jacob knelt down and pointed vigorously to the door so Dora could see. 'Yes, that's right. Keep your eyes closed. I just need to open your shirt so I can listen to your chest. I'll close the bedcurtains in case the maid comes back with the warming pan. You know what these rural servants are like. They never knock.' He untied the curtains on the side nearest the door. Dora rolled out, got up and grinned. She mimed dusting herself down.

He scowled.

'Is anything wrong, doctor?' Gatskill asked plaintively. 'You've gone very quiet.'

'Not at all.' He now started making more noise to hide Dora's exit, kicking over a stool. 'Sorry – I didn't see that there. Right. Lie still.'

Jacob made his examination, treating this as he would a real patient now that he had got this far. Gatskill's pulse was a little elevated for a man who was reclining so he offered advice on how to treat it. His prescription was to rest and not drink too much alcohol. Other doctors would have bled him to lower the sanguine element in his body, but Jacob was sceptical of the efficacy of this method. Soldiers on the battlefield bled plenty and it did none of them any good. Gatskill attempted to pay him for his advice but Jacob had not sunk so low as to take advantage.

'No, no, I really don't want anything.'

Gatskill got up to show him to the door. 'Except me putting in a good word for you with Mr Pennington?' He tapped the side of his nose.

'Er, thank you. Always wise to be on good terms with as many people as possible.'

Jacob made a rapid retreat to search for his errant partner. He was going to have words with her about being one of those 'fools' who 'rush in where Angels fear to tread' – Pope had obviously had Dora in mind when he wrote his 'Essay on Criticism'.

Chapter Thirty-One

Henley-on-Thames

When Jacob announced their plans for an expedition, at breakfast, Leighton baulked a little at them going alone to Henley to convey the news to the Jenkins family.

'Don't you think it my pastoral duty?' he had asked, tapping the top of his boiled egg. Jacob was reminded of a disgruntled bear as his old friend grumbled at being left behind.

'Really, Leighton, we can't leave West Wycombe without one of us to keep watch and the coroner is expected imminently to view the body,' Jacob reasoned. 'You need to be here. Besides, if you had murdered someone and were still in the area, wouldn't you be watching the comings and goings at the scene of the crime? We need to know if anyone shows particular interest.'

Leighton dipped his toast in the egg. 'All my parishioners will swarm like wasps to jam. It's already the talk of the village.'

Dora was keeping quiet, Jacob noticed, letting him handle his friend.

The Persephone Code

'Then please use your instincts. Look for someone whose interest feels discordant – the killer hornet amongst the wasps.'

'I'll do my best, Sandys. But perhaps you should stay, and I should go with Miss Fitz-Pennington?'

Jacob rose from the table with a sardonic chuckle. 'A very good try, Leighton, but you were the one who entered holy orders, not me. This parish is your business.'

Now rattling along the road heading for the Thames, Jacob wondered why he hadn't explained their side trip to Medmenham Abbey. He could have told his friend about Dora's discovery of the link to 'The Rape of the Lock' but something held him back. Instinct told him that the fewer people who knew about the riddles, the better. Leighton was a good sort, but Jacob wouldn't put it past him to mention it to the coroner, Vane or some other gentlemen at the ball when he spoke out about the need for an enquiry into the murders.

Sitting beside him in the hired carriage – which was in truth not much better than a cart – Dora was chewing on a grass stalk. She was back in her women's weeds, as she called them, but her stance was still that of the boy she had played, slumped with her boots up on the footboard. Jacob was leaving her alone to her thoughts until they were clear of the village. His attempts to chastise her last night had failed miserably. She had just laughed and shown him the package of letters. He might as well berate a millstone for all the good it did him to try to control her.

Once they were well beyond the parish grounds, he turned to her.

'Did you read your brother's letters?'

'I made a start.'

'Anything?'

She shrugged and pushed a stray lock out of her eyes. 'My brother had many lovers who liked to write in praise of his ... prowess. It is not something a sister likes to contemplate.'

'I could read them for you?'

Dora sat up, her face sober. 'No. It's the last service I can do my brother. I'll see this through. What's the plan for today?'

'I'm glad you asked. Things almost went badly for you last night because we hadn't discussed our strategy.'

She gazed out at the trees. What did she see there, he wondered. Sometimes, he saw new leaves tingeing the woodlands green after the barren stretch of winter, but mostly he regarded them as symbolic of a harsh world of broken branches and cut timber. Was her soul less cynical than his?

'*Almost* is the word I cling to,' said Dora, turning back to him with a brilliant smile, proving that her experience of life had not yet sapped her. 'A tree that's *almost* fallen is still standing. A play that *almost* goes wrong is a success. A dish that *almost* gets broken is still whole.'

'An admirable attitude but, in my world, a leg that almost rots off, or a life that is almost saved, casts a different shade over the word.'

Dora elbowed him. 'You're no fun.'

'Whereas you are a pantomime of laughs.'

'Thank you, thank you, I'm here all week.' She bowed to her imaginary audience. Jacob was struck by a wild urge to kiss her *into* next week, but they were on a public highway and had serious news to deliver. Perhaps tonight at the ball they might be able to snatch a few moments for romance and explore this attraction that lay between them. It felt like the first moments of lighting a fire. Would the tinder catch, or would it be a false start, leaving damp wood and a smoke-filled room? He was eager to find out.

'Did any names in your brother's letters seem familiar? I might know the ladies in question, and they might still be in the area. We haven't considered that he might've been killed by someone with an additional motive. He stands out as the only highborn victim.'

'Like a jealous husband? It is an angle worth pondering. I'll make a list for you when we get back.'

He corrected the lead horse's drift towards the hedge. 'You are unlikely to have time before the ball.'

'I still don't have a dress, so tragically it looks like I get the night off.' She sounded very pleased with the prospect but, after the trouble she had got herself into last evening, he wouldn't leave her in the rectory on her own for any money.

'That is under control. Unlike this wretched horse.'

Dora laughed as he admonished the leader with a tap on its flank.

Their mood sobered as they arrived in Henley. Since becoming a stop on the coaching routes to London, the town had grown and there were many pubs and inns to check to find out from where Jenkins's sweetheart might've come. Matt himself was more easily identified.

A bargee lounging on the dock by his Thames barge scratched the back of his head, dislodging his cap.

'That big daftie? Aye, I know where he lives. Don't tell me he's got himself into trouble. If he has, it will be a mistake, or an accident. That poor lad barely has the sense to tie his own bootlaces.'

'The address?' asked Jacob.

The bargee rubbed his fingers together. When they were filled with a shilling, he gave an address off Friday Street.

'His dad is a maltster. A good man. I often carry his malt to London.' He then spat in the Thames. 'Shame it's a dying trade. Barely keeps a man in shoe leather.'

In line with the bargeman's verdict on the malting industry, the house in Friday Street had seen better days. A brick and timber construction, it had once been a fine establishment but was now subdivided into many houses that were little more than hovels. Jacob paid a loitering boy a penny to mind the cart – that was preferable to letting the loiterer drive off with it as soon as their back was turned.

Dora touched his arm. 'Jacob, if you don't mind, I think I should ask after Mary while you deliver this news.' She must have seen his expression. 'I'll stay if you prefer?'

Jacob shook his head. She was right. It would be better if he spoke to the father without an audience. No one was likely to have followed them so far, which meant that the danger for them in splitting up was minimal.

'I'll meet you in the marketplace in an hour.'

She squeezed his arm in sympathy, then headed off to the nearest inn.

He hated this part of being a doctor. With a sigh, he knocked on the door.

'Who is it?' called a gruff voice.

Jacob opened the door only to have his lungs filled with the unmistakeable odour of barley going through the malting process. The entire ground floor of the house was covered in a layer of grain and a man was slowly pacing across it with a three-pronged rake, creating little furrows to help the seed germinate. The expanse of barley between them seemed an impossible ocean to cross bearing this news. He was about to change this maltster's life for ever.

'Mr Jenkins? I'm Dr Sandys.'

The man removed his cap. 'How can I help you, sir?'

'Is there somewhere we can talk?'

'Next door. I've a little kitchen that's comfortable enough. I'll meet you there.' The maltster continued to the end of his furrow and then dropped the rake. He pointed in the direction Jacob should go. Returning to the street, Jacob checked the cart was still where he had left it and went along to the next door. Jenkins opened it before he could knock.

'Come in, sir. Can I get you anything? I make a little of my own brew with the malt if you'd like to wet your whistle.'

It would be churlish to refuse the man's offer. Jacob sat down at the scrubbed kitchen table and looked for signs of a wife and children, but he appeared to be living a bachelor life. This was the worst of all worlds: Matt had likely been an only child.

'How do you like it, sir?' the man asked anxiously.

Jacob realised that Jenkins had him down as a prospective buyer for his malt. He sipped. 'It's excellent. You do fine work.' He cleared his throat. 'Mr Jenkins, I'm afraid I've come as the bearer of bad news. It's about your son.'

'Matt?' The man laughed with weary resignation. 'What's he done now? Is he in gaol? Did that lass take him for all his money and run off leaving him with her debts?'

'There's no easy way to say this, sir. Matt is dead. He lost his life sometime early yesterday or late the night before.'

'Dead?' Jenkins said the word like Jacob had said Matt was pregnant – something so outlandish it could not be true. 'No, that's not Matt. The boy might be slow but he's sturdy. Nothing could lay him low.'

'I'm afraid something did. He was murdered.'

The old man set the beer mug down with exquisite care.

Jacob rushed on. 'We think he was asking after his sweetheart, Mary, was it?'

The old man nodded.

'But she was probably already dead. Someone likely killed her a few months back – it remains unsolved. The only thing we can think is that they silenced Matt to stop him asking questions. You also should know that they tried to blame Mary's death on him.'

'Bugger that! My lad wouldn't harm a fly!' Jenkins shoved the table from him as he stood.

'I know. I assure you, most heartily, that I'm doing everything in my power to get to the truth and make sure no one believes such a terrible thing of Matt. May I ask one question?'

'How can that help? There's no mistake, is there? He's a big lad – like a ... like a hayrick. Gentle. Heart as big as a ... as big as...' Jenkins collapsed into his chair and started howling. 'No, it can't be Matt! My boy!'

Jacob felt the pressure of emotion in his throat. It wasn't his place to break down when he gave such news – that wouldn't help the father – but when he met loss like this he wanted to bawl at the unfairness of life. He gave the man a few minutes to sob, resting a hand on his arm in sympathy. Words and explanations were superfluous here.

'I'm so sorry, Mr Jenkins, so sorry.'

The man looked up, tear tracks running down the wrinkles on his cheeks and into his beard. 'It's the innocents that suffer, isn't it? Not old crocks like me who are useless, ready to be thrown out. It should've been me! I should've gone looking in his place, but he was moping and said he had to search for her and I thought, what harm could befall him going just a few miles away? It would be an adventure and teach him something of life.' Fresh tears fell from the tired old eyes. 'And Mary too? I didn't approve of the girl's goings-on, but she wasn't so bad, always smiling and joking, and as kind as the day is long. What happened to her?'

'That's what I'm trying to find out. Mr Jenkins, could you please tell me if Matt could write?'

'My Matt? No. There was no point sending a lad like that to the dame school. He can't even read, though I tried my best to teach him. Why do you want to know?'

He would have to tell the father enough so that Jenkins could go to West Wycombe prepared. If he heard what they were saying at the George and Dragon, there'd be more distress and maybe even bloodshed. 'We think the one who killed Mary tried to make it look like your son was the murderer. They left a note giving the idea that Matt confessed to the deed.'

'Who is it?' The man was up on his feet again. 'I'll skin 'em, I

The Persephone Code

will, and douse 'em with vinegar – then end their miserable life exactly how they killed my boy. How did he die?'

'He was knocked unconscious and hanged.' He left out the evidence that pointed to a slow death and the bizarre place where it occurred. The man had enough to deal with without those details. 'The rector of West Wycombe is tending to him. Matt is in the village mortuary. You can go and get him once the coroner has seen the body, or we can send him to you.'

The maltster grabbed his hat. 'I'm going. I'm going to find out who did it while I'm at it.'

With the mood the man was in, he might well start laying about with his fists and try to beat the truth out of the locals. 'We're doing our best to discover the identity of the criminal but so many wild rumours are flying that no one yet knows the truth. Other girls besides Mary have died. I take it that Matt hadn't left Henley before a day or two ago?'

'Never. Not on his own. He wasn't good at finding his way without someone with him. This was the first time I'd let him … let him go without me.' Pure devastation settled on the man's features.

Jacob hated to think of the guilt the father would feel but it was useless telling him it wasn't his fault. 'If you want a straight answer rather than gossip and speculation, speak to Reverend Leighton. Tell him I sent you to him for an explanation.' Jacob trusted his old friend had experience with the bereaved and could lift the burden of guilt.

'I'm fetching my son home. You'll show yourself out, won't you?' Jenkins left abruptly, not even closing the door behind him.

Jacob got up more slowly, feeling weary of the world and its cruelty. He dug in his pocket and left a guinea for the beer. In truth, he meant it to be put towards the burial of Henley's gentle giant, who'd had the misfortune to love his Mary unwisely and to cross paths, unluckily, with a killer.

Chapter Thirty-Two

Dora realised she had made an error starting with the most reputable inns in town. Asking after a barmaid who serviced male customers out the back was not something a respectable establishment like the Royal Oak or the Angel on the Bridge would countenance. She was given the sharp edge of the innkeeper's tongue for even having suggested such things might go on at the Angel – or anywhere in Henley. They were all pure as the driven snow here.

No one in Henley was admitting to their seedy underbelly. Hypocrisy was not dead, even if two of their young people were.

She paused in the market square to reconsider her tactics. Henley wasn't like London. It was too small a place to have anonymous street walkers who could pick up passing trade; the prostitutes had to be more discreet for the sake of their customers. Added to that, a common lad like Matt had clearly had the opportunity to get to know Mary. Both these facts pointed to a humbler place. However, Mary had also been scooped up by the Hellfire Club for one of their parties. How had that happened? They were rich gentlemen. They didn't trawl from the bottom;

they skimmed from the top of the female talent in a place like this. That suggested someone was running a bordello on the sly, established enough for passing gents to know they could recruit girls for their party from there, but not so exclusive that the girls rose to the level of courtesans who wouldn't give Matt the time of day.

She needed local information, but people were hardly going to admit to a respectable woman where the local brothel could be found, not at eleven o'clock in the morning. It was a man's world, so Jacob might've stood more of a chance getting the information, but Dora didn't want to admit defeat. Pondering her choices, she wondered where the most likely source of gossip would be. Where better than at the milliner's shop?

Making suitable adjustments to her appearance and bearing, she sauntered in, letting the door clang behind her. The people in the shop, assistants and customers alike, turned with the instinct of a pack of dogs sensing a stranger bitch on their territory.

'All right, ducks?' she said to the woman behind the counter. 'You got some flash nabs for the noddle, ain't ya?' The thing about collecting information was not to appear to want it or else you'd end up paying, like Jacob had with the bargeman. Dora didn't have shillings to spare. You had to make them want to pay to get rid of you. She was good at making herself objectionable.

The milliner's assistant hissed when Dora fingered the satin ribbon. 'Don't touch that!'

'How's I to know if I wants it if I don't 'ave a little poke – not that kind of poke, missus.' She elbowed a stout lady in the ribs. 'Naughty!' She was the only one laughing.

'I doubt we have anything for the likes of you in here,' said the assistant.

''Ow do you know that? I might want me a Sunday bonnet, like this one – all spriggled and spraggled. Something to catch the curate's eye.' She flipped at the silk flowers adorning one capote bonnet. 'I'd like mine trimmed with scarlet.'

'There's a surprise,' muttered one waggish lady, prompting her companions to titter with laughter. They were her Greek chorus. How nice.

'Oi, what's you laughing at? My money's as good as yours, I wager.' She leaned on the counter, treating the sole male amongst the assistants to a view of her cleavage. 'Don't you agree, handsome? If I take you out back, will you sell it to me at, say, half price?'

'I... I...' The poor man flushed. From his reaction, she guessed he probably picked his amours from amongst his own sex so wouldn't know what to do with her even if she were the woman she pretended to be.

'Madame LaTour! Madame LaTour!' called the youngest of the assistants, making a run for the stockroom.

Good. They hadn't taken long to break, not like the dressmaker's she'd invaded in Lincoln to retrieve a stolen cloak. It took them a while to admit they sold stolen goods from under the counter.

'Oh lah-di-dah, a French woman in Henley! No wonder your bonnets are only one season out of fashion.' She winked at the stout lady. 'Am I right? You go to town, don't you, ducks? I probably know your husband, eh?'

'Insupportable!' The woman picked up her basket and hurried out.

The milliner rushed in to see what was amiss in a fluttering of handkerchief, lace and ribbons. 'Mon Dieu! What eez 'appening 'ere?' She had the worst French accent Dora had ever heard – and she'd seen a lot on stage.

'This ... this woman is importuning the customers!' said the young man. Much more of this and he'd be the first to swoon.

'*Au contraire, mon petit chou, j'essaie d'acheter un bonnet.*' Dora chucked him under the chin before turning to the milliner. *'Ma soeur, comment vas-tu?'*

'I am not your sir! Now get out! Be gone!' The milliner reverted to what was likely her real accent. 'This shop is not for your sort.' She even flapped her apron at Dora.

'My sort?' Dora pretended confusion. 'Where the hell *does* my sort go in a little place like this, eh?'

The customers hissed at the profanity. Easily shocked, this crowd.

'You'll be welcome at the Broad Gates with the other doxies, but you most certainly are not here!'

Huzzah, the result she wanted! She made a moue of disappointment.

'All right, I get the hint. See you later, sunshine?' She blew a kiss to the assistant.

Dora had to admit that had been more than a little fun. She'd always loved acting – doxy or duchess, all were masks that could be worn for a while, trying out another personality. It was liberating to be so rude.

She found Broad Gates a few doors along on Market Square. It gained its name from the archway built for carriages to pass into the courtyard out the back, but it had obviously come to mean something indicative of lax morals. No one here would be a hero in Bunyan's *Pilgrim's Progress* and choose the narrow way. The front room had the appearance of a normal bar, with ale on tap for the working men who made up the customers. Walking under the archway, she saw the inn was well provisioned with small rooms for customers to take their ease in more carnal fashion. She waited until a couple came out of a room, the man kissing the girl on the cheek before heading back to the market. The working girl played bashful until he had exited via the gateway, then she dropped her pose and her face turned sour.

See, everyone has an act.

'Not up to much then?' called Dora, approaching her before she could go inside.

The woman assessed her quickly and assumed she was of the same profession. 'Nah, but his money's sweet. Tips well, that one.' She brushed her skirt smooth. 'You looking for work? We've room for another girl. You look like you'd make good tips too.'

Was that because Mary hadn't come back?

'Thanks, but no.' Dora decided she'd try the truth on this straight-talking barmaid. She looked like she'd appreciate it. 'I'm actually here with someone.'

'Lucky you.' The girl lolled against the wall, evidently pleased to take a break. 'I wouldn't mind a gentleman of my own, rather than any Tom, Dick or Harry who wants to scratch an itch on market day.'

Dora leant beside her, both watching the world go by beyond the courtyard. 'Not a gentleman like that, I'm afraid. More of a travelling companion.'

'Don't give up hope. He might come up trumps for you.'

Dora was in danger of getting off her point. 'My name is Dora. Would you mind telling me your name?'

'Telling won't cost you nothing. I'm Cathy.'

'Cathy, we're trying to find out all we can about a girl who came from here. A Mary something?'

'Mary Wheeler?'

'I'm sorry but we don't know her surname. She had an admirer – a young man called Matt Jenkins.'

'Big Matt? Aye, that's Mary.' Cathy's face clouded. She was no fool. 'What's happened to her?'

'We think she's dead – at least, a girl we think was her was found in West Wycombe.'

'You don't know? What blinking use is that?'

'I'm sorry for being vague, but I only just found out about this myself. Matt Jenkins came looking for her earlier this week, and someone killed him. His body was found yesterday and that's when we started putting this together.'

The girl sat on a low wall, all strength gone from her legs. 'Killed Matt – and Mary? You're saying both of them were murdered?'

'Yes.'

'Why? He was as harmless as men come!'

Dora noted that she was less surprised to hear that Mary had died. Theirs was a dangerous trade.

'We believe he was asking questions about Mary – and that was a subject that the killer wanted left alone. So they stopped him.'

'I don't believe it – I mean, I do, but I don't want to. What's the world coming to?'

Dora let that comment hang between them, before returning to the subject. 'Wheeler, you say her name was? Did she have any family?'

'Not that she ever spoke of.'

'She wasn't from round here?'

'Came up on one of the barges from London. I always thought she was running from something – poverty, a man, who knows? When was she killed?'

'Maybe you can help us find that out.' Dora didn't want to confuse her by mentioning the two other female victims. 'Do you remember when she left?'

'It must've been just before Christmas. Yes, definitely; it was the week before because Jerry was right put out that he was left short-handed at one of his busiest times.'

'Did she say where she was going and who asked her?'

'She said she'd met a gent who invited her on a lark. Asked me if I wanted to go too but I didn't fancy it. Sounded too good to be true. She thought he'd introduce her to other rich men and she would be made for life – or at least a year or so. That's better than what we've got to look forward to here.'

'No other details?'

'Only that there would be a party somewhere and she'd get new togs – silk ones. That was very important to her. A silk gown and stockings. She could flog them after and eat for a month.'

That appeared to be confirmation that she had, as they suspected, been recruited for a Hellfire party. 'And where did Matt fit into her plans?'

'Oh, he didn't. She humoured him because he was sweet and gave her money when he could, but she would never've married him.' Cathy's eyes glistened and she wiped a wrist over them, annoyed by her tears. 'Not because she thought herself too good for the simple lad, but because she considered herself too … spoiled. Yes, that was her word.'

Dora was getting a picture of a desperate girl who hid her true feelings with a flashy show of spirits, readier to believe in good fortune than her more cynical friend.

'She should've taken the boy's offer,' Cathy said.

'Yes, I really think she should. Thank you – you've been a great help.'

'Where is she?'

'She's buried in the churchyard at West Wycombe.'

'Can you see that she gets a headstone?'

A shout came from inside the pub:

'Cathy, move your arse. Got a customer for you.'

The girl grimaced at the prospect but headed inside.

'Actually, forget the headstone, miss,' she said over her shoulder. 'Just get the bastard that killed her.'

Chapter Thirty-Three

Jacob began to worry that something had happened to Dora. There was no sign of her in the marketplace and he was beginning to attract the attention of the locals as the news about Matt Jenkins spread. He'd already had to fend off questions from a couple of maltster pals of Mr Jenkins.

Then he saw her, emerging from the rear of the Broad Gates Inn. She cut a magnificent path through the people gathered for the market, the expression on her face daring anyone to hamper her. She also looked distinctly more... He struggled for a word and came up with 'disreputable'. It had to be the way she'd removed her neckerchief and coat so that her figure was on display.

She jumped up onto the cart beside him.

'You achieved your quest?' he asked her.

Dora nodded. 'Let's get out of here.'

The cart began moving. Like her, he was more than ready to leave Henley. A pretty town it might be, but it had some very ugly news to absorb.

'I think I can guess how you went about your mission,' he said. 'I hope you weren't importuned?'

This elicited a reluctant laugh from her. 'Lord no, though I think they would consider me as the importunate one.' She then quickly caught him up on what she had learned about Mary Wheeler.

'We have confirmation then that she was enticed away for what sounds like a Hellfire party. And Matt's father also corroborated what we had imagined to be the poor lad's motive for venturing to West Wycombe.' Jacob touched the whip to the leader's flanks to remind the horse it had a job to do. 'Next stop: Medmenham Abbey. What do you think we'll find there?'

Dora replaced her neckerchief and coat, with these slight touches assuming the character of a decent woman out for a drive with her husband or brother. She was a chameleon – another fact to add to the many fascinating things about Dora Fitz-Pennington.

'We can hope that it will lead us directly to what my brother wants hidden until we can take it to Sheridan.'

'I sense a "but".'

'But, knowing Anthony, he wouldn't make it that easy. He liked to make me work for my answers.'

With that sobering thought, Jacob directed the horses along the road following the big bend in the Thames that led to the Abbey. The river was glimpsed to their right in breaks in the hedges, a glittering snake winding its way through the pastureland.

Dora stood up as they approached, steadying herself on his shoulder.

'I think I can see it over the tops of the trees. It's a ruin – just a crumbling tower.'

He was tempted to yank on her skirt. 'Please take your seat, Dora. I can't answer for the roads and I'd hate for you to be bounced out onto your head.'

She sat down and folded her arms. 'Why on earth stage your orgiastic revels in a draughty ruin?'

'You'd have to ask Sir Francis Dashwood about that.'

'Well, he's long dead, so what do you think?'

She sounded almost personally offended by the noble gentleman's demise some decades ago. 'I think he was picking up on our ancestors' love of the ruin in the landscape. You couldn't have a gallery of a noble house without several depictions of the fallen splendours of Rome or Greece.'

'Ah yes. I've seen my fair share. When I was in the Pennington fold, naturally.'

'How did you come to leave?'

She was silent for a moment, such that he wondered if she would tell him.

'I left because my father gave me an ultimatum: I was to cease my childish criticism of his abhorrent business practices and become a dutiful wife to his plantation manager, or leave. I left.'

'He wanted to send you to the West Indies?' Jacob glanced at her defiant profile. Her father was a fool.

'He'd always planned this as my future apparently. Get rid of the embarrassing bastard by giving her as a reward to his man out there. He had the gall to say I would like it, being back with "my" people. That's when I realised what I should have known from the start.'

'And that was?'

'I was always a foreigner to him. My mother's blood was the only thing he saw in me. That man does not know how to love.'

'He sounds impossible.'

'A mild verdict but I'll accept it.' She huffed out a breath and rolled her shoulders. 'Tell me about your father. Viscount Sandys.'

'I've been more fortunate than you. He was and remains a distant father but not unkind. I'd say he is primarily known as a cultured man. My father collected many classical landscapes on his Grand Tour, being from the same generation of taste as Sir Francis. Which brings us back to Medmenham Abbey. An old Cistercian Abbey was the English equivalent of classical grandeur.' He turned down the rutted lane leading to the monastery. 'Not that it was ever one of the great houses, not like Fountains Abbey or Rievaulx. When it was dissolved by Henry VIII, there were only two monks living there, and not much in the way of worldly goods.'

They cleared the trees to see the ruins on the grassy lawn that led down to the Thames. The sun was out and it did indeed make a picturesque spot. At least four arches of an old cloister remained and a square tower. The stonework waged war with the ivy and shrubs that tried to invade. The stones were losing as a green-leaved army clambered up the ramparts.

'A couple more decades and it will have quite mouldered away,' said Dora.

'Unless someone chooses to repair it. I fancy this is a prime spot so close to the Thames. The next owner will take it over if the present Lord Dashwood sells.' Jacob jumped down and tied off the reins of the lead horse.

'Shall we let them graze here?' suggested Dora. 'Before the return journey.'

With her capable help, Jacob led the horses from the traces and let them take their rest by the cart.

'Any idea what signs your brother might've left?' he asked as they headed for the buildings.

'I think I'll know it when I see it.' Dora bit her lip. 'At least, I hope so.'

He laced his fingers through hers. 'Dora, we can only do our best. This was your brother's fight, not ours. We've only been drafted in as his seconds when he fell.'

'But I want justice for those who have died – for all of them,

The Persephone Code

not just my brother. For Mary and Matt, not to mention the ones whose names we don't know.'

'So do I. And I have more confidence in you than you have in yourself.'

She looked up at him. 'You do?'

'You know what I thought when I saw you striding towards me in the marketplace in Henley?'

'Here comes trouble?'

'Yes.'

She laughed.

'But I also thought how fierce you were, an Athena, goddess of war and wisdom. These Illuminati, these Hellfire fools, they do not know what they have taken on. They dismiss you as just a sister and that is going to be their downfall. You are fully able to solve this puzzle. Trust yourself.'

'And I trust you to help me.' She reached up and brushed his cheek. He couldn't resist the invitation. He gathered her to him and kissed her until they were both breathless. Unable to pass on the opportunity, he kissed his way down her neck, exploring each spot for her reaction – beneath the ear, at the place where her neck met her collarbone, then lower. He wanted nothing more than to lay her on the soft grass and explore all the wonders of her body, to unlace that dress and rest his face on her breast so he could worship her beauty. There was no one else around so his mind had already gone there, which played havoc with his control. His hand gathered her skirts, exposing her legs to the breeze. Beautiful smooth skin, a curve of a buttock under his hand. Just a little more and—

She pushed him away gently but firmly.

'Jacob, we can't.' She brushed down her skirts, hiding her face from him. 'Not here.'

Jacob took deep breaths. He wanted to howl with frustration, but she was right. They had a job to do. Pleasurable though a dalliance by the river might be, they could not indulge their feelings now. He was definitely falling short as the kind of gentleman he aspired to be.

'I apologise.'

'No apology needed. I just wish this was another time, and another place.'

He then recalled, as she must have done, that this same abbey had seen many other sexual dalliances, some of them perverse and possibly murderous. She was right. They should not sully what they had between them by letting their attraction run its course here. Plus, he hadn't considered yet what role she might take in his life. He did not want his conversation with Gatskill to be prophetic of the kind of arrangement a man such as him would make with a woman of her station. He must curb his impulses.

He adjusted his clothing and thought of cold mornings in the surgeon's tent. When he had regained his balance, he bowed.

'Lead on. Let us find this clue your brother has left for us.'

'*If* we are right that it is here at all.' She headed into the building by the nearest door.

They found one room that was sufficiently intact to be a place for ceremonies and parties out of the worst of the weather. It was hard to say when it was last used but the inscription over the door – *Fait ce que voudras* – do what you will – was evidence of Hellfire activity.

'What do you think became of the baboon?' asked Dora, running her fingers over the stone. 'The one in the box dressed as a devil.'

'After bringing Lord Sandwich to his knees in penitence? I hope it ran off, jumped on board a barge and headed back for warmer climes.' Jacob moved a bench but found only orange peel and an old cork behind it.

Dora stood in the centre of the room and looked up at the

vaulted ceiling. She turned slowly, examining the ledges and window niches.

'There!' She pointed to the end of a silk rope that dangled over the edge. 'It matches the one in my brother's bedroom. Can you reach it?'

The niche was about twelve feet up, probably a plinth for a statue at one point in this building's history. Whatever saint had once inhabited it had long since fallen. Jacob piled two benches on top of each other and found he could reach the cord if he stretched to his fullest extent. His fingers brushed the tassel, then clasped it.

'Careful – we don't know what's on the other end!' warned Dora.

He pulled it steadily. Something metal rattled and bumped. Rather than risk yanking it down on his head, he groped until his fingers met a handle. He lifted it down.

'A lantern.' Dora took it from him and examined it more closely. 'Pierced tin, and made for a candle. It would cast a pattern on a wall at night.'

Jacob was inspecting the silk rope. 'There's something in the weave. It has been untwisted then retwisted. One moment.' He cut the threads at the end and shook out the strands. A slip of paper fell out. Dora snatched it up before it could be blown away.

'It's a map of England. In fact, I recognise it. We were both taught from Middleton's *System of Geography* – that's the page for our country.'

'Are there any marks on it?'

She walked to the door for the best light. 'None that I can see on the map, but Anthony has written something in pencil along the bottom. "Modest doubt".' Dora closed her eyes. 'I know it. It's from Shakespeare. *Troilus and Cressida*. The sentence completes – "Is called the beacon of the wise."'

'Let me look at the lantern.' Jacob studied the pattern cut into the tin. At first glance it seemed to be just a pretty flower pattern, then he noticed that one of the piercings had been made larger, spoiling the symmetry. 'Is this the wise beacon? He's made one of these bigger. In fact, it's a cross.'

'Anthony is making it obvious for me.' Dora looked from the map to the lantern. 'So if we lit the candle and held up the map to the pattern it casts, that might tell us something? Do you have your tinderbox?'

Jacob was as eager as her to solve the puzzle now rather than wait until dark. He ran back to the cart to fetch his box. Between them, they managed to light the candle and secure it back in the socket. The pattern danced on the wall. Dora held up the map but that was ridiculously small compared to the light speckles.

'I don't know how to hold this.' She tried moving it further away, then close to. 'The cross could indicate anything on this map. At the moment, it is out at sea.'

'There has to be something that fixes it in place – a piece of information that we aren't yet seeing. Bring it closer. Let's make it so the shadow is the same size as the page.'

Now the fiery flower shone intensely on the map.

'The cross mark lies to the southeast of the centre of the flower. Where would your brother consider as his centre?'

'Here – the caves?'

Jacob tried lining that up and it gave them an answer somewhere in the Channel.

'It will be worse if we try our family home in London,' said Dora. 'He can't have travelled to France to hide this thing.'

'But he could have sent it there with a courier? Unlikely, but not impossible.' He lined up London with the centre and the cross fell near Calais. 'We have to leave that on the table to be considered. It would be a good way of getting it away from his enemies.'

'To send it to the great enemy of Napoleon's empire? That's strange logic.'

'What about where he was born?'

'Our estate near Liverpool? Try lining it up a little to the east of the city.'

As they watched, the cross danced into a blank space on the map.

'Lincolnshire. What connection did he have there?'

'None at all, as far as I know,' admitted Dora.

Jacob rubbed his temple. There was something at the back of his mind, some memory that refused to make itself known.

'I think we need to sleep on this. Maybe the solution will present itself if we don't think about it directly.'

Dora blew out the candle and they let their eyes adjust to the gloom again. 'I thought we'd solve this today. I thought we'd get rid of this part of the business and concentrate on finding the murderer.'

He held open the door for her. 'I was never so sanguine. Something tells me that finding one will find us the other.'

Chapter Thirty-Four

West Wycombe

Safely returned to the rectory, Dora contemplated the dress Jacob had found for her. It wasn't completely awful – rose silk with seashell-shaped trimmings; a little too sweet for her – but whose was it and how had he got hold of it? Jacob was something of a mystery to her – reticent yet passionate, as though the emotions were bubbling away not far under his cool exterior. That embrace they had shared outside the abbey had been one of the most memorable in her life and they'd only got as far as kissing. What would they be like if they wound up in a bed? Sensing her wits fleeing, she had cut it short, much to her regret at the time. Now, in the sanity of her bedchamber, she knew it had been the right thing. He was the son of a viscount and a collector of manuscripts, and she an actress who specialised in forging – there would be no common ground. The disadvantages of an affair – loss of respect, danger of pregnancy, hating herself afterwards – meant she was playing with fire each time she gave in to the attraction she felt for him.

She slipped into the silk gown. It felt like a caress as it slid down her body. She fastened the cream sash under her bust and fixed a matching ribbon in her hair. Her stockings were a disgrace – plain cotton and darned – but the skirt hid them. However, one essential item was missing. Maybe she would have a reprieve after all?

There came a knock at the door.

'Yes?'

Jacob stuck his head around the jamb. 'What about these?' He held out a pair of evening gloves, slightly yellowed with age.

'These belong to my chaperone, I guess?'

'Yes. And you now owe me for the difficulty I had persuading her to part with them for an evening.'

'I will take care of them.' The provision of gloves had spoiled her plan to cry off with the excuse that her arms were not decently covered. Accepting now that she had to go, she took the gloves and squeezed her hands into them. 'I'm just afraid I'll split them.'

Jacob held out an elbow. 'You look very well indeed.'

'Thank you – and so do you. Don't tell me you borrowed that from Reverend Leighton?' Jacob was wearing a dark blue long-tailed jacket that even Beau Brummell would not despise.

'No, of course not. I sent a note to Sir Fletcher. He obliged me by sending your gown and my jacket.'

She should have thought of that. Vane was the only person in the neighbourhood who could outfit a lady and gentleman at the last moment.

'Have you left the lantern in a safe place?' she asked.

'In my room.'

'But that's not safe!'

'Safer than drawing attention to it. No one knows we have it – not even Leighton. I've put it on a shelf in a dark corner. If anyone does search my room while we are out, they are far more likely to rummage through my saddlebags and scatter things about in their hurry.'

So he had been nursing that grievance, had he?

She grinned. 'Time was of the essence. Neatness was not.'

Walking into the ball between Reverend Leighton and Jacob, Dora tried hard not to be impressed by the magnificent arrangements. The entrance hall was filled with flowers and attentive servants to whisk away cloaks and hats. They were ushered through to the music room, where the dancing was already underway. This was a large chamber with a white marble fireplace, salmon-pink walls and an exuberantly painted ceiling.

'Don't you think it odd,' whispered Dora, 'that the pictures on the walls are so respectable but up above there is an orgy of the gods going on?'

Jacob blinked and then looked up. 'I'm so used to seeing such motifs that I've become impervious, but you are right. I think that is the banquet of Cupid and Psyche, after Rafael.'

'Nobody wore clothes at their feast?'

'It would seem not.'

Fortunately, the guests were more conventionally dressed, though Dora did notice that the female guests were drawn from the wild widows of society and the demimonde rather than the ranks of respectable wives and virginal daughters. The colours were bolder, the dresses more daring and the behaviour more forthright. Her pink dress moved in her estimation from 'sweet' to the same hue as the goddesses above. Just as well her own skin tone was darker, otherwise she would look semi-naked.

'Is Vane one of the club, do you think?' Dora asked.

'If he is happy hosting such a gathering, I'd be surprised if he was not. Speak of the devil...'

Their host approached. Dora bobbed a curtsy as Leighton and Jacob bowed.

'Delighted you decided to come!' Vane said expansively.

Not that he'd left them much choice, thought Dora.

'And I see my wife's gown does fit. I'm so pleased that I could assist with such a little matter that stood in the way of your enjoyment.'

Had he forgotten that she was in mourning? The pink was hardly appropriate for her situation. Still, she had to remember that they were here for her brother, not to kick up their heels and forget him. Vane stood at the head of a list of people whom she suspected of being involved in his death. She had to draw comfort from the thought that her purpose here was to avenge Anthony by exposing his killer.

'Sir Fletcher, you mentioned that you would introduce me to those who knew my brother best,' she said with what she hoped was a winning smile.

He took her hand prisoner and placed it on his arm. 'Absolutely, my dear, and you must dance at least one set. Sandys, I am unashamedly stealing your partner from you. I imagine you and the reverend would like to join the card players in the next room?' With that heavy hint that their chaperonage was no longer required, Dora found herself taken from her friends. He was as skilful as a collie separating a herd of sheep.

'I believe they are about to start a cotillion.' He led her swiftly across the floor. 'Ah, here is another couple to make up our four. Bates, may I make known to you Miss Dora Fitz-Pennington?'

Bates, a rotund man with high colour and a mop of brown curls, almost fell over himself bowing.

'It is an honour. I've heard so much about you from your brother. Please accept my condolences at this sad time.' His voice was a pleasant tenor, with a hint of Wales in his accent.

Dora blushed and gestured her hand towards her gown. If

only there had been another chance to meet him. 'Thank you. I would have stayed away but Sir Fletcher promised me that I would meet his friends and I couldn't pass up the opportunity.'

'Pennington would not have it any other way. He would urge you to dance, to drink and to be merry in his honour.'

Bates was correct, of course. Her brother would despise moping.

He turned to the lady on his arm. 'May I present my good friend, Miss Mary Wheeler.'

Only the very strictest stage training prevented Dora from showing her shock at finding the Henley woman very much alive.

'Miss Wheeler.' She bobbed a curtsy. 'Lovely to meet you.'

The young woman who was supposed to be dead smiled broadly, displaying a gap in her front teeth that suited her earthy charms of a milkmaid complexion and an abundant figure. 'Miss.'

'Let us join the dance, shall we,' said Sir Fletcher, unaware he had just handed her a very unexpected piece in this puzzle that they were assembling.

Dora looked about for Jacob but couldn't see him. He had probably gone to the card room as instructed and was doing his share of enquiries in there with the gentlemen. She rather stumbled through the first few moves before she reminded herself that she had a part to play. If Sir Fletcher realised that his introduction to Bates' partner had produced this confusion, he might become too interested in why. Far better for her to acquit herself well and look for an opportunity to question the lady.

The dance took up her concentration for the next ten minutes. The cotillion was a familiar pattern but she hadn't been to a ball of this refinement before. The rough and ready dances she attended in local assembly halls and public houses put much less emphasis on accuracy than on enjoyment. Hopefully she did not make a spectacle of herself, following her partner's lead. The second dance of her pair with Sir Fletcher passed quickly as her

The Persephone Code

confidence grew. She spent it wondering how to get Mary on her own and debating whether she should tell her what had happened to her erstwhile suitor. The ballroom might be the very definition of the worst place, especially if the killer himself was in attendance, but when else would she get the opportunity?

She curtsied at the end of the set, hoping Sir Fletcher would release her from his attention but he seemed unaware she wanted to escape.

'Miss Wheeler, I fear I might have torn my hem. Would you accompany me to the retiring room?' she asked, a little desperately.

Mary looked surprised by the sudden request, as well she might. They had no prior acquaintance.

'Nonsense, my dear, one of my maids can fix that for you. Let's not bother a guest.' Sir Fletcher made it sound like she had insulted the woman with a request for menial service. 'Let me take you to one now.' Patting her hand, he steered her out of the ballroom.

'But surely you can't leave the ball! You're the host,' Dora protested. Damnation, this was the opposite of what she wanted.

'As the host I can do very much what I will.'

Was that an echo of the Hellfire Club motto? Dora very much did not want to go off into the parts of the house where there were no other guests.

'Not to worry. My hem can wait.'

'I believe it is my wife's hem, so I say that it cannot. She will have my head when she gets back from town if she discovers a favourite gown spoiled.'

Dora glimpsed Jacob standing by a card table, observing play. Their eyes met briefly and she sent him a desperate look. He moved rapidly to intersect with their path.

'Ah, the gallant companion returns.' Sir Fletcher sounded

highly amused. 'Sandys, I fear I must deprive you of your partner for another short time while I take her to the sewing room.'

'Miss Fitz-Pennington?' Jacob asked.

'I'm all right.' Dora forced down the flutterings of panic. If he knew where she was, then that meant he would come looking if there was a delay. 'You really must meet my brother's old friend, William Bates, and his lady, Miss Mary Wheeler.' She tried not to put too much emphasis on the name, common enough in these parts, but hoped he got the message.

'I must?' His momentary puzzlement cleared. 'Indeed, it would be my pleasure.'

Sir Fletcher looked over the heads of the dancers. 'You'll find them by the refreshment table, I believe. Now, Miss Fitz-Pennington, let's see to that hem so we can return for the next set.'

Unable to back out of her lie, Dora allowed herself to be led away.

Chapter Thirty-Five

Vane steered her down a corridor lined with Dashwood portraits and took her through a library.

'The sewing room is this way?' She glanced over her shoulder. The bright lights of the ballroom spilled out into the passage but where they now walked was illuminated only by the occasional candelabra, separated by pools of darkness.

'I think we both know there is nothing wrong with your hem,' he said coolly.

Dora's mind raced through the possible motives for bringing her here then. A dalliance was the least threatening.

'I really should get back to Dr Sandys. I promised him the next dance.'

'In here, please, Dora.' The overly familiar term of address signalled that the pretence was dropping from him like an actor stepping offstage.

'I'd prefer to return to the ballroom.' She pulled away but he held tight.

'My house, my rules.' With a hand at her back clutching the material of her dress, he propelled her inside his study. The air held the tang of tobacco and she looked about her at the shelves of books and a large desk, trying to get the measure of the man. A full-length portrait of Sir Francis Dashwood hung opposite so that sitting at the desk would mean looking up at him each time you raised your eyes. This was wrong.

'Then it is best I quit your house now as I do not take kindly to being forced.' Dora pulled her arm free and turned to leave.

'Not until you've heard what I have to say. If you leave, you will never find out what happened to your brother.'

Her hand stilled on the doorknob. She turned to look at him. His jade-green eyes were as cold and hard as tombstones.

'What do you know about Anthony's death?'

Satisfied that her curiosity was caught, he sat down in an armchair beside the hearth and gestured her to take the seat across from him. She perched on the edge, hands folded in her lap. Rising again, he took one of the new-fangled cigars from a box on the side table and lit it from the candle on the mantlepiece before resuming his position. It looked like she was being given a glimpse behind the man's mask, here in this room that had no signs of his wife's influence.

'I think we both know that my knowledge of your brother's end is extensive.' He gestured with the cigar, the tip etching a glowing circle in the air.

'Is that a confession?'

'Do you think me simpleminded?'

'I think you a villain.'

He laughed. 'My dear, you've played too long on the stage. The real world is not divided into heroes and villains. We are all just people – selfish, driven by appetites, maintaining a veneer of what we call civilisation so as not to scare off the ladies. We battle to make reason king, but you must know that we are baser creatures under all that, and there is no shame in coming to terms with the truth.'

'You belong to the Hellfire Club?'

'Oh no. I despise them heartily. I came here with the very purpose of destroying them; undoing the work of that monster.' He gestured to the portrait and paused for a taste of his cigar. 'Boys squeaking at the devil they only half believe in. Your brother was one of those, as you know.'

'So your allegiance is to the Illuminati?' Dora took pride in her cool tone.

His eyes shone with pleasure that he was facing a worthy adversary. 'Ah, you worked that out, did you? Or was it Sandys? My men said you nimbly gave them the slip twice in the north, thanks to his intervention.'

Dora rather thought she could take the credit for those escapes but let him believe that. The last thing she wanted was for him to take her seriously as a threat. *Act your part, Dora*, she chided herself. She let her spine sag just a little and dipped her chin.

'He said they bore the symbol of the Eye of Horus.'

'He recognised that? It is a rather obscure mark. I wonder, is he one of us too?' Vane stroked his chin, pondering. 'I don't claim to know all the members in England.'

'He's an antiquarian and knew it from his travels in Egypt.'

'Ah. Pity.' He puffed on the cigar, inspecting her through the billow of smoke.

Dora crushed the pink silk of her skirt beneath her fingers. 'Why have you brought me here, Sir Fletcher? What can you gain from it? People know I'm with you – Dr Sandys saw us leave. I came in with the rector and I am his guest. You can hardly hope to make me disappear without bringing suspicion upon yourself.'

'Indeed.'

How much danger was she in exactly? 'Did you kill those women?'

'No. All those I end deserve their punishment. Their deaths are not on my conscience.'

She rather believed him. 'Then why?' She wished she could remain as silent as he did because it was the position of power in this conversation, but she wanted answers. Studying her, he let the stillness continue until it was unbearable. Then he smiled.

'Congratulations, my dear. You have accepted the position of my latest mistress.'

'I've what?' Where had that come from?

'Tonight we will leave for my house in London. My wife has gone to Bath for her health so you will be welcome. There you will lead me to the key that your brother left you.'

A sickening certainty settled in her chest. He was the one who had read the letter.

'Key?'

'Don't play dumb, Dora. It doesn't suit you. Why do you think I sent people after you? Your brother left you a letter in my cottage and in it he wrote that you would know the key. That key leads to great power – but only if found in time to be of any use. Events in the field make it less relevant each day it sits hidden.'

'I don't understand.'

'I don't need you to. All you need do is be a pretty step along the way for me. Though I have to say that he used his last words to beg that we leave you alone, which was foolish when the letter pointed us directly at you.'

If he knew what Anthony's last words were…

'What did he say?' she asked quietly, as her hatred for Vane mounted to giddy heights. He had killed her brother – this was practically a confession!

'"Not Dora". Quite touching really. He didn't mind me approaching your father. Said he would like to see that happen, but you he wished to keep above the fray.'

'And did you approach my father?'

'Your objectionable sire is alive and well, never fear.'

He hadn't answered her question but Dora thought it likely

from the amused glint in his eye that he had already tried Ezra Pennington and discovered nothing from him.

'And if I refuse to come?'

'That would be unfortunate.'

'How so?'

'If you refuse to cooperate, your good friends, the rector and the doctor, will be shot in a freak accident by my people, who will mistake them for poachers as they return home tonight. So sad.'

'I'll warn them.' She got up.

'Really? You will run out there raving about how I threatened to kill my guests? How do you think that would go? I will be close at your heels to overhear your wild accusations. My servants will restrain you for your own good and I'm sure I can persuade the rector, if not the doctor, that you would be better taken to an asylum before you do more damage to my reputation. Women are locked up for less. It really isn't a fair country.'

Frustration built. She wanted to kill him for this. 'They won't believe you.'

'Would you like to put it to the test?' He waved to the door, daring her to run. 'Shooting is not the only way of removing obstacles such as your friends. Houses do burn down very easily.'

Dora remembered the Illuminati arsonist, Peter Fosse, who'd had no qualms about setting fire to a barn to get to them – and decided Vane would be very likely to carry out his threat. If not he himself, some lackey who would do it on his orders. Just how guilty was he though? How many deaths was he responsible for?

'Did you kill Matt Jenkins?'

'Matt who?'

'The boy found hanged in the caves. He was just a poor lad, no threat to anyone.'

'He won't be missed then.' Vane stubbed out his cigar. 'Come, which is it to be? The asylum or the trip to London as my new mistress?'

That was one thing she would never do. 'No—'

'In name only. I have no desire to have you in my bed.'

How much was that promise worth? Very little. Dora wanted to scratch his eyes out but she had to think quickly. He'd had time to set this trap for her. Being bundled off to an asylum would remove the possibility of escape. Doubtless he had doctors in his pay who would swear she was mad and she would lose all rights and be subjected to humiliating treatment. She knew full well what went on in Bedlam and such places. Could she turn the trap so it caught him? If she went peacefully with him, she would be uninjured and could find her chance to slip away. He wanted to find whatever it was her brother had kept from him. He had no idea about the clues she and Jacob had already found. Taking him to London was moving him away from the lantern and the map, giving Jacob a clear run at solving that part of the puzzle.

If the worst came to the worst, she could look for a chance to kill him. People of her station did not expect the courts to do the job for them. Kill him then flee to America. That might be the best plan of all. Certainly the simplest.

Both ideas required him to let his guard down around her a little. She had to play to the expectation he had of her. Gentlemen tended to assume that actresses were easy of their virtue and happy to do anything if the money was right. Let him think so of her because it would fool him into believing he understood her.

She changed her stance, tilting her shoulders back to display her figure to advantage, her movements more sinuous. *Thank you, Cleopatra, for an education in how to be seductive.*

'All right, Sir Fletcher, I'll come with you. There is no need for us to be at odds. It is actually a timely invitation. I am in need of a change. The north is too parochial; it is time I went to London to seek my next protector.'

He raised a brow. 'I was under the impression that Sandys was your protector?'

The Persephone Code

'He lives in the Lakes. What use have I for lakes and mountains, a place where there is no society that would receive one such as I?'

'You are shrewd. You would only ever be his guilty secret, stuck in some cottage somewhere having to cut your own wood and bake your own bread.' He chuckled at the picture he conjured. 'Good. Then let me phrase this another way: if you help me recover the secrets your brother hid, I will set you up with a goodly sum so you can take your time looking about you for your next gentleman. I can even make some introductions.'

He would be her procurer, would he?

'How kind of you. That is generous indeed.' That sounded too gushing. 'Not that I need the assistance.'

'Indeed not. Your charms speak for themselves. As does your level-headedness. We have an agreement?'

This was going to slaughter any chance she had of keeping Jacob's friendship.

'We do.'

'Then you will understand if I prefer you not to return to the ballroom. I welcome but do not trust your change of tune. You will leave Sandys a note so he does not follow you – a message I will dictate and you will not deviate by a single word. I have a coach ready for you. It would not do for us to be seen leaving together – for my wife's sake. I'll join you in town tomorrow.'

That was excellent. She could search his house in London, slip away and not even see him again.

'I'll be sending a guard with you, naturally.' He cleared his throat and a familiar red-headed man entered from the library. 'I believe you know the Honourable Peter Fosse?'

Chapter Thirty-Six

Dora had not returned, though their host had – some ten minutes ago.

Jacob prowled the edges of the ballroom, his eyes travelling up repeatedly to the ceiling she had pointed out. How had he taken for granted the pictures of fleshy gods in all the houses he had visited, even his father's? Now they appeared to be a warning. The story of Cupid and Psyche, for example, was it a lesson not to look too closely at your lover or suffer for the presumption? The most memorable moment in the story happened long before this feast, when Psyche dared to hold a candle to the face of her mysterious husband and found she was married to a god, not a monster as she had feared. Yet her ensuing sufferings were immense, cast out as she was and made to undergo trials to prove her worth. So was Cupid not a monstrous god for all his beauty? Were the Dashwoods saying something about themselves? We can behave as we like; your role is not to look too closely?

It could apply to the current occupier of the mansion too, surely?

Impatience grew, then anxiety. He wanted to tell Dora about

The Persephone Code

his conversation with the resurrected Mary Wheeler but there was no sign of her. She wasn't dancing or lingering by the refreshments. Nor was she out on the balcony or among the card players. Leighton said he hadn't seen her since she quit the ballroom on their host's arm. That left Jacob no choice but to approach Vane. Suspicious though they were of their host, he surely could not have done anything to a guest, not during a ball?

He fixed on his social smile.

'Sir Fletcher, I have mislaid my companion. Have you seen her?'

Vane nodded a farewell to the men he was talking to. 'Ah, Sandys, I was hoping for a word. Please, come.' He led him out onto a balcony overlooking the garden. 'Would you mind if we talked man to man for a moment?'

'Is there another choice?'

'Quite.' Vane's smile was tight, humourless. 'It is about Dora.'

The use of her Christian name came as a jolt. 'Miss Fitz-Pennington?'

Vane tapped his fingers on the stone rail of the balcony. 'I have to admit that I was smitten by her when you called on me yesterday. I pity her vulnerable situation, particularly now her brother is taken from her.'

'She is not without friends.'

'True, and I have volunteered to be one of them. A very special one. If that treads on your toes, then please forgive me. Passion only is my excuse.'

Jacob couldn't quite get his whirling mind around what was being said. 'Dora?'

'Yes. Putting it bluntly, she's accepted my protection and has gone ahead to London to take up her new role as my mistress.'

Jacob reeled. As far as he knew, all Dora felt towards this man was suspicion. Had Vane coerced her? What had he done to her?

'I don't believe you.'

'Ah. She said you would be angry as she suspected you were rather expecting to offer her similar terms, but she prefers life in London to the Lakes. She wished to avoid a painful interview with you and instead left you this note.' He handed over a folded piece of paper. 'Sorry, old boy, but all's fair in love and war.'

Vane returned to the ballroom, leaving Jacob standing on the balcony. The other guests who had wandered out here gave Jacob interested glances but he turned his back on them. The orchestra struck up a lively number and the floorboards thumped with the rhythmic jumps of the dance. He shook open the note.

Dear Dr Sandys,

Please forgive my hasty departure. I have decided to take the opportunity that has presented itself so unexpectedly and start a new life in London under Sir Fletcher Vane's protection. Thank you for your escort from the north and I send my best wishes and thanks to Reverend Leighton. A servant will come to collect my few belongings as I am leaving tonight.

I wish you well with your future endeavours. It will be best to forget we ever knew each other. Should our paths cross, I will not acknowledge the acquaintance and suggest you do not also. Please don't be a bore and make our acquaintance out as anything more serious than the chance encounter of two strangers who quickly tired of each other.

Yours

Dora Fitz-Pennington

Sandys crushed the letter in his fist. This did not sound like the letter of a reluctant lady. The tone was practical but also exuberant. With his inability to work at his profession, his weakness for opium, he knew he was no prize for a woman. He could hardly be surprised that she had jumped on the better offer.

Stop those uncharitable thoughts! He thumped the balustrade. Those were stupid deductions, not true to the Dora he knew. The letter had been written to prick his confidence. He was falling for the ruse when she expected him to see through it, surely? What about murder, her brother, the Illuminati on their tail? There was no mention of any of that. He scanned the letter again. Was there some hidden message, some plea that all was not as it appeared?

He rested his palms on the stone rail and hung his head between his arms.

Yet it was a rare actress who did not succumb to the lure of taking an easier route to riches.

No, he wouldn't believe it. Vane had some hold over her. She might even be in danger.

Furious that Dora had agreed to this even under duress, he stuffed the mangled letter into his pocket. He would follow her and get the truth from her own mouth before he believed her words.

He was about to storm into the ballroom and find out if she had left already, then realised what a ridiculous figure he would cut.

He had been feet away from her all evening. If she had needed his help, why had she not appealed to him?

The infuriating woman was the only one with any answers.

Leighton appeared at his side before he could cross the chamber to go after her.

'Sir Fletcher just told me not to expect Miss Fitz-Pennington back. His words were coded but am I right in thinking she has accepted an immoral proposal from him?' His face was wrinkled with pastoral concern mingled with distaste.

Jacob's irritation at his friend's phrasing made his retort sharp.

'She is protecting her interests. Morals are a luxury of those who do not have to wonder where their next meal is coming from.'

Leighton sighed. 'Indeed. I fear you are correct. Our Lord had a special place at his side for the sinners and he despised the hypocrites.' He looked away at the swirling couples – many of the ladies of the painted variety associated with the Magdalene. 'I just wish she had applied to me before taking this course of action. I would have done all in my power to help.'

'As would I,' muttered Jacob, then more loudly, 'Still, she's gone and we can't ask her tonight.'

They headed for the door though the dance was far from over.

'You intend to ask her? Go after her and so forth?'

Of course he did. There was still the crime to solve and the mystery of what Pennington had hidden from his murderer. Dora had not returned for the lantern which had been her first concern when leaving this evening for the ball. Was Vane isolating Dora so she would be easier to manipulate? He might be dangling promises before her in exchange for information. Surely she must realise that Vane's offer was only valid for as long as she was useful to him? If he was Pennington's murderer, or knew the identity of that person and was protecting him, she was in grave danger.

'You look troubled,' Leighton said. 'Forgive me if I am encroaching on private affairs, but I was under the impression that you and Miss Fitz-Pennington had tender feelings for one another. This must come as a serious disappointment to you.'

'A disappointment, but not serious.' His tone was glib. He didn't want Leighton to know how deeply this abandonment had cut.

'Do you think you've made any progress with your investigation?' They walked out to the area that had been lit for the convenience of guests and headed for the quiet path back through the park.

'Some,' hedged Jacob. 'I find our host a likely candidate. He knew Pennington better than he admitted and has been very interested in us since he heard of our arrival.'

'Sir Fletcher?' Leighton shook his head. 'Then think again. A man more opposed to the Hellfire Club you would struggle to find. He thinks them childish and despises them. The gentlemen of the area who are of that persuasion know better than to invite him to their revels.'

'Revels is rather a tame word. I note that some of them were here tonight. I met William Bates. You mentioned him yourself as one who brought Pennington into those circles. Why would he associate with someone who despises his club?'

Leighton chuckled. 'My dear Sandys, you mistake a gentlemanly difference of opinion about how they entertain themselves for something as divisive as a religious principle or two nations at war! The Houses of Parliament are filled with gentlemen who openly oppose each other's views and yet will appear alongside each other at the same dinner parties and balls, even some of the same clubs in St James's.'

'If Vane is not a member of the Hellfire fraternity, then what is he?'

'Need he be anything? He works for the Alien Office. He follows the motto "Keep your friends close and your enemies closer".' Leighton waved back towards the ballroom where the dancing continued. 'I would not be surprised to find some French officers in there, captured and released on their parole not to act against our country, awaiting a prisoner exchange. I've met several since Vane came to the parish. A very civilised arrangement that I hope our officers enjoy in France. Vane oversees the exchanges for Spencer Perceval's government.'

Jacob well understood that Vane enjoyed intrigue. No one who helped run the government intelligence service out of the Alien Office would pass up the opportunity to observe the enemy or turn them into an agent on release. But what if Vane's loyalty wasn't to king and country but to something quite different?

'Could he be an Illuminati?'

Leighton gave an unbridled laugh at that. 'Illuminati? Good

gracious, Sandys, Sir Fletcher is a sensible man; his career is in Whitehall. He's obsessed with hunting and, unfortunately, as we now see, with the same weaknesses as many a man who does not keep his marital vows. Look elsewhere for your culprit.'

Jacob was about to make a reply to this overly complacent statement when a crack split the night. Leighton went down with a cry of pain, clutching his side.

'I've been shot!' he gasped.

Jacob swore and hunkered down beside him. He located the entry wound. Not a mortal wound but not negligible either.

A second shot smashed bark from the closest tree.

'Poachers?' asked Leighton.

'There are people here, goddamn you!' Jacob shouted.

The reply was a third bullet, this one hitting a statue of a young Greek and carrying away his trident. Not poachers.

They were sitting ducks unless Jacob could get them into better cover than this bush. There was a white-domed structure on a little hillock ahead – the Temple of Venus, one of the many follies that dotted the garden. That would have to do. Pulling Leighton's arm over his shoulder, he lifted the man.

'Here, press this to the wound.' He handed Leighton his cravat wadded up into a pad. 'Just a little way. I'll put you somewhere safe, then get help.'

'Thank ... you,' rasped Leighton.

A fourth shot was their reward for breaking cover. Jacob flinched, memories of past battles coming back to him – the feeling that the next bullet would have his name on it; flashes of those who fell at his side when it sailed past him and indiscriminately hit another. There had been guilt in that relief.

Reaching the temple, he took Leighton round to the small aperture at the base, another of the anatomical jokes of the Hellfire founder but much more easily defended than the open temple. He propped Leighton against the wall.

'Stay here and make no sound. You won't be seen if you don't move. I'll draw them away.'

Leighton clutched his hand.

'Sandys, I'm sorry I dragged you into this.'

Too late for regrets. 'Hush now. They will only find you if you give your position away. I won't be long.'

Jacob reversed course up the hill, making sure his silhouette was seen in the colonnaded temple. A fifth shot hit poor Venus, chipping her breast.

'Piss-poor aim, thank God,' he muttered as he sprinted away. The shooter was in the woods between him and the house, so he ran for the carriage drive, banking on other guests being present. Failing that, he'd run to the village and appeal for help at the George and Dragon.

That was if the dragon firing at his friend George did not get him next.

Chapter Thirty-Seven

Road to London

Now she knew what it felt like to be the mouse under the cat's claws.

Peter Fosse stared at her from the opposite seat in Vane's carriage. Something malevolent was building between them. She had chosen to sit with her back to the direction of travel rather than next to him but wondered now if that had been the right choice. It was hard to appear nonchalant with his gaze boring into her. She buttoned her coat. Silk ball dresses did not make a good defence against such looks. Thank heavens for her greatcoat.

She was tempted – oh, how she was tempted – to ask how was his foot. Prudence warned against mentioning that sore subject.

Hiding her smirk with her gloved hand, she looked out of the window at the passing countryside. Then she remembered that she had promised to return the gloves, cherished possession as they were of Leighton's elderly aunt. Thinking of preserving the fragile kid skin, she peeled them off her fingers. When had the lady ever worn such an item, she wondered. They were very fine, with pearl buttons.

'If you are thinking of seducing me to win my favour, think again,' said Fosse.

Better not to address that comment. She folded the gloves and slipped them into one of her pockets. The coat was the only possession that she'd had with her when she had embarked on this unexpected journey. Her thoughts turned to her bag left at the rectory. Was it too much to hope that it would be packed up without anyone – and she meant Jacob – looking at the keepsake book?

Consternation rose as she remembered she still had the forged Jonson manuscript tucked between the pages. If Jacob didn't immediately think it a fake, then he would surely swiftly put it together when he saw the company it was keeping with the samples of handwriting.

'You don't look well, Dora,' said Fosse. 'Carriage travel not agreeing with you? Perhaps try sitting forwards?' He patted the seat next to him.

Nothing would make her put herself within reach of his hands.

She had to distract him. Besides, she wanted information.

'Why do you do it?' she asked instead, keeping her tone light as if this was mere social chitchat.

'Do what?'

'Run around with the Illuminati?'

He hissed. 'You dare speak of us so lightly?'

'I have no idea who you really are or why I should care.'

If she was hoping to provoke him into an explanation, she had failed. Her reply conjured a smile.

'Good. We don't want to be known by the likes of you.'

That told her, didn't it? Time to poke a little harder. 'Who is in charge? Napoleon? Talleyrand?'

'We aren't working for the enemy.'

'And yet you do the enemy's work in England? How does that square with not being a traitor?'

'I've taken an oath not to kill you, but I can still make you suffer.' With a vicious smile, he lunged at her, but she slid aside so he merely got a fistful of skirt. Her heart was pounding, a match to the fast thumping of the carriage. This wasn't good. She should have left well alone.

He yanked the skirt up and groped her thighs with cold hands. Her outrage soared but had nowhere to go; nowhere to retreat to.

'Time for payback for my foot,' he growled, the sour scent of a man in rut filling the carriage. 'As a whore, you understand this currency best, don't you?'

Panic rising, she tried shoving him off, but he resisted easily, his thumbs pressing into vulnerable flesh, trying to force her legs apart. Her hands were trapped between their bodies.

Dora tried to headbutt him, but he jerked back.

'Get off me! Driver! Help!' She shrieked until she was hoarse.

He laughed cruelly. 'They won't help you. They'll just want their turn.'

This wasn't the first time she'd had to fight for herself. She had to do something – and quickly.

His lips were slobbering on her neck, teeth nipping, then biting. What was she – a bloody apple? She reached for the most incendiary thing she could say.

'Did you kill my brother? Or was that your master?'

Pressing her down with his bodyweight, he grabbed her throat and squeezed. 'I have no master.'

'You ... keep telling ... yourself that,' she gasped. She dug her nails into the backs of his hands. 'I'm sure he didn't give you orders to rape me. If you do this, I'm out. He needs me and I'll tell him exactly what you did and why I won't help him.'

'Bitch!' He shoved her away from him. 'We're on a shared

mission. There is no servant or master in our circle.' But Vane scared him. Good to know. That might be her only shield.

Dora rubbed her chest. His grip had left bruises there and on her thighs. Bastard. 'Mission? To do what, beat up defenceless women?' Had he been the one to kill the girls? Her neck suggested he could have.

Breathing heavily, Fosse resumed his seat. 'To break the world … and rebuild it as it should have been.' He wiped his mouth on the back of his sleeve as though one taste of her had been disgusting.

The feeling was entirely mutual.

'How should it have been? Freedom to rape and kill?'

'Men of reason should be in power, not fat princes and senile old lords.'

'That's it? Oh yes, I can testify to how reasoned you are. Not a vile passion or criminal urge in you.' Her laugh was dark, and somewhat desperate, as she straightened her clothing. She found Matt Jenkins's knife still in her pocket and grasped it in a shaking hand. If he came at her again, he'd get a surprise. 'You have no political creed? No aims other than the transfer of power to yourselves?'

He looked furious to be asked to drill down deeper into his shallow pond of ideas.

'Things will be much better once we have sound people at the helm.'

'Better for whom?' she asked.

They completed the journey in fuming silence. She did not let go of the knife for a single second.

The carriage arrived in London in the early hours of the morning. Dora jumped out quickly, only to be escorted up to a bedroom and locked inside. At least Fosse hadn't accompanied her, instead handing her over to a stern-faced footman. It was a profound relief to see the back of Fosse. Never again would she allow herself to be in a room or carriage alone with him. His attack had shaken her, particularly as his veneer of civility had been so quickly abandoned. Her miscalculation had almost cost her dear.

Taking off her coat, she went immediately to the window to examine the chance of escape should he come at her again. Her hand trembled as she tried the latch. Closing her eyes a moment, she took deep breaths, demanding that her body steady itself so she could think. The chamber was on the second floor, giving a view across a wide street in one of the wealthy areas of London. She didn't recognize it but guessed she couldn't be far from Mayfair, with its elegant classical facades and the black iron railings keeping the commoners away. The climb down would require a rope of some kind – curtains or bedsheets would serve. If she avoided impaling herself on the railing of the basement enclosure, she would survive. That was a comfort – her life's mission had always been to make sure she had a choice. Not that she was planning on leaving so soon. The Illuminati might think they were using her, but she had resolved to use them – at the very least keep them busy so Jacob could get there first. He had the lantern and should be working on the next clue. If he beat them to the goal, he would use it to crush Vane and his conspirators.

Big words for three o'clock in the morning, Dora, she thought. *You, who barely avoided being raped but an hour ago.*

Sitting at the dressing table to trim the candles, she caught sight of her appearance in the trio of mirrors. Her hair was tumbling down, her neck reddened, and she looked shaken – a tree caught in a spring storm, its blossom ravaged. The assault had awoken memories of the worst time in her life, recollections she avoided like stagnant water. Added to that, the last few days had been one endless journey. She'd lost count of the miles.

'No weakness,' she told her reflection.

That Dora looked back at her with fear rather than defiance. She turned away to the bed.

Sleep first, and then she would gather her strength for the fight ahead.

The next challenge came at breakfast. This was going to be a civilised kind of prison, she realised, on entering the dining room.

'Dora, how did you sleep? I hope you had a good journey?' asked Vane from his position at the head of the table. He did not rise on her entrance. She chose the seat halfway down the table – a neutral position – continuing the ruse that she was cooperating with her situation. They were the only two in the room. If Fosse had slept here, he had not yet emerged. If he entered the room, she worried that she would not be able to maintain her composure. He revolted her to her very soul. Vane, however, did not look as if he'd suffered from his late-night journey. He'd probably slept in his carriage, something she could not have afforded to do.

Had he asked Fosse to attack her, she wondered. It was a very effective way of making her see Vane as the lesser of two evils.

'I slept very well, thank you.' She helped herself to some bread and spread on blackcurrant jam. 'The journey was uneventful.' A footman entered, bringing her a silver teapot and cup, and placed it so she could pour for herself.

'I believe you and Dr Sandys were already working on finding what your brother hid before he died.' Vane cut up his bacon with precise movements.

Dora poured her tea. 'We were.'

'Tell me what you have discovered so far.'

How much to tell him? She wouldn't put it past him to have watched their movements since they arrived. Had he even had them followed to Henley and Medmenham Abbey? 'You know of my brother's letter so you will understand that he left us a puzzle. We have been looking for a key.'

'You searched his house and went into the caves. Did you find it?'

He would be suspicious if she played too dumb. 'I'm convinced it isn't an actual key, but an item that would act as a key to the mystery.'

He nodded, satisfied. 'That much I concluded. I've searched the caves most thoroughly and there was nothing left behind or hidden in any of the tunnels. None of the keys your brother left do anything but open doors I've already identified.'

That suggested he might well have taken the missing key to the caves. Jacob was right to have questioned its whereabouts.

'We went to Medmenham Abbey. Dr Sandys said it was worth trying.'

'I know you did. It should have occurred to me to search it.'

She was glad she had ventured this information first and not been caught in a lie. 'How did you know?'

He waved his fingers negligently. 'Fosse followed you but was instructed not to interfere. He said you disappeared inside for some time.'

Dora struggled to remember exactly how visible the chamber was that they were in to test the lantern. It was entirely possible he had no idea what they had been doing.

'Apparently the place acted as something of a love potion.' Vane smirked at her.

He'd offered her a plausible explanation. 'It does have that reputation,' she said with the brazenness that suited her adopted character.

'Did you find anything else there, apart from the vigorous

attentions of the good doctor?'

Vane was enjoying this. How to mislead him while appearing to play along? She was no blushing miss to be put out of countenance by insinuations that she enjoyed sex.

'We did wonder if the clues in the letter pointed to "The Rape of the Lock" by Alexander Pope. That led us to Hampton Court.' Wasn't she being helpful?

'Very clever – yes, yes, the language of the letter.' Vane rubbed his jaw. 'Hampton Court. Did your brother have friends there? Did he visit?'

An idea came to send him on a wild goose chase. 'I don't know, but he always admired the maze. As a boy, he was proud of having mastered the way to the centre.' Finally, a bite of her breakfast went down easily.

'Interesting.' Vane folded his linen napkin. 'I have to call in at my office but perhaps I can find time today to pay it a visit.'

The footman returned and presented Vane with a calling card on a silver salver. Vane read it then flicked it onto the table.

'I hope you are ready to receive a visitor, my dear. It appears that Dr Sandys did not take his dismissal well and has brought your belongings personally.' Vane didn't give her a chance to refuse. 'We'll see him in the library,' he told the servant.

Entering on Vane's arm, she saw Jacob standing before the mantlepiece, examining the artworks – pictures of allegorical scenes, a muscular swan grappling with a reluctant Leda, a shepherd wooing a shepherdess whilst the sheep went wandering. Tall, aloof, hands behind his back, dishevelled hair bringing a hint of the wild with him to stuffy London – Dora had to give Jacob credit for doing a very good job of projecting unconcern. Seeing him, her spirits couldn't help but rise. Had he come to help her escape Vane's trap? He must know her note was written under duress. She had to warn him that he was in danger and let him know that she was here to avenge her brother, not throw over Anthony's cause. She was relying on Jacob understanding that she had higher moral standards than to accept an offer of protection from a murder suspect.

'Dr Sandys, you really needn't have bothered bringing Miss Fitz-Pennington's things yourself,' said Vane genially.

'I had business in town.' Jacob's tone was curt, lacking any warmth. 'I came to report that there was an unfortunate incident last night as we left your ball. Reverend Leighton was shot.'

Giving a choked gasp, Dora's gaze went to Vane. 'You bastard!' A cannonball of outrage was loaded and ready to fire. She wanted to explode him, to see him erupt like a direct hit to the powder magazine of an enemy vessel. He'd promised her she was protecting her friends by coming with him, but he'd gone ahead with his threats anyway!

'A moment,' said Vane to Jacob. Drawing her aside, Vane spoke low, for her ears only. 'Calm yourself, Dora. The clergyman is not dead, just winged.'

'But you promised—' She'd march right over to Jacob and out of this damned house!

'I only promised not to kill them. I said nothing about delivering a warning.' He'd known full well that hadn't been the spirit of their bargain. 'If you wish me to carry out my threat, please, carry on protesting.' He waved as if to say the floor was hers.

The spark was snuffed out. Dora fell silent. In his own house with his loyal servants around him, he could kill both Jacob and her, and there would be none to carry the tale to the authorities.

Vane must have seen her realisation in her expression as he whispered a patronising 'Good girl'. He turned back to his guest.

'Forgive Miss Fitz-Pennington; the news distressed her. I heard the melancholy tidings from my servants. I understand Reverend Leighton is not too badly hurt, and you emerged unscathed.' Vane sounded regretful, probably because Jacob had survived. 'Poachers – damn scourge on the estate.'

'He will recover.' Jacob turned to her. 'I thank you for your letter. Do you confirm that you are here of your own free will?'

What could she say? None of her reasons for being here had changed. She still had a task to perform.

Vane gave a gruff laugh and put his arm around her, squeezing her shoulder in warning. 'Dr Sandys, a gentleman accepts a lady's word on such matters and does not pester her further.'

'I wish to speak to her alone for a few moments.'

'You can hardly expect to conduct a private interview with my mistress? I did warn you that I am territorial about such things.' Vane leaned down and whispered in her ear, 'Careful.'

'Dora?' Jacob said softly. Vane's grip on her shoulder, however, reminded her that one failed attempt on Jacob's life would not stop another. She had to get him out of this mess by acting as if he no longer had anything to do with it, and maybe one day she could rebuild the bridges her next words would burn.

'Dr Sandys, I thank you for bringing my things. I wish Reverend Leighton a speedy recovery. Please go back to the Lakes and forget everything to do with my brother and … and…'

'Private matters that are no concern of a man with no connection to any of the parties involved,' Vane said smoothly. 'Well said, my dear.' He kissed her full on the mouth – for Jacob's benefit rather than because Vane felt the stirrings of passion for her, Dora hoped. The kiss was entirely heartless. 'As you told me last night, dearest, you are happy in my care, all your needs met, am I right?' He placed his finger on the pulse in her throat, perverting a tender gesture into one of pure threat.

'Y-yes,' she whispered. She wished for a spike to drive through his lying tongue.

The answer fired up Jacob's anger, turning her kind lover bitter. 'Are you sure, sir?'

'Sure?' Vane looked puzzled.

'Sure you're satisfying her needs?' Jacob said the words with the same innuendo with which Vane had loaded his. Dora closed her eyes, braced for the pain of what insult he might lob at her. 'It is just that I've discovered Miss Fitz-Pennington is very good at faking.'

Dora went cold. That changed everything. He knew about the Ben Jonson letter and the book of handwriting samples. She wanted to shout at him that this really wasn't relevant, that matters of life and death were at stake. Fooling a few collectors with more money than sense was not something about which she felt guilt. Or only a little.

Vane missed the subtle message Jacob was sending and took it as part of their battle to prove which was more virile. 'Maybe you had that problem, but I assure you I'm quite skilled at producing a genuine reaction.'

Yes, like terror that he would strike down the one man who had been kind to her.

'Jacob...' Dora began, but what she could say she did not know. Beg his forgiveness? That would only keep him here.

'I believe Dr Sandys is ready to leave.' Vane gave a nod to the footman waiting by the door.

Jacob glanced at the servant. 'Last chance, Dora.'

'I ... I have to stay here. For now.'

'Good girl.' Vane kissed her again, this time with more satisfaction. Motivated by pure spite to make Jacob jealous, Dora had to endure it, or Jacob would intervene and suffer the consequences.

Jacob nodded once, as if her permitting the embrace confirmed something for him. He was not looking at her. 'Vane. You're welcome to her.' With that, he strode out.

Still clasped firmly by Vane, Dora waited until she heard the front door close before she let out the breath she held. Vane continued to press her close, his musky pomade turning her stomach.

'Hmm, that was really quite stimulating, don't you think, to have the hot-blooded doctor panting after you?' Despite his previous protestations that he had no interest in her, Vane had not stopped his caresses now they no longer had an audience. 'But you're mine now – Sandys will spread the word – and I don't let other men play with what I own. I want you to understand that.' He pushed the sleeve of her dress down so he could run his tongue along her collarbone and dip deeper to her breasts. His invasion was hell to bear. She dare not push him away, even while her instincts screamed that she should shove him headfirst out of the window.

'I understand.' She hoped her agreement would be enough to stop him taking this further.

Nipping her shoulder in what was laughably called a love bite, Vane raised his head to study her expression. It had been another test, she realised.

'What? No squeak of protest? I'm enjoying this biddable version of Miss Dora, a woman far more to my tastes as a mistress.'

There was nothing good that could be said in reply to that.

He patted her bottom. 'Now, let's find the key and have done with this miserable business. Then you and I can come to a new arrangement, hmm?'

Dora thought longingly of her little trunk of belongings left with the troupe, and her place in the wagon going from theatre to theatre. 'Of course, sir.'

'Fletcher. You can call me Fletcher.' He chucked her under the chin. 'Though I don't object to *sir* in the bedroom.'

Chapter Thirty-Eight

The West End, London

Nero gave a snort and shake of his mane that summed up Jacob's disgust at the world. He couldn't believe it of Dora – wouldn't. And yet she had put up with Vane's advances, not gone to Jacob's side when he gave her the opportunity.

Surely she had to know that she had thrown in her lot with a man who was in all likelihood her brother's killer?

Jacob reined Nero in to let a carriage pass, the scenes in the drawing room playing a horrid merry-go-round in his head. She did know, didn't she? That moment when she had seemed genuinely shocked that Leighton had been shot – what was he to make of that?

Passage clear, he continued riding.

At first, he'd been convinced she had accepted Vane's offer to further her brother's cause, but then he'd seen her forger's kit and doubts had crept in. It was formidably detailed and he was even now wondering if he'd bought pieces by her at auction. He'd have to return home and go over his library with a fine-tooth comb. He'd been tempted to burn what she had so laughably called a 'keepsake' – would have done so if it hadn't held part of the clue to a man's murder. He would certainly see her prosecuted if he ever caught her practising her pernicious art again. It wasn't the fools whom she persuaded to part with their money – *caveat emptor* was an excuse there – but the falsifying of history. If we couldn't know the truth about our past then the foundations on which we built our reality were nothing but a sponge of lies and inventions. Fact and fiction had to be separated. People like Dora did untold damage muddling the two.

The discovery of her hobby reminded him of all the roles she had so quickly adopted on the journey – wife, doxy, respectable lady, boy. He did not fool himself that he was so irresistible that a woman as talented as Dora would fall for him so quickly. He had to ask himself if she had been playing a role of lover with him? Had she read his attraction to her and acted it back to manage him?

Dora Fitz-Pennington, actress, forger, seeming friend, was entangled in some convoluted plan of her own. But for what purpose? They had been working so well together; why run off in this direction where he could not follow?

An acquaintance hailed him from outside the grand entrance to the Royal Academy.

'I say, Sandys, you're a sight for sore eyes!'

'Brunton.' He forced himself to make a polite nod in exchange. He urged Nero swiftly on, in no state to pass the time of day. The man was a well-known gossip. News of Jacob's arrival would be doing the rounds of the clubs in half an hour. Damn him. He didn't want people – he wanted his Dora, the old one who laughed with him and cut him down to size with her sardonic wit.

Had he misjudged her all along? Had it only ever been about playing him and everyone else for what she could get? He had known her for barely a week. Had he fooled himself so completely?

No – or yes? He despaired at understanding her motives. One thing was clear. For whatever hare-brained reasons of her own, she had left him for that man's protection and there was nothing he, as a gentleman, could do about it.

Fury carried Jacob across Town to Grillon's Hotel in Albemarle Street where he engaged a room and stabling for Nero. Sensing his mood, the staff hurried to obey, doubtless wondering what offence they had caused to have prompted such a glower.

Dora had left him. That fact emerged from his confused feelings about seeing her putting up with that man's pawing and preening.

He was in too much of a temper to deal with his family by going to their London residence. Too many questions – too many filial duties expected of him – when he was more determined than ever to expose a murderer.

Dora's desertion was a blow – not to his heart because he refused to admit that had been vulnerable, but at least to his pride. He was usually a good judge of character. The signs had been there, though, hadn't they? A pretty face had made him forget his caution.

An actress, a forger, a faker – how had he expected anything better of her? He had to shore up his defences against her by repeating that reminder as this step had shown she could hurt him deeply.

He had worked himself up into a worse temper by the time the efficient servants brought hot water for shaving and coffee. The ritual of both soothed him and, when he'd emptied the coffee pot and restored a smooth chin, he had calmed down.

Dora had made him no promises. Indeed, she had warned him not to trust her. Her desire to expose her brother's killer had been genuine while it lasted but she had looked to her future and seen that her interests lay in pursuing her career in London. All of that was logical – but not true.

She surely understood that Vane was mixed up in the business, if not the killer. Vane, as a government official, was weaving a web of intrigue in which she had been caught. The spymaster was working to his own agenda, but it would be hard to persuade others of that because the man was one of them.

Jacob paused at the window, gazing across at the Royal Institution where the wonders of science were demonstrated weekly before the public. The street was quiet, the explosive work hidden behind the classical frontage.

Was that what she was doing? It would be just like her to think that placing herself inside the viper's nest was the best way to expose its secrets.

Jacob thought it the best way to receive a deadly bite.

Turning from the street, he donned his jacket.

Putting the mystery of Dora's motives aside as something he could not solve that day, he considered his next move. She appeared to be in no immediate danger and had elected to put herself out of his reach. However, they still had not solved the 'beacon of the wise' hint that Anthony had left. Jacob needed somewhere to start so the map made sense. He had to know what Pennington had been thinking. Hellfire Club members were his best source as Dora's knowledge was out of date and now she was out of reach. At the ball, Jacob had talked to the missing girl, Mary Wheeler, and was as surprised as Dora had been to find her alive. Mary had confirmed that she had been living with William Bates since she had left Henley and clearly had no idea that Matt had followed her and died because of it. It was hardly news he could break at a ball. Bates himself was the only member of the Hellfire Club that Jacob knew, but he had expressed firmly that Anthony had not died due to club activities. He'd said it was pure bad luck. Footpads. That old chestnut.

Either Bates was genuinely ignorant, or he was hiding something. Jacob guessed the latter. The Hellfire Club possessed some incendiary information which it was doing its utmost to conceal – something that Vane and the Illuminati wanted. But what? If it was so dangerous, why keep it?

The answer came to him in a flash. Insurance.

Wilkes had taught them that you kept incriminating information in order to blackmail someone to keep them quiet. If you wanted to protect your activities, you held information about the men in power who could send in the investigators. Any politician whose name was on that list, or member of the church hierarchy, would do much to stop that coming out, including turning a blind eye.

He needed someone he trusted, someone who would tell him the truth about the Hellfire Club. Only then would he understand what was at the end of the long puzzle trail that Pennington had left behind.

A visit to Brooks's club was on the cards.

'Knighton.' Jacob stood in front of his old friend separated by the barrier of *The Times*.

Ben Knighton folded down the broadsheet, then cast it aside in surprise.

'Good God, Sandys, has hell frozen over?' He held out a hand and shook Jacob's hand warmly. 'I'd given up any hope of seeing you again.'

Knighton was a short man but muscular – the kind of person you'd want on your side in a game of tug o' war. He still had the scar on his lip that Jacob had given him in their knockdown fight about the Eton Monks, the schoolboy attempt to ape the Hellfire Club.

The Persephone Code

'Good to see you too.' And Jacob realised it was. Knighton had always been a straightforward fellow: passionate but honest. Jacob decided he had been too abrupt in his decision to sever all ties with his friends in town.

'Please, join me. Have you had breakfast?' asked Knighton.

Hearing that Jacob had not, they removed from the library to the dining room. There were things Jacob missed about London, and a well-cooked breakfast in a gentleman's club was one of them.

'I heard you joined the army.' Knighton peppered his eggs.

'I did.'

'A surgeon?'

'Yes.' Until his addiction became too serious that he knew he had to break with that life and remove himself from temptation.

Jacob savoured a mouthful of bacon, realising he'd missed a few meals and was very hungry. He wasn't going to tell his old friend about the months of weaning himself off his drug of choice, and how that had worn him down. The poets talked about the strange dreams and soporific effects of opium-eating, lending it an artistic glamour; no one talked about the constipation and insomnia, the loss of libido, the craving that drove you to take more and more. Only over the last twelve months had he recovered his old self and he was determined not to go down that path again.

'You always were an original.' Knighton chuckled. 'Always admired the hell out of you for that.'

'And you?'

Knighton grimaced. 'As you would expect. Ever the dutiful son. Went into the family business. Speculated in canals for a few years, then came to my senses.'

'You have manufactories in Derby, do you not?'

'Yes, doing very nicely thank you.'

'Married?'

Knighton raised a brow. 'Of course! Why else do you think I'm hiding out here?'

Jacob let the conversation meander a little while he wondered if he was wrong in assuming Knighton would have anything to do with the Hellfire Club. Perhaps he had grown out of such things?

He reached for a fresh slice of toast a waiter had just delivered. 'Did you by any chance know Anthony Pennington?'

'The Bullroarer? Oh yes. He was a great friend of mine. Terrible what happened to him. How do you know him?' There was a glint in Knighton's eye. He was giving Jacob an opening to say he'd known him from the club.

'I am acquainted with the rector at West Wycombe.'

'Ah yes, I see. Pennington was quite close to him at the end, I believe.'

'Knighton, I need your help.'

Ben was no fool. He mopped up the last of the yolk and pushed his plate aside. 'I see. This wasn't a chance meeting?'

'No, sadly not. I know you are a good man, but even good men sometimes need to be wild from time to time. So long as no one gets hurt.'

Knighton nodded. 'You've changed your tune. I got this because you couldn't see the joke.' He pointed at his lip.

Jacob smiled. 'I won't apologise. It was a good fight. You blacked my eye.'

'And from the fading bruise, it looks like I wasn't the last person to do so.' A point to Knighton. 'Did you ever ask what it was about you that made people want to punch you?'

'Probably my charm.'

Knighton gave a huff of laughter.

'I understand that some people join certain clubs to have a dangerous kind of fun. I joined the army, so I understand the impulse to take chances.'

'To use your words, as long as no one gets hurt, what's the harm?'

'Indeed. But someone has been hurt. Several someones, in fact. And they seem to be connected to the activities out at West Wycombe.'

Knighton's face shuttered. 'I've not been out there for some years.'

'But you know those who still go?'

'I couldn't possibly say.' Damn inconvenient word of a gentleman.

Another line of questioning was required.

'I don't want you to give up any secrets, but please help me understand. What could have gone wrong? Something happened and men are killing for it. Three women have died; whores, so no one cared – hazard of the trade. I understand that, even if I don't agree. But add to that the unexplained deaths of three men, yet no one investigates. A man falls from the church tower some months back, and they say he's a Peeping Tom and got what was coming to him. One dies in the caves and they say footpads. Another is hanged, and they say suicide. I can't understand why this isn't a bigger scandal.'

Knighton did not look surprised. 'That's easy. The powerful protect themselves.'

'It shouldn't be that way.'

'You always did have an idealistic streak under your cynicism.'

'I prefer to call it a desire to see justice done.'

Knighton folded his napkin. 'One of the victims was Pennington?'

Jacob nodded.

His friend sighed. 'I suppose I have a duty to my brother-in-arms as well as to the existing members.' He leaned forward, lowering his voice. 'Look, once you are in the Club you never leave. They know things.'

'What things?'

'I can't tell you. I really can't. You can't leave but you can –' he searched for a word '– fall by the wayside. I stopped going because the parties took a darker turn about four years ago. The guests were using opium heavily – in all forms, very strong – and the rituals had become dark. Not the parodies that I had been used to. We had fun dressing up as monks, tupping the ladies dressed as nuns. It had been a carnival – *bouleversant*. That largely stopped and it all became too serious. Some were convinced they were summoning demons and that blood sacrifices were needed. They treated the opium dreams as prophecies that needed fulfilling.'

'They killed people?'

'Never.' Then he made a telling correction. 'Not when I was present. There were animals slaughtered on the altar, that kind of thing, but I have no stomach for such flummery. I merely wanted the kind of party I couldn't have with my wife. She's of a Methodistical turn of mind and barely allows me wine with my meals.'

'And the meetings carried on without you?'

'Undoubtedly. Pennington stayed involved, though even he was worried about the new members who were dabbling in satanism. "You don't *dabble* in satanism," he used to say. "You sell your soul to the devil or not at all."'

'Why did he stay?'

Knighton smiled bitterly. 'Because it was his home, the thing that gave his life purpose. He believed in the club's grand history of dissent from societal hypocrisy and thought he could wait for this to pass. He carried out his duties as our Hades but kept out of the ceremonies, leaving those to the initiates.'

'Initiates?'

His friend showed impatience at Jacob's failure to catch on. 'You have to understand that the Hellfire Club is just the first circle of hell. The real holders of the power and influence reside in the lower circles.'

'And they are?'

'How would I know? I just know they are there – and I have a healthy fear of them so I don't ask questions. I suggest you do the same.' He signalled the waiter to sign for their breakfast.

'And if I can't? How would you go about this?'

Knighton glanced around, checking no one was in earshot. 'I'd find out who was supplying the women and the opium – that will lead you to who's really in charge.'

Chapter Thirty-Nine

Seven Dials

There are some roads in life that you swear you will never walk down again but fate sends you that way once more.

Jacob looked up at the ruined warehouse on the edge of Seven Dials, the pillar in the meeting place of seven roads, and swore at his bad fortune. He'd once come here far too often, and far too desperately. Not far north of Covent Garden and the theatres, this was one of the most dangerous areas of town, nicknamed the Rookeries because so many of the poor flocked here to shelter in the tumbledown buildings. Would she even still be in business, he wondered. A year was a long time in the life of an opium trader.

Of course, opium was not illegal. You could get it freely in any druggist's, barber's or stationer's – laudanum, Kendal Black Drop, lozenges, crystals for smoking – so many different forms of the same poison. What you couldn't always find was the place to smoke it privately and indulge your dreams. Your local shopkeeper might question your daily return to obtain more for medicinal needs and notice the change in your person. He might caution against it, or even, if he had a conscience, refuse to sell it to you. Mother Clerk, a renegade from Russia, was burdened by no such qualms.

Would he find the strength to resist?

Taking a deep breath, Jacob entered.

It was a shock to see that nothing had changed. On pallet beds, skeletal men, and a few women, stretched out, lost in their dreams, interchangeable with the addicts who had lain there three years ago. Some waved their hands at phantoms; others lay completely still, eyes wide open, gazing at the brain-fevered sights they saw – whether pleasure domes or monsters, only they could say. Some might even have sunk into a slumber from which they would not waken. The thick, flowery smell of smoke stuck in Jacob's throat. He'd once loved this scent more than any other – perhaps he still did? Part of his cure had been to train himself to associate it with nothing but horrors. He forced his brain to register that, under the scent, was the smell of the unwashed bodies and sickness of those who'd lost the will to look after themselves.

He passed quickly through this hell to the inner sanctum where Mother Clerk used to be found. The chances that she was still here increased when he saw the way was blocked by a street thug, a retired boxer who was as loyal to her as a guard dog.

'Nokes,' said Jacob, giving the man a nod.

'Dr Sandys? Wot a sight for sore eyes!' the boxer rumbled. 'What the 'ell 'appened to ya? Took your custom elsewhere, did ya?'

'I moved into the north country.' Better not to insult the woman of whom he wished to ask questions. 'I wouldn't have left the Mother for any other.'

Nokes nodded, accepting that, and removed himself from the door. 'Yer in luck. She's in a rare mood today.'

Jacob walked in. Cold sweat gathered between his shoulder

blades as recollections of previous visits jostled to the front of his brain like troops disembarking from a transport ship to take a beachhead. Part of him wanted to flee, fearing he lacked the courage to face down temptation. Only military discipline made him go on, heading straight into this barrage to carry out an order.

Mother Clerk sat by her fire. She was a handsome woman with a square jaw and long, aristocratic nose. Jacob guessed her to be in her late fifties, her dark hair grey-shot and face largely free of lines, though her smile was spoiled by her browned teeth. Dressed conventionally and put in a church congregation on a Sunday, she would not be thought the head of a string of opium dens in the capital. Sitting here though, in her red silk dressing gown and beaded slippers, she looked as louche and dangerous as she was. If a customer failed to keep up with his payments after two warnings, Nokes would ensure he would disappear from the smoking room and end up in the Thames.

Jacob gave her a respectful bow. 'Mother Clerk.'

She stretched lazily, hands over her head. Her joints clicked. 'Jacob, you've returned. Come here, dear boy.' She patted the stool at her side. When he was younger, he had been pleased to sit there, enjoying her gossip and her wickedness. She must have seen the distaste in his expression. 'No? Then do take that chair.' She pointed to the one opposite hers.

'How's business?' Jacob asked. He moved around the many small tables inlaid with mother-of-pearl that grew like toadstools in her den. His skin itched to take just a little to smooth off the rough edge of the day.

'Very well indeed. So many desperate souls to help.'

'Hunger and war will do that to a nation.' Jacob removed the cushion from the seat and sat down.

'Quite so.' She touched her fingertips together and studied him. 'You look well.'

'Thank you.'

'You aren't here for the black drop?'

Yes! shouted an inner demon. Jacob shook his head. 'I've given it up.' He had made himself change, forcing his natural wildness down under the strictest of discipline, but every day was the day when he might fail.

She tapped her lips. 'How interesting. I don't think I've ever met a customer who successfully left it behind. I can't even break myself of the appetite.' She gestured to the clay pipe that lay unlit beside her. 'Though I've cut down.' Her eyes twinkled in amusement. Faithless and amoral – and happy to be that way – Mother Clerk found life to be one long, dark joke. 'So we all rattle on to our ignoble ends, except you, my stalwart Jacob, doctor, hero, conqueror.' She chuckled at that image while he shook his head.

Jacob reached into his breast pocket and drew out four guineas. He placed them beside the clay pipe and quickly folded his hands before he reached for it.

'Are you wanting to return to your old ways?' she queried, watching his struggle with wry enjoyment. 'I would caution you not to, but then that would be bad for business.'

'That's for information. And if you don't know, then it is still yours. A sign of my appreciation.' She had always loved flattery.

Smiling coquettishly, she disappeared the coins into a pocket. 'Very well. What do you want to know, my sweet Jacob?'

'A friend of mine died in the Hellfire Caves in West Wycombe. His killer has not been found.'

'Ah.' She said no more so he continued.

'It has been suggested to me that, if I could discover who organised the parties, I would stand a better chance of finding witnesses to the circumstances of his death.'

Mother Clerk picked up the clay pipe and used an ember from the fire to light the sticky black opium in the bowl. She puffed a couple of times to set it burning. 'You're talking of Anthony. Another dear boy.'

'I am.'

'His friends wouldn't kill him. They loved him.' She waved the smoke away, sending the perfumed cloud towards him. She was taunting him. Like a crab in a bucket, she wanted to claw down the one who had crawled up the side to escape. His grip on the rim was weak.

'I'm not saying they did. But I think they know why he was killed.'

She took a great inhale and held it, before expelling. Her eyes were already glazing over.

'Please, Mother Clerk.'

'I despise violence. I don't understand it.' She looked down at the pipe. 'This brings me peace. Everyone should just smoke a little – and love a little.'

Fine words from a woman who destroyed so many by supplying their death-bringing habit, he reminded himself. 'I want to stop the violence that hurt Anthony. He'd want that, wouldn't he?'

She smiled, adrift already on her opium dreams.

'No confidences broken, just information,' he pressed.

'I can tell you –' she nodded with great solemnity, the archbishop of her trade '– that I have supplied the Hellfire boys. Dear boys. So funny and naughty.'

'Anyone in particular?'

'Willy Bates, he comes here. I'm not as fond of him but he's reliable.'

'I saw him last night. He was Anthony's friend.'

'Oh yes. Thick as thieves, those two. A few years back, when he moved to the country, Anthony arranged for me to send parcels monthly for collection at the George and Dragon. Said the dragon needed something to smoke.'

'Under what name?'

'Archbishop or High Priest Cave, a foolish name like that. Anthony arranged the payment and never missed one.'

'Why not in his own name?'

'He said it was for someone else.'

'But he didn't say whom?'

She shook her head. 'I thought he meant Willy. He was pretending to be a country gentleman at the time. Are you sure you don't want a pipe, for old time's sake? On the house?'

He hated that he hesitated. 'No, but thank you.'

'Humour me – take this and I'll answer one final question.' She held out a little bottle of opium tincture. He could take it and throw it away on the first opportunity.

He stood up and pocketed the bottle. She smiled in satisfaction, having won her point. 'Final question: have you heard of Sir Fletcher Vane?'

Her dreamy happiness vanished. She scowled. 'Him? That government spy? Don't make me think about him.'

'Why?'

'He's a devil. Wants to stop all my lovely naughty boys having their fun. And the girls. Why can't he leave people alone?'

'Not a customer then?'

She cackled. 'Him? I wouldn't sell the black drop to him if he begged me on his knees.'

'Why?'

'He's a killjoy – and a killer.' Her eyes returned to their usual shrewdness. 'If you're asking about him and dear Anthony in the same breath, then you know that already.'

Chapter Forty

The West End

Vane had gone to Whitehall, whence he would take a boat to Hampton Court on the trail of her honking wild goose.

Dora prowled her bedchamber. The worm of worry had been burrowing that he would be cross when he returned empty-handed. That might not have been her wisest idea, though she had felt so clever at the time. There was a reckless streak in the Penningtons that she had inherited. She might have been better off playing ignorant.

Not that Vane looked like someone who kept ignorant people around.

Already anticipating that she might have to escape quickly, she'd not unpacked her bag, though she had confirmed from a quick rummage through it that the keepsake book was missing. Forging a clever document did no harm to anyone; even the collectors were pleased as long as they didn't find out they'd been fooled. Damn Jacob. It was not only a tool of her trade, but it was

The Persephone Code

her last link to her brother. He'd better not have destroyed it or she'd ... she'd...

She couldn't think of something strong enough, though kicking him in the groin would be the first step in her revenge.

Jacob had deigned to leave her brother's letters in her bundle. Thank you, Dr Judgemental Sandys. He had no idea what it was like to struggle to live, nor what had driven her to forgery.

Think of Anthony, not that infuriating man, she chided herself.

The letters were in a different order from how she'd left them, so it appeared that Jacob had read them through and tired of them quickly. Erotic letters to an unmarried man from his lover, and copies of the ones he sent in reply, were not the stuff of blackmail.

Her heart missed a beat. Or were they?

Dora slumped in a padded seat by the window, the letters in her lap. She pressed her fingers into her eye sockets to relieve the headache, then looked back down while her vision was still blurry. The writing danced and teased. What was it about these letters? No names. The tone was educated, sophisticated jokes and Latin tags, even the occasional Greek phrase that she did not know. It was obvious now that these were not messages from your common or garden mistress. Anthony could hardly have found a bluestocking to bed.

Her thoughts tumbled into a new shape.

Lady Tolworth had called him Bullroarer but said she hadn't known him in the biblical sense, though they had flirted.

Anthony had always reacted coolly whenever Dora had teased him about his future wife and his tribe of little Penningtons, saying he'd never settle down and live the hypocrite life like their father.

The last girl Dora knew for a fact that her brother had bedded was the kitchen maid from Butterworth Manor years ago. The servant, an older girl with several admirers below stairs, had succumbed to his pleas to initiate him into the mysteries of the flesh when he was home from school one summer. Anthony had been sixteen and annoyed that he had been one of the few at Westminster to lack that experience. The assignation had happened in the orchard one hot summer night, and he had boasted of it to Dora, infuriating her with the superior knowledge of an elder sibling. From his hints and mentions of particular friends, Dora had understood that the boys made their own entertainment after hours at boarding school, the young ones serving the older in the Greek style.

Could her brother have been...?

She looked back down at the letters. Love between members of the same sex was an accepted part of life in the theatre, as at boarding school, though the laws of the country made it punishable by death. Schoolboys were allowed their experiments, a phase one ignored before the serious business of marriage, but adult men had a far more difficult time if their love tended that way. Society cut such men dead even if it did not have the evidence to prosecute. A Molly. A backgammon player. A sodomite. None of the names were nice ones.

She considered the name. He wrote to a Greek mythological figure – Persephone, counterpart to Hades. Anthony had boasted loudly of his conquests to anyone who would listen and had developed the reputation of a philanderer, a rake, but had he actually done any philandering? Had it all been an act? A disguise?

Oh, Anthony.

Sorrow swamped her as she felt the return of that familiar tide. She knew in her heart that this was a correct guess. Little wonder that he had gravitated to the Hellfire Club, where 'buggery', as the law cruelly termed it, was celebrated rather than condemned. No one cared what members did during an orgy – that was rather the point. He could be open about his appetites and have it put down to daring. He'd died to protect the safe place he'd made for his love.

Hurt grew. He should have known he could tell her. She would have tried to help him. He should have abandoned the half-life he lived and joined her theatre troupe. He could have lived freely there, no questions asked; other actors did so. Now it was too late. His room for manoeuvre had been squeezed to the point where he had met with someone – most likely Vane – whom he knew to be dangerous. The threat of exposure, ignoble trial and possible death sentence explained what she had struggled to understand: why Anthony had been in the caves for that rendezvous in the first place.

None of these letters were proof of an illegal liaison; their code was too careful. However, Vane must have found proof and lured Anthony to his death. Who else but the killer would know Anthony's last words?

Not Dora. It made a chill run down her spine just thinking of that desperate utterance.

Suddenly, she laughed.

Anthony, you sharper!

Her brother had made his killer the unwitting carrier of his first clue. Not that he could have foreseen that it would be conveyed to her in person. His mind had settled on what was the most important thing to him at the moment of death. It hadn't been 'Not Dora' but 'Knot, Dora.' Anthony had expected her to go to the house and see the rope on the bed, the missing curtain tie, and follow the letter to the abbey where the knot could be found tied to the lantern.

'I already followed that, Anthony, but you've led me down a blind alley,' she whispered, tucking the letters back into a neat pile and hugging them to herself.

Then her eyes went to the address on one of the last letters. Her brother had been travelling in the month before his death, taking a trip to Richmond in Yorkshire, collecting his letters from public houses along the way. Had he come north to see her on stage and been a silent witness when they performed there? How else could he have come by the reviews he'd snipped out of the local papers. Such newssheets rarely survived to come as far as London. Perhaps his lover had lived near Richmond and he had decided on a final visit to warn him before what he knew to be a dangerous meeting.

It made her ineffably sad to think of Anthony sitting with his lover in that gem of a theatre, watching her but not making himself known.

Curious now about this lover who was the last significant person in her brother's life, Dora put the letters in order of the return trip. It was a relationship still at the stage when being apart required a daily letter to express how much the lover was missed. Anthony kept copies of the letters he sent to 'Persephone', or perhaps they were first drafts? There were many crossings-out as he composed his witty remarks.

Dora's fingers hesitated over the second to last letter. Anthony had sent it from The Cardinal's Hat, Lincoln. She remembered in Medmenham Abbey how the scattering of dots and the cross of the lantern had fallen in the countryside of Lincolnshire when lined up with their old home in Liverpool. Had she been thinking about this the wrong way? It wasn't where Anthony considered home now, but where they had been home together once upon a time.

Yet was she any further on? He'd left her the whole of Lincolnshire to search with his 'beacon to the wise' clue.

And right now, she didn't feel very wise at all.

Vane stormed into her room at dusk, vulture-like in his black cloak.

'What a bloody waste of my time!' he said. He threw off his cloak and made straight for where she sat by the fire. 'As I suspect you knew. Are you playing me for a fool?' He hauled her up by the front of her gown.

'I thought you Illuminati were supposed to be governed by reason?' She tried to unlatch his fingers, alarmed by this abrupt change of treatment.

'I'm running out of time for your games. You will tell me what you know – and tell me now.' He hauled her towards the bed. Her mind flashed up the images of the three strangled women buried in West Wycombe.

'I'm not playing a game!' Fear coursed through her.

'No? Your brother is. That bastard had his hands on secrets that would blow up the kingdom – and what did he do? Confide the secret in his whore of a sister.' He shoved her down, but she rolled and scrambled off the other side of the mattress.

Vane really must not have liked the trip to Hampton. She looked desperately around for a way to defuse this, tempted to throw a jug of water over him as though to douse a fire. 'But I don't know anything. Can't you get that into your head?'

'I don't believe you.' He'd completely lost whatever pretence to rational action he could claim. He cornered her between the wall and the bedhead. She groped in her pocket. 'If I don't get those plans before the summer campaign starts, then they'll be no earthly good to me! And neither will you. Enough playing nice.' He slapped her, making her head jerk to one side, her cheek burning. He backhanded her with the return swing. Pain ricocheted through her skull. 'Tell me! Or do you want to go the same way as your stupid brother?'

Dora would take that as a confession. She grabbed the hilt of

Matt's knife that was still in her pocket and shoved it into his belly. Cloth gave way, then flesh. Warm liquid coated her hand. Vane gasped in shock.

'Go to hell, you murderer,' she spat.

Chapter Forty-One

Dora raced down the street away from Vane's mansion, cursing her impulsiveness. She would be hanged! She'd stabbed a baronet and important government official. Her plan to use her stay in his house to expose him had ended in the worst way, blown up in her hands like a misfiring musket. Any word she laid against him would be rejected as that of a criminal who doth protest too much.

The moment the knife had slid in she was already regretting her action. Grabbing a linen towel from the washstand, she had thrust it at Vane to staunch the blood, leaving him with the knife in the wound.

'I'll get you help,' she'd said as she rushed out, having just enough presence of mind to grab her things on the way. As a last-minute thought, she also grabbed his cloak as a disguise.

'Go to your master!' she'd shouted to the footman standing in the hall. 'He's injured.'

As the man headed upstairs at a run, she'd opened the front door and fled. Her knowledge of London was limited. She'd avoided it most of her adult life. Childhood memories were of the mercantile districts of the City; here, in the fashionable West End, she was at sea. Once around a corner, she slowed, aware that running was the worst thing she could do. Glancing down at her hands she saw that they were stained with blood. She covered herself in Vane's cloak, pulling up the hood. It had the same Illuminati fastening as her attackers had worn in Kendal. How apt.

Where to go? She had very little money and no friends here, unless Jacob could be persuaded to forgive her deception? But how to find him? Would anyone help her flee? Should she go to America?

Out of the blizzard of questions came one thought: the only place that felt like it might show her a welcome was one of the theatres. Her people.

That was a plan – and certainly better than lingering in the street to be arrested and dragged off to gaol.

Asking directions of a street sweeper, she set off for Covent Garden.

Walking across the square amongst the discarded cabbage leaves and bruised apples, the market long since packed up for the day, she paused between the two theatres at the eastern side. Covent Garden theatre itself, or Drury Lane? None of the names on the playbills for Covent Garden were actors she had met before, more's the pity. Sheridan, owner of Drury Lane, had been mentioned by her brother. He at least might have some inkling of what was at stake and help her for Anthony's sake. Mind made up, she headed for the Theatre Royal.

It was humbling coming to this famous stage door, known by actors as the entry to the pinnacle of a career. Sarah Siddons may have decamped to Covent Garden, but under Sheridan, Drury Lane had glittered golden for decades.

Until it burned down in 1809.

The Persephone Code

The response of Sheridan had been widely reported and had now grown into a legend. He'd taken a chair and a glass of wine to watch the flames devour his theatre, which itself had only lasted fifteen years since the last rebuild. He had declared to reporters that a man should surely be allowed to take a glass by his own fireside. Typical Sheridan – laughing in the face of disaster. Now the theatre was being rebuilt on an even grander scale. The fire had ruined Sheridan and he had been ousted from the management by a new circle of investors led by Samuel Whitbread, but Sheridan would still be near his baby even if no longer in charge of her future. For all his many careers – politician, playwright, society wit – he always came back to the stage.

The new theatre was almost complete. The classical façade was painted white, the noticeboards for the performances already erected, and she could hear hammering inside. A carpenter was unloading planks from a cart parked by the door.

'Excuse me, sir, I am looking for Mr Sheridan. Is he here today?'

The man gave her a quick survey, eyes pausing briefly on the bruises that had to be forming on her face. 'Here to audition, are you?' He had her down as one of the many country lasses who made a name for themselves in the provinces and then came to the big city to make their fortune. It was a suitable cover story.

'Yes. I'm from the northern circuit.' And she wasn't even lying.

'Hmm. Good luck to you.' He sounded sceptical of her chances. 'At this time of day, he'll be at his club. You'll have to wait for him outside as they don't let girls in.'

'Do you know which one?' Even Dora, unfamiliar with London, knew that St James's played host to several fashionable clubs for gentlemen.

'Nah, lass, but Jeremy will.' He gave a whistle and the doorkeeper came out of the building.

'What?' Jeremy looked like he ate carpenters for breakfast rather than answering a summons from them.

'Old Sherry. Which club? The mort's asking.'

Jeremy gave her a tired look. Dora wondered how many hopefuls he had to deal with each week.

'It won't do you no good. Our list is full,' Jeremy said sternly. 'But you can try Brooks's.'

Dora wondered at herself, lurking in the shadow of a doorway outside the club. If you wanted to escape attention for stabbing a baronet, then it was probably a bad idea to moor yourself in the heart of a gentleman's London. Few women came here, and certainly no ladies. She was able to wait without being harassed because the cloak hid her identity, but there was only so long her study of a playbill she'd picked up from Covent Garden could excuse her loitering. The Palladian building in front of her, with its decorative pediment that suggested a classical temple, reminded her of the theatre she had just left. At least the performances at Drury Lane were known to be make-believe. In Brooks's, men came to perform to their peers, trying to impress them and forge connections that would further their fortunes. It was all acting.

A chill breeze made her clutch the cloak more tightly. Would she even recognise Sheridan when he emerged? She'd seen a print of him, taken from his portrait, but that had shown the younger man. He was often featured in cartoons, but there he was a caricature. She knew to look out for a man with a flushed face and expressive eyes, but that wasn't very helpful from a distance. This was a stupid idea. Was she better trying her luck down the docks and stowing aboard the next ship to Boston or Philadelphia?

And what would happen if she ran into her father?

Then a man stumbled out of the club – reddened complexion,

familiar expression. Sheridan? Dora hurried to catch him but men suddenly peeled out of the shadows.

'Mr Sheridan, my account!'

'You owe me seven pounds!'

Her voice was lost in the clamour. Sheridan ran to the nearest cab and climbed inside to avoid his creditors.

'Not today, gentlemen!' he called as the jarvey flicked the horse into motion.

She had missed her chance. Despair swept over her. What now?

And then Jacob strolled down the street, heading for the club.

She had not anticipated seeing him here, but, of course, she should have thought of it. He was from out of town and would naturally frequent one of the clubs to meet friends and catch up on the news. Gentlemen often used their club for any correspondence that needed to follow them.

Which made her wonder if anyone had collected her brother's post?

'Jacob!'

He looked around on hearing his name. Spotting her across the street, she was devastated to see that he hesitated a fraction, his face set in unforgiving lines. A carriage passed between them and she almost expected to see him go inside, turning his back on her. When it cleared, he was crossing the road. Thank God.

'Miss Fitz-Pennington.'

The formal tone almost broke her. She swallowed a sob. 'I need help.'

He glanced down at where she clutched the cloak. 'That's blood! Where are you injured?'

She gave a dark laugh. 'Not me. Not much.'

He raised his hand as if to touch her cheek, then dropped it quickly. 'Lovers' quarrel?'

'No! You didn't really think—'

He scowled. 'I didn't know what to think.'

'He said he'd kill you if I didn't stay with him.'

Comprehension softened Jacob's expression. 'Oh, you foolish woman.'

'I thought I'd be able to find proof he killed my brother. I did, but I … er…' She held up her hands in evidence.

Jacob was quick to catch on. 'Let's summon a cab. We've got to get you off the street.' He raised his walking cane and a hansom cab pulled away from the rank.

'Where are we going?'

'Does that matter?'

On the short journey to his hotel, she related to Jacob the events leading to her stabbing Vane.

'Did you kill him?'

'I think not. It was only that little blade belonging to Matt Jenkins.'

'But it stopped him in his tracks. If I weren't so angry with you for getting yourself in this mull, I'd congratulate you.' He looked up as the cab slowed. 'Put your hood back up. I'm smuggling you in. Keep walking whatever anyone says. Room 15.'

They got as far as the foyer when the bellboy hailed Jacob.

'Dr Sandys? I've a letter for you.'

Jacob pressed the key into her hand and nudged her onwards. 'I'll be with you in a moment.'

Dora felt a little better out of public view and behind the door of his room. She went immediately to the washstand and scrubbed her hands. She'd played Lady Macbeth and was not surprised to find herself murmuring 'out, damned spot!' at a particularly stubborn stain. That made her laugh, then sob, until she regained control of herself, inch by inch.

Jacob tapped on the door and she let him in. If he noticed her tear-stained face, he was too gallant to comment.

'A letter from Leighton. He's joining us tomorrow.' He put the note down on the sideboard and poured two glasses of wine from the decanter. 'You look like you need this.'

'You said he was injured?' She downed it in one and returned for a refill.

'A flesh wound. As long as it heals well, it shouldn't bother him. He said he'd received worse from his profession.'

'When he was a chaplain in the navy?'

He gave her a brief smile. 'No, a parishioner's cat once scratched him very badly. He has never lived it down with his congregation.' Jacob waved her to a chair and sat opposite her. 'So.'

'So,' she said in the same tone. 'Why did you doubt me, Jacob?'

He gave her a rueful smile. 'Doubt is my middle name. I doubt everything – God – good fortune – you – and me most of all. I wasn't convinced you'd jumped ship to someone we suspected of murder—'

'Thank you for that much,' she grumbled. 'Nice to know you think so highly of me.'

'*But* I did doubt that you had been sincere in our dealings together. The keepsake—'

'Ah.'

'It was a blow when I was already reeling.' His eyes flickered up to her cheek, then away. 'Did he…?'

'No, Jacob. The only one who came close was that weasel Peter Fosse, my gaoler on the journey to London.' She realised she was squeezing the stem of her glass too hard. Any more pressure and it would shatter. 'Do you have a knife? I've discovered I don't feel safe without one.'

He didn't protest or tell her not to be silly. He simply got up and went to his bag. Returning with one of his pistols, he gave it to her.

'You can have this. We both know you can use it.'

'Thank you.' Her feelings for him had been growing over the time they had spent together, but that moment, thought Dora, might be the precise second when he became very dear to her indeed. She wouldn't use the sentimental language of novels – love was bandied about too easily in those pages – but he was her comrade in arms. Her heart's companion. Her equal. It was good he doubted her. She could never be with someone too credulous as she would flatten them without even meaning to do so. 'Before my disaster, I did learn some things. I don't think Vane killed Matt Jenkins.'

'You are sure?'

'No, but I asked him and he deflected. I think he would have used it to threaten me, as proof that he'd kill again very easily. He did admit to killing Anthony.' She then told him about her realisation that 'Not Dora' had been for her ears, a desperate last clue.

'So we are on the right track,' said Jacob.

'There's more. Something from my brother's letters. He was travelling home from Richmond in Yorkshire and passed through Lincoln. You'll remember that Lincolnshire was one of the locations on the lantern map.'

His eyes lit up. 'A very good thought.'

'I was also wondering if there were further letters waiting for him to collect at one of his clubs. If we can pick up the ones sent by his lover, then it might give us an idea where he stopped to hide his secret.'

Jacob nodded. 'True, but they won't hand them over to someone unconnected with him and you can't go knocking on those doors yourself.'

'You could probably retrieve them if my father hasn't thought to do so. That's if you carry a letter from him giving you permission.' Dora gave him a pointed look.

'You mean…?'

'Jacob, if I can mimic people as unknown to me as Ben Jonson, I can certainly copy my own father's bombastic style.'

Chapter Forty-Two

Jacob struggled with his conscience. If he encouraged her to do this, he would lose any moral high ground he had occupied in condemning her fabrications. Not that he thought he really deserved to feel superior to anyone with his shadowed past. It was about the principle of preserving the truth, and not about him.

Dora must have sensed his uncertainty. She gave him a sardonic look.

'I know what Anthony hid – and it's big.'

'Oh?' Jacob took a gulp of wine, feeling he probably needed the preparation. 'How do you know?'

'From something Vane said. One of Wellington's men must have given the Hellfire Club the plans for the next phase of the Peninsular Campaign as his surety.'

Jacob swore fluently and colourfully with words learned in his army days.

Dora grimaced. 'My thoughts exactly. Vane is planning to share the plans with Napoleon in exchange for the emperor's support for his ambitions. He has set his sights on ruling us all.'

'And that would mean Wellington would be outflanked, the British army smashed to bloody pieces and Napoleon's rule secure from the Atlantic to the Russian border. You may not have heard the news but even now the French emperor is massing troops on his eastern flank. Russia has not yet beaten him in battle.'

'So what's a little forgery in the scales against that? Could he do it?'

'Vane?'

She nodded.

'He's been developing a network of agents in France for years via the Alien Office. I'd say he would be peculiarly well placed to turn it against us if those military secrets came into his hands.'

He got up and went to his saddlebags. Was this how she had started, making a forgery because she had a pressing need? But what damage had she done since? She had spat in the face of truth, distorting what we knew about the great people of the past. Yet here he was about to encourage her to commit another crime! What did that say about his morals?

Then again, sitting on a high horse only made you a target for unseating. Promising himself not to regret it, he took out the keepsake volume.

'I assume you have what you need in here?'

She took it from him and hugged it to her chest. 'Indeed. It was the very first hand Anthony and I learned to mimic. It was the only way to survive our childhood.'

He could well imagine what doors to mischief having a note from a father would open. 'Then by all means, write me a letter. I put Europe's future over my disapproval of the means we employ.'

She shot him one of her gamine grins. 'See, Jacob, what a corrupting influence I am on you?'

And God help him, when she smiled at him like that, he enjoyed the journey far more than he should. He had thought opium was the greatest danger to his character, but perhaps it was Dora?

He left her alone to write her note while he sent out for a change of clothes for her, tipping the staff to keep silent about the woman he had smuggled in. Thankfully they would be thinking the obvious and not imagine she was a wanted woman.

Or was she?

'I believe I should head out for a while, Dora,' he said, taking the forged letter from her. 'I'll deal with this, naturally,' he tapped the message, 'but it struck me that maybe you don't need to fear imminent arrest. Vane would not want the fact that he had you in his house to be bandied about, not if he is hell bent on finding the hidden cache of plans. His ambition will be to get you back and use you to find out where they are – as we are doing.'

Some of the worry dropped from her shoulders and she sat a little straighter. 'Really? I was already imagining a new life for myself in America, out in the wilds, growing corn and churning my own butter.'

He smiled at the thought. 'You may wish to travel there one day, but hopefully not as a fugitive. Let me see what is being said around town. If Vane has kept quiet about his injury, then I think it will be safe to venture out if we are cautious. You'll be hidden here as I've not told anyone but Leighton where I'm staying and he isn't due in town until tomorrow.'

When Jacob returned two hours later, he came as the bearer of good news. Dora's name had so far not been mentioned in any of the clubs, and no one was talking of an attack on Sir Fletcher; even Anthony Pennington's name roused little reaction beyond a 'poor fellow' from his old drinking pals. If Dora did have to go out, a disguise and a couple of stout footmen should keep her relatively safe. If he had his way, though, she would stay within doors as long as possible until they could be certain which way the wind blew. Vane was as changeable as his namesake.

Entering his room, he immediately backed out again. In his absence Dora had ordered a bath to be prepared and she was soaking in it before the fire. He glimpsed golden skin being rubbed by a sea sponge. Never had he been so envious of a sponge.

'I do beg your pardon.'

Her reply was to laugh. 'Jacob, don't be a goose. I'll wrap myself in a towel to save your maidenly modesty and you can come in.'

Imaging her damp body swathed in a thin linen sheet was somehow worse.

'It's safe!' she called.

It was very far from that. He came in, studiously keeping his eyes away.

'I am sorry to shock your sensibilities further, Jacob. I thought you'd be gone all evening.' She sat by the hearth, drying her hair, quite at ease in this situation when he didn't know his moves.

'I came back because I found out what I needed.' He filled her in on his discoveries.

'I'm glad.' There was a pause when only the crackle of the logs disturbed the silence. The atmosphere was pregnant with possibilities, their attraction burning hot once more now that he could no longer stave it off with news. 'Jacob, you don't need to be shy around me. Travelling as I do is more like being in the army than a convent. We room together, get changed quickly in the wings, so a little bit of naked flesh is normal.'

'It's just...' He didn't know what the completion of that sentence was unless it was 'with you it's different', as he was damnably attracted to her.

She sighed. Was she disappointed? Had she been hoping for

another outcome? 'I'll put something on, and you won't look so out of countenance.'

Was he really going to let her do that, just to make him more comfortable? Why was he holding back from something they both wanted?

'Please, don't.' Jacob went to her and knelt before her. 'Dora? I'm sorry I doubted you.'

'I wish I could say in return that I'm sorry I'm a forger, but I can't. I can say I'm sorry it makes you unhappy.'

'And I hate to admit it has been very useful. Pax?'

'Yes, pax.'

He ran his fingers down her long neck and smooth arms, fingertips dancing on fingertips. Everywhere he touched felt like silk. 'You are beautiful.'

She smiled. 'Even with my swollen cheek and bruises?'

'Especially so. Wounds honourably gained.'

She raised her hand to his face where his own black eye was fading. 'What a pair we make.'

'I couldn't agree more.' He pulled her forward, waiting for that little nod of acceptance, then tugged at the knot holding the towel to her chest. It fell away, leaving her naked from the waist up. Her breasts were perfect sumptuous mounds with dusky nipples that he wanted to suck and play with. He bent his head to worship her. She gave a little shiver of appreciation.

'Don't stop, Jacob.'

There was no chance of that. He moved lower, licking her belly button and along the sensitive line above her quim. Her scent was intoxicating.

'You have too many clothes on,' she said, pushing his jacket off his shoulders.

He'd quite liked the frisson of her naked while he bent over her fully clothed – some foolish erotic dream of his – but decided that she was right. For what came next, he really needed to match her state of undress. They'd always met as equals; this should be no different.

With his help, she tugged the shirt over his head. 'Your magnificent scar.'

He'd never heard it called that before. 'I've always thought it ugly.'

'Nonsense. It's proof of your courage.' She kissed it, trailing her lips from his shoulder to his navel, changing their position so she knelt before him. This woman was driving him wild. He'd have to stop her, or this encounter would be over far too soon. He scooped her up in his arms and stood, the towel falling away.

'My courage,' he said as he laid her on the bed and settled between her legs, 'is nothing to yours.'

She smiled up at him and stretched her arms above her head.

'Then prove it.'

Sometime later, lying with his arms around her as she slept, Jacob reflected on the responsibility he had just assumed. They'd not stopped to discuss the basis on which they bedded each other but he was not a man to walk away from a lover. A woman always took more risks with a relationship – ones of health and reputation, not to mention the possibility that they would bear a child. Struggling to keep himself free of opium, he'd not wanted a family or a woman of his own, preferring to keep his liaisons uncomplicated while he recovered. For the first time the prospect of having a lady in his life no longer seemed so frightening. He might even be able to tell Dora about the worst parts of himself and see if she still wanted him after that. They might have a future together and he would never make her feel the humiliation of being his mistress, though that was how the world would see her.

With his support, she need never dabble in forgery again, thus he'd be doing collectors a favour.

Maybe she'd even want to make an honest man of him and marry him?

'Stop it. Your thoughts are keeping me awake,' grumbled Dora, kissing his left nipple.

'I'm not saying anything.' He rubbed his fingers up and down her arm.

'You don't need to. You are a serious man, Dr Sandys, and do not bed women lightly. You are tying yourself up in knots worrying about me, aren't you? Admit it.'

He smiled at the ceiling. That was exactly what he had been doing.

'You mustn't. I wanted this, but neither of us owes the other anything.'

That made his heart chill.

'You don't want to stay with me?'

She tapped his breastbone. 'If you mean as your mistress, then no. As your friend, I am happy to stay exactly where I am.'

His smile returned. 'Trust me, I don't do this with my friends.'

'You don't?' She got on top of him, bringing her warmth to straddle his very interested cock. Her rocking was making all coherent thought flee. 'You don't let your old army pals do this?' She slid up and down him.

'No!' His voice was strained.

'You don't let your friends get this close to you?' She lined him up with her entrance and sank down so he was buried deep within.

'Definitely not.'

'Oh?' She raised a brow, her hair falling around her like a wonderful, dishevelled mane. 'Do you want me to stop then?'

'Minx!' he growled. Flipping her over as she laughed, he

showed her exactly how much he didn't want her to stop. Eventually she was the one begging him for mercy.

They had a late supper and only then did they return to the matter that had brought them together in the first place. Her idea had been rewarded with a letter waiting for Anthony from 'Persephone'.

'Do you think your brother would have entrusted the cache of secrets to her?' asked Jacob.

'No,' she said firmly.

'So certain?'

'It's not a "her". I think he was exchanging letters with another member of the Hellfire Club. They used the group as a cover for their love.'

Different forms of love were not a shock to a doctor. Jacob had only to recalibrate his understanding of Anthony Pennington's character and motives for what he did. It made perfect sense. Hide an illicit love in an illicit organisation. 'I see.'

She pointed to a passage in the letter. 'And look here. Persephone says they hope he found time to stop and see the sights on the way. I think they're asking for confirmation that my brother hid the documents.'

'Then Persephone would know where?'

'Maybe not. Anthony was serious about his duties.'

'But if we discover who Persephone is, we'll be able to ask him.'

She shrugged. 'Yes, or we solve it from the clues Anthony left. I don't think my brother meant me to know about his relationship.'

Reluctantly, Jacob rose and put on his jacket and boots. 'We should meet with William Bates and Mary Wheeler. They should be back in town by now. I think they know more than they realise.'

'Answers like the identity of Persephone?'

'Exactly so. I'll send a note and ask them to meet me in Hyde Park tomorrow morning.'

'You mean "us".'

'Dora—'

'Jacob.' She smiled at him, and he sensed he was not going to win this battle.

'No, it's too risky. Everyone will be there.' Society liked to show off during the season on the carriage ride and walks of the park.

'Exactly. Safety in numbers. Few in the Ton know what I look like. I'll just be an anonymous ladybird. Vane could strike here as easily as at the park.'

Vane would undoubtedly be fuming. His men could come for her once they saw Jacob leave the hotel and he doubted the staff would be able to stand in their way.

'You must wear a veil.'

'Of course. I'll send out for a suitable hat.'

'I suppose a chance encounter on a less frequented path is much less likely to attract attention.' Their adversaries had shown they were quite willing to remove anyone who got in their way. Mary, Bates, Dora and even himself were far safer conducting business in public where no one would dare strike them down.

Or so he hoped.

Chapter Forty-Three

There was a flash and glitter to the crowds that flocked to Hyde Park for their morning's exercise. Society had wrapped itself up like a present in bows and coloured cloth then spread out under the blue skies and spring sunshine. Men were smartly turned out but they were mere foils to the rainbow of partners on their arms. Fashion dictated that the ladies were dressed in narrow-skirted white gowns with cropped jackets decorated with military frogging; the fabric of the jacket matched that of the bonnet trimming. It was as though all the females had risen that morning and reached for the exact same design, like donning a uniform to face the big guns of society gossipers. To Dora, they looked like ranks of variegated soldiers as they sauntered on the arms of their beaux beneath the new leaves of the plane trees.

Dora glanced down at her own disreputable military coat, picked up in a second-hand shop in Carlisle. At least she had the frogging, if nothing else.

'No one is going to mistake me for a ladybird,' she said. 'Or else you will earn a reputation as a cheap gentleman who does not keep his mistress in style.'

'Let's keep them guessing about us,' said Jacob, swinging his cane. He was looking quite dashing in a dark blue jacket and frothy white cravat. She'd enjoyed playing valet that morning. 'Come, we'll take this path. I'd prefer not to stay where we might meet someone I know.'

'Ashamed of me?'

'Far from it. But my mother and sisters are dashed inquisitive.'

He led her away from the carriages and walkers who followed the Serpentine Lake and headed towards Grosvenor Gate. Here, where the park had been landscaped into open spaces, riders exercised their horses. They paid little attention to those on foot as they put their thoroughbreds through their paces. Jacob raised his cane, having spotted Bates and Mary Wheeler walking towards them from the north. Mary's pink silk jacket worn over snowy muslin was a daring shade, denoting her demimonde status. She had gained her desire – the hope that had made her quit Henley. Despite realising her dream, the girl's expression was far more guarded than it had been at the ball.

She had heard about Matt, Dora realised.

'Bates, Miss Wheeler,' Jacob said, bowing. 'Thank you for meeting us.'

'What the hell is going on, Sandys? Heard you and Leighton were shot at,' said Bates. 'Damn suspicious business. Decided the country wasn't safe for us.' He patted Mary's hand.

'I'm afraid I have to agree. We've all stumbled into something that is far deeper, far nastier than we first thought.' Jacob glanced at Dora for permission. 'Look, Bates, I think the less you know about the specifics the better.'

Bates gave him a sour smile. 'How did you know that was my philosophy of life?'

'And you have Miss Wheeler here to protect.'

Mary squeezed her man's arm. 'Matt didn't deserve it. He was a good lad. Harmless. You'll catch the bastard, won't you?'

'We're trying,' Dora assured her.

'Meanwhile I'd not accept any more invitations from Sir Fletcher Vane, if I were you,' added Jacob.

'He's the cove that did it?' Mary's soft features took on a surprisingly murderous expression.

'We're not certain,' admitted Dora. 'He's involved, we do know that.'

'My dear, leave it to Dr Sandys to see the guilty punished. He's a sound man. Got good family to back him,' said Bates in an undertone.

Mary ignored him. 'Whatever you need, doctor, miss, I'm ready and willing.' She was fierce. Dora liked her all the more for that. That was the quality that had taken her from a girl from the back room of a pub to this position of kept mistress, the peak of her career.

Jacob took a quick survey of the park, checking their conversation wasn't attracting undue attention from the riders racing each other across the turf. 'What we need now is answers. Bates, I take it Vane didn't frequent Hellfire meetings?'

Bates gave a bark of laughter. 'Him? No. He was interested, wanted the gossip, but he never applied to be a member. We don't encourage the curious, though with Vane I always felt it was his role in government intelligence gathering that made him want to know everything. I told him he had to join if he wanted to know more – but then he would've been vowed to secrecy so...' He shrugged.

'And yet he moved into the big house, and had a key to the caves? Didn't that strike you as a strange choice for a man who had no intention of throwing in his lot with you all?'

'There have been many tenants at the Park since the Dashwoods moved out. They haven't interfered before. Vane's a patriot, a good huntsman, throws a decent party, but his tastes don't run to the sulphurous kind. He's too ... conventional.'

'You're wrong. He stinks of brimstone. Vane killed my brother,' Dora said, thinking it high time that Bates had his illusions about Vane shattered.

Shock punctured Bates's complacency. 'You know this for a fact? Why haven't you told the authorities?'

'I have no proof apart from his confession to me.' Right before she'd knifed him.

'But you must tell them; at least make them aware. The Bow Street magistrate's a good chap. He'll listen to you, Sandys, if not the lady.' It was telling how much trust Bates put in authority. Mary's and Dora's gazes met and Mary rolled her eyes. No one of their station in life would be so sanguine.

'Perhaps,' said Jacob, 'but first may I ask another question?'

Bates gestured for him to go ahead.

'Did Anthony arrange for Mother Clerk to send you parcels for collection at the George and Dragon?'

Dora wondered what this was about. 'Mother Clerk?'

'I'll explain later.'

Was that a flash of shame on Jacob's face?

'Opium dealer,' said Mary, rendering explanations unnecessary. 'Ruthless Russian but reliable. Everyone goes to her.'

Bates looked puzzled. 'No. I made my own arrangements.'

'I see.' Jacob sounded like he was ticking off a mental checklist. 'Do you know with whom Anthony Pennington was in love? The one he called Persephone.'

Bates looked away for a moment. 'You know about Anthony?'

'We worked it out,' said Dora. Was this one of the ties of friendship that Bates had with her brother? It was a ticklish thing for a man about town to admit. 'I wish he'd told me. I wouldn't have cared.'

'He found it difficult.' Bates toyed with his watchchain. 'Couldn't leave it behind with his schooldays.' Ah, so they had once been lovers, surmised Dora. 'It didn't fit with the image that others had of Anthony, nor he of himself.'

Mary looked confused at this conversation that was going on over her head. 'What are you talking about, Willy?'

He smiled down at her with tolerant affection. 'Anthony's knotty love life.'

She snorted. 'Oh yes. He liked to tie people up.'

Mary's mind was wonderfully literal, Dora realised.

'Men and women?' she asked, knowing Jacob might be too polite to go there.

'Oh yes. Those who liked a little pain with their pleasure. He was very good with the whip.' Mary gave a little shiver.

Dora hid her grimace. There were things one simply did not want to know about one's brother. 'Did he have any particular male friends?'

Mary frowned in thought. 'He did like arranging threesomes in the caves, but I always said no. Jessie was in one with him and another cove. Wasn't he close to that lieutenant, Willy? What's his name? Alex something?'

'Alexander Smith, a lieutenant colonel in the 1st Battalion 2nd Foot Guard,' supplied Bates.

'Is he, by chance, one of Wellington's aides-de-camp?' asked Jacob.

Bates looked at him sharply. 'How the devil did you know that?'

After separating from Bates and Mary, they walked towards the gate.

'What now? Find Smith?' asked Dora.

'I think so.'

'He will have heard by now. Maybe he will be here for Anthony's funeral?'

'That's a good thought. Leighton likely knows the details and I'll persuade him to take me with him.'

'An explanation for your own attendance?'

'Exactly.'

She pressed his arm. 'I'd like to go—'

'You know you can't!'

'*But* I know I can't. Can you be there for me?'

He nodded.

'Thank you.' She leant her head against his shoulder briefly.

'*You!*' A horribly familiar voice pulled her out of that quiet moment. 'So it's true! You dare to show your face in London?' Three men stood in the gateway on the point of entering the park: her father, Gatskill and Sir Fletcher Vane. The baronet looked smug.

Vane wasn't dead then, nor even seriously injured. The little knife had been foiled by the many layers of clothing a gentleman wore. Dora didn't know if she was pleased or not. Had he planned this confrontation as retaliation? She was surprised he knew her father well enough to be seen in public together. The ugly pain of seeing her father after so long she would ignore until she was alone, and Vane wouldn't see how it affected her.

'How are you, Father?' she said, not rising to his melodrama.

'You dare speak to me?' His eyes glittered with the expression that always heralded an explosion. As children it had meant a beating. At least now she need no longer fear that.

'You did just address me. I was replying.'

'Sir Fletcher warned me you had come on the town.' That explained his appearance with Vane: yes, they were looking for her. Vane wanted to recapture her, but her father? He wanted to grind her into the dust. Nothing had changed. 'The only reply I want from you is your heartfelt apology for your scandalous behaviour. If you are asking for me to take you back, then, yes, I will.' He put his hand to his heart, a histrionic gesture that had no real sentiment behind it. 'I will provide for you, but in seclusion in the country away from society. Any other words are a waste of your breath.'

He still laboured under the misapprehension that she cared what he did or thought. 'We already covered this ground five years ago. I don't want anything from you but your absence.'

He flushed scarlet. 'Jezebel!'

'Really, Father, one would think you would remember your own daughter's name,' Dora said.

Jacob angled his body so she was sheltered from her father's glare. 'I will not allow you to speak to my companion like that, sir.'

'Won't allow me?' Ezra Pennington spluttered. 'Is this the impudent dog you told me about?'

'He's the son of Viscount Sandys,' Gatskill said hurriedly. 'A powerful man.'

'I don't care if he is God himself!' roared Ezra. He always enjoyed his tempers, Dora remembered. He liked nothing better than to feel aggrieved and therefore justified in lashing out at everyone. He always saw himself as the victim, and everyone else as at fault. 'He's living out of wedlock with my daughter, flaunting her in society. He must answer to me for that insult!'

Jacob sent her a look of commiseration. 'I see you did not exaggerate.'

Vane, however, aped an expression of offence on behalf of the injured father.

'I agree, sir, it is not the behaviour of a gentleman. Sandys must answer for it. Do you wish me to be your second?'

The suggestion surprised them all, not least Ezra. Merchants didn't usually settle their differences on the field of honour. They preferred damages of the monetary kind.

'A duel?' asked Ezra, perplexed.

'Of course.' Vane was so very smooth, so very civilised, cleverly herding the merchant in the direction he wanted him to go. 'You stated he had insulted you. I naturally assumed that was what you meant.'

And wouldn't that suit him nicely? thought Dora sourly. Jacob could be killed, leaving Dora vulnerable once more. Or Ezra could be hurt, and Jacob would have to live down the ignominy of duelling with a father who had so recently lost his only son. If word got out, he'd have to flee the country to escape the opprobrium. Either way, Jacob would suffer, and Dora would be left unprotected.

'Very well,' said Ezra, struggling to pull off a glove. 'Let us settle this as gentlemen. Tomorrow at dawn.'

Dora sidestepped Jacob and intercepted the glove before it could be thrown at his feet.

'Don't be ridiculous, Father.'

'Ridiculous?' His ire strangled his words so that all he could do was gargle and splutter.

'I have no honour to besmirch. You had me out of wedlock, remember, so you have no right to preach morality. Anyway, you are no longer my father.'

'I ... I...'

'You made that plain when your household wore a black armband for me. I died to you five years ago. Resurrecting me now to take pot-shots at a stranger is beyond even your usual absurdity. You could die.'

His expression changed as her words sank in.

'Dr Sandys served in the army. He is a crack shot. I'm sure you'll agree that I am not worth losing your life for.' She stuffed the glove down the front of his waistcoat. 'Good morning, gentlemen.' She swept on past them. 'Oh, by the way, Sir Fletcher Vane is the one who killed Anthony. You really should choose your friends more wisely.'

Chapter Forty-Four

Leighton rested on the daybed in his suite at Grillon's, listening as Jacob caught him up on the events of the last day. Dora sat very quietly at the window seat, looking out on the street below. Jacob was aware of her, like a beacon shining at the edge of his consciousness, even while he discussed the investigation with his old friend. After her magnificent set down of her father, she had become withdrawn.

'Do you think your father believed you about Vane?' the rector asked Dora when Jacob concluded with the events in the park.

She gave them a wan smile. 'Of course not. I just hoped to take the wind out of his sails.'

'And you did. No glove was sent after me so I think we may put aside any threat of a dawn appointment tomorrow,' said Jacob.

Leighton made a harrumph of disgust. 'Duels are against God's law. The whole practice should be outlawed.'

'It is illegal already,' said Jacob, 'just not prosecuted.'

'Would you have fought if I hadn't stopped it?' asked Dora.

'In a heartbeat. Your father is a fool. You are worth dying for.' He held her gaze, willing her to see that he meant it.

'I'd very much prefer you to live for me.'

There was a speaking silence which Leighton broke with a delicate cough. 'I agree with Miss Fitz-Pennington.'

Dora held up a hand. 'Please, reverend, call me something else. The name Pennington sits more uneasily than ever on me.'

He nodded. 'I agree with *Miss Dora*. Our aim is for us all to live through this debacle. We have no time for duels or family quarrels. Our priority is for the Hellfire secrets to be put back in safe hands.'

'Indeed.' Dora toyed with the curtain tie. 'Jacob, there was one thing I didn't understand. What did you mean about Mother Clerk?'

Dora had sprung on him the question he'd been dreading. He had hoped she had not noticed that part of the conversation with Bates.

'She supplied the Hellfire Club parties.' Jacob glanced at Leighton, then let his shoulders slump. If he was to have a future with Dora, he couldn't hide something so big from her. He'd prefer not to do this with another person present, but he'd put this off long enough. She had to know the kind of man he was. 'I have a confession, which with the reverend here is rather appropriate. Mother Clerk was also my supplier, which is how I knew about her. I gave up being a practising doctor because I was over-indulging in opium.' He looked directly at Dora. 'I'm not the battlefield hero you think I am.'

Dora looked like she'd stepped through a door in the dark and fallen down a set of basement stairs. 'You've given up the poppy as well or are you still in its thrall?'

That was a fair question. She was probably realising how this explained so much of his behaviour. As Mother Clerk said, she'd never known anyone succeed in leaving it behind as opium preparations were ubiquitous in society, rather like alcohol.

But before he could think up the right reply, Leighton was there before him.

'I have many parishioners with the same weakness, Sandys. You aren't alone. This Mother Clerk runs one of those dens of iniquity?'

Jacob nodded. He wanted to talk this out with Dora but this wasn't the time. 'She was supplying the Hellfire Club with their drugs, even out in West Wycombe.'

'Which means we have important people out of control where the enemy might get at state secrets? That sounds a recipe for disaster.'

'Time is short,' said Jacob. 'We must act.'

Leighton nodded. 'And Bates is right. It would make sense to alert the authorities to what is going on so they can get a message to Wellington that his orders might be compromised.'

'And see my brother's friend hanged as a traitor? No, we can't do that.' Dora hugged herself. Before she might have looked to him for comfort. Jacob felt the yawning chasm between them but was powerless to bridge it.

'But we cannot let those plans fall into the hands of the enemy.'

'I'm not suggesting we should, sir. But there is still a chance we can find them first.'

Jacob mentally worked through their options. 'You said that the funeral is in three days' time, Leighton, so we cannot wait. We need to make our move now. We're ahead of Vane, far ahead. He doesn't know about the Lincolnshire link.'

'Lincolnshire?' queried Leighton.

Dora turned to him. 'My brother stopped somewhere along the way on his journey back to West Wycombe. We think he left the papers near Lincoln to keep them out of Vane's hands.'

'Interesting. Very interesting.' Leighton looked up at Jacob. 'I do think we must first tell someone in authority about our suspicion just so that the military can exercise caution, before we go in search of the papers. We needn't name any names. Think how it would look if we were intercepted with such incendiary stuff in our possession!'

Jacob nodded slowly, seeing his point. 'They'd think *we* were the traitors.'

'And Vane would twist it to make it so.'

'We can do it without losing any time.' Jacob headed to the door. 'I'll ask to see the Bow Street magistrate while the hotel arranges for a carriage. It should take no more than an hour. Bates said he's a good man.'

'And then we travel to Lincolnshire?' asked Dora, still not looking at him.

'As fast as we can,' confirmed Jacob.

Feeling the sands of time slipping away, Jacob dispatched the messenger to the livery stables, urging haste, and headed for the magistrate's house. At this time of day, those incarcerated in the cells underneath Bow Street would be facing their summary justice or sent on to the Crown court. Jacob hoped to catch the judge's attention between cases.

He arrived at the tail end of a case. A boy, who looked no more than ten, was found guilty of picking pockets in the market. The magistrate referred him to the Old Bailey and informed the nipper that he was facing a sentence of transportation. His hunger-pinched cheeks and prematurely old expression suggested he knew exactly what that would mean.

And Bates had said the magistrate was a good sort? Jacob would have preferred the boy be sentenced to a decent meal.

Unfortunately, he wasn't able to right all the injustices of the world, though it stuck in his craw to admit it. Living in the Lakes had been his way of avoiding this daily reminder. He wished he were back there with nothing more pressing than a mountain to paint. Instead, he was trying to rescue the nation from imminent danger.

Summoning an usher, he sent a note to Sir John Reed, begging a moment of his time. The magistrate unfolded it, looked around the courtroom over the crowds watching the proceedings, and settled on Jacob. He gave him a nod.

'Court will adjourn,' he said abruptly, rising from his seat.

The usher led Jacob into the magistrate's private quarters next door to the courtroom. The magistrate had taken off his wig and set it on a stand, where it held court over the gathered piles of documents and a pen in an ink dock. The usher remained in the room, arms crossed. The small hairs on the back of Jacob's neck prickled.

'How are you feeling, Dr Sandys?' asked Sir John in a strangely familiar tone. Jacob was certain they'd never met.

'Well, thank you, sir. I'm here on an urgent matter.'

'So your note said. A glass of wine?' He poured two, one for himself and one for his guest. 'Do sit.'

Jacob quickly understood that a hurried explanation was not going to be allowed. He accepted the hospitality. 'Thank you.'

'Now tell me what's on your mind.'

'I've come to report a threat to the kingdom.' As soon as he said it, Jacob's confidence that he would get a hearing suffered a blow. He was stepping out on a rickety bridge over a torrent. He should have ignored Bates and Leighton. They didn't yet have enough evidence for this conversation.

'Indeed.' The magistrate continued his genial tone, not at all alarmed. 'What kind of threat?'

'I want to report that the plans for Wellington's latest offensive are in danger of falling into the hands of the enemy.'

'And you know this how?'

'There's been a series of connected deaths in the parish of West Wycombe.'

Sir John sipped his wine. 'Ah yes, poor Pennington. I read something about that. Footpads in the Hellfire caves, wasn't it?'

'No, sir. I believe that Sir Fletcher Vane, the tenant at West Wycombe Park, is responsible for Pennington's death, and maybe others.'

Sir John grimaced. 'I see. A respected member of the government is implicated. And why would he kill Pennington?'

'You know that West Wycombe hosts the gatherings of the so-called Hellfire Club?'

Sir John gave an encouraging nod. Was that a patronising smile?

Jacob ploughed on. 'Pennington was the warden of the Hellfire Club and kept the secrets that its members lodged as surety. They pledged these as assurance that they would hold their tongues about its activities. Pennington hid these secrets, one of which was the military orders gained from an officer close to Wellington.'

'Which officer?'

'I'm not certain.' His bridge rocked but he remembered Dora's words that they should protect her brother's lover. 'Vane found out and attempted to blackmail Pennington into revealing the location of the cache of secrets.'

'Surely, as a member of the government, he should do exactly that to protect the plans?'

In for a penny, in for a pound. 'Unfortunately, his loyalty is in question. I believe he was doing it for his own reasons, not to protect the war effort.'

'Again, I have to ask why?'

'Vane is an Illuminati. He seeks to bring the government

down.' Jacob knew he had lost his audience, but he had tried. 'Believe me, I know how this sounds, but it's all true. I swear it.'

Sir John nodded in a friendly fashion. 'And now you've got it off your chest. Feeling better, eh?'

Of all reactions, this was one Jacob did not know how to meet. 'What?'

'Stay calm, Dr Sandys. One of your colleagues has been summoned.'

'Summoned why?' He had to get out of here.

'Take it easy, sir. I'm a friend of your family; I mean you no harm.'

Jacob couldn't understand how this connected to his information. 'You have to warn the government – Vane's superior at the Alien Office at the very least. I can't give you proof yet, but lives are at stake. They need to take preventative action.'

'Oh dear, oh dear. I was warned that you were running around town in a fugue state, visiting opium dens and flinging aspersions at everyone you encounter. Broken by your wartime service, they say.' Sir John frowned. 'It does not reflect well on a gentleman to listen to gossip but I see it is true. How sad for your poor mother.'

'My mother?' This was a nightmare. He had to leave.

'Vane said you even drew a knife on him and stabbed him. He lodged a complaint yesterday. Mr William Bates reported similar concerns but said you'd likely hand yourself in to me if I waited.'

Bates was working with Vane. He should have seen it! How else would Vane have known where to find them in the park?

The usher set his hands on Jacob's shoulders, pushing him back down in his seat.

'Rather than press charges,' Sir John carried on with utmost reasonableness, 'we have agreed that you should be secured for your own safety.' He nodded to the usher, who was to be Jacob's gaoler. 'Do it.'

A second burly man entered the office, carrying a straitjacket, and Jacob understood with cold certainty where this was heading.

'I'm serious, Sir John! There is a plot! You must listen to me!'

'Keep calm, Dr Sandys. Don't make this worse.'

Jacob struggled, desperate to make a break for it, but the two ushers were experienced in handling difficult criminals. They had him pinned on his front and stuffed into the straitjacket before he got in any good blows. Once that was fitted, his choices were taken away from him. They heaved him to his feet.

Jacob breathed heavily through his nose, trying to regain his poise. Sir John was not the enemy.

'I understand why you think I've run mad, Sir John, but I'm telling you the truth. Please contact Reverend Leighton; he can be found at Grillon's Hotel. He will verify my story.'

A small flicker of doubt chased across Sir John's genial face. 'I suppose religious counsel should not be withheld from those in distress.' Then he shook his head. 'But Vane is a good friend of mine. A hunting fellow of the old school. You need to be cured of that brain fever of yours before you kill someone.' He flicked his hand. 'Take Dr Sandys away. I must return to court.'

Chapter Forty-Five

The Great North Road

Jacob should have been back by now. Dora fretted with the curtain fringe. The carriage was waiting on the street below and couldn't stay there much longer as it was blocking the traffic. She hadn't found the right words to say to him after his revelation and she worried that he had been wounded by her silence. She was annoyed with herself for that.

Yet her withdrawal had not been without cause. Jacob had used the same supplier as her brother. Anthony had fuelled his mad moods with opium and seeing what it did to him had taught her the bitter lesson that opium-eaters were devious, even fooling themselves that they could reform. When she walked out on her family, the chief reason Anthony had not defended her was that he did not want to be cut off from the funds that paid for his habit. He hadn't stepped up to be her big brother, putting the poppy first. Was Jacob merely another addict? He wasn't the upright doctor set on putting society straight that she had thought.

Could she rely on someone travelling the same path to hell as her brother?

'Miss Dora, please, come away from the window. Worrying does Dr Sandys no good.' Leighton looked up from the atlas. They were plotting their route north to calculate where they would need to change horses. He'd made meticulous notes and it appeared he was nearly finished.

'I fear something has happened to delay him.' She took the seat opposite the rector at the little table.

Leighton checked his pocket watch and grimaced. 'You might well be right. I will go and enquire.'

Dora reminded herself that the mild-mannered rector was in fact a man of generous frame, probably able to hold his own in a tussle should it come to that. Still, his open expression made her feel as though she was sending out a lamb to confront a wolf pack. She reached out and placed a hand on his sleeve. 'Be careful, sir.'

'Naturally. You'll find that few doors remain closed to a clergyman for long. I carry the protection of the church with me. Wait for us here.'

He sallied out, leaving the room in a ticking silence. That came from the clock on the mantlepiece, a timekeeper with a friendly expression. The hands stood at ten past twelve. The morning had already passed.

They ought to have been on the road by now.

Dora twisted the atlas towards her and picked up Leighton's list. He'd carefully printed out the miles between staging posts and the turnpiked roads that would make for the speediest journey. Something about his script caught Dora's attention. It was familiar – the oval shape of the O, the straight tail to the Y.

Then it hit her.

Matt Jenkins' note. *I am sorry I killed them I did it Forgive me.* She would swear it was his hand. She had noticed at the time that the message had included capital letters as if the writer could not bear to leave all rules of grammar behind. A meticulous writer like Leighton would have given in to that impulse to make it comprehensible even while aping the hand of an uneducated man.

The pieces in her head shifted into a new pattern. Leighton, the writer of the message, and therefore ... Matt's killer? No, that seemed impossible. There was no motive. He was the one who had brought Jacob to West Wycombe to investigate the deaths. He'd hardly want himself caught, hardly kill again just before they arrived.

Unless...

Dora began packing up the final things for the journey, her body knowing her decision even before her mind had accepted it.

He might well have wanted her brought within reach. Had he calculated that involving Jacob in carrying the message would inevitably bring them both to his rectory?

Hand shaking, she took up the list and packed it along with the atlas. Whatever the truth, they'd foolishly told Leighton everything upon his arrival in London, despite keeping the details from him for so long. They should have stuck with their first instinct. Now he knew about the military plans and the likelihood that they were in Lincolnshire. He was as keen as they were to get to them. For what purpose? Nothing good, she was sure of it.

His part in this was murky. Only one thing was crystal clear: she had to get to the plans first. The men she was with had all proved unreliable or worse. She couldn't even wait for Jacob to come back. In fact, while he was distracting Leighton and Vane by carrying his complaint to the magistrate, she had been given what might be her only opportunity to get a head start on them. She could work out who exactly Leighton was serving as she made her way north.

She shrugged into her coat, fingers pausing on the buttons. Jacob would think she had abandoned him. And he would be right.

But the safety of the nation came first. Napoleon could not be allowed to massacre British soldiers, men and boys like her brother, just because she was afraid of being misunderstood.

She took up her bag and left the room.

At first the coachman refused to leave without a gentleman.

'I was told to wait for Dr Sandys,' he said gruffly.

Dora had taken the precaution of rifling through Jacob's saddlebags and had liberated some of his money to fund her dash to Lincolnshire. At least he wouldn't be able to spend it on drugs. She held out a sovereign.

'Dr Sandys has been called away to a patient,' she said firmly. 'He is no longer able to accompany me. Here, this is for your trouble.'

The coachman caught the tossed coin, bit it to test its worth, then pocketed it. 'All right, miss, in you hop. Same journey, I take it?'

'Yes. The north road, as quickly as you can.'

When the carriage cleared the West End and started through the newly developed streets of Somers Town and Camden Town, she began to relax a little. She had got away without being stopped. All she had to do now was work out what Leighton had to do with this mess and where exactly in Lincolnshire she was supposed to search.

Making use of the daylight, she opened the atlas and began to trace her route along the Great North Road. There had to be something more, some clue she wasn't seeing. She checked back through the line of reasoning they had followed.

Anthony's letter had led them to Medmenham Abbey where they had found the lantern and the map.

She took these out of her bag, smoothing the page flat on the open atlas.

His last words to Vane had reinforced that clue, telling her to look for the missing curtain tie used for knotting the lantern on the end. Then he had dared to write a fragment of Shakespeare on the torn-out map, leaving her to conclude the line with 'beacon of the wise'. They had taken that to mean they should use the lantern to gain knowledge.

That was logical, wasn't it?

Or had they leapt too quickly to the obvious answer? Anthony liked to misdirect when setting a puzzle. A clue could have more than one meaning. Anyone with half a brain would have tried to use the lantern to pinpoint a place on the map once they noticed the piercings. Was the 'beacon' something else, something to do with the next clue?

She thought briefly of the ball on top of the West Wycombe church but then dismissed it. That didn't marry with the instruction to go to Lincolnshire.

What kind of beacons were there in a landlocked county? No lighthouses. She didn't think it lay on the route of the new shutter telegraph that linked the Admiralty to the coasts. Those went to the east and south coast, not to the north. Was there a line of beacons to warn of enemy invasion? If so, why Lincolnshire? That was hardly on the front line of the nation's defence and was supposed to be remarkably flat – hardly ideal for a beacon.

Dora pinched the bridge of her nose, willing herself to be cleverer. If she didn't work it out before she arrived, her head start would be wasted and her enemies would catch up.

Feeling for the pistol in her pocket, she discovered it had gone. Had Jacob taken it back? If so, when?

This was going to end badly, she knew it in her gut, and yet she had no choice but to go on.

Chapter Forty-Six

Bedlam

Jacob hunkered down in the corner of his cell in Bethlem hospital, Moorfields. He knew this place well, having visited during his medical training. How on earth had he ended up here as a patient? It was the grimmest place in London behind one of the most impressive facades. It looked like a palace from the outside, but within it was rotten. The signs of dilapidation had been evident when he had visited as a student, but now the place was one good storm away from collapsing.

He racked his brains to work out how to prove he wasn't a raving lunatic – not like the poor man in the cell with him who was preaching to the walls, alternating that with hitting his head against the bricks. His skull, protected only by a thin froth of white hair, was scarred with what Jacob could only presume were previous collisions with hard surfaces. His clothes were in rags, remnants of a once fine shirt and stained breeches. Maybe he too had not been insane when he was committed? Being in this hellhole made the man's self-harm seem a logical response.

Screams and sobs rose up like wild animal cries in a jungle, coming in billows of hysteria then ebbing away. It was like winter inside, though spring was in progress in the parks and fields beyond the walls. Worst of all though was the smell. The warders had long since given up nursing any of their charges, too intent on making a penny or two from the visitors they smuggled in to gawp at the unfortunates. The public were now restricted to those who had a ticket from the governor, but he must be doing a roaring trade in handing those out. At least ten society people had paraded before his cell, expressing insincere words of sorrow while they enjoyed the antics of his cellmate. He himself had attracted no attention by pretending to be asleep. He didn't know if he wanted to see someone he knew or not. If word of this got back to his family, they would act, but they also might believe the lies the magistrate had been fed. They'd seen him in the worst stages of his addiction and very little since, so that door was already half-open to belief. He might find himself whisked off to some private asylum from which it would be far harder to break free.

No, he needed his wits to get out of here – and his friends – not his family.

''Ere 'e is, sir. Sitting quiet as a mouse now but 'e roared like a lion when we dragged 'im in.' The warder, whom Jacob had mistaken for a court usher, stood in the doorway, Leighton at his side.

Thank God.

'I'm sure he did, young man,' said Leighton, 'as would you if you were dragged away by strangers. He is amongst friends now and I will vouch for him – as I have already done with Sir John Reed. He agreed he should be released into my care. This is hardly the place for the son of a viscount.' Leighton cleared his throat. 'Now, er, Jacob, you'll come quietly with me, won't you?'

Jacob was about to agree when his cellmate started shrieking.

'Devil! Satan! Beelzebub! Belial! Mammon!' He tried to dash his brains out against the wall. The warder rushed in and pulled him back but the man continued shouting, 'Moloch! Mulciber!'

Leighton followed the warden inside. 'I fear the poor man will recite all the lesser devils from *Paradise Lost* before he quietens. Perhaps you should let me take Dr Sandys away?'

'All right, sir. Send word where you take 'im so I can tell my governor. We can't lose sight of dangerous lunatics.'

'I will endeavour to do so instantly.' Leighton helped Jacob up. He was still in the straitjacket and would prefer to have that off at once but he knew better than to pause even an instant when the prison door was open.

They hurried out into the dank corridor between the cells. Leighton threw his own cloak over Jacob's shoulders.

'My word, Sandys, I leave you alone for one meeting and look what happens!'

Head down, Jacob limped after him. The warders had given him his second beating in a week and he felt every blow they had landed.

'I was betrayed. Bates must be working with Vane. They had set a trap by sending me to the magistrate. Can you get this damn jacket off me?'

They paused when they reached the staircase. Leighton quickly unbuckled the straps so Jacob's arms were free.

'If anyone stops us, you are coming quietly with me to a private asylum in my parish. Make no mention of plots and offer no violence to anyone.' They started down the stairs.

'I think I've learned my lesson.'

Yet as they reached the main doors, they suddenly came upon Vane entering. For the moment, the great hall was empty, just the three enemies wrong-footed by encountering each other where they were not expected to be.

Leighton smiled. 'Vane, I'm glad you got my note.'

Or maybe someone did expect this?

Recovering, Vane unscrewed the top of his cane, withdrew a dagger from the hilt and pointed it at Sandys.

'What's he doing out of his cell?' He raised his voice. 'Warder!'

Before Jacob could respond, Leighton reached into his pocket, took out an all too familiar duelling pistol and shot Vane point-blank in the face. The report echoed around the hall. Vane crumpled, mouth open in shock. Death had been instantaneous.

'Quick,' said Leighton, moving swiftly through the open door.

Jacob was frozen with horror but he could only follow dumbly. Being present at the killing of the man he'd been accused of stabbing would end with him being blamed, he had no doubt.

But Leighton?

Reverend George Leighton of West Wycombe had just shot a baronet as coolly as a pirate finishing off the captain of a ship he had just overhauled.

Once outside, they slowed their pace and Leighton hailed the first hansom cab he saw. He gave the driver orders to return to the hotel. Behind them, they could already hear the alarm bell ringing in the hospital.

Jacob struggled out of the last straps of the straitjacket and stuffed it under the cloak.

'You shot him!'

'He was an enemy of England, a traitor. I did the world a favour.' Leighton glanced behind. 'Good. No one is following us.'

'Who are you?'

Leighton gave him that benign pastoral smile which now struck Jacob as the expression a tiger might give its prey before biting through its neck. 'I am your friend, George Leighton. Are you really disturbed in the mind after all, Sandys?'

Jacob shook his head. 'I don't understand why you killed him. Denounce him to the authorities, yes; get him to talk so we can find out who else is planning to overthrow the government, absolutely. But kill him? You get none of those answers.'

'I killed him because we have to get to those papers before anyone else does.'

'The military plans?'

Leighton gave him the long-suffering look of a teacher to a dull-witted pupil. 'No, that's no matter, not now I've done away with Vane. He was the mastermind behind that particular plot. It will wither without him.'

'But we met at least three other Illuminati. They will want revenge and might well pick up where he left off.'

Leighton snorted with disgust. 'Imbeciles. The Illuminati think they are so clever, when in fact they've been my cat's paw for some years now.'

'Your cat's paw?'

'They weeded out the weak members when I pointed out those I wanted gone. Not that I meant them to go for Anthony, not so soon at least. He was a good follower, if not worthy of the Second Circle. He was a trusty gatekeeper to our realm. No, the idea to target Anthony came from Vane with his idiotic scheme to betray the nation. He needed killing for that alone.'

Some questions Jacob had been considering for some time now had their answer.

'You are the one really in charge of the Hellfire Club, aren't you? The archbishop, the High Priest of the Caves, the one to whom Mother Clerk sent the opium. You barely bothered to conceal your identity.'

Leighton cocked his head. 'How is the old she-demon?'

Jacob was still marvelling at how blind he had been to what was really afoot in West Wycombe. 'Hiding in plain sight – not even bothering to hide. I imagine half the village knows what you get up to.'

'Only a few. The Second Circle is for initiates of the deeper mysteries of our craft, not the common herd.'

'And the women who died?'

Leighton smiled sadly. 'Occasionally I get young girls coming to me for help – usually they are those who have been cast out of their parish when they start to show so they don't burden the vestry with the cost of raising their bastards.'

'Those victims were pregnant?' That made it doubly evil – so vile that it took Jacob's breath away.

'I showed them how they could be of service. Sometimes sacrifices are required. Dying at the point of ecstasy is the greatest gift we can offer Our Master.'

'That is obscene.'

'You don't understand the power of sin. You need to sin in order to be forgiven. Those who sin much are forgiven much.'

'Don't twist the words of the Bible to your own perverted philosophy. You're mad.'

'No, just dedicated.'

'You are crazed if you think you'll get away with this.' Jacob contemplated leaping from the hansom cab while it was still moving.

Leighton gripped Jacob's forearm, demonstrating more strength than he had hitherto revealed. 'Do not. If you want to live, you must do as I say.' He nodded to the streets. 'Where would you go? You've just shot a baronet and broken out of Bedlam. Bates will back my testimony.'

'He's working with you, not Vane?'

'Indeed, though we did have Vane hoodwinked for a while. No one will take your wild words seriously and I will say you forced me away with you.'

Jacob sank back against the leather seat.

'Good man. Now, once we've fetched the delectable Miss Dora, we will be on our way. Save your questions until then.'

He didn't want a woman within a thousand miles of Leighton, especially not one he cared about.

'I'll come, but leave her out of your plans.'

'Oh no, I'm very much afraid she cannot be omitted from my plans, not now she knows about the Hellfire secrets. Both of you have a choice: give us a secret about yourself that we in the Second Circle can hold as a surety of your silence, or…'

'Or?'

'Join Vane in the afterlife.'

Chapter Forty-Seven

Dunston Pillar, Lincolnshire

By the time Dora had reached Grantham, she had decided on the strategy to find her needle in a haystack. Anthony had always been logical when setting puzzles. Her brother so far had located his clues in places associated with the Hellfire Club – first West Wycombe, then Medmenham Abbey. Was there any reason to think he would break the pattern? Dora thought not. She needed to find out if this region had any associations with the club and let that guide her.

Getting out at The Angel Inn, she stretched and rubbed the small of her back. The turnpike was a good road but no matter how fine the suspension on a carriage was, it couldn't prevent discomfort setting in after hours of travelling north. Fortunately, The Angel was an old inn, well used to travellers, and already the servants were hurrying out to deal with the new arrival. The efficiency suited her needs.

'My lady.' The ostler tugged his forelock.

Dora almost laughed at the unexpected term of address, until she remembered that a woman who could afford to travel in a carriage on her own and command the finest teams of horses at each stage had to be a lady. Her shabby greatcoat would be put down to the eccentricities of the rich.

'Yes?' She called on her Olivia, the countess from *Twelfth Night*.

'Will you be staying with us tonight or leaving directly? Just, I haven't got a team available this late and will have to send for one.'

Her driver and groom would need a rest after a day and a half of continuous driving. Both were grumbling.

'I'll be staying here.' Out of the corner of her eye she could see the driver sag with relief.

'Very good, m'lady.'

She swept into the inn. There was no alternative but to bluster through the fact that she had no maid with her. Fortunately, Jacob's purse was not yet empty.

'My good man, supper and a room for myself, and suitable accommodation for my servants.' Let him only find out she meant just a driver and groom when she had secured her place.

'It would be our pleasure, ma'am.' The innkeeper was a jolly sort, flushed and rotund like an Edam cheese. 'Will you dine in your room?'

'That would be satisfactory.' The less she was in the public eye the better.

Money was a miraculous thing. Dora pondered the joys of hot water for washing, a big bed with clean sheets, and carved teak furniture. The walls were decorated with prints of local views, many featuring the cathedral in Lincoln. The care taken over the room was a welcome change – no fleas, no snoring companions, no sacks of onions. Normally she squeezed into a bed in the attic with Ruby, thinking herself lucky to have a roof over her head.

A soft tap came at the door.

'Come!'

The innkeeper himself brought her tray and efficiently set about placing the supper on the table.

'Are you travelling far, milady, if I might be so bold as to ask?' He unfolded a linen napkin with a snap and put it on her lap.

She glanced at the pictures for inspiration. 'Only to Lincoln. I am an antiquarian' – sorry, Jacob – 'interested in history and I believe the cathedral at Lincoln is a marvel?'

'Oh, indeed, milady. Tis a treat.' He poured a glass of red wine.

'Excellent.' On impulse, she pulled her keepsake book out of her bag and put it on the table, tapping the cover with her forefinger. 'I sketch too. Are there any other local landmarks that I might wish to take in on my travels?'

'Before you get to Lincoln?' He stood straight and scratched his chin. 'It's unfriendly country round here. Bleak, some might say.'

She gave a little laugh. 'Oh well. I believe that my brother mentioned a connection of some kind to the Hellfire Club in the area. Caves or whatnot? Maybe a ruined abbey?' She was fishing but what else could she do?

The innkeeper looked puzzled. 'Hellfire? You mean Sir Francis Dashwood?'

She almost wanted to shout with relief but contained herself with a slight smile. 'I believe I do.'

'Well, that Sir Francis might've been a devil down south, but up here he did us all a service. The Dashwoods owned land round these parts, and houses. Old Sir Francis was a great improver.'

'He was?'

The innkeeper pointed to an engraving on the wall, tucked in one corner. 'That there is the Dunston Pillar. One of only three lighthouses built inland – we're very proud of it. Over ninety-two foot it was in its prime.'

'An inland lighthouse?' How bizarre.

'Aye. It used to have a lantern on top to guide travellers across the heath. Then a couple of years ago, now the roads are better and the highwaymen chased off, they decided to change the lantern for a statue of the king. The pillar belongs to the Earl of Buckingham now and he's a patriotic sort. He was the one who put up the statue. You can still go and see it – sketch it if you like. Many visitors do. It's about twenty mile off if you take the Leadenham road to Lincoln, rather than going by Newark.' He lifted the lid on a beef stew. 'Will there be anything else, milady?'

'No, thank you. This is splendid.'

The door closed behind him, and Dora jumped up and spun on the spot, unable to contain her exhilaration. Yes! That was exactly what she was looking for, and Anthony had even made it blindingly obvious with his 'beacon of the wise' clue – only she had had no idea that inland lighthouses existed.

Anxiety crowded back in after her moment of triumph. Now that she saw the answer herself, she wondered whether someone more familiar with Sir Francis Dashwood would work it out more quickly?

Should she set off now?

But her driver was exhausted and no fresh team of horses was available. It would be more prudent to set off early after giving them time to recover.

Sending down word that they would leave at dawn, Dora locked and barricaded the door in case her enemies did catch up with her. All she could do now was wait for sunrise.

Dora managed to sleep, which was a welcome change after the frantic pace of the last few days. Her dreams, though, were horror filled with glimpses of Jacob drowning in a stormy sea as she ran away with the rope. Waking while it was still dark, Dora thought the night terrors were not hard to interpret. Her conscience niggled that she had abandoned Jacob – and stolen from him. He would think she was running from him after his revelation – and perhaps she was?

Rising rather than risk the dreams again, she was ready before the carriage.

Two hours later, when the sun sat low on the eastern horizon, she saw the pillar in the distance. The closest comparison she could think of was the etchings of obelisks that had been found in Egypt: a rectangular pillar tapering only a little at the top. Where the beacon had once blazed, King George III now surveyed the heath. Since the poor king had finally been declared insane and replaced by the regent, it did seem emblematic of the age to exchange a beacon of light for one of confusion.

The carriage drew up and Dora wondered how to conduct her search. The tower had tea pavilions either side of it, but these were empty at present. The door to the tower itself was locked with a note referring visitors to the nearby cottage. She sent the groom to knock and he returned with the custodian of the key, an elderly man in faded livery.

'My lady wishes to see the tower,' the old man said. 'Early bird, eh?'

'If it is not too much trouble.' She made a quick guess as to whom this particular St Peter was. 'I am an admirer of the follies left to us by Sir Francis Dashwood. I've come from West Wycombe Park and was told I could not neglect calling by the pillar on my journey north.'

The old man chuckled. 'Aye, he was a rare one, was Sir Francis. Not that this was a folly – it was useful in its day.'

'You knew him?'

'I remember him from when I was a boy. That was when he married Miss Ellys of Nocton. We had a whole ox to celebrate.' He put the key in the lock, moving with the slowness of his great years.

'Do you remember the tower being built?'

'Aye. I was a youngster then, a servant here on the Nocton estate. We all marvelled at the idea, laughed even, but it caught on, like most of his notions did. And later, even when the roads became safer, they kept it going. Even held grand parties here.' He grinned. 'Not that I can tell a young lady about those.'

Dora looked away with what she hoped would be understood as maidenly confusion. Really, she was hiding her grin. 'Indeed, I've heard rumours.'

He pulled the door open. 'They're all true, miss. Never you doubt it. But nothing for you to worry about now. They're all gone, those Hellfire men. The Earl of Buckingham has seen to it, putting our king on top.' He gestured to a staircase that wound up inside. 'You may go up if you wish. The views are mighty fine.'

'You are not coming?'

'My knees won't take it anymore. I won't be going to the top again.'

Which meant her brother would have gone up alone too. 'Then I will take a quick look.'

'There's no hurry – but there are many stairs. Watch your footing. I'll wait here. Shout if you need rescuing and I'll send one of your men after you.'

She paused at the door. 'It was my brother who suggested I come here. Anthony Pennington? About three weeks ago?'

The old man blinked. 'Oh yes, I remember. He came early, like you have, before the other visitors arrived. He spent a long time at the top. I was worried he'd met with an accident, but he said he had been transfixed by the view.'

'Worried?'

The old man smiled sadly. 'Aye, I don't allow those up who look like they might cast themselves off the top. It's been known. Poor John Willson, the mason, was killed dead putting up that statue. You aren't going to jump, are you, my lady?'

'Do I look the sort?'

He chuckled. 'No, I don't think you do.'

Leaving the old man to enjoy the oblique rays of morning sun at the foot of the tower, Dora began the climb to the summit. The walls were smooth, with small porthole windows to let in light. There was nowhere to hide so much as a scrap of paper, let alone a bundle of documents. Anthony must have known that. He must have had a plan. Her gut told her that it would involve the new statue at the top. It would suit the Hellfire humour to hide such incendiary secrets under the feet of the monarch.

Glad she had thought to replace the pocketknife she had left in Vane's belly, she pressed on to the summit.

From the topmost window, Dora saw that, indeed, the view was mighty fine. George, who occupied the entirety of the summit, looked down, rather than out, a fold under his chin not the most flattering portrayal of the monarch. His shoulders were decorated in the ermine of bird droppings. Running her fingers over the walls of the chamber under the statue, she looked for signs that the stonework had been disturbed recently. She found what she sought in the brickwork directly under the statue plinth. Some structure, possibly the old lighthouse lantern, had been removed and the stone filled in with mortar. One patch looked much newer than the other marks.

Checking for sounds on the stairs that would indicate other visitors arriving, she got out her knife and scraped at the mortar. It came away more easily than she had expected – a sign that Anthony had not intended to leave the documents entombed here for ever, only until collected. When her blade hit metal, her excitement rose. Clearing the last of the mortar, she pulled out a tin. It was the sort a gentleman might use for the transport of personal correspondence and coin. She wiped off the dust and opened the lid.

The secrets of the Hellfire Club looked back at her.

What now? Anthony had told her to take the bundle to Sheridan, but what would he do with the secrets? Would it not be better just to destroy them so no one could take advantage? Yet what was it that she would be destroying? There could be deeds to land, or even wills, for all she knew.

Taking a seat on the steps, she methodically began to read her way through the contents. The military plans were there. Reading how Wellington planned to push up through Spain, she was more determined than ever that Vane would never get his hands on these. There were routes, relief lines, transport ship numbers, names of the commanders, codes to be used – all the minutiae of a campaign in the summary that had been prepared for Spencer Perceval and the cabinet. That proved to be the most innocent of the documents gathered. Her brother admitted in his to his love affairs with men – a capital offence. A bishop gave evidence of his selling of church positions – that would lead to him being defrocked at the very least. A merchant confessed that he had started his business with a fraudulent loan; another man admitted to a murder committed in his youth. Every single document held within it was information that could destroy lives.

And then she came to George Leighton's entry. In it he named himself as the Arch Priest of the Second Circle, performer of all the rites of the Church of the Antichrist. He gave no details of his sins, but even that confession would see him charged with blasphemy by an ecclesiastical court.

The final pages in the pile were the list of current members. They looked like they had been cut from an older book. Dora had plenty of experience using a razorblade to remove pages so recognised the signs. There were too many in the Hellfire List to remember but the smaller group of the Second Circle had only thirteen names. She memorised them quickly. A government minister. An admiral. A society hostess. A member of the Prince Regent's inner circle. And, of course, Leighton.

She almost missed the name at the bottom, added on almost as an afterthought, or perhaps as the newest member. William Bates.

Anthony's friend was far more deeply involved than he had admitted. It was he who had sent Jacob to the magistrate.

Her worry for Jacob shot to the moon. He'd been late and she hadn't stayed to see why. And she'd left him with only Leighton as his ally. She had to get back to him.

Slipping the box into one of the big pockets inside her greatcoat, she hurried down the stairs, trying to stop it clanking against the wall as she ran. She could feel the weight of it pulling on her left shoulder – like she had a keg of gunpowder hidden inside her coat, and yet she had no idea to whom it would be safe to hand it. Would Jacob know?

It was as though her fears had conjured him. When she reached the bottom, she found Jacob waiting for her in the doorway.

'Jacob!' She rushed into his arms and hugged him tight. 'You're safe! Thank God!'

His arms squeezed her, but she could sense his tension.

'Miss Dora, how delightful to meet you again,' said Leighton, his crocodile smile stretching his lips. He was standing in the sunshine as if this was all some pleasant excursion.

She looked about for the porter or one of her men but none of them were in sight.

'I sent your people away, explaining that you'd travel with us from here on. You will, won't you?' He gave her a sly look, silencing her instinctive protest. 'Otherwise, I fear the letter I left denouncing Dr Sandys as the murderer of Sir Fletcher Vane will be released and you both will be hanged.'

Dora looked up into Jacob's strained face. 'Vane's dead?'

He gave a slight nod, confirming Leighton's threat.

'You killed him?'

Jacob's eyes went to Leighton, who smiled an acknowledgement.

'*"It was I," said the sparrow*. What is it to be?' Leighton said affably. 'A guest of Newgate Prison or the Hellfire Club?'

Chapter Forty-Eight

The Great North Road

Jacob watched Leighton closely, waiting for a moment of inattention. He needed to talk to Dora, to come up with a plan so that, when they made their move, they both knew what to do. The man had to go to sleep eventually but he kept up a stream of inane chatter to a stony Dora as they both sat side-by-side on the forward-facing seat.

Go to sleep, damn you!

Jacob and Leighton had been travelling relentlessly since they discovered Dora had gone ahead of them. Leighton had paid above the odds to have fresh teams of horses brought to them swiftly so they had made good time. Following her had proved a simple matter as a woman travelling alone in a carriage was not a common occurrence. The landlord at The Angel had even been forthcoming about her destination when Leighton said they were her family hoping to catch up with her.

Beacon of the wise. Of course. It was obvious once you knew

The Persephone Code

there was such a thing as an inland lighthouse. How had he missed that in his travels? wondered Jacob.

Watching Leighton charm the information out of the innkeeper, Jacob had realised that the rector was an even better actor than Dora. He played the genial gentleman to the hilt. Jacob despised him for it.

After catching up with Dora and relieving her of the box, Leighton had given them no choice but to get back into the carriage. He was taking them south and appeared to be in a hurry. He'd not shared with them their destination, only that they would have to offer up a secret or face the noose.

'Why, Leighton?' Jacob asked after they passed Stilton.

'Why what, Sandys?' Leighton checked his pocket watch. 'You need to be more specific. Don't you agree, my dear?'

Dora kept her gaze fixed on the view through the window.

'You are a man of the cloth, a believer, I assume,' continued Jacob. 'Why risk eternal damnation with the Second Circle? Is it worth your soul? How can you bear the hypocrisy, standing up in church every Sunday?'

Leighton smiled his hateful, superior smile. *'Was wir verstehen, das können wir nicht tadeln.'*

'You quote Goethe to excuse yourself?'

Dora stirred. 'What does it mean?'

'"What we understand we cannot blame,"' said Leighton. 'God made us in His image, with our darker side and impure impulses as well as the good. He even created Satan, splitting off part of Himself, to give expression to the fact that Creation is also capable of evil.'

'The Manichaean heresy? Really, Leighton, I thought that had been argued out in the fourth-century Church,' drawled Jacob.

Leighton ignored Jacob's scorn. 'I live in both the light and the dark. I am a good rector to my parish and preach sincerely; I do good works, but I also acknowledge that my soul is steeped in sin. I have split off that devilish part of myself, even as God has done.'

'You are insane.'

'No, merely curious. I have urges which I must understand so I explore them. You may discover that I am the only honest person you will ever meet, the furthest from a hypocrite.'

'Yet you have killed at least three women in your exploration of your urges?' said Jacob.

'Not I alone.'

So others in the circle were complicit. How deep did this go? 'And the man who fell from the church tower?'

'He unfortunately spied on one of our meetings in the golden sphere. We had no choice.'

'What about the lives of those you killed? Do you not value them?'

'That is not my place. God sees even the fall of the sparrow; how much more will He care for the lives of those unfortunates.'

Dora turned from the window. 'There's no point reasoning with him.'

'Even the Devil can quote scripture,' agreed Jacob.

Leighton laughed. 'Listen to the pair of you – a bastard actress of no great talent and a doctor who can no longer treat anyone, looking down on me. You became addicted to the very medicine you were meant to give to others! What a weakness that betrays.'

Jacob felt the wash of shame inside him. He'd not yet spoken to Dora about what she felt about that part of his life. Hadn't she fled from him at the first opportunity? He feared she had, even though he had been relieved she was no longer at the hotel waiting for them. But Leighton then had run her to ground and now it was too late.

'At least his fault only harmed himself. He didn't have to kill others to protect his guilty secret!' said Dora hotly.

She had defended him! A flicker of hope rekindled.

'Oh, but I don't feel guilty,' said Leighton. 'I feel ... liberated.'

'Liberated from what? Morality?' retorted Dora. Jacob wanted to cheer her for her splendid disdain.

'Let me explain.'

'I don't want to hear it.'

Leighton apparently liked the sound of his own voice too much to oblige her.

'When I first joined the navy as a chaplain, I was so trapped in my rules and my desire to please. And I was entirely miserable. Then I joined the Mediterranean squadron under Bickerton in 1802. Do you have any idea what it is like to serve aboard a warship?'

'How could I?'

'Then I'll tell you what that's like: hell. We spent months patrolling the waters near Egypt to prevent the French pressing their ambitions in that region. We had orders, but no provisions with which to carry them out. Men sickened and died; the ships were falling apart and in dire need of repair. And did the government care? No.'

'It's war, Leighton. You were not the only one to suffer,' Jacob said bitterly.

'Indeed not, but I saw how under the shadow of death men are capable of great generosity and great meanness, sometimes the two contrary qualities in the same person. I realised that I had only ever known men in a civilised state. This was the first time I really understood what we are – something only the refiner's fire reveals when facing death or survival.'

'And yet you lived. What a pity.' Dora's tone was dry.

'I lived. Supplies arrived just in time before the crew mutinied or starved. The expedition was declared a great success. I returned a tempered soul, the steel put into my character having passed through the furnace. The opportunity arose to move to a parish and I saw at once that West Wycombe was the best place to further my explorations.'

He made it sound as reasonable as an explorer setting off like Mungo Park to discover the interior of Africa.

'Are you not at all concerned that the Illuminati are on to you?' asked Jacob.

'You have to understand, Sandys, that the Illuminati is a loose network of people who give themselves that title – gossamer threads spread across Europe. There is little at the core to bind them. There are occasionally enough of them to score a significant victory, providing funds to their preferred leader or exploiting a crisis, but I've always regarded these efforts as more misses than hits. And in England, it will take a while for that hydra to regrow its head now that we lopped off Vane's.'

'And yet you don't see that *you* are the monster,' Dora murmured.

'We all are, my dear.'

'Speak for yourself.' She turned up the collar of her greatcoat and showed her protest by burrowing down inside to sleep. Jacob followed suit, though he had no intention of dropping off. Perhaps Leighton would subside if he had no audience? Jacob watched him through slitted eyelids. His old friend hummed a little, tapped his waistcoat, read a little from a book. Eventually boredom caught up with him and he nodded over the page. The book began to slide. Jacob caught it just before its fall would wake him up.

He gently squeezed Dora's knee. She mumbled something, far into her dreams. He tapped her slowly but steadily, not wanting to startle her awake. Her eyes fluttered open. He held a finger to his lips. She nodded her understanding.

'Thank you for defending me,' whispered Jacob.

'I'd defend anyone against him.'

'I'm sorry.' He wished he had better words and assurances that she might believe.

'I'm used to it. Don't worry.' That didn't sound as though she had really forgiven him his weakness. 'What are we going to do about our situation?'

'We need a plan.'

She rolled her eyes.

Yes, it had been rather obvious.

'Is Vane really dead?' she whispered.

He nodded.

'And they think it was you?'

He repeated the gesture.

'Shame we can't just strangle Leighton now and be done with it, but I guess that would end up on the gallows for us both. We have to prove your innocence.' She said this last partly to herself. 'But how? Who would believe us? The box?'

'That is the best proof we have,' agreed Jacob. 'We can take it…' He paused as Leighton muttered something in his sleep. 'Take it to my oldest brother.'

'Your brother?'

'He sits in the Lords and can use his parliamentary immunity to pass it to the right people in government. I should have gone to him first, not the magistrate.' His damn pride had stopped him going to family. 'We need to expose the rot to daylight. He can also vouch for us.'

'But how to get the box – and how to get away?'

Jacob had seen Leighton pass it to the footman to stow out of reach.

'The signal to run is when you or I get hold of it.'

'Improvise an escape?'

'We don't have a choice.'

Leighton shifted and his head bumped the window, waking him. He blinked.

'I do detest coach travel,' he said, as if they were a party of pleasure. 'Where are we?'

'We have passed Alconbury,' said Jacob.

'Excellent. We should be there in time.'

'Time for what?'

'For your appointment to become members of the Hellfire Club.'

Chapter Forty-Nine

Hellfire Caves

The atmosphere at the rectory had changed. Dora didn't think she was imagining that the place felt colder, like a hearth when the fire has gone out leaving only ash.

Her door opened with no knock. Dora grabbed a fire iron but it was only Leighton's elderly aunt entering with the housekeeper. Could she recruit them to help her escape?

Dora put down the poker.

'I have your gloves.' Dora said, offering the evening gloves she'd kept safe since the ball.

'Thank you, young lady. These do remind me so much of dear Sir Francis.' The old lady pocketed her relic and smiled benignly.

Helen Leighton remembered Sir Francis Dashwood? Dora recalled that she had wondered why the elderly aunt had such lavish items as pearl-buttoned kid gloves but had never followed up on that discordant note. That had been a miscalculation. Now a new picture was forming. Had Helen been one of the original Hellfire Club members? She and Jacob had been thinking about the men when they discussed the original circle, but the orgies would not have been possible without women, some of them society ladies in disguise. Helen's presence in her nephew's household, and how the rector had been introduced to the club, suddenly became clear.

That would teach her to underestimate her own sex, thought Dora sourly.

'George says you are going to one of his parties,' Helen Leighton said brightly. 'How wonderful for you. You may wear one of my old robes.' She signalled to Mrs Stock, who laid the dark grey nun's dress and deep red scapular on the bed. 'If only I were young again.'

The housekeeper scowled. 'I trust you understand the honour Miss Leighton is doing you?'

Was that jealousy? Had Mrs Stock wished to attend but never been invited?

'Oh, I am fully sensible of the privilege.' Her fury at these people kept her scornful rather than succumbing to the fear – she'd use anger to stay sharp. 'Tell me, Mrs Stock, how long have you been covering up the deaths of young women for your master? You've never felt it your duty to report him to the authorities? Not even when they scratched his face in their struggle to live?' She'd not forgotten that suspect story of a cat scratch.

'They got what was coming to them. Harlots, all of them.' Mrs Stock snapped out a wimple from its folds and placed it next to the gown.

'They were girls who came to him for help – mothers to be – who thought the rector a kind man.'

Mrs Stock huffed.

'It takes two to fornicate but only one to murder. Surely you must have realised what he's been doing when you prepared their bodies for burial?'

'Oh indeed. He was making their miserable lives count for something.' She gave Dora a cruel smile. 'As doubtless you'll discover.'

Dora gave the women up as lost causes. They were as deep in this cabal as Leighton himself with his terrifying nonsense about his duty to explore his darker urges and how that unholy act was somehow permitted. She turned her back to them.

'Be ready by eleven,' Mrs Stock said, 'or I'll stuff you into the gown myself.'

Sitting over an uneaten meal in the dining room of the rectory, Jacob acknowledged that he had reached the end of his strength. Over the last week he'd been beaten up twice, imprisoned in Bedlam, shot at and travelled hundreds of miles on very little sleep. This felt like the third day of a pitched battle when the stretcher carriers had brought in a new batch of casualties, and his hand was already shaking as he performed yet another amputation.

As the sun set red and gold behind Leighton through the distorted glass panes, the rector acted as nothing unusual was happening, spearing a bread roll and buttering it. All Jacob could see was arterial blood spurting with his knife as he made a mistake on a young subaltern.

The daytime nightmares were back. Devil take it! He couldn't afford this mental collapse. There was no Lake District to retreat to for recovery, not when lives were at risk.

'More wine, Sandys?'

He did not reply. He had to rebuild his walls, get a distance from the suffering, but it was his brain that was betraying him. He had to be on his best game to save Dora and rescue this situation. On his own strength, he was nothing.

'There's a set of evening clothes laid out for you in your room. You'd best change for the party. You are in for an exciting night,' said Leighton, clearly disappointed in his guest's reticence. Was the clergyman expecting Jacob to be enjoying his impending humiliation in the Hellfire Club?

Mutely, Jacob rose and went upstairs. His things were set out as promised, though his pistols were missing, of course. His travel paint set was there though, on the dressing table. He went over to it and lifted the lid.

Merely to check it hadn't been tampered with, he told himself.

Inside was the little bottle of opium drops Mother Clerk had pressed in his hand. He'd slipped it in so it could masquerade as the oil he used to mix with the pigments. Why had he not got rid of it?

Because it was instant access to brilliance and calm. The door he'd promised he'd never walk through again.

Should he reject the help in front of him at this critical moment? That was just his pride speaking.

He remembered the look Dora had given him when she'd found out about his reliance on opium. She already thought him an addict; what harm if he was one again for an evening? If he could save Dora by boosting his abilities, that was worth this slight misstep. Just the once. He really needed it.

His fingers reached for it unbidden.

After some hesitation, Dora did get dressed in the nun's costume, though she drew the line at wearing the veil. They had to get the document box before they fled and that was likely to be where the Hellfire Club met. If they had to pretend to go along with joining, then so be it. As soon as one of them got their hands on it, they could run.

She picked up the cross that had been left for her to wear as a necklace. The cross was inverted. *No thank you.* She tugged it up by its chain, then realised it had quite a heft to it, being made of brass. She slipped it into her pocket. You never knew when a garrotte might come in useful. She certainly didn't want to leave it lying around to be used on her.

Mrs Stock escorted her down to the hallway where Jacob and Leighton waited. It was a relief to see her one ally was still standing.

'Jacob!' Dora went to him, but he just smiled vaguely at her. Something was wrong. 'Jacob?'

'Do I detect the signs that the good doctor is revisiting his opium-eating days?' Leighton said blandly. 'I hear relapse is particularly hard on a former addict.'

'What have you done to him? How much have you given him?' She'd seen people overdose on opium drops – the blue lips and fingernails, the depressed breathing. Sometimes the body quietened so much it just stopped. She rubbed the back of his hand. He felt very cold.

'Do not blame me. I was planning to offer him some at the party later. He must've had it with him all the time.' Leighton smiled sweetly at Dora. 'I believe we all know the secret Sandys will hand over to the club, do we not?'

'Jacob, what have you done?' Dora shook his arm.

'So long since I've known peace,' he said in a mild voice.

'Did you even measure it out?'

'Very strong. Stronger than I'm used to,' Jacob murmured, not sounding bothered by the admission.

'Jacob, you've got to move. Let's walk this off.' She needed to stop him collapsing into a lethargy from which he wouldn't wake. She was furious with him for doing this when she most needed him. He was just like Anthony!

'Exactly so, my dear.' Leighton selected a cane from the stand by the door. 'We can walk to the caves. Please put your coat over your rather fetching costume. We wouldn't want the parishioners to talk now, would we?'

She was very pleased to oblige him as her coat had the kind of pockets useful when smuggling documents out of the cave. Half supporting a swaying Jacob, she followed Leighton to the caves, Mrs Stock at her back.

'Jacob,' she hissed, 'I am so angry at you right now but you've got to work this out of your system!'

'Evening, Rector,' said one man returning home late. 'Have you heard about Sir Fletcher?'

The little party from the rectory paused to allow Leighton to make appropriate noises of concern.

'Indeed, so sad. Killed by a madman, they say. I'll open a condolence book in the church tomorrow so we can send our best to his widow.'

The effrontery of the man! Dora seethed. She would love nothing better than to denounce him but there was only one villager in the lane and he would surely not believe her.

'That is very decent of you. Goodnight, sir.' The man entered one of the cottages and shut the door.

The brightness of the lights increased as they approached the cave entrance. Lanterns were suspended on hooks all the way along the tunnels leading to the secret places underground. Mrs Stock stayed at the entrance and locked the gate behind them.

Damn. That would make getting out more difficult.

'Only admit members,' Leighton cautioned his housekeeper.

'I know the drill, sir.' She took a seat on a barrel by the entrance, on guard duty.

As Leighton led the way along the tunnel, Dora tried to rouse Jacob.

'Do you know where you are?' she whispered. 'Jacob, please, wake up!'

'Dora. I adore Dora,' he muttered. 'I want to kiss your feet, nibble your toes. Come to bed with me.'

He was clearly away with his dreams as he would never say anything so sentimental in his right mind.

'Jacob, please. Try to shake this off!'

They reached the banquet hall where the party was already in progress. It was hot from the braziers and the candles melting on every ledge and tabletop. The participants stank of perfume and sweat. Mary Wheeler was there, pouring drinks for the company, dressed in a diaphanous gown that displayed her figure. Three other women stood in the niches, striking poses like classical statues, their breasts exposed and drapery slipping seductively off them. When a bell tinkled – held by one of the men – the women moved to take a new pose to the cheers of the onlookers. In the larger nooks, couples were already engaged in vigorous intercourse, watched by the those who got their pleasure by peering in from the passageway at the back. The biggest crowd was gathered by a quartet who were managing some complicated entwining of limbs to make their sex into a round game. Someone collapsed, bringing down the circle and causing much laughter and cheers.

If it had been just sex, this would have been bawdy but harmless. Did these people know that lives had been lost? Dora wanted to scream but she wouldn't be heard over the excited talk and cries of ecstasy. They would merely assume it was another fantasy being played out.

William Bates stepped out of the crowd. Of course he would be here, the flea-bitten rat.

'Your excellency, you've brought us fresh meat, I see?' Bates pulled her coat from her shoulders and dropped it on the floor. 'A very superior sister.'

'Bugger off, Bates. You know I am not here willingly,' snarled Dora.

'And that is what makes it such fun.' He put his hand to her throat and squeezed. 'May I?' He addressed the question to Leighton.

If her being raped in public was the secret that Leighton thought would keep her quiet, then he had another thing coming to him. Such a vile act would make her shout their wickedness from the rooftops. And she would fight it. By God, she would fight! She had vowed never to be a victim again.

'She's not for you.' Leighton seemed entirely unmoved by the scene around him, like a vicar at a wedding of strangers. 'She's Sandys' pledge. Help me take them to the inner sanctum.'

What did that mean?

Bates took over supporting Sandys while Leighton prodded her along with his cane. Their passage attracted a few interested stares, but what did they see? A woman play-acting a nun – half the ladies present who were dressed at all bore some resemblance to this blasphemous fashion – and a drunken man being carried by a friend. She had to think of a way of getting them both out of here, but her mind was coming up blank. Dora kept her eyes open for the document box, but this didn't seem the right place for it – too many people not from the innermost circle, too many flickering shadows and confusion to keep the secrets safe. She would wager that Leighton would have them in the unholiest place, which was why she didn't resist as he pushed her onwards.

The smaller chamber, the one where they had found Matt Jenkins hanging, was set up as a satanic chapel. Lewd pictures decorated the walls, fire burned on the altar, and a great cross hung upside down on the back wall.

'Immediately above us,' said Leighton, pointing with the silver tip of his cane, 'is the reverse image of this: the altar in the church, the cross, the pictures of saints and angels. Think of it like an image on a pack of cards. This hill is the only place in England where both halves of mankind are found. Here is the true heart of

Our Master's kingdom on earth and He will reward his true believers.'

Trembles made her knees weaken. Damn her legs. They needed to get ready to run, not fold. This was all going too far. She had thought Jacob would be here with her to thwart them, not away in his dreamland. Time was running out. 'You are deluding yourself, vicar. All you have waiting is a very hot place in Hell.'

But nothing she said dented Leighton's self-confidence.

'Prostrate yourself before the altar – on your back.' He pointed to the place in the centre of the chamber.

'If it is so holy to be ravished before this altar, why don't you offer to do it?' Dora tried to back away but Leighton propelled her forward.

'Oh, I have. Many times. Most enjoyably. Tonight is Sandys' initiation.' He kicked her feet from under her and she landed hard, bruising an elbow. She tried to scramble up, but he pinned her by straddling her, knees on her arms. He was practised in subduing women.

She spat at him. 'This won't make a difference. I'm not some society miss who will be shamed by such an act.'

He ran a finger down her cheek and neck, pressing on her windpipe.

'Indeed not. That is why Sandys here will kill you at the moment of coitus – or believe he has. That will silence both you and him – though he is the only one to keep breathing. We shall enjoy watching that.' He got up and Bates shoved Jacob down on top of her. 'Think of it as your greatest performance, Dora.'

Chapter Fifty

Jacob was underwater. That was the only explanation his befuddled mind could suggest for how he could float along, glimpsing strange oceanic sights. Mermaids swayed in a cavern, scraps of seaweed that might be silk fluttered, fat fish with white bellies and dark backs swam by. The noise was too much, too sensual and gross. He wanted to lie down in the dark and enjoy the hum of happiness in his bones.

Amazing – to be able to breathe underwater. How clever he had become.

And the swimmer at his side. Dora. He adored Dora. Had he said that aloud? She was wearing a strange robe. When had she become a nun? Or was this some erotic dream that would see him waking with a wet nightshirt and empty arms, embarrassed like a boy of fifteen? Dora wasn't fifteen. She was all woman, witty and warm, the most vibrant person he had ever met. He wanted to strip those clothes from her and lick her from toe to breast. Had he said that too?

Now he was lying on top of her in a dark place, in the light of a thousand fires. She looked scared, not pleased to be with him. He didn't want to alarm her. The dream was shifting to a nightmare.

'Dora?'

'Don't do this, Jacob. It's the opium.'

Opium-eater. He had been one once and had vowed never to be so again.

'Sandys, you have to tup her. It's that or we kill her.'

But opium suppresses the libido, he wanted to tell them. All doctors know that. It used to make him brilliant but now he just wanted to cuddle her and sleep. He dropped his head on her breast and sighed. She smelled so good under those musty robes.

'What's wrong with him? Is he a Sodomite? He's lying on her like a beached whale.'

What were those men doing in his bedroom?

'Sod off,' he murmured.

He could feel Dora trying to push him off her.

'Sorry, darling, too tired. Can't do it tonight.' He rolled over so she could breathe.

A sharp object jabbed him in the solar plexus.

'Wake up, Jacob!'

Dora was on her feet, holding an ornamental cross like a blunted dagger. He looked up and saw a hook swinging above his head.

Alarm shot through him. The hellfire caves. Matt Jenkins. Images danced into his brain and flitted like bats.

'I'm not your lamb for the slaughter,' Dora said fiercely.

'Bates, subdue her,' Leighton said, almost bored.

The other man moved towards Dora but she skipped behind the altar and seized one of the burning vessels. It held a reservoir of oil which gave off a powerful scent.

'Come any closer and I'll show you hellfire!' she shouted.

'Foolish woman. We can just outwait you. That will only burn for another few minutes.' Leighton moved to block her on the right as Bates moved to the left.

Hang on, this wasn't right. He was a gentleman. He shouldn't just lie here while his lady was fighting for their lives. He pulled himself up by one of the hangings. It came away from the wall and flopped over him. Hadn't Dora once showed him a clever trick? He threw it over Leighton's head.

'Now, Dora!'

Dora cast the oil over the rector. That hadn't been what Jacob had meant at all. He'd meant she should run to him. The hanging went up with a whoosh. Leighton screamed, unable to fight his way out. Bates rushed to help him but Dora threw the second bowl over him, setting his jacket on fire. He dropped and rolled, yelling in agony.

Jacob pulled a second hanging from the wall, meaning to extinguish the flames on the screaming men. He wasn't thinking straight but he couldn't watch another man burn to death.

'I got them, Jacob!' Dora called. He glanced up and she was holding a box. 'What shall I do with them?'

'You've set them on fire!' he said, shocked by the rapid developments.

'Good idea. We can't take a chance. No one should get their hands on any of this.' She opened the box and tipped the pages out into the last remaining bowl of burning oil. It spilled, setting the altar cloth alight. 'Time to go.'

Jacob dropped the hanging onto the rector. Leighton was writhing like a soul in torment. It might be too late. Bates was groaning. He at least was still alive.

Dora took his hand. 'Come with me.'

'What about them?'

'They can save themselves.'

That made weird sense. 'You're better at rescues than I am.'

His feet weren't cooperating so they staggered up the

passageway back into the banquet hall where the party was still in progress. Mary Wheeler approached them.

'Have you seen Mr Bates?'

'Yes. He just tried to rape and strangle me,' Dora snapped.

Mary went white with shock. 'He ... he...'

'You have to choose: help me get Jacob to safety or go up in flames with the rest of them.' Dora jerked her head at the crowd.

A billow of smoke issued from the passageway they had just left.

'I say, I think something is on fire!' said one fat fish, pausing from his suckling of his mermaid's breast.

There was no bravery amongst this shoal. That proved to be the signal for their evacuation. Panic ensued – screams, overset tables, fish ... no, *people* running naked for the exit.

Time jumped again. Jacob found himself supported by Dora on one side and Mary on the other, heading up to the surface.

'This is good – she won't see us,' Dora muttered.

'Who?' asked Jacob.

'That female Cerberus.'

'I admire a woman with a classical education.' His dream was turning rather splendid again after those dark moments. He could smell the fresh air and feel the coolness of the night. Carried out on the wave of people fleeing the caves, they passed the gates and stumbled on. Dora commandeered a carriage, pushing a startled coachman from his box, and Mary guided Jacob to a seat. When the coachman protested, she told him she was taking her passenger to hospital and he wasn't going to stop her. He should instead help evacuate the injured.

'You really are splendid,' Jacob said, gazing up at Dora. 'Athena.'

'What's wrong with the doctor?' asked Mary.

'Opium. Check his pulse.'

Cool fingers pressed into his neck. 'That would explain it. Poor man. He'll feel rotten in the morning.'

'I'd say it serves him right but even addled he proved useful.'

'Do you know how to drive?'

'I've driven a cart.' The carriage rocked as Dora released the brake. 'Keep him secure.'

'Is carriage driving the same?' Mary cradled his head in her lap. He would prefer Dora do that, but she was busy.

'We're about to find out.' Dora cracked the whip, and they began to move.

Chapter Fifty-One

The West End

Dora drove them all the way to Lady Tolworth's house in London. She had debated going directly to Jacob's family but, if the authorities were after him for the death of Vane, they wouldn't think to look for him at the home of a society lady with whom he no longer had any relationship.

Lady Tolworth's butler proved to be up to an emergency even though they arrived at dawn, wearing the most inappropriate clothing imaginable. At least Dora had grabbed her coat on her way out.

What would she rescue from a burning building? It seemed her coat was the answer.

That was now wrapped around Mary. Even the unflappable butler might have baulked at allowing a nun and a half-naked wench into the kitchen. Lady Tolworth was summoned, the family physician sent for to see to Jacob, food and beds offered. Dora refused a separate room. She was worried that Jacob might stop breathing if he was left, even though the doctor assured her that the dosage was working its way out of his body. He recommended coffee to stimulate the heart.

'I should bleed him to settle his humours.' The doctor got out a pan and scalpel.

'No ... no bleeding,' Jacob moaned.

Dora moved to stand beside the bed. 'Let's try the coffee first, shall we?'

The physician looked to Lady Tolworth. 'Your ladyship?'

Dressed in her nightgown, with her blonde hair around her shoulders, the noblewoman still managed to command the room. 'Thank you, Mr Edmunds. I will send for you if he worsens but we'll do as Miss Fitz-Pennington suggests.'

The doctor departed, grumbling about female know-it-alls, leaving the two women and a slumbering Jacob between them.

'This is bad. I leave you both for a day or two and Jacob is accused of murder. What on earth have you been up to?'

Dora opened her mouth but found only nervous laughter escaped.

'I think you need a brandy, not coffee.' Lady Tolworth rang for a decanter. Once it had been poured, Dora chugged back a mouthful. The slap of the alcohol cleared her head, enough so she could recount the events of the last few days. Lady Tolworth's eyes grew wider and wider.

'There is no danger the plans will reach the enemy?' Trust the lady to see the most important point.

'No, your ladyship. I burned them.'

'And that horrid rector?'

'Him too, though it is possible he survived. Jacob tried to save him.'

'He would.' Lady Tolworth patted Jacob's hand. 'Even out of his mind with opium he still seeks to help others.'

'You knew about the opium?'

'We all have our weaknesses, dear. No one is perfect – and we shouldn't expect them to be because too high expectations will break them.'

Was that what she had done?

Jacob turned over and muttered, 'Dora?'

Lady Tolworth gave her a smile that had tears behind it. 'He's yours now, my dear. Look after him.'

'I ... I'll try, but I don't even know if I can stop him being accused of murder. I got carried away in the caves, fearing I'd not get out with the documents while carrying Jacob. So I burned them all. Will anyone believe us?'

'You make a good point.' Lady Tolworth went to the desk, sat down, and began writing.

'What are you doing?'

'Sorting this out. You've already done so much, getting rid of Vane and Leighton, but I know Sir John Reed. His brother-in-law holds a parish thanks to my patronage so he should be well disposed towards me. I will also send the current Lord Tolworth to the parliament to find Jacob's brothers. One of them is in the Lords, another in the Commons. They will make sure the accusations go away. Is there anyone else who poses a threat?' She looked over at Dora. This was a woman who should have been in charge of an army, not just a household.

The two most guilty were dead or near to death. 'William Bates, if he got out. I also know the names of the Second Circle. They are all dangerous. And then there's Peter Fosse and the other members of the Illuminati.'

'A long list then. We'll start by clearing Jacob's name.'

Dora must have dropped off to sleep because she woke when Mary brought in a tray of coffee and breakfast. The young woman had changed into a maid's dress and apron and seemed content with the alteration.

'Are you all right, miss?' Mary asked, placing the tray on the desk.

'I think so. I feel like I've just come in out of a terrible storm.'

Jacob's eyes opened. He sat up with a jolt, panic in his expression. 'Dora!'

Dora patted his arm. 'Hush now. You're safe.'

Mary carried over a cup of strong coffee. 'The doctor said you were to drink this.'

'I've been ill? No, no, we were in the caves... What the hell happened?'

'You were under the influence.'

He groaned and shut his eyes. 'I'm an idiot. I thought it would give me an edge to carry on but it must have been ten times its usual strength. A little gift from Mother Clerk.'

'You could've died of an overdose.'

'That was probably her game and part of me thinks I deserved to. I promised never to go back to it.'

Dora had a choice: agree with him and make the break now — who wanted to throw in their lot with an addict? — or accept that he had his weaknesses just as she did. She could help him clamber back on the straight and narrow way.

'I agree it was extremely foolish, but you managed to be helpful even so.' Practised now at relating the events of the last few hours, Dora recounted what had occurred as he settled back on the pillows to sip his coffee.

'You are well? You weren't harmed?' His gaze went first to her, then to Mary.

'We are both well, thank you.'

'Miss Dora is a wonderful hand with the horses. Drove all the way to London, she did.' Mary bobbed a curtsy. 'I'll leave you both to...' She waved her hand, indicative of the soft words she expected the two lovers to share.

'You don't have to go back to that life, you know,' Dora said as Mary went to the door. 'We'll make sure you're looked after.'

Mary rested a hand on the knob. 'I think it might be time I looked after myself, don't you?'

'Then we'll help you do that too,' said Jacob.

When the girl left, Dora and Jacob just looked at each other. His eyes were sad, haunted.

'I'm so sorry.'

'I managed, and you did help by throwing that hanging over Leighton.'

'I was taught by the best. But I let us both down.'

'Jacob, neither of us are heroes. You overestimated your ability to resist your addiction and it almost led to disaster. It is going to take a while for us both to come to terms with that, rebuild trust. But I'm also not perfect.'

'You're not?' He brushed the back of her hand.

'I have a little problem with honesty. In fact, I enjoy making my forgeries.' Clouds gathered on his brow and she carried on quickly to head off the argument. 'Think of it as my addiction.'

'Then let me help you channel it in less harmful ways.'

She smiled at that. 'All right. Let's see if you can do so, and I'll help you with yours. By the way, Lady Tolworth is sorting out your position so we should be able to return to the world without fear of you being arrested or locked up again.'

Jacob drained his cup. 'I can feel that already – my heart is racing. I'm also sorry that so many have got away with crimes. If we don't know their names, they can continue to pervert justice.'

'Oh? What good would the names do?'

'I was thinking on our journey south that we could denounce the Second Circle and send a letter to the papers. It makes even more sense now as they will be reporting the events at the caves and trying to work out what has been going on. A clergyman caught in the flames of a satanic ritual, he and another man reported to be severely burned but hanging on to life, several society figures spotted fleeing half-naked – I know a few editors from my school days who would love to publish that scandal. Give them the information and they will do the work.'

Dora closed her eyes and recited the names she had memorised.

'That's them? How can you remember that?'

'I learn and retain at least three plays a week while we are on tour. A list of thirteen names is child's play.' She moved the breakfast things off the desk in preparation to writing the names down. 'I can do it in Vane's handwriting, if you'd like?'

Jacob groaned.

'No, no, this is a good use of my skills, the kind of thing you should be encouraging. We could come up with a story of our own as to how he was murdered by the Hellfire Club to ensure his silence but heroically left this list behind. It would keep us out of it.'

'He'll die a martyr.'

'He's dead so what does that matter?'

Jacob rubbed the bridge of his nose. 'Maybe that would be for the best. Let Vane carry that burden. He can be the one to skewer Leighton, Bates and the rest. I can imagine that neither of us would welcome the notoriety.'

'I hope the newsmen can find the identities of the women who died and make sure their graves are marked.'

'If they don't, we will.' He threw back the covers.

'Feeling better?' Dora smiled as he crossed the room to pull on his breeches.

'Miles better.'

'We survived.'

'We did.' He tugged her up from her seat and kissed her. 'Thank you.'

Dora sighed with contentment. It had been so long since anywhere in the world had felt like home. Standing in Jacob's embrace was for her where she felt most peaceful. They weren't perfect, but they were good enough for each other. That would do.

He rested his chin on her head. 'We make an excellent team. I don't want this to end.'

She leaned back so she could see his face. 'Who says it has to?'

Epilogue

11TH MAY, 1812

The Houses of Parliament, London

'I'm not sure I'm ready to meet him,' Dora whispered as Jacob conducted her through the doors of Parliament. It was an impressive building, full of men in dark suits under gothic arches. *It's just another kind of theatre*, she told herself. *You have every right to be here.*

Jacob squeezed her hand. 'He's been summoned to a secret meeting of the War Cabinet to answer for his actions but he asked to meet you first, in case they decide to put him away in a military prison.'

'They won't, will they?' Her alarm pounded in her ears.

'I think not. He is well connected and, as the papers were destroyed, they will prefer to pretend it didn't happen. Most likely outcome will be that he is stripped of his rank and booted out of the army, though they'll make up some other excuse for it. I doubt any public record will be made of the near miss of losing our war plans to the enemy.'

The Persephone Code

'What's he like?' Jacob had already met him in his gentleman's club to arrange this rendezvous but she was dying of curiosity.

'I liked him. He told me that your brother never stopped talking about you.'

Dora wrinkled her nose to dismiss the stinging sensation in her eyes. 'He did?'

'You were the only one in his family that he was proud of – himself included.'

'That sounds like Anthony.' She sniffed, pressing her wrists to her eyes.

A handsome man with golden hair and side whiskers stepped out from behind a statue. This had to be him. If he walked into a ballroom, the ladies would swoon. His coat was a splash of crimson against the grey stone. Gold epaulettes, gold embroidered leaves on cuffs and collar, gold buttons: no wonder her brother had been dazzled. Golden to Anthony's darkness. Persephone to his Hades.

Alexander Smith, lieutenant colonel in the 1st Battalion 2nd Foot Guard, bowed, a stoic expression on his face. He was ready for anything, even her contempt.

All the words Dora had prepared fled. She simply held out her hands. This was the man Anthony loved – the one who had brought him happiness in the last months of his life. Nothing else mattered.

Alexander's rigid posture vanished and he hugged her to him, letting go of the sobs that he'd not been able to share with anyone. 'I'm so sorry, Dora,' he whispered. 'So sorry.'

She found herself crooning soft words to him, nonsense about it didn't matter when of course it did. The man had almost betrayed his country. And why? Because he'd wanted a safe place to explore his love for Anthony and they had both thought the entry price worth paying. He had not known, of course, that the secrets of the club were about to be attacked. He had done it all for love.

Yet another fool like all the rest of us, thought Dora. He was a good match for her brother in that regard.

They went to one of the benches at the side of Westminster Hall.

'There is so much I want to ask you,' admitted Dora, 'so much I want to know about my brother.'

'I'd be honoured to tell you what I know.' Even Alexander's voice was attractive – a bass with a Yorkshire accent.

'Why did my brother not give you the secrets to guard? Why hide them?'

'He came to me in Richmond with that hope but he found I was about to be called back to my regiment in Spain. We agreed it was best to put the box somewhere no one would suspect without solving the clues he left – hints only you would decode.'

'But why not give them to Leighton instead? I thought he was a friend?'

'The Arch Devil himself?' Alexander curled his lip. 'He was never a friend – and Anthony knew that. Leighton was taking the Hellfire Club too far. It should have been an amusing and ribald pastime. Leighton wanted something far darker, truly satanic, and he was using the secrets to blackmail anyone who protested.'

'And he killed to get his way too?'

Alexander nodded. 'That we did not know for certain, though Anthony had his suspicions. I think that was why he asked you to send the box to Sheridan.'

'Yes, I didn't understand why he didn't simply burn them all himself.'

'That I can explain. Anthony wasn't trying to destroy the Hellfire Club but put it back on the right track. There are many men who can only be themselves there and that is incredibly precious. Sheridan is one of the old members, though he stopped coming some time ago before the darker turn. Only he has the authority and public position to make the right decision about what to do with the pledges. We thought he could reign in Leighton and appoint a new infernal Archbishop to protect people like us. But you both put an end to Leighton instead.'

Jacob grimaced. 'If you call putting a man at death's door from his injuries, we did.'

'The bastard's not dead yet?' Alexander sounded disappointed.

'He soon will be – the government would prefer that to a trial.'

'And Bates?'

'Someone arranged for him to be pressganged as an ordinary seaman in the navy. We won't be hearing of him again.'

The ruthless way the government had got rid of the criminals without resorting to public trials had both shocked and impressed Dora. Vane was lauded as a hero, Leighton a madman who burned himself to death, and Bates was out of the picture. Life would continue without a hitch in anyone's step.

'Sir, sir!'

They turned, but it was not Jacob being called, rather a harried-looking man heading towards the Commons. His white hair was swept back from a high forehead, his clothes a funereal black. Dora glimpsed worried grey eyes shadowed by fatigue. Jacob drew Dora aside.

'That's the Prime Minister, Spencer Perceval,' said Alexander, standing to bow.

So close to the centre of power – she had not expected that. This parliamentary world was foreign to her. Dora bobbed a curtsy as Perceval swept past and Jacob bowed. The crowd of petitioners followed, beggars after much more than pennies: trading rights, government contracts, investments. One badger-haired man of stout appearance and fierce expression caught her eye.

'And there's my father with his cronies,' she said in a low voice. 'I should have anticipated that he would come here to lobby the government. He is a frequent pest of those in power.'

'That's to be expected. Your father is part of the rising class and has the money,' said Jacob. 'Old families like mine will soon be extinct.'

'Your father?' asked Alexander, peering over the heads in interest. 'I've never met him in the flesh.'

'And trust me, you are very much better that way,' she said.

Just then, a man with bushy sideburns stepped out of Ezra's crowd in the lobby. He levelled a pistol at Perceval's entourage.

Dora watched in horror as her father lunged forward with a cry. 'No, Bellingham!'

Bellingham ignored him and shot the Prime Minister in the chest. It was so sudden, so strange. Dora, who had seen so much death on stage, couldn't scream; had no prepared speech for her reaction. Perceval also seemed unable to connect the pain in his body and the blood spreading on his waistcoat, to the fact that he had been shot. He even managed to walk on a few steps until he collapsed at the feet of the MP for Norwich.

'I am murdered,' he said in shocked tones.

The lobby erupted.

Guards rushed forward, Alexander amongst them, using his uniform to control the stampede. Members of the public were pushed back to give the injured man room. Dora clung to Jacob.

'I can't believe this. I thought we had stopped them.'

Jacob drew her swiftly apart from the chaos.

'I must get you away.'

'Shouldn't you help?'

'Heart shot. There is nothing a doctor can do.'

'Is it the Illuminati?'

He glanced around him, searching for further attackers. 'You don't have to pull the trigger to be responsible for creating the atmosphere in which such things happen. That's what we are fighting against, you and I.'

Tripping up the steps to the exit, Dora glanced behind her. Alexander had gone, swept up in the drama of the assassination. The only still points in the lobby were the murderer, sitting quietly on a bench awaiting arrest, and the dying prime minister, his head on an aide's lap.

There was a lot of work for them to do.

ONE MORE CHAPTER

YOUR NUMBER ONE STOP FOR PAGETURNING BOOKS

The author and One More Chapter would like to thank everyone who contributed to the publication of this story...

Analytics
Abigail Fryer
Maria Osa

Audio
Fionnuala Barrett
Ciara Briggs

Contracts
Georgina Hoffman
Florence Shepherd

Design
Lucy Bennett
Fiona Greenway
Holly Macdonald
Liane Payne
Dean Russell

Digital Sales
Lydia Grainge
Emily Scorer
Georgina Ugen

Editorial
Arsalan Isa
Charlotte Ledger
Janet Marie-Adkins
Jennie Rothwell
Tony Russell
Caroline Scott-Bowden
Kimberley Young

International Sales
Bethan Moore

Marketing & Publicity
Chloe Cummings
Emma Petfield

Operations
Melissa Okusanya
Hannah Stamp

Production
Emily Chan
Denis Manson
Francesca Tuzzeo

Rights
Lana Beckwith
Rachel McCarron
Agnes Rigou
Hany Sheikh
Mohamed
Zoe Shine
Aisling Smyth

The HarperCollins Distribution Team

The HarperCollins Finance & Royalties Team

The HarperCollins Legal Team

The HarperCollins Technology Team

Trade Marketing
Ben Hurd
Eleanor Slater

UK Sales
Laura Carpenter
Isabel Coburn
Jay Cochrane
Tom Dunstan
Sabina Lewis
Erin White
Harriet Williams
Leah Woods

And every other essential link in the chain from delivery drivers to booksellers to librarians and beyond!

ONE MORE CHAPTER

YOUR NUMBER ONE STOP
FOR PAGETURNING BOOKS

One More Chapter is an award-winning global division of HarperCollins.

Sign up to our newsletter to get our latest eBook deals and stay up to date with our weekly Book Club!
Subscribe here.

Meet the team at
www.onemorechapter.com

Follow us!
@OneMoreChapter_
@OneMoreChapter
@onemorechapterhc

Do you write unputdownable fiction?
We love to hear from new voices.
Find out how to submit your novel at
www.onemorechapter.com/submissions